# Also by Omar Tyree

# Also by The Urban Griot

# For the Love of Money

A Novel

# Omar Tyree

Simon & Schuster
New York · London · Toronto · Sydney

SIMON & SCHUSTER
Rockefeller Center
1230 Avenue of the Americas
New York, NY 10020

Copyright © 2000 by Omar Tyree

SIMON & SCHUSTER and colophon are registered trademarks of
Simon & Schuster, Inc.

For information about special discounts for bulk purchases,
please contact Simon & Schuster Special Sales:
1-800-456-6798 or business@simonandschuster.com.

Designed by Deirdre C. Amthor

Manufactured in the United States of America

10  9  8  7  6  5  4  3  2  1

ISBN-13: 978-0-7432-7887-4
ISBN-10:    0-7432-7887-9

For my family,
friends,
and all of the readers out there
who praised
and slandered me
for Flyy Girl
since 1993.

Well . . . I'm back
And I heard that you missed me.


Truly yours,
Tracy Ellison Grant

# Happily Ever After

*Is a fantasy*
*that will not come true*
*unless the pages of the book*
*stop turning.*

*But in real life*
*the pages ALWAYS turn.*
*So you get over it*
*and you keep reading.*

*Or*
*you ignore the new pages,*
*rip them out of the book even,*
*and you throw them away.*

*But then you become*
*lost*
*with no desire*
*to be found.*

*And in the wilderness*
*you become a casualty*
*of your own stubbornness*
*instead of a survivor.*

$'s $

*For
the Love
of Money*

# April 2000

$ $
$

*I* was nervous, and shifting my body weight from left to right while I stood in front of a packed auditorium at Germantown High School in Philadelphia. I hadn't been back to G-Town since I graduated from the school in 1989. I made sure that I looked good that morning too. I was dressed in a tan Victoria's Secret suit with brown leather Enzo shoes, skin-tone stockings, French manicured nails, newly plucked eyebrows, and my hair was wrapped shoulder length and flipped at the edges. I wore the seductive G perfume, and looked simply ravishing! However, this was Philadelphia, a city where they brought you back down to earth, *especially* high school students. So after I was introduced to them as Tracy Ellison Grant, a Germantown grad with a master's degree in English from Hampton, a Philadelphia schoolteacher, a scriptwriter for several television shows, and finally the screenwriter, associate producer, and star of the Hollywood feature film *Led Astray,* I took the stage and was visibly nervous about what they would ask me about my life and my business. Since I was a new American star, my business was no longer mine.

I took a deep breath and forced myself to step up to the microphone at the wooden podium. I looked out at five hundred students and faculty members. Like Tupac Shakur, all eyes were on me. I didn't know *where* to begin.

I said, "Wow! Germantown High School. It's good to be back."

The microphone was loud and clear. The auditorium had been renovated with dark brown wooden chairs, and the floor was shiny and clean. For a second, I had flashbacks of Diana Ross in *Mahogany*. I could feel it. I was no longer with the people. I was somewhere up . . . *there*, and trying to get back down, but they were not helping me. All they did was stare at me in hushed silence, waiting for me to say something that would validate their preconceptions of stardom. I felt like a tightrope walker in the circus, fifty feet up in the air. My audience was filled with many who prayed for me to make it to the other side in style, while others jinxed me for a big, sloppy fall, so they could walk out and talk about me.

*I told you she ain't shit! She ain't no better than none of us!*

I told myself, *You're thinking too much, Tracy. Calm down and just . . .* talk! *You're stronger than this.* Much *stronger!* I just had to convince them that I was still cool like that, and down-to-earth. The stardom hadn't changed me. Or did it?

I held my head up high and said, "It's been a long road for me." I smiled and continued, "If you read *Flyy Girl*, then I guess you *know* half of it. But I went through a lot more to make it to where I am today, and a lot of people didn't think that I could do it. A lot of people were jealous, and a lot of them are *still* jealous.

"But I had some good friends and some good breaks along the way, and I just had to keep my head strong to make it," I told them. "You have to set out to do what *you* want to do in order to become who *you* want to become, regardless of what everyone *else* is doing.

"So I held on to my goals and kept moving forward." I

said, "I just had confidence in myself, and I had friends who supported me, as well as the haters who didn't. And if *you* want to be successful in whatever it is you want to do in *your* life, then you can use mine as an example of how to go for it, by learning from all of my mistakes and taking from all of my strengths."

That was the gist of my short speech that morning before Stephanie Lletas, the veteran schoolteacher who had invited me back to Germantown High, stood up to address their questions to me. My short speech was just the tip of the iceberg.

"For those of you who have questions, we have two microphones set up in both aisles. We'll need you all to stand in single-file lines," she addressed them. The students all called her Mrs. Let. Mrs. Let was all business even when I was a student there, *and* before me. She dressed sharp every day, knew her stuff, and didn't *take* no stuff! I admired her. I couldn't stomach being a schoolteacher in Philadelphia for *two years*, let alone teach for *twenty*. She even offered to pay me an honorarium, but I told her to keep it. I wasn't so big that I couldn't speak at my old high school without a fee.

The lines behind the microphones backed up with mostly girls, then the questions began:

A tall girl grinned in her jeans and short-sleeved pink shirt. She was as nervous as I was.

"In your book *Flyy Girl*, you were waiting for Victor Hinson to get out of jail at the end, and I just wanted to know what ever happened between you two."

I smiled. Everyone who read my book wanted an answer to *that* question.

I said, "By the time he got out of jail, he had legally changed his name, found himself a new woman, married her and had children. And I had to get over it."

They were all in shock, or at least the students who had read my book. No microphone was needed.

"He up and dropped you just like that?" another girl shouted toward the stage. A few boys in the background began to snicker. I guess that a lot of the young studs considered it a norm for a man to play a woman.

The sisters, however, were outraged and hanging on my every word. If only I could film the pain in their faces and record their collective moan. They really wanted their love story to remain a reality, but life was not that simple. Especially in the nineties with so many failed relationships. Hopefully, the new millennium would bring brighter days for black love.

"He had his reasons," I told them. I really didn't want to get into it. There had been many nights of pain regarding that chocolate-coated man named Victor, but the sweetness had faded away. I had to move on from him. I even wrote a poem about it: "When the Sweet Turns Sour."

After I answered the Victor Hinson question, it seemed like *half* of the line reclaimed their seats. I wished that I could create some beautiful love fantasy to offer them instead, but I couldn't. Fantasies were for Hollywood.

The next question came from a short girl wearing glasses.

"Do you still write your poetry?"

"Yes I do," I answered. "I used to perform a lot of my poetry right here in Philadelphia before I moved out to Los Angeles."

"Are you thinking about publishing any of it?" she asked. She looked like an aspiring poet herself, studious and introspective.

"Yes I am. So keep your eyes open for it in the future," I told her. "I just don't know what I want to call it yet. I thought about calling it *Griot Sistah*, but I haven't decided on it," I added with a smile.

The first guy in line asked me, "How hard was it to break into Hollywood?" He even had a tape recorder in his hand.

I grinned at him. "Why, are you planning to be the next Spike Lee or Robert Townsend?" He looked like a do-it-yourselfer, too strong-willed to wait. Hollywood would make you wait until you couldn't stand it anymore, but everyone wanted to be lucky, "Lucky Like Me," another one of my many poems. Poetry was what kept me sane, during my insane years of dreaming about fame and fortune.

The young brother said, "Yeah, I want to make movies one day," and cracked a smile. He was being modest. You *had* to be modest in a predominately black high school in Philadelphia. They *forced* you to be modest: the snickering, the eye-rolling, and the doubting. It was what made me so nervous about returning that morning, and so hard headed when *I* was a teenager. *To hell with the crowd! I'm going to be me!* This young guy was smarter than that, and his modesty protected him from the wolves.

I said, "It *can* be hard to make it in Hollywood if you're not prepared for it. *Very* hard. But that's with anything that you do. You have to learn as much as you can, always ask questions, and keep your dream alive until you make it," I advised him. "Some people get their break early, some people get their break late. And I was just fortunate because I never stopped working."

Another guy was ready to ask me a question, and he could not even stand at the microphone without acting silly. I could tell that he wasn't about anything before he even opened his mouth. He had that slick-ass, I-know-it-all look, the kind of guy I learned to curse out in a heartbeat.

"In your movie *Led Astray,* when you were naked, was that *your* body, or was that a body double?"

That was just the kind of question those immature guys were waiting for. A roar of laughter launched through the entire auditorium while the teachers shouted and scrambled to maintain order. The girls hissed at the boys for acting stupid, just like *I* would have done, but that only added to the noise. Mrs. Let motioned to have the student removed from the auditorium, but I stopped her.

"No, he has a legitimate question," I responded. "I'll answer him." First I had to wait for everyone to settle back down.

I composed myself and asked, "Has anyone seen Spike Lee's movie *Girl 6*?" A few hands went up, but far less than I expected. Philadelphia teenagers were mostly too damned cool to raise their hands unless you spoke to an advanced class, or at an advanced school. Some students needed extra motivation for everything.

"Well, in the movie *Girl 6*, the main character was repetitively asked to take her clothes off, and she wouldn't do it, and so she didn't get the role. But the moral of the story was that there are many immature and oversexed *men* who run Hollywood, who have never grown up. And actresses end up having to cater to that immaturity," I said. "Just like with these rap videos; they just *have* to see some ass and some tit, even though it's not in the song. So I'm *glad* that he asked me that question, because now I can tell everybody here that *men* need to grow the hell up!

"Why does the woman have to get butt naked and raw just for you to like the damn movie?"

The crowd went wild behind my frank explanation. I turned and had to apologize to Mrs. Let for my candor. She waved it off and told me to keep going. However, it wasn't as if all of the girls in the audience agreed with me. When the crowd settled down, a girl wearing a Muslim head wrap begged to differ. She stepped to the microphone and said, "I'm saying though, you could have told them no. We have to learn to respect *ourselves* like that. We can't just tell guys to grow up and mature if we're still gonna shake our behinds and whatnot in front of the camera, and *be* the hoochie mommas in the videos and movies. *We* have to start saying *no* to that!"

"THAT'S RIGHT! TELL HER!" a number of the guys shouted in her support.

I couldn't really argue with the sister, but I was embarrassed and my ego made me argue my point anyway.

"You know what? The irony is that if we *don't* get in the film at all, and someone else does the role who may not necessarily *care* about voicing their concerns, then we never get to change anything. So we have to learn to transform the imagery into something more than just naked sex."

I guess my argument sounded weak because the Muslim girl jumped all over it.

She frowned, shook her head, and said, "No! You change the imagery by walking off of the stage and not doing it." She walked away from the microphone and left me steaming.

I said, "That was the same argument we had in the thirties and forties about playing maids and Aunt Jemimas. But you know what? We *were* maids and Aunt Jemimas in real life, and we didn't make a *tenth* of what they did portraying one in a movie. So don't just focus on the image, try to change the reality. That's what *real* art is supposed to inspire us to do: change our realities."

That ruined the entire event for me. I was on the defensive for the rest of the lecture. There were a few questions about my friends Raheema and Mercedes, which they had read about, and I gave them half-assed answers without much feeling. I was a damn wreck. All of my doubts that morning were consuming me.

I couldn't wait to get the hell out of Germantown High School that morning. I felt so damned small! A mouse hole was too big for me. I knew better before I ever agreed to do the sex scenes in the movie, and it was *my* original screenplay. Artists have to be brave and stand up for their work. Maybe I wasn't as brave as I *thought* I was. Was I still the too-fast Tracy of my younger years, chasing Hollywood fame for my own personal high and fortunes? Or was I really the artist that I claimed to be, with something original to offer to the people? I was still confused about that. Was I doing it for the love of the art, or for the high of the money?

When the lecture was finally over, after signing autographs, Mrs. Let walked me out the door and tried her best to console me. "We all have our crosses to bear, young sister. The more you try to do, the heavier your cross becomes. That's why so many people decide to do so little, but that doesn't change the size of your cross. God will find ways to test you anyway."

*Ain't it the truth,* I thought to myself. I thanked Mrs. Let for having me and thought about how hard I fought to get to the big screen. I wondered if it was all worth it. I walked off by myself to climb into my rental car and slip away before anyone else could notice me.

**$ $ $**

My mother told me how much my young cousin Vanessa admired me. She was a sophomore at Engineering & Science High School in North Philadelphia, where my brother Jason graduated a year earlier. She had read my book *Flyy Girl* six times and memorized it. She was my first cousin Patricia's oldest daughter. Trish and I had never been close, going all the way back to my sixth birthday party, but can you believe she named her first daughter Vanessa Tracy Smith? The girl even had the nerve to look like me, subtract my light eyes. Vanessa had brown eyes so dark they looked black. She was a shade or two lighter than me, with dyed light hair to accentuate her allure. The family had all been telling her for years how much she favored me. I was flattered and looking forward to seeing Vanessa again, but the visit to my old high school had dulled my excitement a bit. I was no longer in a good mood. To make matters worse, since North Philadelphia was not exactly my cup of tea, I got lost trying to find E&S High School and ended up running late.

When I arrived, Vanessa was still waiting for me out on the front steps of the school with two friends in tow, just like I would have been. I smiled and wondered how long she would have made her friends wait had I run even later.

"Oh my God!" one of her friends shouted. The other girl was more reserved, but they were both ready with their notepads and pens in hand for my autograph. I signed them immediately and told them to stay smart.

Vanessa played it cool. She cracked a smile and asked me if I had gotten lost again. I had told her previously that I could not find E&S to save my life, even when my brother was there.

"Well, I'll see y'all in school tomorrow," Vanessa told her two friends. They looked like your typical girl power clique, all pretty and knowing it. They were various shades of brown like a box of chocolates, but they were nowhere near as flyy as *my* crew would have been back in the eighties. They were just . . . plain. The nineties generation was more flyy in attitude, and were much more reserved about it, like in a secretly snobbish sort of way. In the eighties, we were flyy physically, mentally, *and* with our attitudes. We were all out in the open with it, wearing all of our gold, designer glasses, silk shirts, Gucci gear, expensive coats, and plenty of fancy hairdos. We rubbed it all in people's faces: *I'm flyy, and you're not!* Which of course resulted in many of us getting flat-out robbed by the jealous haters.

I was figuring on giving Vanessa's friends a ride home before she quickly dismissed them. However, since E&S was an academic high school, many of the students who went there lived nowhere near North Philadelphia, but Vanessa did. She lived right off of Girard Avenue, across the bridge from the Philadelphia Zoo. Although, I didn't imagine that she hung around there much. Vanessa was more of a traveler.

She followed me over to my rented Ford in the parking lot and looked around as if I was driving something else. I was used to that. Hollywood was *full* of car watchers.

"It's a rental car," I told my cousin. "All I need to do is get around in it. I'd rather not have all of the extra attention of driving a nice car while I'm home anyway."

Vanessa smiled off her disappointment and shrugged. "I guess you can get tired of so many people watching you," she said.

I nodded and opened the car doors. "You know I don't have to answer that."

She said, "But you got a lot of attention *before* you moved to Hollywood."

"And *you* don't?" I asked her as we climbed inside.

She shrugged again. "I have *other* things to do."

*Like what?* I thought of asking, but we had plenty of time for that. I would be in town visiting for two weeks.

"What kind of car do you drive out in Los Angeles?" she asked me.

I was afraid to even answer, but I answered her anyway. "A Mercedes."

Vanessa grinned. "What color?"

"Black."

She nodded. "I like the dark blue ones."

*Have you been in one?* I thought. Why was I holding back with her? I forced myself to ask her anyway. "Are you into cars or something?"

She nodded. "I'm into a little bit of everything."

*How about teenage sex and fast men? Are you into that?*

I was assuming everything and I couldn't help myself. I just started to laugh.

"You're not trying to play out all of the things I did in *my* life are you? Because that's *not* the way to succeed," I told her. I felt hypocritical as soon as the sentence left my mouth.

"No, I haven't done any of *those* things," she said. "But I *do* want to live nice."

She *did* live in North Philadelphia. I was a Germantown girl in *my* days. That made a big difference in perception *and* in lifestyle.

I was hungry so I decided to stop off at a steak shop for that nationally known Philadelphian treat: a cheese steak with fried onions, salt, pepper, and ketchup. Vanessa ordered a fish sandwich with cheese fries.

"You don't eat steaks?" I asked her.

She frowned. "Mmm, sometimes, but not a whole one."

I looked over her body size. She was not my five foot eight height. Vanessa was closer to five foot six, and she did not have a body like I did at her age.

"How much do you weigh?" I asked her.

She grinned. "Why, I look skinny? I weigh a hundred and ten."

At five foot five *and a half,* one hundred and ten pounds *was* thin.

"You better eat some of this steak, girl," I teased her. "You're not Calista Flockhart."

"Who?"

"The girl who plays Ally McBeal," I told her.

"Oh. I'm not *that* skinny. I just don't want to be like my mom."

I didn't know how to respond to that. Her grandmother, my Aunt Marsha, was big, and my cousin Trish had followed in *her* mother's footsteps. They both chose men who didn't stick around. Vanessa had every reason in the world to want more. I just didn't want to encourage her in the wrong way.

"Well, just don't overdo it," I told her. "Good exercise will take care of any extra pounds before you even let it get that far."

By the time we finished our food, it was close to four o'clock. I had an appointment in Jenkintown, Pennsylvania, at six. I didn't want to be caught in rush-hour traffic trying to make it, but I couldn't take Vanessa, and I didn't want to rush away from her either.

"You know, I have an appointment I need to get to soon, but let's say I pick you up from your school again on Thursday and we hang out then. I'll try and see you all this weekend too."

I wanted to butter up the pot, but Thursday was my only promise.

Vanessa nodded. "I have an assignment to finish today anyway," she said.

I couldn't tell if she was brushing me off or if she felt

slighted in some way. I was sure that she could get along without me though. She struck me as a big girl, and big girls don't cry.

I stood up and tossed our food in the trash bin. "Well, let me drive you home then, and I'll pick you up again on Thursday *on time*," I emphasized with a smile.

Vanessa hesitated. "Can you drop me off at the main library on Vine Street? I have to look up a few things."

Was she really going there for homework? I would have it *bad* if I ever had a daughter. I had too many recollections on my mind from my own reckless days as a teen. I mean, Vanessa *did* go to Engineering & Science, one of the top public high schools in Philadelphia. She had good grades at that. How could I doubt her?

"Yeah, that's no problem," I told her.

We were less than five minutes away from Vine. I dropped her off at the front steps of the main library and made sure she was okay. She didn't talk to me much on the short ride there.

"Are you okay?" I asked her before we parted.

"Yeah, I'm okay. I just have a lot of things to do."

"You're introverted, aren't you?" I asked her.

She looked squeamish, as if she didn't want to answer. That told me all I needed to know.

"Well . . . yeah, I guess so."

That was another difference between us. I expressed *myself all* of the time, with my words, *and* with my actions. Vanessa was more of the sneaky type. They were more dangerous because you could never quite tell about them. My old next-door neighbor Mercedes was that way, and her story was tragic.

I was still not convinced about my little cousin's library visit, but I had things to do as well, so I had to let it go.

"Okay, I'll see you Thursday," I told her.

She just smiled at me.

I drove off and couldn't get Vanessa off of my mind. Sure, she was my cousin and all, but I thought of her more as a girl who looked up to me, and someone ready to flower, who may just need a little more attention. A lot of girls needed more attention.

I drove all the way to Jenkintown thinking about how hard it was to be a grown-up and a role model. I was a role model whether I liked it or not, because I was an African-American star in a land where too many of us were not given the opportunity to even breathe. It seemed unreal. How in the world did I do it? Everyone was watching and talking about me. That's a lot of pressure on a person.

I returned my rental and caught a short taxi ride to the Jenkintown car dealership. I was more than a half hour early for my appointment. I guess I overestimated travel time in Philadelphia because of all of the traffic jams in Los Angeles that I had become accustomed to. I figured I could get in and get out with the vehicle that I wanted to buy, but my original salesperson (a brother named Byron) was not there. Whenever you deal with two different car salesmen you end up starting all over again. I already liked my price, so I planned on waiting around a few minutes, until I saw the platinum-colored Infiniti SUV I had wanted for my father. Boy was it sexy! I just had to take another look.

"Can I help you with anything?"

I turned and faced a young, eager white guy in a dark suit and tie. He looked straight out of college.

I said, "Has anyone put a bid on this SUV?" I wanted to see if the other salesman had set aside my name and price for that platinum Infiniti like I had asked him to. I was also curious to see if I could even sweeten the deal, or if the new salesman would try and screw me. I had read in a magazine somewhere that African-American women got the worst deals in the country on new cars.

"No, not that I know of," he answered me.

"Are you sure? Because I wouldn't want to take someone else's car."

He smiled and said, "It's not someone else's car until they've driven off the lot with it."

"But what if another salesman was already working with it?"

That poor guy had no idea how deep I was about to dig him.

"Well, in that case, we would have a record of it."

Two things crossed my mind. First, if my initial salesman did not take me seriously, then maybe he didn't record it. Second, if the new guy was a wheeler-dealer, then maybe he would lie about it even if it *was* recorded, or talk to his boss about *unrecording* it if the price was right. I thought of a lot of different imaginary plots as a writer. I couldn't help myself. It kept me sharp.

I planned to stir up the plot a little more. I said, "I'll tell you what. What price would you give me if I could buy it today in cash?"

"In cash? Tonight?" He looked hungry enough to eat for four.

I said, "Yes," and allowed him a full view of my style of dress and my purse to entice him.

"Ah, I'll be right back. I'll have to go see." He began to walk away, but then he turned, too quickly, and looked desperately at me. "Ah, would you like to walk inside with me?"

"Why, do you think that I would leave?" I asked him with a grin. "I want to finish looking at it."

He nodded, and realized his own eagerness with a smile.

"Okay, I'll be right back out." He turned to face me once more before he made it inside. "I'll get the keys and let you take her for a ride."

I nodded to him and grinned. "Okay."

Byron, my initial salesman, showed up just in time to make it *more* interesting. Life was all a game anyway, especially when you have the money to play, so I was enjoying myself.

He said, "Hey, you know what? After I talked to you last night, I wrote your name and number down and said, 'Tracy Ellison Grant? I wonder if that's the one who played in that movie *Led Astray*?' Then I thought about it and said, 'Damn, she *is* from Philadelphia. What the hell was *I* thinking?!'

"I apologize for that, sister. I really do," he said. "Let's go ahead and make this deal."

The brother was raw energy, excited like a new boyfriend on that first private night. He even looked like a winner in his light gray pin-striped suit and burgundy striped tie that jumped out at me. I had gotten Byron's name and number from a friend who had gotten a good deal from him. I didn't make a big deal about my star status. I wanted to use that as my ace in the hole.

Out walked my new salesman with the keys. I didn't even know his name.

I said, "You know, I had talked to Byron last night about this car before I came in. I just wanted to see if he had set it aside for me."

The white guy looked crushed, but he tried to play it off.

"Oh, well, okay. Byron, you talked to her yesterday?" He had to make sure I wasn't pulling a fast one on him just to give a brother a sale.

Byron had betrayal written all over his face. He quickly played that off too.

"Yeah, I talked to her. She wasn't supposed to be here until six."

"I was running early," I explained.

Byron snatched those keys away as if he had to feed a greedy wife and eight kids.

"Yeah, man, I got it."

The manager walked out and said, "Excuse me. You say you're interested in this Infiniti?" He was a tall white man with gray edges invading his thick, dark hair. He wore a dark suit and tie himself. I guess Byron wanted to stand out and look a little jazzy at work with the light-colored suit.

The manager moved toward the keys as if he wanted to give me a personal look through, but Byron beat him to the driver's-side door with them instead.

He said, "I talked to her about this SUV last night. She's an actress. Tracy Ellison Grant. She has a book out too. *Flyy Girl*, right?" he asked me. He damn sure wasn't giving up those keys. I mean, if you want to see some *real* acting you should visit one of these hungry car dealerships.

The manager got the picture and said, "An actress? Oh." He gave me a long stare. I knew what was coming next. "So, what have you starred in?"

The first young white guy stuck around just to be nosy. I guess his feelings were hurt at losing a golden sale. I was sure that he would talk about me. He would probably call me all kinds of names, but I was used to that. Some people just had to grow up.

Byron jumped back in and answered, "*Led Astray*. It was about this black woman who was trying to make it out in Hollywood, and how she got all caught up in the game, and decided to play her *own* game."

All of a sudden, the brother was my public relations rep. His manager and coworker were still nodding, both dying to have those keys in hand.

"Well, you ready to take it for a ride?" Byron asked me. He was as eager to get away from them and secure his sale as they were to try and take it from him.

First the boss had to chat me up with the usual: How long had I been acting? How does it feel to be a star? He apologized for not knowing any of my work, and then he promised to look out for me in the future. He thanked me for doing business with them, asked me how I found out about the dealership, and just went on and on.

I was so happy to climb inside of that beautiful Infiniti that I didn't know what to do with myself. People will outright talk your ear off sometimes. I only listened to all of his jabber because I wanted to sweeten my final sale price at the end of the night. You can't expect to do that with a nasty attitude.

When we pulled off, Byron got *real* on me and started talking that black talk.

"You see that?" he asked me, shaking his head with a grin. "They were scheming to take this damn sale. I'm glad you looked out for me like that, sister. I didn't know you could make it out here early. If I would have known that, I wouldn't have taken my break until *after* you came."

I smiled back at him and toyed with all of the gadgets in the car.

"Oh, she's nice, ain't she? This is top of the line here," he told me.

"Why do men refer to cars as 'she'?" I asked just for the hell of it.

"Because we're men," Byron answered. He laughed, a strong hearty laugh. Maybe it was *too* hearty. He was really pleased with his sale. In fact, he seemed to think more about the sale than explaining to me the features on the car. I wanted it anyway so I let it ride.

"They didn't know who you were," he said. "They don't even watch black TV shows, let alone go to see black films. I get so tired of telling white folks about black culture around here that I just don't feel like commenting on it sometimes. But I *have to* because we're Americans too. You know what I mean, sister? We're Americans too.

"I know that they *think* that we're not, but we are," he continued. "Hell, the only black stars they know around here is Bill Cosby, Will Smith, and Allen Iverson."

After a while, I just blocked the brother out and listened to the sound system. He caught on to my deaf ears and got back to telling me about the car. Brothers can drive themselves crazy about race sometimes. Not that *I* don't ever think about it, but *damn*!

I said, "Byron, actually, a lot of white people *do* pay attention to our culture, but they do so on their own time. They're coming around. Just have a little patience."

He laughed more civilly and said, "Just have a little more patience, hunh? It's just like a sister to say that. I guess we need to give them another four hundred years."

I grinned and changed the subject. He didn't understand me, and I didn't understand him. That was exactly why I wasn't married, because I didn't have time for man-woman misunderstandings every damn day of my life!

We drove back to the dealership, and they gave me a six-thousand-dollar deal. They took the initial price of thirty-nine thousand dollars down to thirty-three, all because I was paying it off in cash. In fact, since I was not planning to finance it, I probably saved more like *twelve thousand* in the long run. Money talks, but then they tried to sell me everything else to knock the price back up, maintenance plans, additional packages, extended warranties, car phones, anything to make an extra buck.

I finally said, "Look, this car is a gift for my father's fifty-first birthday. If he wants to get anything extra put in it, then he can come back and get it himself."

"If you get it included today, it'll be a lot cheaper than as a separate package," the manager told me.

I said, "It won't mean a thing to him if he knows he didn't pay the thirty-three thousand dollars for the car. What's another thousand for toys?"

They were starting to get on my damn nerves! The next thing I knew it was close to nine o'clock at night, and I still hadn't signed all of the paperwork yet. Damn car salesmen! They need to be shot!

The manager noticed my agitation and finally decided to close the deal. Byron was smiling his brown behind off, but he didn't look so handsome to me anymore. He had ruined my short-lived fantasy. They *all* do. Maybe my standards were too high.

"Would you mind if we took a picture of you while you stand next to the car?" the manager asked me before I pulled off. He had a camera in hand already and they were all smiles at the dealership.

I snapped, "For what? So you can show me off with the car and talk about it?" I was tripping because I was pissed off already! Why the hell would I want to take a picture after being there for nearly four hours?! I was tired of their faces and breath, smelling of coffee and cigarettes.

The manager looked at me and said, "Well . . . yeah, I guess so. It isn't every day that we have an actress in town."

I told him, "All right, well, can you make it fast? I have to get home already."

He snapped their damn picture and I drove the hell out of there, a happy camper at last!

**$ $ $**

I drove back home with that Infiniti, riding high, windows down, and was loving it! I imagined that my father would love it too, and so would Vanessa. That's why I couldn't take her with me. I didn't want her eyes to get too big. I thought that I could take her shopping on Thursday, but then I would have to buy both of her younger sisters something. That would lead to me treating *all* of my cousins to gifts, first *and* second generation, as if it was Christmas. Damn! Money is a pain in the ass! However, since Vanessa was introverted, I thought that maybe she wouldn't tell anyone.

I laughed at myself for being so petty. I could afford to buy everyone a gift. As long as they weren't all forty thousand-dollar cars. My father deserved it. He had been pampering my mother for the past ten years. I guess he still had a guilty conscience for walking out on us like he did. Once I had made it to college at Hampton, my parents were traveling to the Bahamas, Florida, the Pocono Mountains, Ontario, and just having a *good* old time!

I said to myself, *Damn, how come that couldn't happen when I was still at home?* I went straight through school during the summertime to finish college early while working year-round as an RA at the dorms. I just wanted to get college over with. Then my girl Raheema started talking about grad school, and my behind did two more years for a master's degree. Can you *believe* that? I never said that I didn't *like* school. It was better than sitting at home and doing nothing.

I was so busy thinking about my life that I barely paid attention to traffic. I almost cut off a delivery truck and wrecked my father's gift in an accident before I could even surprise him with it. I made it back to Germantown on Chelten Avenue and stopped off for a raspberry-flavored iced tea. I climbed back in the Infiniti, buzzed the windows back down, and cruised for home.

When I stopped at the stop sign of this small, dark street on the way to my parents' house, two dingy brothers ran up to me from separate sides of the street. The one on the driver's side stuck a damn gun in my face.

"Get the fuck out the car and leave the keys in!"

*I'll be damned! A carjack just five blocks away from home!* I thought to myself.

I sat there like a zombie and said, "This is a brand-new gift for my father." I couldn't even move for some reason, and I was saying the wrong thing, but I couldn't help it. I was in shock.

"I don't give a fuck! Just get the fuck out!"

The gun barrel had me frozen. Would I be shot right there and die over a damn CAR? I decided to open the door slowly to climb out. I was near tears already.

The brother on the passenger side said, "Wait a minute, man. She look like, um . . . Tracy Ellison Grant from the movies."

"I AM!" I pleaded to him. I sounded like a big baby, but so what if he could get me out of it.

"Who?" the guy with the gun asked.

"Tracy Ellison Grant, man, from that movie *Led Astray.*"

They just stared at each other for a second.

"I AM, I AM!" I kept pleading to them.

The guy with the gun shook it off and said, "She can *af-*

*ford* to lose this motherfucka then. Are we gonna do this shit or what, man? We ain't got all fuckin' day!"

"Naw, family, let her go. I ain't goin' out like that, man."

"Yeah, listen to him," I said. "Don't treat your sister like this. I love my people."

I actually said that to them.

"Well, pull over and give me forty fuckin' dollars before the cops come, and I'll let you go. A nigga need somethin' to eat, since you love your *people* so much."

I had running boards on each side of the Infiniti, so they both held on to the car as I pulled over and into the next block. I pulled out exactly forty-three dollars and some change. That was all I had on me. That damn crook had called out the right number. Forty. If I believed in the lottery I would have played it straight, 4-3-0.

"This all you got?" he asked me.

"That's it. That's all I have on me," I told him, teary eyed.

He looked to his friend and frowned. "Come on, man, let's bounce."

The one who saved my car had one last thing to say to me.

"Hey, sis', keep this to yourself, aw'ight? Or put it in your next movie or something, 'cause remember, I didn't *have* to say nothin'." He even smiled when he said that, wearing a black and silver FUBU jacket of all things. I heard that FUBU stood for For Us By Us. If it did, then I guess the positive message got lost somewhere.

Talk about a damn plot! The best ones jump up and smack you right in your face. I could barely hold on to the wheel when I drove home. Once I arrived, I parked in front of the house and calmed myself. My block was much safer and better lit than parts of Chelten Avenue. Germantown was a damn schizophrenic neighborhood!

I had to get myself together before I walked inside to face my parents. I didn't want them to panic and bug me all night about it. I just needed time to calm myself down. I came up with the wildest idea to call my agent in California from my cell phone. She usually worked late, and it was only after six in Hollywood, so I called her at her office.

"Hello," she answered.

"Hey, this is Tracy."

"Hey, how are things going back in Philly? Did you have a good day? What time is it back there now? It's dark already, isn't it?" she teased me. "Remember, you have that radio interview tomorrow morning. So make sure you get plenty of z's tonight."

I took a deep breath to stop myself from breaking down and crying again.

"I was almost carjacked," I told her.

She stopped breathing while waiting for the punch line.

"Wait, you're kidding me, right?"

A carjack wasn't my kind of a joke.

I said, "I want you to get in contact with Omar Tyree about writing that part two to *Flyy Girl*. I think it's time for us to really sit down and talk about it."

"Tracy, you're serious."

"Yes, I'm fuckin' serious!" I shouted at her. We were cool like that. My agent was my girl. I could vent to her when I needed to and she could give it back to me, but this was not the night for it.

"Okay, okay. I'll call his agent first thing tomorrow morning. Now in the meantime, tell me what happened. Did you call the police?"

I said, "Really, I just don't even feel like talking about it right now. A lot has happened to me today, as well in the past few years, and I just want to put the shit in a book or

something and forget about it. I don't know." I was bab-
bling, but I was serious too. I had a lot more shit to talk
about, and those fucking piss-ass Hollywood interviews
were nothing but sound bites: "So how did you make it?
What's it like to finally be a star? What are you working on
next? Who is your other half, by the way? Are your parents
proud of you?"

What the fuck did *they* know?! They didn't know shit,
nor did they care. Another damn interview would follow
mine next week, next month, or whatever. After a while,
celebrities all sounded the same. I needed a new tell-all
book. I thought that maybe I would call it *Shit Happens,
Good and Bad, and Then You Die.*

My agent was screaming, "Tracy! Tracy, are you there?!
What's happening?!"

*I'm losing my fucking mind, that's what's happening!* I
was thinking to myself. I heard my girl loud and clear, I
just couldn't respond to her. I was in a daze. It was surreal,
like I was on a witch ride, watching myself be tortured and
was powerless to stop it. I hovered over the car from the
outside and screamed at myself through the windshield,
*"What are you doing?! Don't just sit there! Do something!
Dooo something! . . ."*

# Black English (Ebonics)

*"Girrrl, I be trippin' on how*
*you be complainin' about*
*HIM*
*and how he be gettin' fired*
*and be in trouble wit' 'da damn law.*

*And What'sherface?*
*She be gettin' pregnint all 'la time,*
*and yet be fussin' about how*
*they be act'din down at the welfare off'fis*
*when she don't even be bringin' her right papers.*

*Then we be all cryin' about how*
*white folks be act'din racists 'n shit*
*when it be*
*US*
*that be playin' ourselves short in the first place!"*

*Copyright © 1992 by Tracy Ellison*

# June 1996

$ $
$

*I* was turning twenty-five years old in September, and I had just wrapped up my second year of instructing English at East Germantown Middle School. I had no idea what I was waiting for in my life, or why I thought that I could appease myself as a Philadelphia schoolteacher. Nevertheless, that was the career that I had settled on. It was the last week of the 1995–96 school year, and grades were already in, so we were basically baby-sitting the students for those last few days before sending them off for summer vacation. In walked this crazy mother with a scarf around her head and slippers on her feet (honestly), ranting about her daughter's failing grade in my English class.

"You mean to tell me that my daughter could go from a C grade to an F in the *last* report?" she asked me with foul intent. She even had a crowd of young students gathering for the early Monday morning drama.

I was caught off guard by it. I had mailed this woman three letters during the final report regarding her daughter's slippage in my class, her lack of homework completion, *and* her dropping test scores, and I could never catch the woman at home when I called. I always got one of her teenage children, who either told me that she was not at home, or asked me to hold the line for five minutes at a time while I waited for nothing. I considered the girl's situation helpless, because I was *not* going to drive the hell over to her house and knock on her door to look like some maniac schoolteacher. I would probably be cursed out for that anyway, but I guess that's what some parents need you to do nowadays to get the message about their children.

Schoolteachers could get to *my parents* immediately! Was that so damn long ago? Had families become that lackadaisical? Was it an income thing? I couldn't figure it out, and I didn't have the patience for it.

I told the woman, "I've been trying to contact you for two months." I was very civil with her. After all, she was my elder.

She said, "You expect me to believe that?" as if I was lying to try and cover my ass. The situation was embarrassing.

"Do you have teenage kids?" I asked her. I planned to take the most logical route to why she hadn't received any of my phone messages or mail.

"Yes I do," she huffed at me.

"Do you work during the daytime?"

I hadn't received a work phone number for the parent.

"I work at night," she answered.

"Are you at home when the mail arrives?"

"What the hell does that have to do with you failing my damn daughter on the *last* report?"

She stressed that *last* report thing as if she thought her daughter could just cruise on through my class in April, May, and June, and still expect to pass. Maybe that's why she did it. Her mother seemed to be condoning it.

I looked at her daughter, LaKeisha Taylor, a lazy, attitudinal type of child, and saw exactly where she got her demeanor from. While her mother poured into me with *her* attitude, LaKeisha looked as innocent as a flower girl in a wedding.

"Hold on just a minute," I said, and walked over to my desk. I had copies of everything. I pulled out three dated letters concerning her daughter's lack of progress over the last couple of months and showed them to her mother.

While she looked at those, I pulled out copies of test scores, because LaKeisha had a funny problem of somehow *losing* failing test papers.

"Did you see any of these marks?" I asked her mother.

Suddenly, my innocent student didn't look so settled anymore.

Her mother turned to her and said, "Girl, what the hell is this? How come I didn't see none of these papers?"

LaKeisha didn't say a word, so I had to say *my* piece.

"Well, she told *me* that she lost them."

"But she still had a *C*," her mother continued to argue with me.

"Those test grades do not include homework assignments," I reminded her. "LaKeisha has not completed much of anything this last report. I can show you her entire fourth semester."

"And she can *still* fail with a *C*? I just can't understand that."

I don't think this woman was interested in seeing her daughter's marks at all. She just wanted me to pass her that morning like presto magic or something, but I was not planning on being a magician. Her daughter was going to summer school. That's all there was to it. It wasn't that I disliked the girl, because I had been there myself when I was young, she just hadn't done what she was supposed to do to pass. I had only failed seven students out of nearly one hundred and thirty that I taught that year, because I was very tough on them to learn their work.

"Well, is there anything we can do?" her mother asked me. She had a nerve to try and act civil too, as if that was going to change something. We were four days away from summer vacation. All we were doing was finishing our final paperwork as the students said their last good-byes until September.

I looked that woman straight in her face and said, "She can make it up in summer school." I meant that too. It would be a lesson for LaKeisha in the future.

Her mother returned to sour in a snap of a finger. "Well, who the hell can I talk to about this? Because I don't *believe* she needs no damn summer school."

I could not *believe* what I was hearing.

I asked, "What do you believe she needs?"

The woman looked puzzled for a second. She responded out of spite, looking me over. "She needs a damn teacher who *cares* instead of one who's just working for a *paycheck.* That's what she *needs.* Gon' tell me she can make it up in summer school."

That's when the kids began to laugh and snicker.

"Well, you can go to the principal's office then," I finally told her. Although that wouldn't change her daughter's grade either. I said, "LaKeisha knows the way there," just to add my own spice to the issue.

The woman looked ready to jump me so I stepped aside. Elder or not, I wasn't about to let her kick my ass. I would have broken every nail on my fingers to protect myself.

She looked me over once more before she left and grumbled, "You *think* you fuckin' cute. That's *your* damn problem. Come on, girl," she snapped at her daughter.

I was through! I didn't have the skin to be a schoolteacher in the nineties. At least not at a neighborhood school. Maybe I should have tried a private or Catholic school where more parents were serious about education. However, I thought that would have been a sellout. *I* didn't go to private or Catholic schools. The inner cities *needed* qualified teachers, and I was more than qualified. Many of the inner-city teachers were barely passing their teachers exams. They were just slipping into the system based on need. So I thought I had something extra to offer.

At the end of the day, nearly every teacher in the school had heard about my stand that morning. A few of the older teachers advised me on how to deal with parents, but some of the teachers didn't particularly care about my master's degree and my high standards of instruction. Maybe they felt that passing students kept the peace, but I thought that only set students up to fail in the future.

"I heard what happened this morning," one of the science teachers said to me as I stepped into the hallway and locked my classroom door. I was heading out to my car in the parking lot.

Desiree Johnson had been teaching for four years. She was twenty-nine and had a degree in chemistry from Maryland. We clicked immediately. We both believed in excellence and we were teaching to try and make a difference. Desiree just had a longer fuse than I had, and she had tougher skin. She was athletic and feisty, with a natural short crop of hair.

"Yeah, I guess I might as well get used to that, hunh?" I said to her.

"Unfortunately," she answered. "But don't give up on them, Tracy. It's not the *kids'* fault."

I smiled and shook my head, thinking about the children of students like LaKeisha. If my assumptions were right, she would *definitely* be having them. The boys were already eyeing her, and she didn't have the head strength or the smarts to turn them away. At least *I* was strong enough to *choose* who I wanted to be with. That helps you to *choose* not to get pregnant. Like the saying goes, If you don't stand for something, you're liable to fall for anything.

"So whose fault will it be when *her* children are failing twenty years from now?" I asked my fellow schoolteacher.

Desiree chuckled, taking in my glum outlook. "It's a long cycle that needs to be broken," she said. She was right. I just wasn't so sure that *I* was the one to do the breaking, and with every step we took toward the exit that day, I continued to think, *What the hell am I doing trying to teach anyway?* I still had this inner desire to be someone special, someone who would shine. I couldn't shine at East Germantown Middle School.

We made it out to the parking lot where I was stunned by the broken glass, the graffiti on the walls, and the dullness of the place, as if it was my first time noticing it. I loved Philadelphia, but I realized at that moment that I needed *more* than a regular job. I would suffocate and die there, spiritually. I just needed . . . euphoria, and teaching wouldn't be able to do that for me. I needed that rush of energy that chasing after fast and dangerous guys gave me. I needed the attention that wearing sexy clothes and having things my way out on the streets gave me. I wanted the whole temptation of going for forbidden fruit again, ignoring my parents and doing something wild and crazy. I was just bored out of my mind as a teacher, and I needed a reckless challenge in my life like I had so much of in my younger years.

"So what do you plan to do for your vacation?" Desiree asked me at our cars. She was parked not far from me.

I did not have the faintest idea what I wanted to do for my summer. I said, "Good question. What about you?"

"I'm teaching a couple of summer school classes. After that, my boyfriend and I are going to Hawaii."

"Hawaii?! You *really* picked a place to vacation," I told her. I was jealous. I needed a Hawaii vacation of my own. I also needed the type of boyfriend you could take on a vacation.

"Well, hang on in there, Tracy. It gets easier. The first couple of years are always rough."

"So I've found out," I joked, but it wasn't funny. I had a lot of thinking to do.

I drove home to my two-bedroom apartment off of Lincoln Drive, and took a long look at myself inside of the full-length mirror on my bedroom door. There I was, wearing tailored suits, with manicured nails, jazzy hairstyles, designer shoes, and looking good, just to go and teach middle school students. Not that they didn't need something to aspire to, and someone to show them the way, but maybe that parent was right. I was too damned cute and maybe just a touch superficial for the job.

"Slut!" I cursed myself, stripping from my clothes. I felt guilty. I knew I didn't have the long-term dedication to teach those kids who needed it. I just wanted what *I* needed. Recognition. Was it so wrong to want to feel special and to do something about it?

I sat down on my bed in panties and bra and pulled out my notepad to write a poem about my feelings of mortality. I had always been special. I used to think of myself as a goddess, but suddenly I wasn't special anymore. I could not handle my new reality, so when I had finished my poem, I decided to call my girl Raheema in New Jersey for a little pick-me-up.

Raheema was doing a fellowship at Rutgers University after finishing her degree in African-American Studies at Cornell and her master's at Yale. She was really doing it up! I was proud of her. She was on her way to being one of those big-time scholars who knew something about everything, and I was in luck. I caught her at her office.

"Hey, Ra-Ra. You wanna go to the mall? I hear there's some cute guys up there," I joked with her, reminiscing on our teen years.

She broke up laughing and played her part.

"Tracy, I don't care about that. I have homework to do."

"Girl, this is Saturday. You can do your homework tomorrow."

"I'm going to church tomorrow, Tracy. I don't have time for the mall."

"Well, how 'bout you go to a party with me tonight?"

"For what?"

"What do you mean, 'for what?' So we can meet some guys."

She let out a long sigh and said, "Tracy, how many times do I have to tell you. I am *not* interested in boys."

I broke out of my role-playing and complained, "Raheema, I am just *too through* with this teaching shit! Do you know I had a parent who came up to the school today and asked me why I failed her child when the damn girl didn't do anything for the entire fourth quarter? Some of these parents are a pain in the ass! They want their kids to get a damn free ride in life."

Raheema paused before she said anything. That meant she had a lecture to give me. She was always thinking. That was just her personality.

"Actually, Tracy," she started up, "when you decided to go for that master's degree in English at Hampton, I was really surprised. Then when you came back to Philly and took that teaching job, I just did not know *what* to think. I just *knew* that you would be married and working on your third or fourth child by now. At least that's how you were heading when we were still in high school."

"Yeah, well, you know who fucked that up. Gon' get out of jail and hook up with some damn house mouse," I snapped, referring to my teenage sweetheart and his new wife.

"House mouse? How do you know that Victor's wife doesn't work?"

"I *don't* know. I'm just calling her a house mouse based on what I *do* know," I said. "She's one of those sisters who will do just about anything to satisfy a man's ego. 'Oh, I'll do it, honey. What do you need me to do?'"

Raheema laughed and said, "If I remember correctly, Victor had *you* that way too."

"Yeah, until I grew up and he couldn't handle me on equal terms. That's just how these black men are nowadays. They all want you to be some damned young girl who doesn't know shit. Well, fuck that! Those days are over with for me and I know *too* much."

"So my mother was a house mouse too?" Raheema asked me.

She knew the answer to that, so I was plain honest with her.

"Raheema, your mother was a *big-time* house mouse, and you know it. But she's okay now. So I guess you work through it, but I'm not planning to be one at all. But let's not get into that, because I called you for a pick-me-up, if you have time to chat," I told her.

She said, "Yeah, I have time. I just finished eating a late lunch."

"So what do I do about this whole teaching thing?" I asked her flat out. That was what friends were for, honesty.

Raheema started to laugh again. "Here we go. The same old Tracy," she said. "You want someone else to tell you what to do, so you can go right ahead and do what *you* want to do anyway."

She was right. We knew each other's personalities long before we had our first periods.

"All right, so give me your opinion then," I said, smiling. I felt better already, but I still needed a solution to my problem. What the heck did I want to do with myself?

Raheema said, "Tracy, *we both know* that you are *not* going to be happy until you get *whatever it is* that you want. So I say, stop wasting your time with everything else and go after whatever *scheme* you have in your mind to do. And I won't judge you for it, because that's who you were born to be, just like I was born to be me."

"Well, why does it have to be a 'scheme'?" I asked her. She made it sound like I was still a gold digger.

"Because whatever it is, I'm quite *sure* that it's going to be hard to get. That's just how you are. If it's too easy, you don't want it."

I broke out laughing. Whatever it was that I wanted, it was so hard to get that I couldn't even figure out what it was.

Raheema asked, "Isn't your book *Flyy Girl* being republished this year by a major house?"

Prior to September 1996, my novelized life story was only a local thing on the East Coast.

"Yeah, and I'll be getting more royalties from it," I told her. "I already received my part of the advance."

She said, "That was real cool for Omar Tyree to write your story like that, or should I say *our story,* but I kind of thought that you would follow up with that and become a writer of some kind yourself."

"I *do* write. I still write my poetry," I said. "I just finished one before I called you."

"And how does it make you feel when you write and perform them?"

"Oh, girl, you know my poetry is the shit," I bragged. "That's when I really get a chance to sit down and think and bring stuff together."

"Well, why don't you go for that?"

I said, "I've been told that poetry doesn't really sell like that unless you get a contract to do music with it or something. Everybody can't be Maya Angelou and Nikki Giovanni, you know."

"Well, there you go. It's hard to do, so go ahead and do it then. That sounds right up your alley," Raheema advised me.

I was very hesitant about the poetry thing, even though I knew my stuff was good.

"Or, you could even become a screenwriter or something, because once they put that book out nationally, they might want to take it to film, and that would *really* make us famous," she joked. It was a shock to everyone when *Flyy Girl* came out, especially how people began to like it and talk about it. Most of the people who read it just couldn't believe how fast I was as a teenager, but it was all the truth. However, I had calmed down a lot since then. I was a mature woman, or trying to *be* mature.

"Yeah, I daydreamed about all of that," I admitted. How could I *not* dream of making a movie about my life story?

"Well, what are you waiting for? You need *me* to tell you to go for it? Just get busy and do your thing," Raheema persisted in pushing me. "Once you put your mind to getting what you want, Tracy, *nobody* can stop *you,* and that's the *truth!*"

I tried to play it off and act reserved about her suggestions, but by the time I hung up the phone with my girl Raheema, I was nervous for some reason. I guess I could feel it deep down in my soul. I really *could* make it happen. I had the energy, the talent, the passion, and the drive to do whatever the hell I wanted to do. It was all up to me.

I stood up and took a deep breath. My decision was made already. That's why I was nervous. It was like that single moment before you hit the stage to do your thing. The anxiety. The anticipation. I was filled with it. I wanted to go where the stars were and see just how brightly I could shine, or see if I was only bullshitting myself.

"Well, here goes everything," I said out loud.

I had a college friend at Hampton who moved out to Los Angeles to teach at the elementary level. She was a Spanish minor, she said, to make more money out there. So if I wanted to try my luck at writing, performing poetry, or even acting out in Hollywood where the stars were, then I wanted to have that backup plan, to teach on the side. In hindsight, I guess I wasn't as confident as I thought. I didn't want to become a damn fool and end up broke and struggling out there for some dream. Maybe that's what I was waiting for, a final push to give me the courage to go for it. We all need that extra push sometimes.

As for stardom in New York, where my book was being republished, I never even thought of going up there. That place was like an oversized Philadelphia to me. I went there a few times and was not impressed. It wasn't the kind of place where you could reinvent yourself at a higher level. I needed to go much farther away from home anyway, so that

I could *feel* like I went somewhere. From Philadelphia, New York was only a hop and a skip.

I had never been to Los Angeles, so I didn't know what to expect. I just had to make sure that I stayed away from red or blue outfits, and that I didn't talk too much about my East Coast home. That coastal thing, started up by rap music rivalries, was a damn trip. I wanted to make sure that I was better safe than sorry out there. I loved Tupac *and* Biggie; Death Row Records *and* Bad Boy, but they *all* needed to grow up and stop acting like . . . N-I-double G-As. They were too talented and popular for that.

So I pulled out my phone book and dug up my girl's parents' phone number in Baltimore, and made the call to get in touch with her. She gave me her parents' home number in Baltimore because she knew it would take her a while to get settled out in LA, and it was no sense in giving out numbers that could change.

"Hello," her mother answered the phone in Baltimore. I *assumed* it was her mother, but just to make sure, I kept my introduction simple.

"Yes, this is Tracy Ellison. I went to Hampton with Kendra Dayton."

"Oh, yeah, that's my daughter."

*Good*, I thought to myself. "Oh, well, how do you do?" I asked her.

"I'm fine. So, what can I do for you?"

"Well, I'm a middle school teacher in Philadelphia, and Kendra told me that she wanted to teach in the Los Angeles area, and that I could come and visit her whenever I felt up to traveling to the West Coast."

"Yeah, she *is* a schoolteacher out there, and she *loves* it! You need me to give her your number?"

"Would you please, and have her call me as soon as she gets a chance?"

"Okay. Let me get out a pen and a piece of paper and I'll call her tonight. You know she's still at school out there right now with the three-hour time difference," her mother said. "So I usually call her right before I go to bed."

I wasn't even thinking about the time change. "Oh, yeah, thanks for reminding me."

I gave her my number, chatted her up a bit, and hung up the phone with an energy boost. I felt like someone had just poured a five-pound bag of sugar into my veins. I needed to go out jogging, play tennis, run up and down the stairway, have some good sex, or *something*. I was just burning up with energy!

I couldn't *wait* to plan my trip to California. My phone rang right in the middle of my new excitement.

"Hello."

"Hey, girl. How was your school day?" It was Mike, a muscle-bound weight trainer that I was seeing. I kept real loose ties with him, because I didn't need no macho shit holding me down. In fact, I only dealt with him because he could give a massage like an Egyptian god or something. He could eat a *mean* dish of stew (if you know what I mean) at that.

I sighed and said, "Don't take me back to that place. I was just starting to recuperate."

He chuckled. "It was that bad, hunh?"

"Yeah, that bad," I answered.

I thought about asking him what he was doing and inviting him over for an afternoon sweat-out. He had called at just the right time. Mike had the kind of employment, as a weight trainer with Philadelphia sports jocks, where he had money and plenty of time on his hands. He was always bragging about who he worked with, and who played for the Eagles, the Sixers, or the Phillies. I didn't really pay the shit any mind, myself, because once I grew up and went away to college, I learned to appreciate the power of making my own damn money and not sweating some rich assholes who are mostly out for a pussy chase. Not that *all* of them were like that, but you know what I mean, *and* you know the kind of women who chase them. Nevertheless, I was still a woman and sex was sex. It was good for the soul.

I cut straight through the chase. "What are you doing right now? You have any free time?"

"Later on tonight, but not right now," Mike answered.

I didn't want to set up anything for later though. What if I didn't feel like it later on? Or what if I wanted to start planning things for LA. I didn't need a man in the way of that, especially if he knew that I was going somewhere. Mike tried to play the role like he could be as straight business as I was about our loose relationship, but I knew that he really liked me, and it would all come out as soon as he knew I was planning to relocate. I could already predict his response.

"Well, try and call me later on then," I told him.

"Why don't we just set a time?"

"Why don't we just leave it open?" I asked him instead. "And if we close it, then we close it later on?"

He chuckled again and said, "You're a hard woman to break, you know that?"

He knew what time it was, and he knew that he couldn't hold me down.

I said, "I'm as hard as those damn weights you lift," just to rub it in. I owed that all to Mr. Victor Hinson, or Qadeer Muhammad, as he called himself, for leaving me hanging like he did after getting out of jail and hooking up with someone else.

"You gon' need to soften up *sometime.* Like when I put my hands on you, and everything else," Mike teased me.

What would a man be without a good comeback line, right? I just laughed at him.

"Well, we'll just have to wait and see what happens."

"Aw'ight then. We'll play it your way."

I hung up the phone, and my energy had already settled a bit. I laid back on my bed, still in my bra and panties, and relaxed. Suddenly, I felt kinky. I decided to take my bra and panties off, and turn my oscillating fan on low, and let it blow over my naked body in bed, as I daydreamed of how sweet my future would be out in Hollywood, because Hollywood got swingers.

*You want this?* I asked a chocolate, baldheaded man in my daydream.

*Yes. All of it,* he told me.

I spread my legs wider with my right knee up and stroked my stomach with a sexy grin.

*Well, come and get it then.*

I just relaxed with my daydream and let my fan blow me up and down.

## $ $ $

I never did hook up with Mike that night. I went to the movies by myself instead, and began doing research on the whole Hollywood name game, you know, who was doing what and who was successful at it. Mike wanted to accompany me on my poetry night that Thursday, but I never took any men to my readings. I didn't want to be stuck with him if a deep, *deep* brother did his thing up onstage and I decided to seduce him right there on the spot. Well, the shit never happened because a lot of poetic brothers, who I came in contact with, either brought their own women to the readings, were too artistically busy to just chill, or were unorganized and full of themselves, so no one ever qualified, and that *hunk* of a man, Philadelphia's own Wadud, was happily married already.

I guess I was always fantasizing about something. Hollywood was the perfect place for me.

Right when I grabbed my bag in my seventies-inspired poetry gear—oversized bell-bottom jeans, a rayon shirt, and big shoes (call me a chameleon)—my telephone rang.

I was hesitant to answer it. I had already told Mike no, and I didn't have time for a chat with anyone else, but I answered it anyway, just in case it was something important.

It was. Kendra Dayton was calling me from California. She said, "Tracy Ellison. What's up, girl? My mom called and told me that you were ready to visit California. Sorry I didn't get back to you sooner. It's the end of the school year, and you *know* how that can get."

"Girl, don't even go there," I told her. "I have *so* many horror stories."

"Don't we all. We need a teachers' mental clinic, right?" she said.

I begged to differ. I said, "No, we need a *parents'* mental clinic."

"Ay-men to that," she responded and laughed. "Aaayy-men!"

I said, "Your mother told me that you loved teaching out there."

"That doesn't mean that I don't have any problems."

I laughed. I could tell that Kendra and I would hit it off well if we lived in the same city. I didn't even talk to her all that much at Hampton. We just chatted when we saw each other, but as we had ended up in the same teaching profession, it gave us more to relate to.

"So, can I crash at your place for a week, or what? Do you have a kinky boyfriend that I need to know about in advance?" I joked. I don't know what was wrong with me, but sometimes I just said the first thing that came to mind, particularly when I was pressed, and I was pressed to see Hollywood.

Luckily, Kendra found my joke appealing and laughed.

"They have a different kind of black man out here. They're more laid back," she said. "*Too* laid back sometimes. I dream every now and then of inviting out a few in-your-face Baltimore brothers from home.

"'Hey girl, come here, yo'," she mocked them.

I smiled. "Do they use 'yo' for everything in Baltimore?"

"Yes they do."

"So, you mean to tell me that guys out in California are not really roughnecks like they show in these movies?" I couldn't believe that they could lie that much. Were movies *that much* make-believe?

Kendra said, "Girl, do you think I would waste my time out here with *them* fools? Yeah, they have those crazy gangbangers out here, but I'm talking about *professional* and college-educated men, not no 'hood rats, but they *do* have them out here, and they are just as ignorant as they are in those movies."

"So where do you live out there?" I asked her. I almost forgot about my poetry reading.

"Carson. It's right next to Compton, and right above Long Beach."

"So you're right in the midst of the music makers."

"Yeah, and I'll tell you something else too. All that crazy

stuff they talk about in their music, they're not even lying. Some of these people out here are downright foul, and they use the N-word, the MF-word and B-word in regular conversation.

"On the East Coast, at least we know when to change it up," she said. "Well, they don't change anything out here, and then they want to complain about a lack of jobs. Well, who wants to hire you walking around with plaits in your hair, your pants hanging down, underwear showing, no education, and a filthy mouth with no shame to it?"

I didn't realize that Kendra was so fiery. I didn't know what else to say, but I realized that I was running late.

"So, when are you planning to come out here?" she asked me, right on cue. I had to go.

"I guess in mid July or early August," I told her. "I still have to buy plane tickets. Will you still be there this summer?"

"Yeah, I'll be here. I have plane tickets to fly home to Baltimore next week. I'll spend the last week of June back at home, and fly right back out to LAX. The weather and the terrain is beautiful out here. Wait until you see it.

"We didn't have any palm trees in Baltimore," she joked.

I told her that I was running late for my poetry reading and got her number.

"Yeah, you did write poetry," she remembered. "You think you might want to write screenplays or something out here? I have connections if you do. I know a woman who works with the screenwriters guild."

Man, talk about things moving fast! I began to wonder what took me so long to try that big move to the West Coast myself.

"Well, we'll sit down and talk about all of that when I get out there," I promised her.

I left for my poetry reading with the biggest head in the

world. I just *knew* that I would put my thing down once I got out to California. I was cruising in my black Toyota Camry on Lincoln Drive and heading toward downtown on air. You couldn't tell me anything!

When I arrived at the Philadelphia Arts Bank Cafe on Broad Street, I was still smiling. It was a typical cafe with tables, chairs, coffee, tea, and pastries that opened up for nighttime events with a small front area that they used as a performance stage. You could look right inside from the busy traffic on Broad Street.

Lil' Lez' said, "Damn, Tracy, was it *that* good?" She was referring to sex. Leslie Pina, a half-pint of a sister with the cute looks that made guys love to call her their shorty, could sound as horny as *three* women. When she wasn't doing a poetic rap thing, she usually wrote about love and fucking, and not necessarily in that order.

I said, "This has nothing to do with sex. I'm just feeling good tonight."

She smiled at me and asked, "Are you sure?"

I just shook my head at her and grinned. I found a table with an open chair, which was hard to do, because the place was packed that night. I took a seat right as Stephanie Renee was taking the stage, a poet/performer/writer/singer/actor/events coordinator and publisher of a newsletter called *Creative Child*.

Stephanie's style was part everything, like mine. Humor. Frankness. Love. Community. Dialogue. Human politics. Theatrical, and many times she was very spiritual. Her poems were much more spiritual than mine. She could sing too. I couldn't hold a note to save my life.

I sat there and listened to Stephanie do her thing, and my smile faded away. I thought, *What makes my writing any better than hers?* Stephanie had more range, more performance experience, and had been pushing her creativity for years, but she was more or less local. I wanted to be bigger than that with everything that I did.

Next up was Jill Scott. Jill could be as sexual as Lil' Lez' sometimes, but Jill's shit got raw and real deep on you. In fact, if I had to pick one sister to represent in a national poetry contest from Philly, Jill Scott would be very hard to deny. She cleared your ears and mind out whenever she performed, and filled you back up from head to toe with whatever the hell she was talking about. However, her style could be mundane, because you already knew what you would get with her.

I sat there and listened to everyone's poetry before I did my three pieces. I didn't even feel like reading them anymore. Everyone there would have loved to take their art to the next level, and I was sure that screenwriting and acting would have ten times as many talented and driven people out in California.

I did my first two pieces with little energy, then I introduced my new poem.

"I just wrote this one on Monday, but this is how I've been feeling lately, because I realize that all of us would love to shine on a major stage one day. I mean, that's just the American way. Chase your dream, right?

"Anyway, here it is, 'Recognition':

> *"I had a big date yesterday*
> *with King Kong*
> *on top of the World Trade Center.*
> *Helicopters swung in,*
> *news cameras taped it,*
> *and reporters took notes with flashing light bulbs*
> *all around me.*

*"But my King Kong got pissed off, y'all,*
*with all of the noisy cock blockers.*
*So somebody shot him.*
*And he fell waaay*
*down.*
*BOOM!*

*"Then I cried*
*while the whole world watched me*
*in silence.*
*But when I awoke,*
*I realized that my King Kong*
*was only a little brown Teddy Bear*
*that my momma gave me.*
*And nobody knew me.*
*Even worse,*
*nobody cared*
*to know."*

Simply put, my poem was a short fuse that night that fizzled into nothing. At first the audience just sat there, as if they were waiting for more. I received a slow and steady applause, but they were clapping just to send me the hell off of the stage. I could tell. I guess "Recognition" was too short and melodramatic for them, and I didn't really care *what* they thought because poems serve as references to your life, and they are meaningful whether an audience is into it or not.

A silly-ass brother then decided to be a comedian.

"*I* wanna know you!" he yelled at me as I walked off from the stage.

Lil' Lez' spoke to me again before I left that night.

She said, "I felt you, Tracy. That shit was real. We all feel that way sometimes. I know *I* do. Some people just don't want to admit it. And that's why they didn't get it. It went right over their heads."

$ $ $

I left Broad Street in my car, and was disappointed. I had to pump myself up as I drove back home close to midnight.

"I can do this shit!" I yelled. "Just put my mind to it like my girl Raheema said. *She* knows I can do it, and she's smart. She's the smartest person I know. And she's right too. I'm the most *driven* person that *she* knows. I can do anything I put my mind to."

I found myself cutting down everyone else while pumping up myself. I was taller than her, prettier than her, better than him, smarter than her, and I was going to show them *all* that I was the shit!

"You just wait," I told myself.

Another bag of sugar filled up my veins. I was hyped again, and I had no idea how I would fall asleep that night before my last day as a teacher at East Germantown Middle School. I just had too many battles going on in my mind that night, but there was one thing that I *did* know.

I screamed, "HOLLYWOOD, HERE I FUCKIN' COME!"

I was still defiant, just like I was when I was a teenager.

# Big Girls Don't Cry

*Tears may roll down my face,*
*but tissues wipe them away.*
*Today it rained on my parade,*
*but tomorrow starts a new day.*

# April 2000

$ $

$

**M**y agent was hollering at me through the cell phone, while I sat in a daze behind the wheel of the new Infiniti SUV I had bought for my father's birthday.

"TRACY! Are you still there?! Answer me!"

"Yeah, I'm here. I just blanked out for a second," I told her.

She calmed down and took a deep breath. I could hear her through the phone.

"Are you sure you're okay?"

"If I'm not, then I'll tell you tomorrow. But tonight, I just want to go inside and lie down."

"Okay, well, I'll get right on that call for the book deal tomorrow."

"Yeah," I responded to her, "you do that."

"And what about the radio interview in the morning? Will you still be up to that?"

I had agreed to do the *Wendy Williams Show* on Power 99 FM. That Wendy chick loved to gossip. I would need a lot of energy to deal with her. If I didn't have it, I wouldn't be representing for my hometown, and if I canceled they may take it that I was too big to do the show as promised. It was a no-win situation, and I had to keep pushing forward.

"Yeah, I'm still doing it. I just need to get some rest."

"Are you absolutely sure?" my girl asked me again.

"Don't force yourself to do it if you're really not up to it. We can reschedule. I mean, it's not as if you're promoting anything. You'll be home in Philly for another week, right?"

She had a point, I was just showing up to give the station love, but I just couldn't allow myself to punk out like that. I had to suck it up and keep going. I convinced myself that I would be fine in the morning.

"No, I'll do it, and I'll call you tomorrow afternoon sometime, which will be *your* morning," I joked, to loosen myself up.

"Okay. I'll be waiting for that call."

I hung up my cell phone and took a deep breath of my own. I thought, *Do I still feel like announcing my gift to my father, or should I just let it sit out front for a day and tell him about it after he gets home from work tomorrow.* With *my* bad luck, somebody would decide to steal it right out from in front of the house. I decided to wait anyway, because my parents would be able to tell that something was wrong with me if I didn't show the proper enthusiasm about the gift that night, and in my present state of mind there was no way in the world for me to act all jovial.

I tossed the car keys and paperwork in my purse, took another deep breath, and started toward the house. As I was closing the door to the Infiniti, my girl Mercedes was walking out from her parents' house next door.

"Haaay, Tracy! I knew I'd catch up to you sooner or later."

She approached me for a hug. I was not in the mood for it, but I *had* to hug her, right? She would have thought that I had my nose all up in the air if I didn't.

I said, "Yeah, you caught me," and forced a smile.

Mercedes immediately looked at the Infiniti. "That's real nice. You just got it?"

I guess she could tell that it was brand-new. It had that straight-off-the-lot shine to it.

"It's a gift for my father's birthday," I told her.

She nodded, still checking it out. "Oh, well, that's nice. How much did it cost you?"

Did I really want to answer that question? . . . No. Of course not.

"It wasn't free," I told her. I left it at that.

Mercedes said, "Shit, don't I know it. Ain't nothin' out here for free."

She had lost weight during her period of addiction to drugs years ago, and she had never regained it. Although she didn't look unhealthy or anything. She was just thinner than she was when she was flyy. She still had the knockout looks though. Hell, Mercedes was the one who had turned *me* on to materialism, but I couldn't blame her for everything that *I* went through, and I still managed to turn myself around and go to college.

Mercedes straightened up her act and ended up working at the drug addiction clinic where she first received help. She even worked her way up to a management position there, but she couldn't move up in salary until she went ahead and received more formal education, which she refused to do. Raheema and I had already discussed it. Mercedes was just plain averse to going back to school, and to think that she used to be a straight-A student in grade school. Drugs can really mess up a person's head.

I was really in no mood for chatting with Mercedes that night, so I told her how long a day it had been for me and promised to catch up with her later on in the week.

"Oh, well, don't let *me* hold you up. Go on in and get yourself some rest."

I sensed a touch of sarcasm in her response to me, but I didn't have time for bickering with her, so I let it slide.

"Okay, well, I'll call you up later on."

"Later on, like tonight?" she asked me. She seemed real pressed to talk to me.

I shook my head. "No. I mean, later on like tomorrow or something."

"Oh. Well, all right then, I'll talk to you. I have something important to ask you anyway."

It was a setup. I felt like one of Mercedes' old boyfriends, as if I was about to be used for her personal gain. I had been the same way for a few wild years back in the eighties, so I knew Mercedes as well as I knew myself. However, I let that slide, too.

"Okay," I told her with a nod. I was ready to head in the house.

"So we can talk, right?"

She was trying to twist my arm into promising her something, something that probably had nothing to do with us being girlfriends. You get that a lot when you start making money. Stardom can make you think that everyone is after some of it, and usually, they are, but I didn't bust my ass to make it big in Hollywood just to become a year-around Santa Claus. I'm sorry, but that was not my damn job!

I took another calming, deep breath before I got irritated. "Yeah, we can talk."

Mercedes said, "I don't want to make it seem like I'm bothering you or anything."

It was too late for that, and I was already bothered.

"Just let me go inside and rest tonight, and we'll deal with *whatever* when we see each other again," I told her.

She gave me one of those deep-eyed looks of hers and nodded. "Okay. That's cool."

Mercedes was as good at reading people as I was. She was probably better at it, but I thought she would have matured past the petty shit, especially if she was supposed to be *helping* other people. Excuse my French, but she was thirty-four fucking years old and still playing head games! Was life still that damn trivial to her? When I thought about her while shooting my movie *Led Astray,* I was only acting, but in real life, Mercedes was obviously still going through the bullshit.

I walked inside the house with my old key. My mom and dad were nestled on the sofa watching Chris Tucker's *Rush Hour* on video. I looked at them and just started smiling. They had it good, they just didn't know it. I was envious.

"Tracy, did you ever see this *Rush Hour* movie?" my mother asked me. "That damn Chris Tucker is a *fool!*"

"Yeah, I saw it. He's a big man in Tinseltown. They tried to hold him back but couldn't."

"Why, because they had Will Smith out there already?" my father asked me with a grin. Black men were always suspecting racism. It was as if they had a built-in radar for it. Even my brother Jason was hip to it.

I smiled back at my dad and said, "You know the game, but right now there are just too many black stars out there for Hollywood to continue working from those strict quotas anymore. And if they did, then *I* could have never broken out, because Halle Berry, Regina King, and Lela Rochon were just snatching up *everything* for a while," I joked.

I looked at my parents all snuggled up on the sofa again, and decided that *I* wanted a piece of that. I took my behind right over to the sofa and tried to force my way in between them.

My mom said, "Tracy, what are you doing? You go get your

own man. You're not a little girl anymore to squeeze in between us. What's wrong with you?"

I ignored her and said, "Mom, stop blocking the love."

My father just laughed at us.

"I got two girls fighting over my attention again," he
teased.

Mom gave him the evil eye. "Well, *she's* going back out
to California in two weeks."

I looked at her and said, "Are you trying to get rid of
me, Mom. What do you think I came home for? I need
some love too. I had a rough day," I pouted. I was slightly
offended by it.

She said, "Girl, I was just playing with you. You know I
love you. I just didn't expect for you to run up in here and
jump in between us."

My mother was close to fifty herself and still looked like
a thirty-something honey chaser. She had all of the honey
that she needed with my father though. He was aging the
way that only black men could, like fine, dark wine. After a
minute or two, I decided to step out of the way and return
to my old room. I guess I had a long face when I did it.

"Tracy, you can stay here if you want," my mother compromised. "I heard that you Hollywood types are spoiled,
but God!" she joked to rub it in.

I shook my head and grinned. "I was spoiled *long* before
I went to Hollywood."

My father laughed out loud. "Tell us something we
*didn't* know."

I made my way up the steps and into my old room. I fell
to the small, twin-size bed and thought of all of the memories I had there: Mom and Dad arguing in the hallways at
night, sleepovers with Raheema, Bruce hiding inside of my
closet for dear life, Timmy sneaking up to my room after

school, late-night phone calls on the cordless, and many fantasies about Victor spending the night in my bed with me. I even pulled out my pen and notepad and wrote a poem about it: "My Old Room."

Before long, all of my worries that night had slipped away, replaced by soothing flashbacks of the past, as I crashed into a much needed sleep.

## $ $ $

"Tracy! You have that interview on Power 99 this morning, don't you?"

My mother was standing at my door. I looked up at the alarm clock. It was six thirty-seven in the morning. I forgot to set it.

I mumbled, "Yeah, I know," and didn't budge.

"Well, that Wendy Williams is very popular here. A lot of people listen to her. I listen to WDAS myself. I like the older music.

"Are you doing Mary Mason while you're here, on WHAT?" she asked me.

"On Thursday," I told her. "I do NBC that same morning." I was showing everyone love. It was all a part of my homecoming celebration.

"NBC? With Steve Levy? Well, what are you gonna wear?" my mother asked me.

I smiled and said, "Why, you want to pick something out for me, Mom?"

"No, you do okay with that, because I would *tell you* if you didn't. I just figured I'd ask."

My father stuck his head in the door and said, "I'll see you later on, Ms. Grant."

My mother grinned at it.

"I'll need to explain that today," I told her. "I hear a lot of people are assuming things about it."

My mother shrugged her shoulders. "Do what you have to do. I have to get ready for work myself," she said, walking back out.

I climbed out of bed to pick out my clothes for the day. I didn't plan to look all spiffy for a radio show. It wasn't as if anyone could see me. However, if I *did* look fabulous, maybe Wendy Williams would say something about that over the air. Nevertheless, I went with some loose-fitting blue jeans and a lime green cotton shirt, like an ordinary Josette.

I had to decide whether I would take the Infiniti for the day or catch a taxi. I guess I should have thought about that once I decided to wait an extra day to surprise my father with his birthday gift. The original plan was to take my father's Buick after I gave him the Infiniti. Maybe he could sell the Buick, store it in a garage, or use it just to drive to work at the hospital. That way he could cut down on unnecessary mileage on his new SUV.

Despite the carjack attempt from the night before, I figured I *had* to take the Infiniti. I didn't feel like jumping in and out of taxis all day, and I wanted to make a run to King of Prussia Mall for a big-time sale that they were advertising.

So I took the Infiniti that morning and arrived at Power 99's studio in the Roxborough area around fifteen minutes of eight. I couldn't even get inside of the place. I walked from the front door to the back, and back to the front again, only to have to walk a second time to the back to get in.

"Office hours start at nine o'clock?" I asked the quiet brother who finally let me in.

He grinned and said, "Yeah."

It was a good thing I was determined to do the interview. Otherwise, had I been an egotistical star, I would have walked off and driven back home for more sleep. My parents only lived fifteen minutes away from the station.

I walked in the studio and met Wendy Williams, a tall, big-eyed, busty sister. She had the natural energy of five cups of coffee with plenty of cream and sugar added.

"Tracy Ellison Grant! I'm so glad to finally meet you! Here, have a seat," she said, tossing the belongings of Dee Lee (one of her two male cohosts from the Dream Team Morning Show) to the floor.

"Yeah, just *throw* my stuff on the floor. I don't mind," the light, bright brother cracked at her.

"It shouldn't have been there. You know that's my guest chair."

"Well, just *maybe* I had it set up so I could politely move it for the lovely sister to sit down."

"So, in other words, I busted your groove."

"Yes, you did. Like always."

"Well, Dee Lee, learn to stop *harassing* my guests then."

"Oh, now Wendy, don't you *dare* go there, because I have *nada* to say to you when you invite the entire Philadelphia *Eagles* backfield up in here so you can foam at the mouth."

She broke into a laugh and said, "Oh my God! Just don't tell my husband."

"Treat me with some respect then," Dee Lee told her. "I'm not a punk named Robin to your Batman. I'm like Bruce Lee playing Kato, and I'll kick your ass up in here. Then it'll be me and your husband fighting."

Wendy actually jumped out of her rotating chair and threw a couple of karate moves on him. They were acting as if it was lunchtime or something. They were having *big* fun! Eight o'clock in the morning!

"Excuse us, Tracy, because we *are* adults in here. At least *some* of us are," Wendy joked again.

I grinned and said, "This is your house. I'm just a visitor."

I wish Hollywood was that fun. After you've been on the set for a few days, doing useless repetitions of the same small scenes, the fun just leaps out of it. Until, of course, you wrap and get ready for editing. That's when it begins to be fun again, waiting for your show to air on television or your film to premiere in the theaters. At least for the people who make the final cuts with standout lines and scenes.

When the red light flashed to go back on air at Power 99 FM, Wendy and Dee Lee took their silliness from the break and went right on air with it.

Wendy pushed her chair up to the microphone and said, "Our guest for the day is Philadelphia's own movie star, Tracy Ellison Grant, of the Hollywood film *Led Astray,* who many of you also know from *Flyy Girl,* a book written about her life growing up right here in the Germantown area of Philadelphia, and the fast life of the 1980s. Well, Tracy is here in our Power 99 FM studios everyone, and Dee Lee, my infamous cohost, has already tried to hit on her, but I busted his groove. So now he's all upset with me and he's *threatening* to tell my husband about all of the Philadelphia Eagles that I bring on the show just to flirt with. But it will *never* work, because my husband loves me, trusts me, and he *knows* that everything I do at Power 99 FM is only a business thing, and a business thing alone."

Dee Lee said, "Yeah, right. I'll tell him a few things that were entirely *not* business."

"Yeah, Dee Lee, like what?" she called him out. "What exactly are you gonna tell my loving and *secure*—which is a very big word in working marriages, by the way, for all of you new couples out there—husband?"

"Oh, now, Wendy, don't let me get started on the time you took homeboy in the back and ah—"

"Anyway," she said, cutting him off with a laugh.

"He won't be so *secure* after that," Dee Lee continued.

"Yes he will, because I haven't done anything, and I'll just tell him, 'Honey, these are all lies because I busted Dee Lee's groove with our guest, Tracy Ellison Grant, and now he's trying desperately to get back at me.'

"So, anyway we have Tracy Ellison Grant here in our Power 99 FM studios, and we're going to come right back to her after a break, and before Dee Lee starts making up any lies to get me in trouble with my sweet, dear, and loving husband. Kiss, kiss."

"Oh, *now* she's trying to butter him up," Dee Lee said. "We *all* know what *that* means."

"It means what?"

"It means that you're *guilty.*"

"Yeah, whatever. So, we'll be back everyone, with Tracy Ellison Grant."

As soon as we were off of the air for more music, or *they* were off of the air, because I didn't have a chance to even *breathe* in the microphone, Wendy asked me about the name thing.

"Okay, now I have to ask you about this Grant name thing, because my sources in Hollywood say that you have a husband back here in Philly, and my Philadelphia sources say that you have a man back out in LA. And *I* don't know *what* to think, so I just have to ask you that."

I smiled. "I just spoke to my mother about the name

thing this morning, and it's a real simple explanation to it."

"Okay, well, let's save that for the Power 99 FM audience out there, because everyone is like, so confused about this whole name thing. I mean, some people were even saying that you had added the Grant name on to hide that you had turned into a lesbian. And I said, wait a minute. After reading about your early life in your book *Flyy Girl,* I just couldn't see how you could go from *that,* with all of the cute guys and everything, to wanting just . . . *girls.* You know what I mean? That just didn't add up to me."

Dee Lee looked at me and broke out laughing. "That's Wendy," he told me. "She *will* go there."

"Well, I'm just giving Tracy a chance to clear all of this up, you know, because that *is* what I'm hearing, and before I just jump to any conclusions." She gave Dee Lee a mischievous smile.

He said, "Oh, you've *never* done that before. That's not even your style."

Wendy laughed it off and turned back to me. "Anyway, before I jump to any conclusions, I just wanted to give you the opportunity, in your hometown and all, to set the record straight."

"Or crooked, if the case may be," Dee Lee added jokingly.

"Well, I'll straighten that all out immediately," I told them. I was not the *least* bit amused by it. Can you *believe* that?! A *lesbian?!* Was Wendy just making that shit up for effect or did she really hear that?

We went back on air and got right into it.

"Okay, we're back with our guest for the day, movie star, slash screenwriter, slash author, Tracy Ellison Grant, and the first thing we want to do is have her clear up the whole

Grant name thing, because some people, and I'm not going to say any names, but you know who you are out there, have been saying some cruel things about the home-girl. So we, at Power 99 FM, are going to give Tracy a chance to defend herself."

"That's right. We got your back, Tracy," Dee Lee added.

"Well, I should have had more coffee this morning for this," I began. "So this is how you guys have taken over Philadelphia and killed the Carter and Sanborn show?" I cracked for general purposes. I had to let them know that I was *not* a damn plaything *or* a pushover!

"Oh-kay," Wendy responded.

Frankly, I didn't give a fuck! I said, "The Grant at the end of my name was added because once I went from sitcom writing to screenwriting and then to acting, I found there was a Tracy Ellis and also a Tracy Ells already in the books. So instead of being caught up between those two, I just decided to add Grant. Plain and simple."

"Wow. Just like that," Wendy said. "So there was no funny business going on with the name change at all, it was just a professional thing?"

"Yes, that's all that it was," I responded. "So everyone out there adding their own particular twist to it needs to grow up." I was still appalled by the whole lesbian thing. I wondered how far the rumor had traveled.

Did Mercedes know about *that*? She *was* still connected to the streets more than anyone else I knew. My concentration was blown again. I just couldn't believe how twisted things could get once you become a celebrity.

Wendy said, "So, have you already been asked a bunch a questions about that? Is it an old story for you by now?"

"Actually, I *haven't* been asked a lot about it," I told her. "That's why I knew that I would have to say something to someone sooner or later. I guess I just didn't know what kind of rumors were out there about it, but I did realize that some people would assume I had married someone named Grant. That crossed my mind when I first decided on it."

"Well, yeah, especially for the people who read your book," Wendy said. "We were all thinking, *What's up with this* Grant *thing?* We all thought that you were waiting to marry Victor Hinson. Then the brother went to jail and changed his name to Muhammad, right? So what was up with this Tracy Ellison *Grant?*"

I had to give Wendy one thing: she knew her shit. She had obviously read my book.

I said, "Well, that's all true, but it didn't happen like a big old fairy tale. I had to move on, but that does *not* mean that I moved *into* the closet and tried to cover it up with a name change, for all of the people out there who somehow got it twisted."

I just could not seem to keep my mouth shut about the lesbian matter. It really bothered me. I guess because I was so *un-lesbian*.

Dee Lee jumped in and said, "Well, why didn't you just use your middle name or initial? Isn't that what a lot of other Hollywood stars do?"

I said, "I thought of that, but I wasn't too fond of using my middle initial."

Wendy took my earlier cue regarding lesbianism and ran with it like a fox who had just spotted the rabbit. "Well, let's talk about this fear of being labeled a lesbian when we come back. Because it seems like a lot of successful sisters have been called lesbians at one time or another, simply because they could not be attached to a man."

Once I realized that I had let the cat out of the bag on

the air, I felt like kicking myself in the mouth. Wendy had only mentioned it *off* of the air. Nevertheless, if the rumor was floating around that I was a lesbian, then I had to face it and have it corrected. I couldn't tiptoe around it and hope that those who believed it would know what I was referring to. That idea seemed silly. It would also seem as though I had something to hide. So I *had* to get it out in the open. There was no other way around it.

Wendy Williams had set me up perfectly. Just by bringing that crazy shit up she made me address it. I had no intentions of dealing with something like that on a popular morning show in my hometown of Philadelphia, while my parents, fans, and family members were all listening in. I felt like a damn fool! I began to feel really hot and clammy with a headache coming on. I had to compose myself and deal with it like a professional.

When we came back on the air, I said, "Wendy, you know what this is? It's all about sexism. A woman is not supposed to have her own money without a man being attached to it somewhere. Even Oprah had to bring her man Stedman all up on her show and parade him around so that everyone would know that *she had* one. You remember that?"

I decided to get the hell off of that show as smoothly as I could. I had heard that Wendy *idolized* herself some Oprah Winfrey and would just about kiss the ground that Oprah walked on.

She got excited immediately and said, "Okay, now *that's* true. Oprah Winfrey *is* my girl and all like that, but it's not like I would bring *my* husband or boyfriend all up on my show so that people will know that I have one just to stop the rumor mills. You know what I'm saying? I've *never* had to go *that* far."

"Then again, you've never had Oprah Winfrey's money either," Dee Lee interjected for another laugh.

"But you *do* talk about your husband a lot on the air," I reminded Wendy. I heard that about her as well.

Dee Lee nodded and said, "Yeah, you do."

I don't know where the third member of the Dream Team was that morning, nor did I care. I just had to fight my way through it and still come out smelling at least *halfway* decent. By the end of my interview I had done a fairly decent job of turning Wendy back on her heels.

She said, "Well, this has really been fun. So come back real soon, Tracy, and let's do this again sometime."

I didn't make any promises, and by the time I made it back out to my father's Infiniti that morning someone was ringing me on my cellular.

*Should I even answer this?* I thought to myself. I just *knew* that it would be more bad news. Whoever it was, they had obviously just listened to the show and felt that it was urgent to talk to me directly afterwards. So I ignored it until my cellular phone rang with two more calls.

I finally answered it, about to be teed off again. "Hell-lo."

"Tracy, this is your mother."

"Oh, Mom." She was calling me straight from the nursing home cafeteria where she still worked as a dietitian. I felt like apologizing to her for my attitude, but I didn't because I was sure she had something to say about the show that I may not have liked. My mother always thought that I responded with my heart too much and not with my head. She said that I was a lot like her in that way, and like far too many women who were down on their luck in life. "We have to learn to *think* more before we *do* things," my mother told me. "That's a lesson it took me *years* to learn, and I'm *still* learning it."

She said real calm over the phone, "Tracy, you know you did it again, right?"

I sighed and let her go on. It was no point in arguing with her. That only would have run up my cellular phone bill.

"Now you have to realize that when you decided to become an actress, you became public property for everyone to talk about you, just like when that book came out. You remember how many people were talking about *our* decisions?"

My mother would never let me forget that *Flyy Girl* exposed *her* life as well.

"Yeah, Mom, I remember."

"Well, now you're doing it to yourself again, and if you allow yourself to get sucked into these petty games of *he say, she say*, you won't get *any* sleep at night."

"So, what am I supposed to do, Mom, just ignore it? In my *own* home?"

"Yes. That's *exactly* what you do. Ignore it," she argued. "People who know you know that you're not a lesbian. And those who even want to *think* that don't know you."

"Well, have *you* heard any of those rumors?" I asked her. I was curious to see if she was already ignoring them and hadn't said anything to me about it.

"No I haven't, and don't you think that I would have *told you* something if I heard anything like that. I mean, shit, you're still my daughter, Hollywood or not.

"I wouldn't let *anyone* say that kind of thing about my daughter. Are you *crazy*?!" She sounded as pissed off about it as I was. That made me smile. I felt better about it. Mom had my back.

"And why did you tell everyone that you didn't like your middle name?" she asked me.

"I didn't say that. I said I wasn't *fond* of using my middle initial."

"Well, what's so wrong with using Tracy Louise Ellison?"

I began to laugh as I pulled out from the parking space.

"Come on, Mom, don't start that again. 'Louise' makes me sound like I'm fifty years old." In my mind, all I could see was images of Mr. George Jefferson from *The Jeffersons* hollering "Weee-zaaay!"

My mom laughed with me and said, "Well, 'Grant' doesn't sound that young, either. It reminds *me* of the Civil War, and we weren't *free* back then, you know."

"*Some* of us weren't free," I corrected her.

"*Most* of us weren't," she argued.

I said, "Well, Mom, I don't want to keep running up this phone bill for local calls. I'll talk to you when I see you at home tonight."

"Running up a *phone* bill," she snapped at me. "You mean to tell me that you're making Hollywood money now and you're still concerned about some *phone bill*?"

"Mom, trust me. If you forget that you're talking on these cellular phones, your monthly bill can get up to as much as a mortgage for a house."

She chuckled and said, "Okay, well, I'll see you later then. And by the way, was that new silver truck outside a gift for your father's fifty-first birthday? You know he noticed it. You couldn't find a better place to hide it than that?"

I just smiled. "What made you think that?"

"Girl, I wasn't born yesterday. And your *father* wasn't born yesterday either."

"Well, that's a long story, but I was planning on giving it to him tonight."

My mother paused and said, "It looks nice. Now I can't

wait until *my* birthday," she added, and started laughing again.

I pouted and said, "See."

"Aw, girl, go 'head somewhere. I don't want your money," she told me. "All I did was raise you for half of your life before your father came back in the picture just in time to send you off for college."

I shook my head. I didn't know what to say. My mom was playing the guilt trip on me.

"So now I'm gonna have to buy you *and* Jason a new car," I continued to pout. How could I say no to them? They had all put up with a lot of stuff from me.

My mom said, "You don't have to buy me a new car, honey. Who do you think will be driving that new SUV that you're giving to your father? You don't know the house rules by now? What's *his* is mine and what's *mine* is mine."

We both laughed at it.

Mom said, "Well, go 'head, girl, and save your little phone bill. I'll see you later on at the house. And Tracy?"

"Yes," I said, smiling. She had cheered me up.

"I love you."

I smiled even wider. "I love you too, Mom."

When I hung up to continue with my day, I realized that I couldn't really cry about anything, because if you look at it, I had *everything* to look forward to. So I clicked on the stereo system and popped in a CD. I was curious, but I *refused* to listen to Power 99 FM for a while, because I didn't want Wendy Williams to surprise me with something else. Hell, I was back in a good damn mood, and I *planned* to remain that way!

# A Woman's Liberation

*I grew up a while back*
*and took off my tight jeans*
*and those other little, skimpy things*
*to liberate my body.*

*I put away my*
*old love letters*
*from long-gone boyfriends*
*to liberate my heart.*

*I discarded my false notions of*
*how young ladies should act*
*in male-dominated societies*
*to liberate my mind.*

*I dared to picture myself a heaven,*
*so that I could reach*
*for a better tomorrow*
*to liberate my soul.*

*And then I flew*
*far away*
*like a bird*
*in no cage.*

# July 1996

$ $
$

Whe my airplane reached the city limits of Los Angeles the sight of the small houses with palm trees planted all around reminded me of toy houses, as if the capital city of make-believe was only make-believe itself. I could tell that it was a different kind of place, judging from the clothes that people wore on the airplane, and the many nationalities they represented. It was like a styleless and faceless nation where anything goes. Even the flight attendants seemed spirited in their blue uniforms. It made me feel that LA was a place where you could really be free and let yourself go. On the East Coast we were hindered by rigid dress codes and a more structured approach to life, where breaking the rules led to unpleasant whispers, nasty looks, and cold shoulders. However, on the plane to LA all that I could feel was warmth. I felt relaxed, like in a bubble bath, even as the plane experienced turbulence in our preparation for landing.

When we landed, I undid my seat belt, stood up, and collected my carry-on luggage. As soon as I made it through the bridge and into the Los Angeles Airport terminal I felt overdressed in my coordinated blue and white. Had I just stepped through to the other side of a seventies time warp or what? The people there looked like outright, nonconforming hippies, slackers, and year-around vacationers with nowhere special to go, and no particular time to be there. It even seemed like they were *walking* in slow motion. I just stopped and stared for a minute with a child's grin on my face.

"Hey, Tracy," my friend Kendra said, once she spotted me standing there.

We hugged and broke away.

She said, "Wouldn't you know it. As soon as I step away to run to the restroom the plane rolls in. How long have you been waiting here?"

"Actually, I just stepped off of the plane. And *you* seem to be the only one concerned about the time in here," I joked to her.

"Yeah, I'm from Baltimore."

She didn't look it anymore. The Kendra Dayton that I remembered from Hampton wore a conservative hairstyle with just a touch of burgundy dye, and looked uptight half of the time. In LA, her dark brown face looked relieved and glowing. She was wearing hot pink pants, sandals, and her hair was in long braids past her shoulder. Shit, Kendra looked stress free and sexy, like a Gap commercial mixed with Victoria's Secret. I needed some of that loose, sexy energy myself. I was loving LA before I stepped foot out of the airport!

"So how was your flight?" Kendra asked me.

We started walking toward the baggage claim to gather the rest of my things.

"It was long, but peaceful; just what I needed, more time to sit down and think to myself."

I continued to suck in the wide-open feel of the West Coast as we walked. There were even people soliciting inside of the airport. They would never allow that at Philadelphia International. Nor would people give you the time of day to do it.

I shared my thoughts with Kendra. "So anything goes out here, hunh?"

She smiled and said, "Basically. And that can be a good *and* a bad thing."

"What's so bad about it?"

"It's hard to get people behind anything," she answered. "Like the PTA meetings. Forget about it. Parents come in *more so* to show off and make an appearance than to find out what their *kids* are doing. Then their kids grow up to be the same way. Superficial."

I said, "At least they don't tell you how to *teach,* because that's what happens on the East Coast, *if* you can get the parents to come in at all."

Kendra grinned and shook her head. "I guess it's rough for teachers everywhere."

"Damn right, and they don't pay us enough," I snapped. "But I didn't fly out here to talk about teaching. I came out here to see if I could trade in my piece of white chalk for a fancy black pen."

"Well, I just wish that *I* could write like that," Kendra said. "I'd try my luck in the script game too. There's *surely* more money in it." She looked me in my face and said, "Do you know that if you write for a popular television show for just *two* months you could match the average teachers' salary, that we work *nine* months to make, and that's just writing for the *small-time* shows."

I could not help but to smile. All I could see were dollar signs in front of me and my name rolling through with the credits. The funny thing about all of the scriptwriting talk is that everyone assumed that was what I wanted to do, *and* that I could even do it. I had never written a script or screenplay before in my life. I guess that once you put a book out and write poetry, people just naturally assume that writing for television and film is easily in reach. I kind of went along with the flow, as if I really knew what the hell I was getting into. However, like Kendra said, even writing for a "small-time" show would beat teaching, and I was ready and willing to learn everything that I needed to know.

We found my luggage and pulled it from the reclaim wheel, and I followed Kendra out to her car, a Toyota Camry just like mine.

I dropped my luggage at her trunk and started laughing.

"What's so funny?" she asked me.

"Girl, we even drive the same car."

"Stop! Is yours red, too?"

"No, my Camry is black."

"Oh, because I was ready to fall out. I have thirty thousand miles on this car. I've only had it now for a year and a half."

"I hear that people do a lot of driving out here though."

"Yeah, and I did *more* driving because I was exploring things, seeing what it all looked like. Especially after the riots hit out here and everything. I bought myself a map and started navigating."

"So, you would be the right person for me to ask where things are?" I asked.

"Pretty much. Yeah."

We tossed my things in the trunk and headed toward the front doors. I couldn't wait to get out on the road.

"So, where are you taking me to first?" I sounded like an eager tourist.

"First I want to drive you back to my place in Carson to let you unpack, and then we can do whatever. I'm glad to have some East Coast company out here for a change.

Sometimes the West Coast mind state can get to you, and you start losing touch with what's really going on in the world."

"You mean, it's that bad out here, where people don't realize what's going on?"

Kendra looked at me with a serious grill. "Child, let me tell you, I don't know if it's the warm weather or the earthquakes, but a lot of these people could care less."

I began to wonder what made Kendra remain in California with the way that she talked about it.

"What do you love about being out here in California again?" I asked her with a smirk.

She caught on to my sarcasm and laughed. "I know, right? I get to beating the place up so bad that you would think I hated it out here. But I guess it's that love/hate relationship that you have with things you care a lot about. So let's just put it this way: If I didn't care about Los Angeles, then I wouldn't talk about it so much."

I smiled. I said, "In that case, the brothers from the Nation of Islam love America more than *any* of us with the way that *they* talk."

Kendra laughed loud and hard. "Oh, they *do* love America," she said. "You don't see any of them catching that first boat back to Africa, do you? They would just rather they *control* America than the white man. That's what *their* problem is. They want to be in control of the whole boat."

We jumped on the expressway for Kendra's place. As we drove, I took in the palm trees off of the road. They stood some fifty feet tall and seemed to be evenly spaced.

"I didn't know that palm trees could get that tall," I commented.

Kendra laughed. "Girl, you sound like a kid at an amusement park."

"Oh, this *is* an amusement park for me. Trust me."

"Yeah, that's how I felt when I first came out here. Now you see why I stay out here? It's all in the atmosphere."

We made it to her three-bedroom, orange-painted flat and gathered my things from the car.

"Every single house out here is different, hunh?" I guess I was too used to Philadelphia's uniform designs of red-brick row houses and gray stone twins.

"I like that though," Kendra said. "It gives you a feeling of individuality and uniqueness."

"It reminds *me* of Florida with all of the bright colors," I told her. I had been to Florida a few times for spring break while at Hampton. Florida and California were the only states where I ever saw orange, green, yellow, and aqua houses, but I hadn't been to every state.

Kendra nodded. "Yeah, it does remind you of Florida a little bit, but California is a lot more populated. Every time *I* go to Florida, I always ask myself, 'Where do the people live around here?' They have a lot of hideaway housing in Florida, like they're protecting themselves against floods and tornadoes or something. California's housing is right out in the open."

"What about the earthquakes?" I asked her as we made our way into her modest house.

"The earthquakes?" she responded, wide-eyed. "Oh, girl, let me tell you. When I first experienced an earthquake out here I lived in an apartment complex in Inglewood on the second floor, and I actually thought that the people downstairs were shaking up the house or something. So I was about to grab my broomstick and beat on the floor: 'What the heck are you doing down there?' Then I realized, 'Oh, my God, this might be an earthquake!'"

"How often do they happen?"

She grimaced. "About three or four times a year."

I looked at her and asked, *"Every* year?" She made it sound as normal as a northeastern snowstorm.

She laughed and said, "Most of them are just small shimmers. You get used to it."

She showed me to her guest room that had a brown sleeper sofa and a small color television set. There was nothing to brag about or to complain about at her place. She even had a small backyard with a fence and a basketball hoop. I wondered if Kendra got lonely. She didn't seem like it. She probably enjoyed the peace that she had. You don't get much peace in crowded East Coast cities. Something is always going on. On Kendra's block, it pretty much looked like everyone minded their own business and kept to themselves. I guess it *would* be hard for Californians to come together on anything.

After getting situated, Kendra took a deep breath and said, "So, where do you want to go to first? Hollywood?"

I smiled. "Why not?"

We walked back out to her car and Kendra stopped to look up at the blue sky.

"You see how peaceful this is? In Baltimore there was always something distracting me from realizing how beautiful the sky was."

I nodded. "I see what you mean. I was just thinking about how peaceful it seems out here myself."

We hopped back inside of the car and took off for Hollywood.

Kendra said, "Usually I would take Route 110 to get to Hollywood, but since you've never been out to California before, I'll take the street."

She handed me a map as if I knew how to read it.

"This is where we are right here." She pointed with her finger to the bottom of the map.

Just like she said, Carson was below Compton and right next to Long Beach.

"Long Beach looks huge," I commented. "I thought Compton would be bigger."

"Yeah, because of all those rap songs about it, right?"

I smiled. "I guess so." I looked at where Los Angeles was located, all the way at the top of the map. "How long will it take us to get to LA?" It looked like a two-hour drive. I didn't remember it taking that long for us to drive to her house from the airport, but from what I could tell on the map, the airport was closer to Carson than LA.

Kendra shook her head and started grinning.

"What's so funny?" I asked her.

"You're not used to reading maps, are you?"

I smiled again. "No. I mean, it's not like I have to use maps that much on the East Coast."

She said, "You know what I noticed recently. Women don't really use directions the way that guys do. When I first moved out here and asked people how to get to places, women would say things like, 'You go up there, and make a right at the McDonald's, then when you see a Burger King down the road, you make a left and go straight up.'"

"What's wrong with that?" I asked her. It sounded about right to me. That's how *I* would have given directions.

Kendra said, "That doesn't work too well when you have to travel a longer distance. That's when you have to know east, west, north, and south."

*Whatever,* I thought to myself. *As long as you get there.*

When we stopped at a red light, Kendra looked up to the right, past my passenger seat. "You see that little N and little S at opposite ends of that street sign?" she asked me.

I looked up and noticed it. We were traveling north on Main Street. It even had the hundred that we were on: 21800.

I just started laughing. "I know I noticed that on street signs before, I just never paid it much attention. Especially when you already know where you're going."

Kendra shook her head and smiled. "I know Southern California better than many of the people who grew up out here," she bragged. "You see that?" she asked me, pointing out ugly gray housing complexes that were gated off. "This is South Central Los Angeles. So it's *not* all good out here."

She had *that* right. A ghetto was a ghetto, and it was never pretty.

"So this is where Ice Cube and John Singleton are from?" We were on Broadway, still heading north.

"Or where they *claim* to be from. But South Central is a large area. Some parts of it don't look this bad, but some parts look worse."

I asked, "You notice how ghettos are always gated up or closed in somehow? Even in Hampton, Virginia, they have those housing complexes where it's only one way in—"

"And one way out," Kendra finished for me. "Ain't it a shame? They make sure that you can't run and hide anywhere to escape poverty. They throw it right up in your face."

We turned off of Broadway and onto another main street heading north again.

"This is Figueroa. Ice Cube rapped about this street too. The prostitution and stuff, but it's not like they say it *used* to be. I think they started cracking down on things after the riots hit."

We drove a few miles up, then Kendra pointed out where the LA Clippers play.

"A lot of people go to the Clippers games when a good team like Chicago, New York, Orlando, or Houston come to play. It's a lot cheaper and more practical than going to see the Lakers at the Forum. I even went to a couple of Clippers games out here, but I've never been to a Lakers game."

When we made it downtown, the place looked pretty empty to me.

"*This* is downtown?" I asked. It looked like a ghost town compared to downtown Philadelphia.

"Not much goes on in downtown LA, as you can see. Hollywood runs the show out here, not downtown."

We headed farther north on Western Avenue. I was paying attention to every street sign. I had Kendra to thank for that.

"As you can see, we're now in Chinatown. Or 'Little Asia,' as *I* like to call it, because there's Koreans and Japanese here too. A lot of Filipinos and Samoans also live out here in California.

"Over to your right is Dodger Stadium and plenty of Mexicans," she said. She smiled and added, "That's East LA, Tracy. Oscar De La Hoya town."

I said, "But I thought they didn't like Oscar De La Hoya in East LA, or at least that's what I hear every time he fights on HBO." I liked to watch the fights with my father and his friends.

Kendra nodded. "Yeah, a lot of them don't, because, you know, the white man loves Oscar, and Mexicans can be like us sometimes. The more acceptable you are to white people, the less *your* people want to identify with you, as if Oscar sold out by being too clean-cut and popular."

"Until Oscar dies, right?" I cracked, sarcastically. "Then they'll *all* want to claim him. 'He was the best boxer that East LA ever had.'"

Kendra laughed. "You know it, girl. Just like *we* do."

Finally, we made it up to Hollywood Avenue, but it wasn't two hours like I had thought. It was more like forty minutes. Kendra pointed out everything.

"This is where the stars put their hands in the sidewalk. That's Mann's Chinese Theater. They have a lot of movie premiere events there."

I said, "That place really *does* look Chinese." It had Chinese architecture and everything.

Kendra laughed. "Well, that's why they call it what they call it."

"I wonder what the Chinese people think about that," I said.

Kendra laughed at me again. "Girl, you *sound* like a writer. You're curious about everything."

"And *you're* not? You're the one who brought the map."

We drove up another few blocks

"Okay, now, this is Sunset Boulevard. This is my favorite."

I could easily see why. Sunset Boulevard was the most attractive street, with gigantic billboards for upcoming films, neon lights for shops, stores, and attractions, and plenty of fancy cars driven by unknown producers, directors, studio people, and stars. I couldn't name any of them. I had no idea who was who.

"This is *West* Hollywood, by the way," Kendra told me. "*East* Hollywood looks like any other rundown city."

When we reached East Hollywood, I could see that she was right.

"Damn, you're not lying," I said. "We went right from star town to slum town."

Kendra laughed and stopped herself short. "Hey," she said with a hand up, "*real people* live here, and I don't think they would appreciate where they live being called a slum."

"Okay, I take it back then," I told her with a grin.

"Now let me take you through Beverly Hills," she said.

We turned right onto Beverly Boulevard and headed back west.

"Have you spent much time up here?" I asked her.

"For what? I didn't come out here to be involved in this."

I chuckled. Hollywood didn't look all that spectacular to me either.

"Well, where's the big Hollywood sign?" I asked.

She looked to the right past my passenger seat again.

"You can actually see it from some streets, but I'll show it to you. I'll take you up to Griffith Park and let you look out over everything."

When we hit Beverly Hills *you knew it!* Everything changed to loveliness, and *real* money.

"Damn, is that a *used* car lot," I commented.

They had a car lot with Bentleys, Rolls-Royces, Lamborghinis, Benzes, Beamers, and other fancy rides that were not new, but *definitely* still shiny and beautiful.

"Yeah, used for eighty-thousand dollars," Kendra joked. "And you see these stores around here. I wouldn't even walk in these places."

The stores didn't look all that fancy, but the names Gucci, Prada, Fendi, Chanel, Armani, Boss—like in Hugo—and many more, told you everything you needed to know. DO NOT ENTER UNLESS YOU ARE FILTHY RICH!

I said, "Kendra, you never just walked in and asked what the prices were?" I was only joking of course. It was a black thing to joke about how underprivileged we were.

Bill Cosby was famous for it, the "We were sooo poor" jokes.

Kendra said, "Heck no. They have those buzz-in door things, and if you don't *look* like you can afford anything, they'll just ignore you, or buzz you in and make you feel stupid. 'And what would you like to *look at* today?'"

We broke out laughing.

Kendra said, "Okay, now, let me show you these houses up here."

We drove a few blocks up and it looked as if we had just driven into a rich man's movie. There were beautiful earth-tone colors, palm trees, grass, glass structures, brick, stone, new-world architecture, shapes, sizes . . . *everything!* Heaven on earth was the only way that I could describe it, or maybe I was exaggerating, especially coming from my blue-collar, Philadelphian roots.

Kendra said, "Okay, now let's drive deeper into it."

The blocks began to stretch into more greenery where most of the elegant, larger homes were out of view.

"You see the difference? The richer you are, the more you can hide your house. They even have star maps up here where people actually ride around looking for people's houses to take pictures."

"Did you buy one?" I asked her.

She smiled, looking guilty. "Yeah, but just as a collector's item."

"So you never looked at any of these houses?"

"Yeah, I looked at them, but not because of who *lives* there. I looked at them because they were slamming. Now let me show you UCLA's campus up here," she said.

"UCLA's campus is in Beverly Hills?"

Kendra looked at me with a grin that said a thousand words.

"Girl, when you talk about a *campus,* this is *it!* And you know how people would always say that our campus at Hampton was nice. Well, wait until you see this."

We got back on Sunset Boulevard and headed farther west for UCLA. When we arrived, the campus was five times as large as Hampton's. It was just as green, and twice as fancy. Hampton's campus in Virginia may have been small, and it was *definitely* nicer than most, but next to UCLA there was little comparison.

It took me a while to even speak. When I finally did, I said, "Now this ain't even fair." That's all that I could say.

"Girl, this is about the biggest jock school in the world. They get all *kinds* of athletes," Kendra added.

"Yeah, I would imagine so. All they have to say is, 'Let me invite you to see our campus.' I mean, this is higher learning like a bitch. John Singleton had it right again."

Kendra laughed and said, "Remember the character that Ice Cube played in the movie? He was on campus for like, eight years, right? Just chilling."

"Yeah, I would chill too, but would you give up Hampton for this?"

Kendra was stuck for a minute. "Maybe on the weekends, but not all the way."

"Yeah, right," I said, doubting it.

"I mean, you know, a black education and a black campus meant a lot to me. And we were *hardly* poor at Hampton."

"Yeah, you're right," I admitted as we drove away from the Beverly Hills campus.

"They don't even have black schools out here, and they have a bill coming up this fall that will try and do away with affirmative action scholarships in education. In the *entire* state of California," she told me. "And I'll tell you right now, we won't have enough people to back us to keep it.

"They wouldn't even *try* anything like that on the *East* Coast, because we have *far* too many educated blacks and higher institutions that would not allow it," she said. "But in California, I think they can get away with it. The only person we have over here fighting for anything is Congresswoman Maxine Waters. That sister is all by herself out here."

"Sounds like you're ready to run for office in a couple of years yourself," I teased.

"Maybe I will," Kendra responded.

The next thing I knew, we were on La Brea Avenue, heading south. I guessed that our Hollywood sightseeing was over.

"Where are we going now?" I asked.

"I'm going to take you down Crenshaw. That's a major avenue out here."

"Didn't they talk about that street in *Boyz N the Hood*?" Kendra smiled. "Of course they did."

Once we reached Rodeo, we made a left turn and headed east for Crenshaw. I was loving what I saw on Rodeo. The area looked close-knit, green, clean, and was filled with black people. The closeness of the houses there reminded me of home.

"What neighborhood is this?" I asked.

"Oh, this is Baldwin Hills. It's close to Culver City, where they have a lot of the television studios, and right up from Inglewood, where I used to live when I first moved out here," she answered. "This area and Inglewood remind me the most of home."

"That's *just* what I was thinking," I told her.

"Yeah, Baldwin Hills has their own mall out here too.

That's where we're heading to now. Are you hungry?" she asked me. "They have this soul food spot I want to take you to, and right across the street is the mall, and Magic Johnson's movie theater."

I nodded to her. "Yeah, I heard about that. Is it nice?"

"Yeah, it's nice. He has like nine or ten different shows and a black wall of fame with actors, singers, and of course, athletes on it. We'll make sure that we go to a couple of movies there before you leave, and maybe we'll check out Mann's Chinese Theater too."

"So where is this soul food place?" I asked her. "I'm starving."

We made a right turn onto Crenshaw and pulled right into a small parking lot at M & M Soul Food restaurant.

"This is it," Kendra told me.

As soon as we walked into the restaurant, I noticed more of the long braided hairstyles. It was obvious that they weren't much into fiddling with their hair out in LA. They just tossed in some braids for a couple of months and ran the town with them.

"How long have you had your hair in braids?" I asked Kendra.

She chuckled. "So I guess you noticed that about LA by now, right? I've had my hair in braids for a year now. At first, I just wouldn't do it. I was sticking to my Baltimore roots, you know, but once I got tired of dealing with my hair, I said, 'That's it. I'm gonna do what everyone else out here does, slap in some braids.'"

There were a few old-school brothers in there with Jherri-curls and perms, looking like they wanted parts in the revival of *Superfly,* but I didn't comment on that. As long as they didn't try to talk to me their hairstyles was *their* business.

We ordered from the menu of various styles of chicken,

fried fish, meatloaf, liver, collard greens, macaroni and cheese, corn, rice, red beans, stuffing, gravy, cornbread and biscuits, with lemonade or soda. Neither one of us could finish our order, and when we stood up to leave, we could barely walk.

"Yup, soul food does it every time," I joked, rubbing my belly. "Now we'll both have to find a sanitized toilet in a few hours."

Kendra laughed as hard as she could with a stomach filled with fattening food, which was not hard at all. We drove across the street to check out Baldwin Hills Mall. It was a two-level mall with nothing spectacular, anchored by a Sears at one end and a Macy's at the other.

"Excuse me, are you a model?" this guy asked me before we could even get inside of the mall good. After all, I was five foot eight and gorgeous with cat-shaped, hazel eyes. I considered myself sexier than Tyra Banks too.

I smiled and decided to play along with him. "Something like that," I answered.

"An actress?" The short, stocky, and bald brother, wearing one of those blue muscle shirts that clung to his body like extra skin, was full of it. His pants didn't give him much air to breath down low either. He had no idea who he was dealing with.

"I've been known to play a role or two," I told him. "You want an autograph?"

Kendra held in her laugh.

"How about you sign my card and I leave one with you?"

"What do you do?" I asked him.

"I'm a personal trainer. A lot of my clients are Hollywood types."

He handed me his card. It read "Body Work: *The right build for the right you.*"

I started laughing.

"Body Work. The name works, right?" he asked me, grinning with perfect white teeth.

His name on the card was Derrick Conner.

"I guess so," I told him, still laughing as I handed it to Kendra.

He gave me another one that I signed for him. Kendra was still holding in her laugh, waiting for us to step away from him so we could laugh out loud together.

He looked at my signature and read it. "Marva Patterson? Where do I know that name from?"

By that time, I had to look away before I killed myself trying to hold it all in.

"You think about that on your way out, and I'll keep this card handy. Do you do massages?" I asked him.

"The best in Hollywood," he bragged.

*Well, what's your ass doing down here in* Baldwin *Hills instead of up in* Beverly? I wanted to say, but I kept it to myself.

"All right, well, maybe I'll give you a call then," I said as Kendra and I walked away.

"Yeah, you do that."

Kendra looked at me and said, "Girl, do *not* play with these guys out here. Okay? Some of these guys are stone *crazy.* I mean, they take themselves *to heart* out here."

I was still laughing, but Kendra was not.

She said, "I'm serious, Tracy. Don't do that. This is not Philly, Virginia, or Baltimore. These guys have loose marbles out here."

"In other words, you have a couple of horror stories to tell me about," I assumed.

"Yeah, I do."

Before Kendra could open her mouth to tell me about

them, another brother stopped me in the mall. He looked tall enough to play basketball.

He looked me right into my face and said, "Those contact lenses look perfect on you."

I don't know if that was supposed to be his pick-up line or what. I said, "And you know the best thing about it? I don't even have to take them out at night," and I kept walking. I don't even think the brother got it.

Kendra shook her head. "I can see it now. You're gonna get yourself in a *bunch* of trouble out here."

I laughed it off and told myself to cut it out. I wasn't a teenager anymore. However, all work and no play makes for a dull woman, and I was *far* from being *dull*.

## $ $ $

By my fourth day in California, Kendra and I had visited several of the beaches, seen a few movies, visited Griffith Park, and I even checked out three different places to live for when I moved out there. One was a townhouse complex in Baldwin Hills off of Rodeo. The other two were apartments in Inglewood, but I liked the Baldwin Hills townhouse more, which of course, cost more money to rent.

"All I have to do is put down the security deposit and the first couple of months of rent in September when it's available, and hopefully I'll be set with something in the business by the time Christmas rolls around. In the meantime, I might need you to hook me up with a teaching position," I hinted to Kendra, "just in case I don't have what it takes to write in Hollywood."

"A substitute position?"

We were chilling in the breeze of her backyard, as the sun went down at close to nine o'clock.

"Yeah, just keep an eye open for me and tell me if I need to send in a résumé before I get back out here in late August."

The plan was to fly some of my things out to LA to leave at Kendra's house a week before I moved, and then figure out the most sane way to transport my car and the rest of my things, which would *not* be cheap.

Kendra bought most of *her* things out in LA, a smart idea. It was probably the smartest.

I said, "Maybe I can sell my stuff back in Philly, and then start all over again out here like you did."

"Yeah, but I never had to sell anything. I moved out here right after finishing at Hampton. You might lose a lot of money doing that," she said.

I didn't have any cheap, disposable furniture in Philly either. That was just my expensive luck.

"I'll just have to get what I can get for it," I told her.

"Okay, here she comes now," Kendra said. We were waiting to talk to her "Hollywood connection," a sister attorney who worked for the Writers Guild of America. How did Kendra know her? The woman's sister lived right next door to her. Kendra just happened to live in the right place at the right time.

I got nervous though when the sister walked in and Kendra introduced us.

"Yolanda Felix, this is my friend from college at Hampton, Tracy Ellison."

We shook hands. The sister was as tall as I was, and dressed in a peach business suit. She had long, dark hair and looked more Filipino than black. She had that bronzed-skin, wet-haired, island look. The suit she was wearing was my style too. It was stylish, but not too fancy.

"So you have a book out?" she asked me. She was

straightforward and no small talk. That made me *more* nervous. How was she reading me?

"It's coming back out this September with a bigger publisher," I told her.

"*Flyy Girl*, right?"

I looked at Kendra. She had hooked me up.

"Yeah, that's it."

Yolanda smiled. "I was flyy in my day too. I'd like to read that when it comes out."

"No problem. I'll give you a copy."

"So you want to write screenplays?" she asked. I wondered how old she was.

She waited for me to answer.

I nodded and said, "Yeah, I guess." I didn't sound too confident. I changed my answer and made it stronger. "Yeah, I *do* want to write screenplays."

"Have you written one before?"

"No, but I have a master's degree in English."

For whatever reason, the more I mentioned my master's degree in English, the less value it seemed to have. I felt like I should have kept my mouth closed.

Yolanda said, "Oh yeah? I majored in English at Howard before going to law school."

When she said that, I thought, *Yeah! I worked* hard *for my master's degree in English!*

"So we have something else in common then, besides being flyy and all," I joked. I was all smiles, and my initial nervousness faded.

She said, "If you want to write screenplays, you can't *guess it,* you have to *know it,* backward and forward. You have to be willing to fight for it like it's your own flesh and blood. Especially if you're a *black* writer. If these Hollywood producers and directors have problems understanding *white* writers, then you *know,* they look at *us* as if we're from Mars."

I got nervous again. What if white people just didn't get me? How much power did black people have in Hollywood? I had no idea.

Yolanda said, "And I hope you don't think that your looks will do it all for you. I've seen plenty of pretty sisters *and* white girls get caught up in the physical game and lose. You really have to know what you're doing out here to survive. You hear me? You have to take this business *very* seriously."

Kendra broke in for a second and asked if anyone wanted anything to drink.

"Yeah," I told her. I guess she could see how confused and worried I looked. I knew that I was more than just a pretty face, but still. I didn't know what it took to make it in Hollywood. I was just planning to go for it and figure it all out along the way.

Yolanda asked, "So when are you planning to move, next month sometime?"

I took a sip of my juice before I answered.

"I'll be out here next month, but my townhouse won't be available until September."

"A townhouse? So you *are* serious then."

I nearly caved in from the pressure, but I dropped my head and took another sip of my drink to hide it. I had to convince myself that Hollywood was what I wanted. It was something that was hard and fruitful like my girl Raheema had said. So I composed myself and looked Yolanda in her eyes before I responded, "Yeah, I am serious."

She took out a business card, flipped it over, and started writing names.

"What you need to do is call The Biz or the UCLA Extensions program and get them to send you their brochures on screenwriting and television and film courses. I would take courses at *both* places. The more contacts and references you have, the better. You call me up when you get back in town, and I'll sit down and talk to you about everything.

"We have thousands of aspiring young screenwriters out here, but we could use some that are as serious as you are about it, especially young sisters," she told me.

I just nodded my head, still playing along with it, but when she left, I was shell-shocked.

"Well, what do you think?" Kendra asked me.

I said, "Damn! She was all business."

"I hear they *all* are, or at least the ones who get things done, and I hear that *she* gets things done," Kendra said.

I could imagine. If Yolanda Felix was a proper representation of Hollywood business, then I definitely had to get my act up to par and go out there like I really meant it, because she was *not* playing!

## $ $ $

When I told my parents about my plans back at home that summer, my mother flipped.

"You mean to tell me that you're just gonna stop teaching altogether to go out to California and try to write movie scripts? Have you lost your damn mind?! Do you know how many people dream about doing that and never get anything done. Then they end up right back at home and starting all over again with nothing.

"Tracy, have you *thought* about this?" she asked me, still irritated, "because you're forever leaping before you look, girl. This is not teenage growing pains anymore, this is *your* real life now."

We were all sitting at the kitchen table, me, my mother, and my father. My father didn't have much to say. He just sat there amused by it. My little brother was out running the streets somewhere, enjoying *his* teen years of the 1990s.

"Well, what do *you* have to say about this, Dave?" my mother asked my father.

First he smiled. He said, "Patti, Tracy is a grown woman, and if this is what she wants to do, you can either support it or tell her that you don't support it, and let her do what she wants to do. I don't think she's sharing this with us to gain our permission. I think she's just informing us as her parents."

He was right, because I damn sure had made up my mind already. I wasn't even planning on arguing with my mother that night. I had other plans.

"Well, how do you *feel* about this, Dave?" my mother instigated.

I said nothing. I just waited for dad to answer. It wasn't as if it was going to change anything. I just wanted to hear what he had to say.

"Well, how many people get a chance to put a book out about themselves without being famous first? She did that. So why can't she write movies?" he asked. "I mean, she does have a master's degree in English, so put it to use. A lot of people don't even use what they went to school for. Writing and English go hand and hand, don't they? If she was going to teach middle school all of her life, she could have done that with a regular degree."

My mother was still doubtful. She said, "Well, I hope they don't read your book and get the wrong idea about you, because I heard Hollywood is a sleazy business for a woman to be in."

My father shook his head at my mother's lack of confidence in me, but as far as I was concerned, it was the end of the conversation. I was a grown-ass woman and I could handle myself no matter *what* arena I was in. I wasn't some confused teenager testing the rough waters again. I was a young adult making a simple career move.

I stood up to excuse myself. "Well, we'll see," I declared to my mother. "And now that we know what I'm after, the next thing for me to do is to sell as much of my furniture as I can to get ready for the move."

"And what about your car?" she asked me.

I shrugged my shoulders. "Looks like I'm gonna have to drive it out to California."

My father looked at the disgust on my mother's face and broke out laughing.

I drove back to my apartment complex where I had Mike waiting outside for me in his car. I was ten minutes later than I said I would be. I approached him sitting under his map light and reading a magazine. I blew my horn as I drove by toward the parking lot.

When I met him, waiting for me at the security door, I thought about the personal trainer out in LA and began to chuckle.

"What's so funny?" Mike asked me. Mike was much taller than the guy in LA, and he worked more with athletes. Plus, I knew that he was telling me the truth.

"Nothing at all," I told him.

"That's a lie, but I won't even get into that," he responded.

"Good."

We walked to the elevators. When the doors closed, Mike put his magic hands on the back of my waist and worked his way up to my shoulders and neck.

"You know just what I need tonight," I told him, leaning my head back and enjoying it.

"Yeah, but I can't stay tonight," he told me.

*Good,* I thought. I wanted to rest in my bed and have it all to myself once he had finished with the job. So I was planning on making up a reason for him to leave anyway, but I played it off.

"You can't stay?" I asked.

"I gotta be in New York tomorrow morning. I might even have to drive up there tonight."

"Well, don't exhaust yourself with me," I teased him.

"Oh, I won't. I know how to conserve my energy."

"Just don't conserve *too* much energy," I warned him with a big smile. I didn't want a quickie. I just didn't want him to stay. I wanted my pie and peace of mind too, just like a lot of guys wanted it. Hit and split, right?

Anyway, while Mike worked his fingers into my naked body that night, all I could think about was what he would say or do once I told him that I was relocating to California. Maybe I didn't have to tell him at all, but that seemed too cruel. I knew that he was more attached to me than he let on. I just wasn't attached to him.

I asked, "Have you ever thought about moving away from Philadelphia?"

"Like to where?"

"I don't know, Atlanta or someplace?"

"Sometimes I do, but I like it here," he answered. "What about you?"

"I like it here too, but sometimes, when you stay home too long, you start to feel like you haven't done anything." That was all that I planned to say about my relocation.

Mike chuckled and said, "I know the feeling, but whenever I'm away too long, I can't wait to come back home. So I know that Philly is the only place for me until I feel differently."

He pulled his clothes off and finished the job with our naked bodies clashing. I cooled down and took a shower after he had left to wash the lust away. After I pulled the wet sheets from my bed, I called my girl Raheema at home in North Jersey, well after midnight. Regardless of the time, I had something to say. She was used to my late-night phone calls anyway. Sometimes I would just leave a message for her.

She didn't pick up when I called that night, so I left another message on her machine:

"Well, girl, you said it when we were still living on Diamond Lane, 'Tracy, you're gonna be rich and famous one day, if you keep writing stuff like that.' Remember that?

"Well, I'm getting set to go out to Hollywood and try my luck. And my book by Omar is coming back out this year too. So it took me a little while to get back on track for this, but everything happens for a reason. So here I go. And I'll talk to you when—"

BLOOOP!

The damn machine cut me off. Was that a sign that I wasn't going to make it? I called Raheema right back and finished my message.

"Like I was saying, I'll talk to you when you call me. And I *will* make things happen when I go back out to California. You can *count* on it, or my name ain't Tracy."

I hung up and wrote another poem, "A Mission," before I crashed in a fresh bra and panties on clean bedsheets.

# Camara

*Kiwana named me Camara,*
*one who*
*teaches*
*from experience.*

*But when will*
*I learn*
*from my own*
*lessons?*

*When will*
*you*
*learn*
*from yours?*

# April 2000

$$ \$\,\$ $$
$$ \$ $$

*I* went home and took a nap before leaving my parents' house at lunchtime. I was headed for King of Prussia Mall on I-76 West. The Wendy Williams morning show was no longer on the air by then, and I felt safe enough to listen to Power 99 again. They were playing Will Smith's classic anthem, "Summertime." That song had to be at least eight years old, but in Philly, everybody still loved it. When that song played, I thought back to my college years. I was a lot more subdued at that time, waiting for Victor to sweep me up off my feet when he got out of jail, which never fucking happened. I was a damn fool, saving myself for nothing. So I grew sour and turned the song off, tired of the hurtful reminders of my heart wound. Who the hell needs bad memories on their mind?

When I arrived at the mall, I had to decide where I wanted to park. King of Prussia had to be one of the largest malls in the country, and they were always adding something new to it, including parking lots. I had been going there to shop for as long as I had a license to drive, especially after discovering they had no taxation on clothing. You could just about buy an extra outfit or a pair of shoes from the savings, and I usually did. I planned to hit the mall and splurge in a big way!

I used the restroom in Nordstrom's and entered the

second level of the mall, and a sharp-looking white man with slick dark hair in a tailored gray business suit stopped me immediately.

"Tracy Ellison Grant."

He said my name as if we were old friends, but we were not. I waited for him to explain himself.

"I have to tell ya, I just *loved* your performance in *Led Astray*," he said excitedly.

He didn't appear to be the kind of man who got excited about much. He looked very poised and calculating, like a million-dollar-a-year lawyer.

"Oh, well, thank you," I responded.

"And you wrote the screenplay yourself?" he asked me.

He had even done his homework.

"Yes, I did."

He shook his head, amazed by me, and didn't know what else to say. I was used to the glazed eyes of men, going all the way back to high school. I smiled, because I knew that he would break his neck to take me out, *if* I went that way.

I started to thank him again and excuse myself, but he was not ready for me to leave.

"My name is Tom Slayer," he said, pulling out a business card.

I took it and looked it over. It read "Loebe, Lewis & Slayer, Attorneys at Law." I nodded and grinned at him. I was right again: he *was* a big-time lawyer.

"You don't look old enough to be a partner. I guess you're a real go-getter then," I flattered him. "How old are you?"

"Thirty-eight."

"You're married?"

"Divorced."

"Two kids?"

He nodded. "Yeah."

I nodded back to him. "Your wife couldn't take the pressure?"

He grinned, big and guilty.

"You're the writer. You tell *me* the story. So what are you working on next?" he asked me.

"Shopping," I hinted. He was holding me up, and I was not interested. He pressed his luck anyway.

"Well, how long are you in town? Maybe we could do dinner or something. You know, I can talk about law money and you could talk about Hollywood money. I'm sure we *both* have plenty of stories to tell."

"I'm sure we do," I told him, "but I'm just about booked up with family and friends. Outside of that, I would like some time to myself."

"I know exactly what you mean. Sometimes the days move a little too fast," he said. "But let's say you, ah, hold on to my number, and who knows, maybe I could fly out to Hollywood and you show me around out there. I'm game. Maybe I could find a few stars out there to represent. I'm assuming that you have representation already."

He was smiling like a kid who had just caught a baseball at the Phillies game. He was really putting himself out there for me. That was the difference I had learned concerning white men and black men while out in Hollywood. I hate to say it, but white men were a lot more determined. However, I couldn't get past the history of white men and black women in America to fall for one. White men had had their way with us long enough.

I said, "Yes, I do have a lawyer, but I'll think about that visit," just to get away from him.

"Please do," he told me.

When I walked away, I was afraid to look back, embarrassed to catch his eyes glued on my ripe ass. I wore blue jeans that were not tight enough for extra attention, but not loose enough to hide my curves either.

I just kept right on walking until a short, dark brown sister noticed me.

"Tracy Ellison Grant. I heard you on Power 99 this morning." She shook her head and said, "Girl, don't you worry about that lesbian stuff, just keep right on making that money. *I* sure would."

I told her "Thank you," smiled, and kept walking. I figured that I would never be able to shop in the Philadelphia area at night or on the weekend when the stores were actually crowded. I could barely walk through the mall while it was halfway empty, and King of Prussia was filled with mostly white shoppers who wouldn't notice me. It wasn't as if I was Julia Roberts or anything. I was just a local black girl who had made *one* movie.

I noticed a few more stares as I walked, but I had to ignore them. I couldn't react to everything, but I did feel a bit uncomfortable about it. It was my first shopping spree in the Philadelphia area since my movie was released in February. I didn't want my hometown fans to think that I was stuck on myself. They probably loved me more than anyone. Nevertheless, shouldn't I be allowed to shop in peace like everyone else?

I didn't walk into any shops until I saw the Enzo shoe store on the bottom level. Comfortable shoes were *always* number one in *my* book, no matter *what* I wore.

As soon as I walked in I came face-to-face with Kiwana, my college friend from Cheyney State University during my high school years at Germantown. Kiwana had graduated from Cheyney and moved back to New

York during my sophomore year at Hampton. She had been my number-one positive influence to get me back on track from my reckless flyy years. When we set eyes on each other inside of Enzo's, we just about lost our minds!

"OOOOHHH!" we both screamed, hugging each other like two maniacs.

We fought to get out the first words.

"So how's it been going?" she asked me.

"How's it going with you?" I asked her back.

"Everything is beautiful," she told me.

I stopped myself and said, "Well, I can't say all of that, but I can't complain either. Not really."

"Yeah, because you're the big star now," she said. "Everyone knows what you have to offer."

I immediately felt guilty. What did Kiwana feel about me taking off my clothes for the camera? She had obviously heard about my movie. I guess I underestimated myself and the power of Hollywood films.

I grabbed Kiwana by her arm and said, "We have to sit down and talk. Are you hungry?"

She still had the prettiest brown skin that I've ever seen in my life, and she had put on the perfect amount of weight in her bright sundress, like a mother who had gotten her schedule in order. I couldn't wait to ask her about *everything*, and to get her opinions on *me*. The Lord works in mysterious ways, and Kiwana was just what I needed at just the right time.

"As a matter of fact, there's a Friendly's right around the corner that I was going to hit right after this," she told me.

"Have you picked out your shoes already?" I asked her.

She held up a pair of brown and a pair of black leather sandals and smiled.

"I'm trying to make up my mind about the color I want."

"What size?" I asked her.

She looked at me suspiciously and answered, "Seven."

I got the attention of a saleswoman and pulled out my wallet from my bag. I didn't want to delay our talk for another minute. I wanted Kiwana's full attention, even if I had to buy it.

"Can we have both of these in a size seven?"

"Sure."

"Thank you."

Kiwana shook her head. "I can't let you do that, Tracy. I pay my own way."

"You turn thirty-one on August seventeenth, right?" I asked. I had memorized her birthday. "Just consider this an early birthday present," I told her. "I owe you *a lot more* for what you did for *me*."

"All I did was become your friend, Tracy. I don't deserve a reward for that."

"Yes you do too, because you were the right kind of friend at the right time," I argued.

The saleswoman brought out the shoes, and I grabbed them before Kiwana could.

"Would you like to try them on first?" I asked her with a grin.

"Not if *you're* buying them," she responded.

"Girl, cut it out," I pouted. "It's not like they cost a thousand dollars. I'll even let you pay for lunch, and I'll order enough for two doggie bags just to make you feel better."

She laughed and finally agreed to try on the shoes. They looked good on her too.

Done deal. We headed to Friendly's ice cream restaurant.

"So, what do you think about me taking my clothes off in the movie?" I asked her quietly, as soon as we were seated and looking over our menus.

"Are you ashamed of your body?"

"Of course not."

"Did they force you to do it?"

I had to think about that one. "Well, not exactly."

"Was it written in your screenplay? You *did* write the movie, right?"

"Yeah, but I wasn't supposed to *star* in it."

"Oh, so some other sister was supposed to drop *her* clothes?"

She made me feel guilty again.

"Yeah, somebody else was supposed to do it," I admitted with a chuckle.

"I think it was a good film, actually. It took Spike Lee's *Girl 6* to the next level, because a lot of people slept on that movie. I loved it."

"I did too," I told her excitedly. "I bought the tape and watched it eight or nine times."

"Your movie also reminded me of *I Shot Andy Warhol*, starring Lili Taylor," Kiwana added. "I guess the only people who can really understand the black woman actress are the people who do it themselves, you know."

"Are you still performing?" I asked her. I felt terrible about not knowing. It made it seem as if *my* work was more important than hers. Kiwana had been performing for years. I had just started. I was a rookie.

"I just finished performing *The Women of Honor* on Broadway. I was the only African American in it."

I hadn't even heard of the show before. I felt embarrassed, so I kept my mouth shut and let her continue.

"I'd like to think that things are changing for the better

for African-American performers, but it's just a very slow process," she told me.

"Yeah, I just got lucky by meeting all of the right people," I admitted.

"And you probably used your Tracy charm, drive, and bull-headed determination too," she assumed.

I smiled. "Why, of course."

"Are you ready to order?" the waiter asked us. He was a young brother who was due for a haircut, and he was staring at me. However, I didn't assume anything, especially while in front of Kiwana.

I ordered a chicken dish. She ordered salmon.

"By the way," the waiter said after taking our orders, "I loved your movie. I saw it three times."

Kodak would have loved to capture the picture of the smile on *his* face, even with his lack of a haircut.

I smiled back and said, "Thank you."

"You get a lot more men commenting on your work than women, don't you?" Kiwana asked me.

"It sure *seems* that way," I told her, "but I'm not really sure. I think they're just more aggressive about it. To tell you the truth, I think that most of them would probably love to sleep with me," I teased.

"A lot of them have been *white* men; white men with money," I added. "A lawyer just handed me his card in the mall today, talking about visiting me in Hollywood."

Kiwana just smiled at me and was real poised. She reached into her brown canvas bag and pulled out a picture book of her two daughters.

"Oh, my God! I didn't even get a chance to ask you," I responded. Her daughters looked light, *very* light, like Latinas.

I flipped through the pictures and stopped at a blond-haired white man, looking as proud as he could be, cheesing with the two girls in his arms.

Kiwana read my pause and said, "That's my husband, Martin McNeil."

I was speechless. *Kiwana married a white man, and had two kids with him?!* I couldn't believe it! She had taken me to the African Cultural Festival in Fairmount Park where I had first discovered my love for poetry. She knew African names and had given me one (although I rarely used it). I just didn't know what to say.

"What are your daughters' names?" I finally asked her.

"Our oldest, she's four. Her name is Halimah. It means gentle and kind. I named her that after her father. Our youngest, she's one now. Her name is Safara. That basically means fire, or passionate one." She smiled and said, "Safara was very busy in my stomach when I was pregnant with her."

I still didn't say anything. I just flipped through more of her picture book, asking myself, *Who will her daughters marry?* and *How could a queen like Kiwana slip away from the brothers?* I even asked myself if it was possible for *me* to go the other way and into the arms of . . . the enemy. I didn't know what else to call them. It was because of a long history of mixed children (with white men and black women) that sisters like myself, Raheema, Mercedes, Kiwana, and so many other colored girls had problems with our community and plenty of struggles with darker, more African-looking sisters. I couldn't even look at a sister with my light brown eyes without her assuming a million things about me. Did Kiwana know what she was putting her daughters through by having them with a white man? I was a mess, and Kiwana had still not bothered to explain anything.

"So . . ." I didn't know exactly how to ask her.

"How could I do it?" she asked herself for me.

I nodded. "Yeah."

Kiwana looked up above my head and searched her thoughts before looking me in my eyes to explain it.

"Life is so much more complicated than politics," she said. "Politics are black or white, rich or poor, North or South, Democrat or Republican, male or female. But in reality we are *all* of those things. We're just *forced* to choose."

The waiter interrupted her by setting our food down.

"Are you an actress too?" he asked Kiwana. I was just praying that he didn't ask us for autographs. I wanted to get down to business.

"Something like that, yes," she answered him.

I waited for him to fade away before I asked her, "So what happened to your feelings about Black Nationtime?" She had shared with me a poem of that title years ago.

"I'm still about cultural goals for our community, as well as my daughters *and* my husband," she said. "He understands the importance of breaking down the walls of division. If he didn't I couldn't have married him."

"So you're telling me that he never called any of us a nigger?" I was being childish, but I *had* to ask it.

"Oh, I'm sure that he has," Kiwana answered civilly. "But that doesn't mean he feels that way now, *or* that he can't learn from his mistakes and past prejudices, because he has. Now he fights for the rights, dignity, and history of African Americans and for *all* people, much more passionately than a lot of the darkest brothers who do nothing but put us to shame every day."

"Well, how did it happen? Were you in a performance

together?" Her husband looked like an actor himself. He was good-looking with bright white teeth and a Colgate smile, but still . . .

"Yes, he was. And he continued to ask me out, and I continued to tell him no," Kiwana answered with a grin.

"And then what? Because plenty of white men have asked me out too," I told her. I thought that *I* would have fallen for a white man before *Kiwana* would have. However, I was strictly ghetto for a minute in my teen years. Maybe that ghetto mentality (that still surfaced in me sometimes) wouldn't allow me to be anything but BLACK, and be all the way down with blackness, whether it was negative *or* positive. The ghetto protected you that way. Kiwana was from Queens, New York, and artistically inclined. Maybe she was a lot more open about things than I ever had the chance to be.

She said, "Basically, we began to go out as friends, and I continued to ask myself, 'Why can't this happen if just on a *human* level?' And I set every trap in the book for him to fall off, including taking him to some hard-core New York clubs.

"And he asked me real honestly about that. He said, 'Kiwana, I am very much committed to establishing a long-term relationship with you whether we're only friends or not, but you have to at least be real with yourself as to whether you feel comfortable with me instead of using other means to test me, expecting that I'll fade away. I believe that you owe me that honesty, because I've always been honest with you.'"

Kiwana's eyes looked all dreamy. I guess that was the speech that did her in and made her fall in love on the other side.

She said, "Tracy, as you well know by now, the more

ambitious you are as a black woman in America, the less you find supportive brothers who can handle that. And that's sad, but I just told myself that that's no longer *my* problem, and I decided to move on with my life."

I just started to eat my chicken meal before it got cold on me, but it was too late. I had lost my appetite. I didn't even feel like shopping anymore.

Kiwana continued: "I don't expect for you to see what *I* was able to see, Tracy. All I ask is that you don't treat me any differently than you did before."

I smiled and said, "But what if I want to talk about white people?"

"Then go ahead and do it," she told me. "Just because I married a white man doesn't mean that the whole world has changed. I wish that it would, because I would sacrifice myself in a minute to do that, but it just doesn't work that way."

*It damn sure don't!* I thought. I felt terrible about everything. Kiwana was like a long-lost sister to me. I loved her, but marrying a white man . . . I just didn't know if I could love *that!* However, there were several white men who had stuck out their necks to help me along in my career in Hollywood. I owed them a big thank-you for that, but not marriage. I mean, opportunity is the American way. Or is it not?

*Damn!* I had been home for less than a week, and all kinds of drama was jumping out at me from every direction. I didn't even remember to ask Kiwana what brought her to the area until we separated, and once we separated I had a million other questions to ask her and no way to catch up to her until she made it back home in New York. Hopefully, she would get back in touch with me. I did leave her my cell phone number, but what more did we have to say to each other? I just felt terrible. When push came to shove, my girl Raheema would always end up on the other end of my stressed-out phone calls. In year 2000, she had two kids herself, a boy and a girl. She had married an intellectual brother, and despite what America seemed to represent, good, intellectual brothers *did* still exist. We just oftentimes ignored them, keeping our eyes wide open for roughnecks like my Victor Hinson, while sidestepping the sweet softies in our lives.

*If I only knew in my younger years what I know now . . .*

## $ $ $

When I was done *attempting* to shop, it was close to four o'clock in the afternoon. My girl/agent would be in full swing at her California office. I called her up on the cell phone to get an update on the book deal.

"Hey, it's me, Tracy," I said.

"How has your day been?" she asked me. She sounded really gentle, as if she was still concerned about the carjack attempt from the night before.

"I'm okay. Stop sounding like I have cancer or something," I snapped to lighten up the conservation.

"Did you still do the radio interview?" she asked.

"Yeah, and guess what rumor mill I was pulled into?"

"What?"

"Lesbianism. All because of the Grant name thing."

She got excited and said, "Uh oh! You know what that means, don't you?"

"No I don't. What exactly does that mean?"

"That means that you're a hit! Trust me! In the business of Hollywood, *any* rumor is better than *no* rumor. That just means that people want to know more about you, and as long as it's not true, I wouldn't sweat it. They just want to see you paired up with someone, that's all."

"What if I don't exactly *want* to be *paired up* with some-one?"

"You just bear it and move on to your next project."

"But won't that make producers and directors look at me funny for my next *straight girl* role?"

She chuckled over the phone and said, "Please! Sexual preference is the *last* thing that *Hollywood* worries about. As long as it helps to sell you.

"Just look at Ellen DeGeneres as an example," she pointed out. "She may have been pulled from a conserva-tive television network, but she's had what, four or five movie deals since then? And that goes ditto for her girl-friend Anne Heche.

"Tracy, I would *not* concern myself with that," she told me.

"Yeah, but they're both white. The black community is much less tolerant for that kind of a thing," I argued, just for the sake of arguing. I wanted to hear my girl's complete view on it. After all, I *did* accuse *her* of being a lesbian when we first became friends out in California.

"Remember there was a time when you were wonder-ing which way I went?" she hinted with a chuckle.

I laughed and said, "I was just thinking about that my-self. Anyway, enough of the gay talk; what's the deal with the book deal?" I asked her. I was pressed.

"Well, I called Omar's people this morning, and I was told that he'll take another look into it."

It sounded as if they were stalling to me.

I said, "Tell them he better look into it *fast,* because the plot is thickening." I was getting pissed with this brother.

My life story in *Flyy Girl* was what put his writing career on the map, and he was fronting big-time to continue what we had started. I mean, didn't he realize how big of a book my sequel would be? Maybe he didn't.

My girl said, "I told them that you would want to include some of your poetry. I think that would be a great thing to do. Poetry is really catching on again in a major way, all across the country. Pop singer Jewel's poetry book was even a best-seller a few years ago."

*Yeah, yeah,* I thought to myself. I was really *pressed* to get that book deal *done!*

"Well, just stay on them about it and let them know that we *will* move on if his answer is no. We don't have all year to *wait* for his answer either."

I said, "Omar's a good writer and I respect our history together, but now that I'm big I could get anyone I want to write it."

"Okay," my girl said. She was putting on her "Tracy's the boss" routine with a little woman's high-pitched squeal that I hated. "Can I also tell you that I received a few more scripts for you to look at when you get back out to California, or do you want me to FedEx them to Philadelphia for you?"

I smiled and said, "Okay, cut the shit. I'm just a little hyper about this book thing, that's all. I didn't mean to come off like a bighead."

"Your words, not mine," she responded.

"By the way," I decided to ask her, "would you ever consider marrying a black man?"

She paused. That was all I needed to know. She had probably never even thought about it.

"Why do you ask me that?"

I wondered if her face was turning red, but my agent was a dark-haired Jewish girl. Her face probably didn't turn flushed.

I answered, "No reason. I guess you'll just find out about that when we finally get this book deal," I teased her.

"Find out about what?"

I took a deep breath. I didn't have the energy to get into it.

"Another time, okay? Another time," I told her.

"All right. So what do you want me to do about these scripts?"

I thought about it. "Well, I'm too busy out here to even—" I stopped myself and thought again. *Maybe I could use something to take my mind off of all of the drama around here and think more about my future,* I pondered to myself.

"On second thought, go ahead and FedEx them to my parents' house. I could *use* something to look forward to."

"Okay. Consider it done," she responded again in that sarcastic little voice of hers.

I said, "Would you stop that? I am *not* like that. And if I ever *do* get a big head, I want you to mail me a letter and let me know, so that I can stick it in my purse and read it to myself at least three times a day."

She said, "Hey, that sounds like a good idea," and laughed about it.

I stopped and asked, "So you really feel that I'm getting bigheaded then?" I was definitely concerned about that. A Diana Ross "Super Diva" figure was *not* who I wanted to be, *nor* what I wanted to represent.

My girl said, "Tracy, I'm gonna level with you. If you didn't have the qualities of determination that it takes to make it out in Hollywood, you would have never made it *this* far. Trust me. You *have* what it takes, I just don't want you to overdo it."

I smiled and said, "Thanks for the compliment, but I am *not* being bigheaded."

She just laughed. "Sounds like a guilty conscience to me."

"Whatever," I told her. "I don't have time for your head games right now. So get back to work," I teased.

My girl went right back to that little voice of hers.

"Oh, yes, of course. I'll get on it right away."

I hung up the phone with her and planned to pay my agent no mind. If I was getting bigheaded then so be it, because I still had shit that I wanted to do!

# When the Grass Is No Longer Green . . .

. . . the sun cannot reflect and shine upward.
The dirt looks extra hard and plenty thirsty.
And little boys and girls run inside
with blood gushing from their knees from bottle cuts
instead of grass burns that can be washed away
and kissed.

. . . the trash decorates the streets and sidewalks
with steel gates and wired fences that intimidate,
distracting clear vision on even sunny days,
and claiming to protect its tenants
from bad, outside influences,
while locking in the good ones who dream America.

. . . little girls pick up babies instead of lilies
and daisies,
while their boyfriends pick up rocks,
sticks, bats, knives and guns.
But seldom do they pick up their babies.
Maybe babies are too heavy to hold, like jobs.

. . . Mickey Ds, BKs, TBs, KFCs and Wendy's
are the cleanest and brightest things standing.
Or at least
on the outside.
Because the insides often need sanitation,
including the attitudes of some who work there.

. . . those who have checks may cash them
for a fee,
not to hold and collect dividends,

*but to spend at the next corner*
*on their favorite friends and pastimes*
*instead of saving for a better day.*

*. . . neighborhood fights become entertainment,*
*paid not with golden belts and million-dollar contracts,*
*but with death*
*and deep scars that stop you from running,*
*while mothers cry and wear old dresses*
*to new Churches for their sons' funerals.*

*. . . powerless officials offer Band-Aids*
*for solutions*
*instead of signing budgets to uproot the soil*
*and fertilize the land for grass that grows,*
*and shines*
*which may take for generations.*

*But,*
*. . . no one living there has time*
*to wait,*
*because Yesterday barely made it,*
*Today is holding on by a string,*
*and Tomorrow is forever breaking promises.*

# September 1996 $ $

$

*I* settled down in Baldwin Hills and was lazy as hell for my first two days in California. My car needed a break anyway after driving for four days from Philadelphia to get there. I just wanted to sit outside, suck up the West Coast atmosphere, and watch cars drive by from my second-floor balcony.

I had moved to California in style. I actually had a townhouse! I didn't plan to buy any furniture though, that was for sure. If I didn't get connected with a big job, substitute teaching was *not* going to pay my rent. I needed to make some serious money in order to stay there. I bought only a bed, some cheap dressers, and a few new dishes to eat from. I also bought a new color television set and a high-tech VCR with a stand. You cannot *possibly* plan to break into the business of television and film without *those* two necessities. I had given my previous television set and lower-grade VCR to my brother. The rest of my townhouse was empty, upstairs *and* downstairs. I mean, I was in *echo* territory: *HELLO, HELLO, HELLO!*

I thought about the prospect of not having any furniture for a while and laughed out loud to myself. I was sure that people would tease me about it, but what was more important, having a nice place to live in a nice area, or buying fancy furniture for a crummy apartment in the 'hood? Excuse me, but I'll take the pretty townhouse with no furniture in a *heartbeat*! A lot of people did without furniture in college, myself included. I was used to it. However, my empty place also served as a reminder of how busy I had to get to make sure that it wouldn't *remain* empty. So I had plenty of work to do.

On my third day of officially living in LA, I finally decided to do a little exploring, you know, drive around on my own and see what I could see. I hopped in my black Toyota (which still had Pennsylvania license plates), and drove past the shopping center on La Brea toward Crenshaw. I just figured that Crenshaw was the place to be.

I guess I wasn't paying too much attention to the road when I came up on Crenshaw. I arrived much faster than anticipated. I jumped in the turning lane in front of an old gray Volkswagen Rabbit. I didn't think too much of it though. The young driver was moving slow and listening to loud rap music anyway. It was no big deal in Philly. You just wave politely to the driver and keep on going.

I turned onto Crenshaw and started cruising with my eyes bouncing from left to right as I took everything in: the shops, the people, the buses, the billboard advertisements, and everything. Crenshaw was definitely BLACK, and I felt at peace with my California people as if I was on North Broad Street back home in Philly. All of a sudden, the young guy driving the VW Rabbit jumped back out in front of me. I went to switch lanes so I could have clear vision from my front windshield. The VW Rabbit swerved in front of me again. I moved back to the first lane that I was in, only for this nutcase to jump in front of me for a third time.

I finally got pissed the hell off and started to yell, "WHAT THE—," but I stopped myself and realized that I was no longer in Philadelphia. I thought, *What if this ass-*

*hole has a gun and he's ready to shoot me just for cutting him off?*

The next thing I knew, he had switched lanes again and slowed up so that he could pull up right beside me. He looked and grilled at me, and I didn't know if he was reaching his right hand for his stick shift, or for a gun, but I was *definitely* not planning to wait around and find out. I jammed my breaks in the middle of traffic and tried to make a U-turn.

BURRRNNNMP!

"WHAT THE HELL ARE YOU DOING?!"

BURRRNNNMP!

"YOU CRAZY ASS!"

People were blowing horns and yelling all kinds of things at me, but I made that U-turn and just missed hitting two oncoming cars. I was a nervous wreck from fear. My heart was practically on *fire* it was beating so fast! I was looking for the first police car I could spot to save me, and there was none in sight. My hands began to shake at the wheel while I looked around for that crazy guy in the VW Rabbit who was hounding me.

I didn't see him, but I took off up Crenshaw and made a left turn back toward my townhouse anyway. I was thinking about that crazy movie *Menace II Society*, starring Larenz Tate and Tyrin Turner.

"Please, God, let me make it back home!" I hollered to myself while driving like a lunatic.

When I arrived at my townhouse, I hopped out, ducked down, and sprinted back to my door as if a killer was stalking me. I could barely get my key inside of the door I was shaking so badly.

"Hurry up, hurry up!" I told myself. I finally turned my key and lunged into the house before locking my door. I threw my purse to the floor, relieved, and yelled, "SHIT!"

I could barely breathe, and my chest was hurting. I tossed my hands to my face and mumbled, "Oh my God!" My ass was ready to fly back home to Philadelphia *quick*, because I was *not* driving again in LA. Kendra was right. Those Negroes out there were stone cold *crazy!* Just because I cut him off. It wasn't as if I had done it on purpose. I was even afraid to sit out on my balcony, thinking that the guy would drive by and aim up at me with a shotgun.

Of course, everything I did that day was an overreaction. Nevertheless, how the hell was *I* supposed to know that you don't cut people off in LA. Or at least not young black males who listen to loud rap music. When I sat down on my empty hardwood floor and thought about that, it made me sad. My thoughts about the incident fed into the whole stereotype of young black men, rap music, movies, and violence, but shit, if those Negroes didn't *act* so violent in the first place, the stereotypes would have never been started!

I must have sat there on my empty floor and thought about things for a hour. When I was done thinking, I went and grabbed my handy notebook and began to write the most political poem that I think I've ever written, "When the Grass Is No Longer Green . . ." I used a lot of the information that Kendra had already presented to me, added what I had seen out there with my own eyes, and went from there with my creativity. When I finished it, it was also one of the *longest* poems that I had ever written. However, I wanted to make it even better, so I knew that the initial idea was only a first draft.

I called Kendra to tell her about my crazy drive on Crenshaw, but she was not at home from her school day yet, so I decided to call my girl Raheema long distance in

New Jersey. It was three-thirty in LA, which translated to six-thirty in New Jersey. I called Raheema at home instead of at her office at Rutgers. Knowing her studious behind, she was probably working late at the university. I was surprised when she answered the phone.

"Hello."

"Hey, girl, you busy?" I responded. "I'm officially out in LA now, and *already* I have things to tell you."

"Long distance at that," she teased me with a laugh.

"Well, how else am I gonna tell you, through telegram?" I snapped sarcastically. Raheema and I were forever playing a game of smart mouth with each other, no matter how old we were.

"So what happened that's so important already? You met a big-time Hollywood producer who wants to turn your life story into a movie?"

"No, but I was almost shot at today like a movie."

"Well, that is Bloods' and Crips' town out there," she told me. "You need to find a book called *Do or Die* by Leon Bing and *Monster* by Sanyika Shakur, and read all about it."

That was my girl! Raheema knew something about *every*-damn-thing! She was like a walking encyclopedia.

"Well, let me tell you what happened," I started.

"Actually, I'm getting ready to go out," she cut me off. I guess Raheema knew that I was overreacting. She had dealt with my drama all before.

I stopped short and asked, "You're going out? With a guy?"

We both laughed. Raheema's dating life was *always* news to me. Sometimes I felt that she would join the scholars' monastery and never have any use for the flesh.

"Yes," she answered me, guarded. All that did was make me curious.

"What's he like?"

"He's smart. *And* he's patient. Unselfish. And actually *handsome.*"

She said each thing as if it stood alone.

I asked, "What, he wasn't supposed to be handsome?"

"Let's just say that looks are not a major requirement for *me* like it is for *some* people we both know."

I laughed and said, "Whatever. You have to think about your kids."

"Oh, trust me, I do."

"Okay, well, you don't have time to hear my story, but just let me read this poem to you that I just wrote."

She paused and said, "Okay."

I responded, "It's *not* going to kill you, girl. Just hear me out."

"Read it already," she pressed me.

"Okay, here it is, but I just want you to know that I'm still working on it."

"Revision is always good, now let's hear it."

I read it to her with all of the politics involved and the repetitive flow from the title, and Raheema just breathed over the phone.

I asked, "So what do you think?"

"I think I might want to use that in my future class-rooms," she told me. "Maya Angelou, look out! That piece was *phenomenal!*"

"Aw, go 'head, girl, you're exaggerating," I said with a smile. I was glad to hear it though. I added, "You can use it, just as long as you tell them where you got it from."

Raheema said, "Do you actually think that I would ever use one of your poems and not give you credit for it?"

"I'm just making sure," I told her.

"You are a mess."

"Yeah, whatever. Now go on out with your smart, patient, handsome, unselfish date, and don't do anything that *I* wouldn't do."

"Don't you mean to say don't do anything that you *would* do?" she teased.

I just smiled and said, "Bye, Ra-Ra."

She said, "Isn't your birthday this Friday, September six? What are you doing, something that *I* wouldn't do?"

"Look, girl, it's just another year for me. That'll be my first day of taking a crash course on screenwriting. So I'll be starting the education of my new career on my birthday."

"Well, knock 'em dead, Tracy. Knowing you, I'm *sure* that you will."

I hung up the phone and thought about my first class on how to write screenplays. I began to think of how I could make the Crenshaw driving incident into a scene in a film just like it had inspired me to write a poem. I wondered how much of screenwriting would be the same way, coming up with an idea off of something that happened to you, and expanding on it to make it come to life up on the big screen for everyone else. The theory made perfect sense to me. I guessed that I would soon find out, but first I had to tell Kendra about my day.

When Kendra arrived at home, I was waiting for her to pick up that line and hear me out.

"*Girrrl,* let me tell you what happened to me *today.* You were *absolutely* right . . ."

**$ $ $**

When the Hollywood Film Institute said *crash course,* that's *exactly* what they meant. I paid three hundred dollars (which included the price of several screenwriting books) for two days of instruction to help me figure out what the hell I was doing. We started early in the morning and had classes up until night with several breaks in between.

I arrived bright and early at the film institute in West Hollywood still terrified of driving out in LA. Since I knew that I would be early, I took my notepad with me to look over my Crenshaw-inspired poem again. I had an extra notepad with me to take down everything I could on screenwriting from the crash course.

I read my revised poem to myself, rewritten with all of the perfect words and dramatic breaks for mass appeal in performance *or* on paper. Some poems are no good for performance, just as others are no good for print. I wanted my poem to stand up in both forms.

I had to go to the bathroom right in the middle of reading it, so I went to search for the restroom. When I returned to my desk, I realized what I had done. You *never* leave your creativity unattended. A good creation is worth more than money, and there was a dark-haired white girl reading my shit when I returned. At first I thought she was about to take it, but then she saw me coming and tried to pretend as if she was only noticing that someone had left something there.

"So what do you think about it?" I asked her with a grin. I knew she had read it.

She turned and asked, "Excuse me?"

She was attempting to play the innocent, but she had no idea who she was dealing with.

I said, "My poem. I saw you reading it. What do you think about it?"

She was dressed in casual gear with tan khakis, Banana Republic style. I was dressed casually myself in blue jeans.

She smiled and said, "It's very good. I like how you use the title as your dramatic point with repetition."

"Yeah, I try to do something different every time."

"So you're a poet?"

"I don't really call myself one. I just do it, you know, like the Nike commercials."

She laughed and said, "My name is Susan," and extended her hand to me.

I looked clearly over the top of her thick brown hair with my superior height and shook her hand. "I'm Tracy." This girl must have stood about five foot two *with heels*. I just *loved* being tall, and I had to let her know that I was confident with it. I figured that I had to use *some* kind of an edge out in Hollywood. I would be out of my league out there. It was brand-new territory for me.

"So, I guess we're, ah, here to learn how to write scripts," she said out loud and took a seat in the desk to the right of mine.

"Yeah, I guess so," I responded to her.

I stared up at the huge blackboard at the front of the room, thinking how ironic it was for me to go from being a student to a teacher and back to a student again. However, that was life. When you step it up, sometimes you have to start it all over.

"So, what film school did you go to?" she asked me.

I looked at her and searched her dark eyes. She was making a positive assumption about my education. That was a good thing, but my answer was not.

"Actually, I didn't go to film school," I told her. I left it at that just to see what her response would be.

She said, "Oh," and was speechless. I read that as: *This*

*black girl doesn't have a chance. She didn't even go to film school.*

I had already heard it through the grapevine (Kendra) that Hollywood crash courses were mostly for film majors and people who were already in the business, and not necessarily for fresh newcomers like myself.

After an embarrassing silence, I decided to release Susan from her hushed suspense.

"I majored in English," I told her.

"Oh yeah," she uttered. She was still at a loss for words.

"Then I went ahead and received my master's in it," I added.

Susan's eyebrows raised on that one.

"Oh yeah, a master's in English? I have my MBA. What did you do your thesis on? I'm always interested in that."

It was a good damned thing that I wasn't lying. I would have been busted on the spot!

I said, "The use of common speech for effective human communication as opposed to the rigidness of King's English."

She smiled. "Well, you can't use the King's English in *this* business, I'll tell you that much. No one goes to the theaters with dictionaries in hand."

"Exactly," I told her. "The more you can relate your diction to your audience, the more effective your communication becomes."

"So what do you think about this Ebonics thing that they've been bringing up in Oakland? Have you heard about that?"

Girlfriend was right on the case!

I answered, "If you're an American, then you *should* be afforded the opportunity to learn how to read, write, *and* speak English properly. And if you *choose,* after being educated, to break your diction for whatever reason to relate to whatever group, then fine, but only *after* you've learned the correct methodology.

"That's what our *taxes* are supposed to pay for," I concluded.

My English professors at Hampton would have been proud. I taught from the correct approach to English myself. How else could I be an effective English teacher?

"You know, I was teaching English to middle school students back home in Philadelphia before I decided to try my luck out here in Hollywood," I said. "I just wanted to see if I could make an improvement on the writing of African-American roles."

"Who would know better than an English teacher, right?" she joked.

I asked, "So what brings *you* to a screenwriting class with an MBA? Shouldn't you be in a film production and financing course or something?"

"Well, I've already been through a bunch of those courses, actually. I just want to learn as much about the business of Hollywood as I can, including the writing process," she answered.

She was straightforward and pretty easy to talk to. I think I liked her. By the time we had finished chatting, the class was filling up and it was getting close to start time. Right off the bat, I witnessed up close that Hollywood was definitely a white man's game, because including Susan and myself, there were only five women there out of thirty, and there were only three brothers out of the twenty-five men, with two Latinos up in the house.

I began to feel nervous about my prospects again when the instructor walked in with several screenplays in hand.

He was a tall, slender guy with a full gray beard and a gray head of hair, wearing wire-framed glasses.

He said, "Well, whatever *philosophies* you learned in your film schools, kids, forget about them. I'm here to tell you how we actually *make* films out here. Then again, don't forget *everything* you learned in film school, because you can still use a good twenty-five percent of it."

He waited to see if we would all laugh, and he was unsatisfied with our lack of a response.

"That was a joke, people, loosen up. I mean, this *is* only a three-hundred-dollar course, right? Am I in the right classroom?" he asked us. "It's not like that small piece of property you sold to go to film school at USC."

They laughed a little louder at that, but I had nothing to laugh about. I was paying strict attention.

"Okay," he said, holding up the finished screenplays in his hand, "these are a couple of the screenplays that we're going to look at as we get started here. I have Lawrence Kasdan's *Body Heat,* Steven Haft's *Dead Poets Society,* John Singleton's *Poetic Justice,* and Richard Zanuck's *Jaws.*

"By chance, have you guys seen any of these films?" our instructor joked again. *I* even smiled at that. However, I did wonder how many writers in that room saw *Poetic Justice.* I thought that John Singleton could have used a woman's touch on writing it myself. He should have given *me* a call. I smiled and held my thoughts to myself.

"Okay, as you guys should already know, all successful story writing should have a beginning, an ending, a drive, a few conflicts, and a definitive resolution.

"You want to make sure that you define who your audience is.

"You want to make sure that you define your six dramatic stages. Which are . . . anyone?" he asked the class.

One of the white guys spoke up first. That was an easy numbers game. They dominated the room.

"Act I, Plot Point I, Act II, Plot Point II, Act III, and the Resolution."

It sounded simple enough to me. All I needed were the details on how to do it.

"Now a good, well-defined character with drive, pizzazz, and morality, *or* the *lack* of morality, as the case may be for *some* of you, is a great thing to start from. A great opening scene, a strong theme, and inspiring scenery are also good starting points. However, what you're all here to find out is *what* is needed to pull all of these separate things together to make a successfully executed story."

*Exactly,* I thought to myself as I sat there and took notes. Susan only listened. Like she had said, she wasn't really planning on writing, she just wanted to know as much about the business of Hollywood as she could. My crazy behind was out there to try and make a difference in the community by learning how to write something worthwhile, *and* pay my damn rent. I also wanted recognition for my work, of course.

We went over the entire screenwriting process for both days, met some actual screenwriters, watched films, analyzed successful execution, weak execution, and discussed protecting what we wrote, pursuing agents, pitching your stories, and plenty of other needful things in the film game. We even went over some screenplay ideas of our own. I learned a lot there.

During our breaks I made a lot of small talk with Susan, and two of the brothers who were there. I was even asked out for dinner that Saturday night (the day after my twenty-fifth birthday), and I accepted, if only to make a few new friends. What I *didn't* do was trade phone numbers with Susan after that second day. After I thought about it, I figured that I should have. Susan may have been a real mover and shaker, sitting right under my nose, so I hoped to bump into her again.

**$ $ $**

Richard Mack was my height with low-cut hair, slim to medium weight, light brown, and very talkative. He claimed to be from Detroit, but I begged to differ. He seemed more like a suburbanite to me. I was used to people from the suburbs claiming nearby cities from going to Hampton. Everyone did it. If you lived right outside of Chicago, you told people you lived *in* Chicago and moved on.

Anyway, Rich was not my type, so I planned to stay strictly professional. We went to this scenic restaurant on Sunset Boulevard called The Tropical. They had outside seating and plenty of satarilike appeal.

"So, what kind of projects do you plan on writing?" Rich asked me once we were seated. We both ordered tropical blend drinks with a touch of rum in them. They called them Havanas.

I was skeptical about being too open with my film ideas though. I didn't know this guy like that. He *seemed* honest enough, but still.

"I don't know what kind of projects I plan to write yet," I told him. In reality, I was still thinking about writing something based off of my drive on Crenshaw.

"What did you think about the crash course?" he asked me.

"It was okay," I answered. I was barely paying attention to him, daydreaming about my thoughts for story ideas. I guess I wasn't the best of company that night. I was there physically, but not there mentally. I had a two-month screenwriting course coming up with the UCLA Extensions program later on that September. I heard that UCLA's courses were more in-depth than the Hollywood Film Institute's, and the instructors there were supposedly better connected in the business.

I decided to ask Rich what he knew about it.

He said, "I've been there and done that. You get to work on and complete an actual screenplay. Then you go from there and try to find a writing job."

"So what happened to your job?" I asked him.

He looked shocked at first before he smiled and shook his head. I guess he didn't expect me to be so forward.

"I was briefly writing for a show that was canceled. That's part of the business out here."

"What do you do for money in the meantime?" I asked. I was still concerned about that myself.

He said, "Fortunately, I still have enough saved for a few rainy days from when I was working."

I had about three thousand dollars left in my bank account after paying for the townhouse, and I was not due a check for the republication of *Flyy Girl* until after the publishing date in October. That seemed like forever!

"So, what made you decide to write for Hollywood after teaching English in Philly?" Rich asked me.

"Boredom," I answered. "I needed something more challenging, something that would pick me up in the morning."

He grinned and said, "Whatever happened to coffee?", which I felt was pressed and corny. You don't have to comment on everything a woman says. That's why he wasn't my type; he was too short, too ordinary, and not hardly cool enough for me. I hated to admit it, but that Philadelphian cool that I was so used to was a hard thing to replace. However, that didn't mean that Rich and I could not be associates in the business.

All of a sudden, a lot of the customers started standing up and walking over to the television set in front of the bar.

"What's going on over there?" Rich asked our waitress.

The tall, attractive blonde was ready to take our dinner orders. She gave us the shocking news, blow for blow. "Tupac Shakur was shot while riding in the passenger seat of Suge Knight's car after the Mike Tyson fight in Las Vegas."

I looked at Rich and Rich looked at me. We both had wide eyes.

"And he survived again?" I asked our waitress. Tupac Shakur was always slipping away from fatality, like a real-life ghetto hero who wouldn't stay down. The boy seemed to have nine lives, and every time he escaped from death his popularity increased.

"Oh, I don't know," our waitress answered. "They just said that he was taken to a Las Vegas hospital in critical condition."

Rich said, "Critical condition means that he *did* survive. I heard he wears a bulletproof vest anyway."

"They said he wasn't wearing one tonight," she told us.

I began to wonder if our blonde waitress listened to rap music herself. She sure seemed keen on who Tupac was *and* who he was connected to. He *was* an actor. Our waitress probably wanted to be an actress herself. She sure didn't look like your average waitress.

It was just my luck when the news reports began to talk about feuds between LA's Bloods and Crips as a possible motive for Tupac's shooting. I just couldn't get a damn break out in LA! I still had to drive the hell home to Baldwin Hills.

*Shit!* I thought to myself. I knew enough about retaliation to not get caught up in the crossfire, and I was not planning to go anywhere *near* Crenshaw that night.

Suddenly I lost my appetite. I thought about ordering take-out from my townhouse for the next month until the tension cooled down. You could feel it in the California air as soon as they started talking about the Bloods and Crips.

Rich asked me, "What's wrong with your food?" He was eating like there was no tomorrow. I guess the craziness out in LA didn't bother him at all, but it bothered *me*. I wanted to get the hell out of there, and I was just starting to get my feet wet in Hollywood. I hadn't even taken off my towel to jump in the water yet.

Rich wanted to hang out and show me around, but I had no plans at all for that. I wanted to get back inside the house like a damn mouse myself. I couldn't believe that I was acting so damn paranoid, but like they say, Better safe than sorry. Rich didn't sweat it. I guess he had other women to entertain. So I drove back to my townhouse in Baldwin Hills as nervous as I could be, and rushed to my bedroom to listen to more news about Tupac's shooting. It was all over the radio stations and everything.

All that next week I received phone calls from my family and friends back home in Philly:

"Is everything all right out there? You sure you don't want to come back home for a while?"

Even Kendra was nervous about things:

"I told you, Tracy. I bet you'll listen to me now. These guys out here in LA are not to be played with."

I had definitely learned to believe her, but I was not a punk either. I had relocated to LA to put my thing down in the industry of Hollywood, and that's what I planned to do! If I was shot and killed in the process, then that bullet must have had my name on it. Nevertheless, I prayed in my bed every night that it didn't. I wasn't even a church-going woman.

It was not hardly a pleasing twenty-fifth birthday treat that September in Los Angeles for me, but like they say, Only the strong survive, and I was damn-sure strong. Or at least I liked to *believe* so, and I was prepared to find out.

# The Fast Lanes

*A fast mind leads to*
*fast situations.*
*A fast body leads to*
*fast boys.*
*A fast boy leads to*
*fast sex.*
*Fast sexuality leads to*
*fast reputations.*
*A fast reputation leads to*
*fast propositions.*
*And fast propositions lead*
*your fast ass down*
*empty, one-way streets*
*that have dead ends*
*and nowhere constructive to go.*

*So if I could*
*do it*
*all over again,*
*knowing what I now know,*
*I would choose to drive*
*slowly,*
*and obey the speeding laws.*

# April 2000

$$ \$ \$ $$
$$ \$ $$

After the visit to King of Prussia Mall, I made it back to my parents' house in Germantown right at five o'clock and beat the rush-hour traffic. I was anxious to call up Raheema in central New Jersey (where she still lived after earning her Ph.D. in African-American Studies at Rutgers) to give her the news on Kiwana. Raheema had to pick up her kids from day care, so I knew that she would be home. Imagine that. After all of the daydreaming that *I* did in our youth concerning a husband and a family, and the tear of boys that *Raheema* had, it was ironic that *she* ended up happily married with the husband and kids and *I* ended up single and was hardly even *looking* for a mate. Go figure that out.

"Hello," she answered on the first ring.

"Hey, girl, it's Tracy."

"Haaay, you're back at home now, right? How have things been back home?"

"Drama, drama, and *more* drama," I told her. "I haven't been able to relax at home *yet*. I almost got carjacked. My visit to Germantown High School bombed out. I was accused of being a lesbian on Power 99 FM this morning, and you would *never believe* who ended up marrying a white man?"

"Who?" Raheema asked me.

"Kiwana."

"Kiwana? From Cheyney?!" her voice went high. "Get out of here!"

"I'm serious," I told her. "I bumped into her today at King of Prussia Mall, and she showed me pictures of her two daughters with her white husband and everything."

"Did she have the daughters with him, or were they with a brother?"

"No, they were with the white husband, and both of her kids are *lighter* than you," I added.

"Oh, well, thanks for the reminder, Tracy. Thanks a lot," Raheema cracked. "I forgot how light I was for a minute."

I just laughed it off. Black people would never be able to get away from color complexes, because every day new babies are born with different shades, and we are damn sure not color blind! Raheema even went through a radical stage in college where she got heavily into Black Power, culture, and politics, and started to remind me of Angela Davis or somebody, wearing her hair in a short Afro. She wasn't as outspoken about things as Angela Davis or I was, but Raheema kept it real, and she was very much pro-black.

"Well, I can just imagine what she told you," she said, referring to Kiwana.

"Okay, what did she tell me?" I quizzed her. I loved letting my girl use that brain power of hers.

"She told you that she couldn't find a supportive brother who could handle her strong independence or understand her career as a stage performer."

I nodded to myself with the phone in hand. "Basically, yes, that's what she told me. She said the more ambitious you are as a black woman in America, the less you'll find brothers who can deal with that, and basically, she said that it wasn't her problem anymore and she was moving on."

Raheema was speechless for a second. I heard her three-year-old son, Jordan, asking for help to use the potty.

"Excuse me for a minute, Tracy. You don't mind if I take the phone in the bathroom with me, do you?"

I laughed. "Do what you have to do. I remember those days of trying to potty train my brother Jason."

"Well, Jordan only asks for help when he has to do number two, because he likes to sit on the big toilet like his father."

I laughed again.

"Ernest takes him in the bathroom with him?" I could see it in my head, Raheema's husband taking their son into the restroom and suffocating the little boy with funk.

Raheema caught on and laughed herself.

"We all have to learn. Lauryn is starting to go now, and she's only fourteen months. Would you like to talk to your aunt Tracy?" she asked her son.

"Yes," I heard Jordan speak up.

"Hi, Aunt Tracy." Actually, Raheema had made me his godmother, but "Aunt Tracy" made us seem a lot closer, and it felt appropriate to me.

"Hey, Jordan. Did you enjoy your birthday party last week?" I asked him.

I had just missed it, but Raheema understood. You can't make too many promises when you have a busy schedule.

Jordan answered, "Yes. We had balloons, ice cream; I blew out the candles on my cake. I hurt my knee playing outside in the grass. I'm three years old now. I have a new red bike."

I laughed even harder. He sounded like your typical smart kid. His little mind just lined the subjects up and spit them out, just like my brother used to do.

Raheema reclaimed the phone to continue our discussion.

"The saddest thing about what Kiwana is saying is that it's true," she told me. "If you don't find a black man who basically does the same thing that you do, or something close to it so that they can understand the support that you need and the schedule that you keep, then the courtship can lead to a short, rocky road and a dead end."

I guess Raheema lucked up, because her husband Ernest was an associate law professor and moving his way up at Seton Hall, not far from Rutgers. They were both high achievers in education.

"In other words, you're saying that I'll need to marry someone in the entertainment business now, is that it?" I asked her rhetorically.

"Or at least someone who understands the demands of the business," she said.

Thinking of Seton Hall, I asked Raheema, "Have you heard from Jantel lately?" Jantel, another friend from our high school days, was awarded a track scholarship to Seton Hall.

"Last I heard, she was still trying out for the Summer Olympics in the quarter mile."

"I wonder if she'll be in this year's Olympics then," I said out loud.

"Maybe. They say that women peak later than men. Twenty-nine is a perfect age for the Olympics."

"Not if she's up against Marion Jones. That girl can outright *fly*, and she's still in her *early* twenties," I commented.

Raheema said, "It's just good to know that all of us are doing well."

I nodded. My mind strayed to Raheema's older sister

Mercedes, and my fast-behind friend Carmen from grade school.

"You know your sister wants to sit down and chat with me," I told Raheema.

"You thought that she *wouldn't*? She *always* talks about you. You're *her* idol now," Raheema said with a chuckle. She remembered the times when Mercedes was *my* idol as well as I did.

"You have any idea what she may want to talk to me about?" I was still curious and skeptical about what Mercedes had planned for me.

"Your guess is as good as mine," Raheema responded, "but I wouldn't be surprised if it had some kind of a monetary concern behind it. You know she still wants to make more money than what she makes now at the Nicetown drug clinic."

"I know, right? But I've been trying to tell myself to stop thinking that way."

"*I* wouldn't stop thinking that way. I mean, she's my sister and I love her and all, but . . . To each her own," Raheema concluded. You could hear the frustration in her voice. Sometimes you just have to let people go their own way.

"Well, I hate to cut this conversation short, Tracy, but I have a ton of things to do. If you're free this weekend, how about you drive up here to Plainfield to visit us. It's only an hour and change away."

I chuckled. If I said yes to everything while I was at home, I would nearly kill myself. However, maybe a ride up to New Jersey to visit my happily married friend and spend time with her family would do the trick to ease my mind, because nothing else had.

I said, "I'll have to think about that. It will depend on how tired I am after Friday."

"Okay, well, take your time and don't exert yourself, because I know how much energy you can burn up trying to do too many things, Tracy. So just slow down. Okay?"

"I hear you, girl. Just take a chill pill."

When I hung up the phone, I looked out of my parents' front window and saw my father pulling up right behind his Infiniti SUV. I parked it right where he usually parks his Buick in front of the house. I grabbed the keys and rushed outside before he could start on his way in. It was a perfect sunny day for a surprise.

"Happy birthday, Daddy!" I shouted to him, standing in front of the Infiniti with the keys in hand.

He smiled, stroked his trimmed beard, and acted all cool about it.

"You get a good deal on it?" he asked me.

"I paid for it in *cash*. I *needed* to get a good deal on it."

"How much?"

I couldn't believe he was asking me that. I said, "What difference does it make, Daddy? Just get in and drive it!" I was beginning to lose my patience with everything. Why was everyone making it so hard for me to come home and enjoy myself?

My father took the keys and said, "This is just a high-model Pathfinder. Nissan makes them both. I like that new Cadillac Escalade myself."

I couldn't believe my damn ears! I had nearly gotten carjacked in that Infiniti after working out a good damn deal for it, and after all of that, my father was telling me that he would rather have a *Cadillac*! I was just *too through*!

I said, "Well, Daddy, why don't you go trade this in and buy yourself a damn Cadillac then."

Right as I said that, my mother pulled up from work in her car and parked behind my father's Buick, all lined up in the street in front of our house and the neighbor's next door.

I was so pissed off that I turned away and began to walk back to the house.

"Where are you going?" my father asked me.

I said, "I'm going up to my old room to lay down."

"What did you say to her?" my mother asked him. I guess she could hear the irritation in my voice and see it on my twisted-up face, because I was *pissed*!

"I didn't say anything to her," my father lied.

I stopped in my tracks and turned around to glare at him.

"Oh no you didn't, Dad," I told him. "You are *not* gonna sit here and *lie* right in my face like that." I turned to my mother and said, "He told me that this Infiniti is nothing but a high-model Pathfinder, and that he'd rather have a *Cadillac* Escalade, and then had the *nerve* to ask me how much I paid for it. Talk about being ungrateful!"

"*Ungrateful?*" my father asked. He was still grinning. I guess it was all a joke to him. "Do you want me to sit here and add up how much it cost *me* to raise Ms. Tracy Ellison *Grant*, send her behind away to college for four years, and then help her out while she finishes grad school for two *more* years?"

"To correct your *mis*-information, Dad, I finished college in *three* years," I snapped at him.

My mother began to laugh out loud. "This sounds like a father-daughter conversation here, so let me go inside the house and mind my own business."

"You don't want to ride in my new SUV?" my father asked her.

My mother stopped and looked at both of us.

"I thought you wanted the Cadillac?" she asked him.

He frowned at her as if Mom was busting his groove.

"Come on, Patti, I was just pulling her long legs, that's all."

"No you were not either. You *meant* what you said," I huffed at him. I saw Mercedes drive up in her car, a dark blue Honda Civic. She made a U-turn and parked across the street.

"Well, have a nice drive," I told my parents. I decided right then and there to go out with Mercedes, get something to eat, and see what she wanted to talk to me about.

She stepped out of her car wearing a red velvet dress, as if she had a new important boyfriend, but I had to erase that thought from my mind. Maybe she just decided to splurge with some of her own money for a change.

"Nice dress," I told her.

"Thank you," she said, smiling. "It's just a li'l somethin' somethin'."

"You wanna go out and get a bite to eat?" I asked.

Mercedes looked puzzled. I hadn't even allowed her a chance to cross the street yet.

"Right now?" she asked me.

"You have something you have to do with your parents?"

"Well, not really," she answered. "I'm driving?"

"Yup," I told her, heading over to the passenger side to get in. I was ready to go immediately because I was beginning to feel the emptiness in my stomach from not being able to eat at the mall with Kiwana.

When my father looked over at us in the car, I stuck my tongue out at him and made him laugh. Mercedes chuckled at that herself, and then she commented on her father.

"It's like night and day how *my* father was when we were

growing up compared to how he is now," she told me. "He's all mellowed out and shit now."

She was surely right about that. Mr. Keith was a major reason why Mercedes had lost so much faith in people. She began sneaking around with roughneck boyfriends and having sex, while hanging out late, being flyy, and eventually she slipped into taking drugs because of all of her wantonness and feelings of despair. In the meantime, she had *me* following right in her footsteps, but I never had as much baggage in my life as Mercedes had in hers. I never did any drugs either. I just missed the discipline and love of a father figure until my dad came back home to us.

*And what about you now?* I wanted to ask Mercedes. How had *she* changed over the years? She still seemed jaded to me, but I decided to get around to all of that later on.

"So, where are we driving to anyway?" she asked me.

"Let's go to Bennigan's on City Line Avenue," I told her.

"Oh, that's a bet. Their food is bangin'."

Mercedes still had that slick-ass talk and street appeal. My character in *Led Astray* stole a lot from her flair. I began to smile, just thinking about that.

"What?" Mercedes asked me. She had to be up on everything, eagle-eyed. I bet that her probing into everything could be very tiring.

I asked, "Mercedes, do you ever put your guard down?"

"Hmmph," she grunted with a smirk. "I wish. Put my guard down for what? So somebody can stab me in the back? I already have too many stitches in my back for that shit."

She looked at me and said, "Put it this way. You're all out there in Hollywood now, right? Do you trust those wheelers and dealers out there?"

She had a point. I didn't trust many people in Hollywood, but I *did* have people who had my back out there. You *have* to have faith in *someone*.

I asked, "Do you still smoke?"

She looked at me puzzled again, still trying to read everything.

"I don't smoke all like that. I'll light up an occasional cigarette here and there, but I don't smoke anything *else*, if *that's* what you mean.

"Do *you* smoke now?" she asked me back.

I shook my head. "Never did, never have, never will."

Mercedes paused and started to chuckle. "You smoked in that movie."

"That was just a character," I responded tartly. I wondered if Mercedes actually realized that I had used her as a model for my character. I wouldn't put it past her.

"Still strong-headed, Tracy," she commented. She looked the other way as we made it onto Lincoln Drive.

"You know you left me hangin', right?" she said out of the blue.

*Left you* hangin'? *What is she talking about?* I asked myself.

"What do you mean?" I asked her.

She said, "In your book, you had it all mapped out like you were gonna wait for Victor to get out of jail and marry him. What happened to that?"

"Oh," I responded in relief. I didn't know *what* she was talking about. That was an easy question to answer.

"Like you said from day one, Mercedes, Victor was too fast for me, right? Remember you told me that. You sized *that* relationship up way back when. So it was time to wake up from the dream. I've done that already."

"You know he owns a bunch of stores now," she told me.

I was trying my best to keep my mind *off* of the man,

while staying away from areas where he owned stores. "He has a health food store, a barbershop, and a hair supply store, all on Wayne Avenue. I know all about it," I said, "including the real estate that he owns down at Temple. And I'm happy for him, *him* and his wife." Nevertheless, I damn sure didn't feel like bumping back into him.

Mercedes looked at me and started laughing. "Are you *really* happy about his wife?" I guess she could sense my irritation. I hated talking about Victor, I really did. It was like discussing a third-degree burn to your face.

"Are *you* happy?" I asked her back. She was beginning to get under my skin.

"As happy as I expect to be right now," she answered.

I shook my head and looked away. Mercedes had to be the most doubtful person in the world, and the thing that got to me was that she had so much potential. It was as if she had no desire to reach for anything important in life. She had gotten too used to mud fighting, and I didn't have time for that, so I planned to keep to myself until I received a chance to stuff my face at Bennigan's.

"By the way," she said, before we could reach City Line Avenue, "I wouldn't worry about that lesbian shit that Wendy Williams was talking on the radio this morning. You know good and well you're not some damn lesbo, and so does everyone else. They just do that crazy shit for the ratings."

I laughed to myself and didn't comment on it. Mercedes didn't miss a damn thing!

After we arrived at Bennigan's, ordered our food and drinks, and began to dig in, I had to flat-out ask Mercedes what she wanted to talk to me so urgently about, because up to that point we had only done a bunch of small talk.

Mercedes looked deep into my eyes and asked, "Do you own a house out there in Hollywood?"

I shook my head. "Not in Hollywood. I have a place in Marina Del Rey. That's south of Hollywood."

"But you *do* own a house out there, right?"

"It's not like the houses you see on the *Lifestyles of the Rich and Famous,* but yes, it's mine, it's nice, and I *earned* it," I told her. "Why?"

"Does it feel good to own your own house without landlords fucking with you all the time and not doing what they're supposed to do?"

I thought about how positive Mercedes seemed after she came back home to her family and asked for help to make it through her drug problem years ago, and I guess that the angelic recovery period was long gone.

I asked, "So you want to buy a house?"

"In Yeadon," she told me. "I already saved up half of what I need for a down payment—"

"And you need the other half," I concluded, cutting her off.

She stopped talking and stabbed her cheesecake with strawberry topping with her fork.

"How much is half?" I asked her. I sat there and wondered how much it would take to get Mercedes out of my hair. On second thought, I could have been setting myself up to become her next pusherman, giving her access to something she would crave again and again, my money.

She swallowed her mouthful and said, "Actually, I'm thinking it would be better if you could give me the whole thing. That way I could use *my* money to furnish it and tighten it up with a new paint job and all that."

*Typical,* I thought to myself. Mercedes had some nerve!

"And what about your mortgage payments?" I asked her.

"Shit, Tracy, mortgage payments are like rent. I can do that. It's the damn down payment that stops most people from being able to buy houses, not the mortgage payments."

"You still have to qualify for the bank loan to get the mortgage," I told her.

"And how hard is that to do? It's plenty of people walking around out here with three-hundred-thousand-dollar houses and *terrible* credit."

"Yeah, but they have higher-*rated* credit because they have the income, whether their credit is good or not. And most people with money are going to pay their mortgage, *first.* Or at least those who have any sense."

Mercedes went back to eating her cheesecake while I shook my head again. It was just too obvious of a scam.

"What?" she mumbled through her food. "You think I'm trying to get over on you? We go back too far for that shit, Tracy."

"That's what I'm afraid of," I told her. "You're thinking that I can't turn you down because we're cool like that." *But* are *we?* I asked myself.

"Tracy, nobody's holding a damn gun to your head, so you can do what you want to do."

"And what if I choose to say no?"

She paused. "You just say no then."

I knew better than that, but what could I do? I felt like I was being blackmailed through our supposed friendship, but Mercedes was no friend like Kiwana was. Mercedes had only influenced me to do the *wrong* things, and never the right things. *If you can get somethin' without doing anything with him, then do it. But if you can't, then*

*make sure you play with his mind real good before you do,*
she told me when I was young and very impressionable.
*'Cause see, a lot of guys are stingy until you give them some*
*pussy. But once you do, they start actin' dumb, all in love 'n*
*shit.*

What kind of shit was that to tell a young teenager who
looked up to you? Was that the kind of friendship that I
felt committed to protect? Hell no! However, I *had* used
many of Mercedes' emotions, her reciprocal sexuality, and
her turmoil of drug addiction to play out some of my role
in *Led Astray.* So in a sense, I *owed* Mercedes.

I asked, "So how much do you need?" I just wanted to
hear a number. I was curious to see how much our "friendship" was worth.

"Twelve thousand dollars," she told me. At ten percent
for a down payment, the house was worth one hundred
and twenty thousand dollars.

I said, "I'll have to think about that," and left it alone.

Our conversation was stale for the rest of that night.
Mercedes drove me back home, and before we went our
separate ways, she said, "I know it seems like a fucked-up
thing for me to do, me asking you for money like that, but
we only live once. If you could help me out like that instead of me having to kill myself to buy this house, then
that would mean a hell of a lot to me."

I stopped and thought about her comment before I responded to her.

I said, "You know what? If you don't learn how to have
some faith and dedication in whatever it is that you're *try-*
*ing* to do, then even if I give you the money for this house
that you want so badly in Yeadon, it won't mean a damn
thing. Because tomorrow you'll kill yourself with the next
project that you have no faith in, and you'll start looking

for someone to bail you out again. And I might as well tell you right now, *I'm* not gonna be the one."

"Tracy, I wouldn't even—"

I cut her off with my hand raised in a stop sign and said, "Whatever. I'm telling you now, *I'm* not gonna be the one. And you can blame your father all you want for your problems, but this is *your life* and *your decisions* now. So just like *he* mellowed out, *you* need to get with the program and get *your* priorities back in order!"

I could tell that Mercedes wanted to curse me the hell out before I left. I could read it in her spiteful eyes, but she couldn't do it. Not yet anyway, because I still had something that she wanted. She hadn't changed a fucking bit, and it was getting harder for me to continue feeling sorry for her ass! So I just walked away and left her hangin', hangin' on a damn string, just like *she* was used to doing with everyone else.

# Hollywood, Hollywood

*It makes you hurry up*
*only to slow back down*
*and await*
*a green light*
*that may never come.*

*Limbo City,*
*Bimbo City,*
*this is what it feels like;*
*a rhythmless poem*
*in need of perk.*

*YET, infatuation,*
*anticipation*
*calls your name at night,*
*while you sleep walk*
*toward the fortune*
*AND the fame.*

*Copyright © 1998 by Tracy Ellison*

# October 1996

$ $

$

After Tupac Shakur's murder in September, there were eight or nine shootings in the Los Angeles area (several of them fatal) that were reported as gang retaliations. I had a chance to see the infamous LAPD in action out there (not on the streets myself, but on the Los Angeles news). By October, when things had cooled down a bit, I had enrolled in the UCLA Extensions program for screenwriting, and I knew a lot more concerning what to do and where to go, and more important what *not* to do and where *not* to go in LA. I began to brainstorm different ideas for my first attempt at writing a script for the course that I was taking. I also had received twenty hardback copies of my republished book *Flyy Girl*, with my portion of the advance still on the way. However, that did not mean that I was at peace with things. Hollywood had this greedy edge to it that made you feel unsatisfied with anything less than being an "A-list" star, and I was *far* from it! I was only a novice, trying like hell to learn how to swim in a hurry and make it upstream with *Crenshaw*, an urban love story.

In writing my first screenplay, I nearly spent the night a couple of times while using the computers at Kinko's copy store. Through my years of undergrad, grad school, and teaching, I always had access to computers so I never bothered to buy one. However, it became inevitable once I started writing scripts out in LA. A personal computer was an essential.

My plan for the plot of *Crenshaw* was as follows:

Act I: An aspiring model who is new to the city of Los Angeles accidentally cuts off a young gang member who is on his way to carry out a retaliation murder for a friend who was killed by a rival crew. The gang member, irritated, nearly shoots the model for cutting him off because he was in a hurry and ready to kill someone. Although she escapes unharmed, the timid model is scared out of her wits, and the young gang member arrives a minute too late to carry out his murder as planned.

Plot Point I: The model arrives at her first photo shoot that same day, and unknowingly becomes attracted to the gang member's older brother who is also a budding model.

Act II: The plot thickens when all is revealed and a feud breaks out between the two brothers regarding LA gangs, sissy modeling, the girl's meddling, and her lack of understanding of street culture. Ultimately, all three characters are forced to reevaluate the meaning of life, love, and career aspirations in Los Angeles.

Plot Point II: As the model begins to learn more and becomes sympathetic to the blighted subcultures of LA through her association with her new lover, he is also shot and killed by the rival gang and the intensity of the rivalry escalates.

Act III: The model and the young gang

member meet again at his brother's funeral where their mother cries out for someone to stop the madness on the streets. Meanwhile, the younger brother and his gang friends develop plans to carry out a massive shootout.

Resolution: The model is inspired to action. She tries all of the words in the world to talk the younger brother out of throwing his life away in the gangs, and actually sleeps with him to stop him from joining his friends in the big plan. In the missed attempt at another retaliation, five of his gang member friends are killed, along with nine members of the rival gang. However, a police SWAT team arrests everyone involved, killing several more gang members in LA's worst shootout in years. The young gang member then has nothing left to fight for and has a lot of thinking to do concerning his life. The model goes on with her career with a better understanding of the streets, and the young gang member finally sees the light and thanks her by sending her a diamond bracelet to her photo shoot.

After thinking out all of the details and finishing my first screenplay, I turned it in for review and discussion at the UCLA Extensions course, and it was immediately called a *West Side Story* meets *Colors* and *Boyz N the Hood* with a *Jason's Lyric* and *A Bronx Tale* twist.

I couldn't believe it! After all of my hard-ass work on that damn thing, it was blatantly unoriginal! That made my whole illusion of becoming a Hollywood screenwriter seem impossible. The question was: How in the world can you create something that hasn't already been done and make people want to see it? *Or*, more important, as I learned in the business of Hollywood films and television: How can you take an old dog story, and turn it into a *new* dog with plenty of kicks and tricks with a major *spin* of the plot?

Actually, I had presented a major "spin" in *Crenshaw*. I had written a plot where the girl fucks *both* of the leading men, who were brothers, but that twist of the plot was called highly unbelievable. One silly white guy in my writing course chuckled and said that my screenplay had a pornographic arc to it.

He said, "You're telling us that this hardcore gang member is gonna stop to knock boots and just forget about his plans for the big shootout? I mean, *come on!* Wouldn't his gang members look at him as being pussy whipped if he did that?"

We all broke out laughing. I had to laugh at it too. It was comical and true.

I said, "Hey, don't ever underestimate the power of great sex."

"Oh yeah, well, just point *me* in the direction of *any* model like that. I'd tell her, 'I have nothing left to live for. I'm ready to kill myself. I need great sex to save me. *Please!*' And she'll say, 'Oh, sure, meet me at my apartment at eight.'"

They were having a field day with me, and it was no longer funny.

"All right, all right, let's just settle back down," our instructor told us. He was a dark-haired short guy with a long name that started with a K. Everyone called him Professor K. instead of trying, unsuccessfully, to pronounce his name correctly, and he said that he didn't mind it. He was also well connected in the business, so no one took him for granted either.

After we finished class that day, with everyone planning on sharing my humiliation with their Hollywood friends (I'm sure), my confidence had dropped a level. I was thinking about writing comedy, or even porno movies if they would let me. I thought about any- and everything, but ultimately, I didn't fly out to Hollywood to make a fool of myself and embarrass the people back home who loved me. So whatever I did, it was going to be based on a sane decision.

"Now you know what we're up against," someone said from behind me as I walked to my car.

The sister's name was Juanita Perez. She was from New York, and she looked really into the hip-hop movement with her twisted baby dreadlocks and baggy, colorful clothing. Prior to that day, she hadn't said a word to me. I just took it that she was there strictly for business, so I left her alone.

I smiled at her and said, "I was wondering if you were ever going to speak to me before this course was over. I mean, we *are* the only sisters in here. Then again, with your name being Juanita Perez, I wasn't sure if you were more down with the Latinos or something. I figured that you *looked* brown enough to be black."

She returned my smile. "My father's from Panama, but you wouldn't know it from looking at him. He looks like the average dark brown brother. But with *your* eyes and *your* look, I was thinking the same thing about you; that *you* were maybe a little extra."

I laughed at it. "Girl, I'm from Philadelphia," I told her. I guess she didn't know. "My father is probably as brown as yours. He just happens to have light-colored eyes and he passed them down to me," I added.

"I guess that we were *both* misled then. I'm sorry about that, but I've been burned out here too many times," she said.

"What, with people who didn't identify with being black?" I asked her. We stopped at my car.

"Yes. I was like, where are the real black people out here?"

I laughed and said, "Well, girl, you just found one." I went further with it and opened the trunk of my car. "Matter of fact," I said, grabbing one of my hardback books from the box, "I'll even let you read about it."

She looked at the illustration on the front cover and read the summary inside. She asked, "You have a *book* written about you?" She seemed really excited by it.

I said, "Well, you know, we all went through those flyy years back in the eighties, girl." Juanita looked my age, so I just assumed that she was.

She said, "Don't I know it! I had the big earrings and the drug-dealing boyfriends too. You should think about making this into a movie."

I didn't think too much anymore about making a movie about my life. After learning how skimpy screenplays were written as compared to books, I just figured that my life story was too damn long and detailed for a movie. My story would have been more like six to eight hours than two. They would have had to make a television miniseries about me like *Roots*. So I just thought that it was better told in a book.

I answered, "One day," and left it at that.

Juanita read into it and said, "Oh, I get it. You want to get a few of your other ideas green-lighted first so that you can build up a track record and do what you *really* want to do."

I said, "Yeah, that's it," just to go along with her.

She looked at the book jacket again and asked, "Who's Omar Tyree?"

"He's a writer that I know from back home in Philly. He started his own publishing company, and when *Flyy Girl* came out in '93, based on *my* life story, we sold so many copies that a bigger publisher wanted to pick it up and re-publish it."

Juanita grinned and said, "Word?! It must be good then!"

I smiled, not wanting to toot my own horn. However, when I thought about all of the early sex that I went through in the book, I had second thoughts about giving it to her. It was too late for that. Thousands of people had already read it, and I could count on thousands more who would.

"Well, let's just say that I went through a lot of different changes," I told her, feeling self-conscious. I had already given Kendra and Yolanda their copies. I kept wondering if their opinions would change about me once they read it.

Anyway, Juanita was all smiles. She said, "You know what, there's a party over in Culver City this weekend that I want to invite you to, where we can both meet up with what they call *Black* Hollywood out here. I was just invited to it myself yesterday."

I said, "Oh yeah? I heard about Hollywood parties and whatnot, but I haven't been to one yet. It seems like you need connections to do *anything* out here."

Juanita said, "Well, I'm already used to that from the New York crowd."

I smiled. "I guess so." In Philly, a blue-collar city, we were less concerned about keeping up with the Joneses, but I couldn't say that we didn't think about it at all. That would be a lie. So Juanita and I traded phone numbers before we went our separate ways.

**$ $ $**

"I don't know about going to these Hollywood parties, Tracy. I told you I didn't come out here for that," Kendra was telling me at her house in Carson. I was begging her to tag along with me because I wanted to feel secure with more than one friend there. I also wanted to introduce Kendra to Juanita. I thought that we would all get along well together: three East Coast sisters.

"You know you want to go. Stop fronting," I teased Kendra. I already knew that she would agree to it, if just to see how I would get along there. Kendra continued to think that I was too over-the-top with my actions.

"As long as you don't sneak off in some back room somewhere and leave me," she said with a grin.

I looked at her skeptically. "Sneak off in some back room for what?"

She laughed and said, "I'm just joking with you, girl."

I caught on and said, "I'm a mature woman now. Okay? So don't let that damn book go to your head." I *knew* that *Flyy Girl* shit would rub me the wrong way!

Kendra said, "I know, Tracy, God! I mean, you obviously had to learn a lot from your life to get to where you are now. Everybody went through some of the things you went through in your book."

"Yeah, well, don't throw that shit up in my face."

Kendra stopped and looked at me seriously. She said, "Tracy, if you're going to react like this, then maybe you shouldn't have agreed to put this book out with a major publisher."

She had a point. I had to get over it.

"Okay, that was childish. I admit it," I told her. "I'm just getting defensive now because I'm going to deal with new people reading this book who don't know anything about what I'm doing now."

"And when they get a chance to find that out, they'll leave you alone about it," Kendra advised me.

"Yeah, well, I just hope that these Hollywood guys don't trip like I'm easy to get in bed, because I'm *not*. If you *read* the book correctly, there were *hundreds* of guys who *wanted* to sleep with me, but I only had *five*."

Kendra started to laugh again and said, "Tracy, calm down and let it go. Now let's go to this party."

I was still beefing when we made it to Kendra's car, but by the time we pulled up to the party in Culver City, I had mellowed out.

"Do you think that we're dressed properly for this thing?" Kendra asked me with a grin as we climbed out of her car.

"I have no idea," I told her. "That's why we went with this."

We were both dressed somewhere between formal and casual in our skirts and blouses.

"Yeah, I guess we can't miss too bad. Unless everyone else in here is dressed up in tuxes and gowns, or dressed down in blue jeans."

Judging from the cars that were parked around the private houses in Culver City, it was definitely a money spot. There were plenty of loaded SUVs, Jags, Lexuses, and Benzes parked outside. I even spotted a green Maserati and wondered who the driver was.

We walked right into the large, elegant flat with no problem and blended right in with the crowd. It seemed that most of the people there were playing it safe, dressed casually formal with skirts, dresses, and sports jackets.

The music of choice in the background was Tha Dogg Pound with Daz and Kurupt, which seemed out of place to me. The majority of the crowd were older than us. Maybe they should have been listening to smooth jazz or something.

"They still listen to rap music?" Kendra whispered to me.

I smiled. "That's the same thing I was thinking." However, no one was really dancing to it, just nodding occasionally.

"Ladies," some tall brown guy in all blue said, approaching us with his hands out. He looked as if he had been waiting to receive us all night.

I asked him, "Are you speaking to us?"

"If you're in my house and I don't recognize you, I am."

He said it super cool, but why did we feel like he had just dissed the hell out of us?

I said, "I was invited by my friend Juanita Perez, and I brought my girl Kendra along with me."

Kendra just stood there and had me do all of the talking.

"Juanita *who*?" he asked me.

"Juanita Perez, from the UCLA Extensions course."

I felt like a bigger fool with every word I spoke, and this guy was still looking blank at us.

He shook his head and said "I don't know any—"

I cut him off and said, "Okay, I'm sorry. I can see that this is a know-only party, and since you don't even know who invited us here, I think it's best for us to be on our merry way."

I was so fucking embarrassed! It seemed like everyone in that room was looking at us, but trying to play it cool at the same time like they were not.

"Well, you don't have to leave, just tell me who you are," he told us with a smile.

I guess he could sense how embarrassed we both felt. Kendra didn't have to say *a word* to me, and I just *knew* she would talk about it the entire way home.

I said, "I'm Tracy Ellison from Philly, and this is Kendra Dayton from Baltimore."

He smiled even wider.

"East Coast," he said. "So what brings you out west?"

"I'm just getting my feet wet in the industry," I told him. "And Kendra already lives out here. She's a schoolteacher."

He nodded to Kendra and looked back to me. "You're getting your feet wet in what industry?" he asked me. I still didn't know who the hell he was.

I said, "Well, I'm not out here to cheer for the Lakers. I'm talking about the business of television and film."

I was beginning to set myself, and it never took me long. Who was this guy?

"Oh really? So what do you do for a living until you can get all the way wet? Because you *do know* that some people never get a chance to jump in the pool, don't you?"

"I hear some people don't even get a chance to try on their bathing suits," I teased him. I didn't care anymore, frankly. No damn party was going to make or break me, so I played along with him. I could feel people listening in on us too, but so what? In the meantime, I kept asking myself, *Where the hell is Juanita?*

"And that doesn't discourage you at all?" he asked me.

"What is your name again?" I finally asked him back.

Kendra nudged me in my side. I guess she thought that I was getting too bold and bad for my own good, but to hell if *I* was going to continue to stand there while this guy ran off twenty questions at me. I would leave his damn house before I allowed him to do that. I wanted to at least know who I was talking to. I had dignity, and I was *not* being interviewed for a position. If I was, then I would like to *know* about it *in advance*.

All of a sudden, a shorter brother wearing brown and black stepped out and introduced himself to us instead. "How are you doing? I'm Harold Wiggins, creative producer of Laugh Out Loud Wednesdays on Warner. Let me introduce you to one of our head writers, Joshua Pendleton," he said, motioning to the guy in all blue who had been asking us twenty questions.

That's when we realized that we were the guinea pigs in an ongoing joke. Apparently, Joshua had been embarrassing newcomers with the "Who are you and what do you do?" routine.

He laughed along with a few others in the crowd who had been watching us.

"She's tough. She was holding her own," he joked to Harold.

I said, "Yeah, because I didn't even know who you were, and you were asking us a million questions about who *we* were."

"Well, this *is* my house. Remember that," he told me.

Harold said, "Correction. This is *my* house."

"Well, I still haven't found my friend Juanita yet," I told them.

"You're looking for me?" Juanita slipped from behind me and asked. She was dressed casually formal herself, in black.

"Now who invited you?" Harold asked her.

"Reginald," she answered him.

He looked relieved and nodded to her.

"Oh, okay. Reginald just stepped out about a half hour ago. He should be back soon."

"Who is Reginald?" I asked for my own knowledge. They were kicking his name around as if he was someone important.

Harold said, "Reginald is pretty much a creative talent hawk. He runs around this town and pulls together anyone coming in with raw, untapped talent that we might be able to use."

"If you don't watch out, he's gonna have *your* job soon," Joshua joked to Harold before he slipped away to join the crowd.

Harold smiled it off. He looked in his early forties, but he was possibly younger. Joshua looked thirty-something or younger himself. I couldn't quite tell their ages. They all had a youthful, energized presence about them. I guess you *would* have to be energized in a fast-moving atmosphere like Hollywood's.

Harold looked past us toward some other arriving guests. "If you'll excuse me. HAAY!" he screamed as he moved on.

"God!" I snapped, cradling my ear.

Kendra shook her head and finally spoke up. "Tracy, you are just too much. You *do* have what it takes to make it out here, I'll give you that. Just don't push it too far."

I turned and introduced her to Juanita.

I said, "Well, we have Philly, Baltimore, and New York. All we need now is New Jersey and D.C., and we'd have a full East Coast Nation out here," I joked.

We all laughed and held our space, but it wasn't as if we were doing much there. It seemed like one of those parties where people had to warm up to each other for a full hour before they really started talking. Unless, of course, everyone knew who you were already, because when Martin Lawrence and then Jamie Foxx walked in with their separate posses, people started running to get up close and personal. I just sat there and laughed.

"I can't see *myself* doing that," I said out loud. It looked like a groupie convention from then on, as other A-list entertainers walked in. Or at least A-list for *Black* Hollywood. No one in that place could command the raw income that many white entertainers could. However, as all of the people there ran for attention from the incoming stars, I felt lonely as hell and insignificant. I guess that was supposed to be the time to "schmooze," as they called it, but that wasn't my thing anymore. I didn't want to be *with* a star, I wanted to *be* the star.

"What's wrong with you?" Kendra asked me.

"I'm just thinking," I told her. Hollywood made me feel like I was a nobody.

I looked to Juanita, and she was in her own world too, as if she was searching for someone. When this slim, busybody of a brother walked in she nearly jumped for joy.

"Reginald!" she called out to him.

I read his face immediately. He didn't want to be bothered with her, but his look was snap-finger fast. You had to pay close attention to catch it. Let's just say that I had plenty of experience in reading Reginald's *type* from dealing with so many players in Philly before I even made it to college. In reading guys, I considered myself a veteran.

He walked over with a fake smile and hugged Juanita.

She said, "This is Tracy, the one who I told you had a book out."

When he looked into my face, I read "dog" all up and down his body. It even seemed like he was panting.

"So, you have a book out?" he asked me, searching everything with his rapid eyes.

"*You* need to be the one with the book," I said to him. "*Everybody* talks about you," I bullshitted. I wanted to see if my hunch was right on the dog vibe that I felt from him.

"Was it good things or bad things?"

"*I'll* never tell," I hinted at him.

I caught a look from Juanita that didn't appear too friendly, and I knew immediately that she was screwing him. She probably thought that *I* wanted some, but I didn't. I was just having fun.

"Let me introduce you to somebody real fast," he said to Juanita, pulling her away from us. I guess he was outright rude too.

Kendra turned to me with a grimace and said, "Tracy, what the hell was that all about?"

I played innocent and said, "What?"

"Why were you flirting with him like that, right in the girl's face? You don't plan to be friends with her long?"

I said, "What, you thought they were a couple?"

Kendra looked at me as if I should know better.

"That was pretty obvious to *me*."

"And you think that he's loyal to her?"

She started to chuckle.

"That was obvious too. He looked like he wanted to get rid of her as quickly as he could."

"That's what I was reading," I told her. "So I was just trying to find out if my hunch was right, that's all."

She grinned at me. "Sharpening up those skills from your youth, hunh?"

I laughed admittingly, and responded, "I guess so."

Kendra said, "Well, I don't think your New York girl

read any of your book yet, because *Reginald* is as obvious as they come."

We shared a laugh before this good-looking, caramel brother stepped up to me with a drink in hand.

"What video did I see you in?"

I looked at Kendra. Kendra looked away and grinned.

"Ah, you didn't see *me* in a video," I told him.

"Are you sure?" He actually looked puzzled.

I said, "Yeah, I'm sure."

"Were you an extra in a recent film or something?"

Kendra couldn't hold in her laugh anymore, and that made me laugh right in the brother's face.

"An *extra*?" I asked him as if I were appalled.

He said, "Don't tell me you've starred in a film already and I don't know who you are. Or was it in a television show?"

The brother was making a deeper fool of himself by the minute.

I put my hand on his arm and said, "Don't strain yourself, brother. I just came out here about a month ago. Maybe you just saw someone before who *looks* like me."

"Well, you do look good," he told me.

"Thank you. You do too, but if you'll excuse me, I think I need to go stuff my face before my stomach begins to growl and I turn you off."

"That wouldn't turn *me* off. That would just mean that you were hungry. What's your name, anyway?"

"I'll answer that when I come back," I told him, spotting the table of food ahead of me. I pulled Kendra's hand forward to follow me.

"You know what I'm beginning to notice?" she asked me as we headed toward the barbecue chicken, mixed fruit, drinks, and miniature sandwiches.

"What?" I asked her.

"No one seems to pay me any mind when I'm with you. *Usually,* I get all *kinds* of comments and propositions," Kendra told me.

"Aw, girl, go 'head with that," I snapped at her. "You're the one in here walking around like you don't have a tongue. And I know you do, because you talk my damn head off about education and the lack of black politics in LA."

"Yeah, and I bet these people in here don't even think about those kinds of things. They just take things for granted. That's exactly why the affirmative action bill will be wiped out next month in the state of California."

"You want to go make up some fliers and pass them out in here?" I joked with her.

"Hmmph," she grunted. "Don't waste *my* time and energy."

We loaded up on the food to settle our stomachs and looked around through the crowd again.

"Once you've seen one of these parties, Tracy, you've seen them all. These people are all so *obvious* in here."

"That's the same with the party scene anywhere, really. I mean, do you really care what everyone else is doing, or do we just make casual conversation?" I asked her.

Kendra nodded. "That's exactly why I don't really do parties. It's all nonsense. That's why I have nothing to say in here."

"So you're ready to leave then?" I asked her.

She took one last look around the room and asked me, "Are you planning to mix and mingle?"

I looked around myself at all of the "schmoozers" waiting in line to talk to more important people than us and decided that it was time for me to go. I had seen enough, and felt enough, enough of the cold shoulders and corny come-on lines.

I finished my punch, slapped the empty cup on the table, and said, "Yeah, we might as well go."

"Are you going to say bye to your friend?" Kendra asked, referring to Juanita.

I shrugged my shoulders. "I barely know that sister. I'll just see her in class next week." I just wondered what she'd think after she had read my book.

Before we could make it out of the door, another tall, chocolate brother attempted to grab my hand.

"Leaving so early? I was just about to find out who you were."

I pulled my hand away ever so gently and said, "Maybe another time."

"Do you have a card?"

"Sorry, I didn't bring any with me."

"Well, what studio are you with?" he asked me with a grin, assuming things.

I smiled back at him. "When I finally make it in one, I'll let you know."

He said, "Well, sometimes it's who you know who can get you in the door."

I paused and thought about that, and decided to pass on his game. I wasn't out in California to meet a man, I was out there to do my thing in the industry, and I'd rather get in on my *own* hard work and merit than through knowing someone, especially a fine, chocolate black man. Excuse me for thinking it, but I had a hard time imagining us being only business associates. Maybe that was how Juanita got hooked up with Reginald, but I was not the one for sideshows. I was a main-attraction type of woman.

I said, "I'm sorry, but that's not the way I want to go

about things," and stepped off before he could say another word. Sometimes you just get tired of dealing with new guys.

Outside, Kendra looked into my face and asked, "Do you still want to be in this business? Because you can see how slimy it is. And I'm not saying that *everyone* in the business is slimy, but it just seems to me that the *business* of Hollywood is slimy in itself."

Kendra was echoing my mother, and I didn't even have a chance to respond before Mr. Reginald slipped past us and dashed to his car. He was parked right across the street from the house, a black Lexus coupe with gold trim.

Kendra and I looked at each other and smiled.

On his way back in, Reginald proceeded to throw out his hook and bait, his *real* reason for dashing to his car like that.

"Hey, you two are leaving already?" he asked us.

"Yeah, we've seen about enough," Kendra spoke up for a change.

I smiled at her.

Reginald pulled out two business cards and handed them to us.

"Get in touch with me if you need anything. Tracy, right?" he asked me before he looked at Kendra. "And what's your name again?"

Kendra paused and came up with "Suzanne."

I grinned my ass off and didn't say a word.

"All right, well, you know, get in touch with me. Maybe I can introduce you to some people who are good to know."

*I'm sure you can,* I told myself.

I nodded to him and said, "I'll do that."

"As long as Juanita doesn't mind," Kendra instigated. I

guess she decided to be naughty her damn self since we were leaving.

Reginald froze and looked stunned, but only for a hot second.

"Oh, we're not like that. We're just real cool. What would make you think that?"

This brother was full of it.

"All right, well, I'll just ask her in class next week up at UCLA," I told him.

"Ask her what?"

"You know, if it's okay to go to Hollywood functions with you." I sweetened up the pot and looked at his car. "I've never been in a Lexus before," I lied.

Kendra had to look away again.

Reginald laughed it off and looked nervous. I guess he realized that he wasn't dealing with amateurs.

"I'll see you around," he said, backing away.

"You promise?" Kendra added.

Reginald shook his head and grinned. "You two need to stop," he warned us.

We laughed while we walked away.

## $ $ $

When I got home that night, I was worn out. I looked around through the emptiness of my bedroom and wondered exactly how long it would take me to fill my place up with furniture. I didn't plan on kissing too much ass to get there though. If I had to kiss ass at all I planned to plant my lips right at the top with someone who could green-light whatever I was working on and get me started without all of the bullshit.

I told myself, "There's no way in the world you'll find

me hanging out with *that* set." Was I too real and too forward for the bullshit machine of Hollywood? I guess I would soon find out.

**$ $ $**

Early that next morning, my telephone rang. It was Raheema on the line.

"Hey, Ra, what's going on?" My voice dragged and I was barely conscious.

"I have some big news for you," she said. She sounded peppy, as if she had eaten a big breakfast and was ready to run a marathon.

I looked over at my alarm clock. It was thirteen minutes after seven. I guess Raheema had forgotten about the three-hour time difference from New Jersey to California.

I said, "This better be good, Raheema."

She actually giggled as if she held the biggest secret in the world. I sat up and asked myself, *What the hell is going on?*

Raheema said, "I'm getting married at the end of January. I want you to be my maid of honor. And I'm three months pregnant."

"WHAT?"

She said, "I know, I know, it's a shock, but I was just calling everyone up and letting you all know. I know it's short notice, but my plans are nothing real fancy. I'm sending the invitations out this coming week with the wedding colors."

"Well, how long were you planning on keeping this all a secret?"

I couldn't believe her! I thought I was her girl!

"Tracy, we're grown women now, and we *do* have our own personal lives."

"Obvious*ly,*" I stressed to her.

"Well, we're still brainstorming all of the details, so I just wanted to give you a heads-up on it, and I'll probably call you back this week with more."

"No, no, no, no, *NO!* You are *not* getting off of this phone with me yet. I don't even know this guy's name. How could you do that to me? Does your family even know him?"

"His name is Ernest. Ernest Neumann. And we're going to be visiting my family next week."

"Three months pregnant? So what about getting your Ph.D."

"I'm still going for it. I'm focused."

"You weren't *that* damn focused if you got pregnant."

"Oh, grow up, Tracy. I'm twenty-five years old. Twenty-six is a good age to have a baby. I'm prepared, I'm mature, I'm educated, *and* we want to do this the right way."

"The *right way* would have been a pregnancy *after* marriage," I snapped at her.

"Who are *you* to talk about doing things 'the right way,' Ms. Flyy?" she asked me with a laugh. "Really, Tracy, I have a lot of phone calls to make this morning. I'll catch back up with you later on in the week."

"Okay, okay, just answer me this: Do your parents know yet?" I asked her.

"They were the first people I called this morning."

"And what did they say?"

"Tracy, please. I believe I've *earned* all of the respect in the world from my parents. They know that I wouldn't make any decisions at this point in my life without thinking about it. So they said, 'Congratulations, let's get this wedding under way, and we can't wait for our first grandchild.'"

I hung up with my girl Raheema in slow motion. I felt like a fool again. That girl sat there and told me to go and chase some Hollywood dream, knowing good and well that she was getting good and steamy with the real thing all along. All of a sudden, it felt like I was the last person to graduate into real life. There I was out in Hollywood going to jive-ass networking parties, while my next-door neighbor and lifelong friend was back in New Jersey living a real life, with a real man, and had a wedding and baby on the way.

I was all the way up and feeling outraged!

"SHIT!" I hollered at my empty walls. "Is this shit really worth it?" I asked myself. "Thanks, Raheema! Thanks a fuckin' lot! I feel just great now!"

I stood up, grabbed my robe off the bed, and walked toward my balcony to sit outside and think while a few early morning cars drove by.

It took a while to come to my senses about things, but I figured that I couldn't turn back. I was barely getting started. How much of a fool would I look like if I *did* turn back so soon?

I said, "Well, I made my new bed out here in California, so I guess I have to sleep in it."

# The 4th of July

*It must be a holiday*
*with firecrackers*
*and blazing colors*
*streaking through the night.*

*It must be a barbecue*
*with fire on the grill,*
*burning wings and ribs*
*while little cousins play dodge ball.*

*It must be a revolution,*
*bringing power to the people*
*with raised black fists,*
*Dashikis, and Afros*

*It must be a celebration,*
*giving the crowd a reason to cheer*
*and go nuts,*
*shouting and blowing car horns.*

*It must be someone big,*
*like Will Smith,*
*Oprah Winfrey,*
*or Michael Jordan in town.*

*But all of this commotion for me?*
*Somebody must be pulling my damn leg!*
*Now please, let me go.*
*I have work to do.*

# April 2000

# $ $
# $

 got up at my parents' house and took a shower at five o'clock in the morning so I could be dressed and ready for the morning news on NBC with Steve Levy by six-thirty. When I stepped out from the shower with my towel wrapped around me, my father nearly gave me a heart attack. He was standing out in the hallway in his pajamas waiting for me.

I jumped up in the air and squeezed my shoulders, yelping like a bimbo in a horror movie. "Damn, Dad! What are you doing out here?!" I shouted at him.

He smiled and laughed at me. "I just wanted to catch you before you left this morning, since I didn't get a chance to catch you last night."

I smiled and said, "Yeah, I heard you and Mom in the room last night, doing whatever you two were doing in there."

He chuckled and said, "You should have held your ears then."

"It wasn't as if I was *trying* to hear," I told him. I was embarrassed by it, to tell the truth. Imagine coming home at night and hearing your parents inside of their room going at it. I guess riding around in the new SUV made them feel like newlyweds again.

"I just wanted to thank you for my birthday present,

and to tell you not to take what I said personal," my father said.

I grinned and shook my head. "I wasn't going to sweat that, Dad. It would have worn off eventually, but I *was* pissed about it though. I'm not even gonna stand here and lie about that."

"So, I hear you have a busy morning today."

I nodded. "Yeah, I do. I have Steve Levy, and then Mary Mason after that."

He grimaced and asked, "Mary Mason? Are you ready for her? She's pretty tough."

"So I've heard," I told him.

I never listened to Mary Mason myself. She was on AM radio. The only time I could remember listening to AM radio was during the Lady B Show, all the way back in the early eighties when rap music was just getting started.

"You make sure you watch what you say on her show, and remember to respect your elders," my father warned me.

I laughed and said, "Okay."

He said, "I'm serious."

He was only making me nervous about it.

"Okay, Dad. Thanks a lot. Now can I get dressed, please?"

"Oh, sure. Don't let *me* hold you up. Your fans are waiting for you. I'm only your father."

I looked at him and shook my head. "Men," I said, "just *have* to make the world revolve around y'all."

"Well, you know what they say: You can't live with us, but ya *surely* can't live without us," he boasted playfully.

I stared at him and asked, "Well, what have *I* been doing then?" I had never lived with a man in my life.

"Thawing out in a cave," my father answered me. "And as soon as you're finished thawing out, you're gonna step right out into the sunshine to meet yourself a nice man."

I couldn't believe my father had even said something like that. The nerve of that goodnatured, fifty-one-year-old father of mine to still have such chauvinism.

I shook my head and walked back into my room. I guess men just take their pinheaded views on sex and relationships to the grave. However, I couldn't get an Amen on that from my mother that morning, because she was obviously still in dreamland from my father's handiwork the night before. To be dead honest with myself, I wished that I had someone to make me late for my interviews. Late, and good and happy about it too. So I guess my father knew a little something about women after all.

**$ $ $**

I love how peaceful it is to drive in the morning time before traffic gets thick. I hit Lincoln Drive and made it over to NBC on City Line Avenue in ten minutes. I arrived early and sat in the green room, tempted to drink a cup of coffee.

"You mean to tell me that you don't have a bodyguard with you?" the young weatherman joked with me. I didn't remember his name.

I sat in my mint green suit, brand-new stockings, and mint green shoes (that matched my suit perfectly), and smiled at him, with my legs crossed like a lady.

"How much would you charge me for it?" I flirted with him.

He laughed it off. "Ah, I don't think that my wife would like *any* price that I would charge you. I don't even think she would feel comfortable with me *mentioning* your name."

"Does she know who I am?" I was curious. I kept second-guessing how much white Americans followed black American stardom.

He smiled and said, "Oh yeah, she knows who you are. We saw the movie together out at Plymouth Meeting."

"And what did she say about the movie?"

"Ah, let's just say she needed some TLC that night to make her feel a little more secure."

I bet that many married white women who saw *Led Astray* and had a type A husband (the executive class) needed some TLC indeed with the prospect of a young and sexy black woman out to ruin their husbands' personal lives for her own business sake. Call me a devil's advocate, but that was my favorite spin of the movie.

I smiled at the weatherman and said, "You tell your wife that it was only Hollywood."

"Are you kidding me? I can't even tell my wife that you were on this *show*."

"She doesn't watch?"

"Not all of the time."

I watched him put too much sugar in his coffee. Did I make him nervous?

I smiled and said, "You better watch that sugar before you catch a real sweet tooth."

He caught himself and frowned. "Jesus, look at me. I may as well mix it with two cups now," he commented with a boyish grin.

I guess I *did* make the weatherman nervous. I laughed at it and got myself ready for Steve, who was already on the air. When he received a break, he came out and led me back to the studio.

"Have you gotten your next movie deal yet?" he asked me. I wasn't in town to promote anything, I was just doing a bunch of homecoming interviews, so Steve was looking for an angle. He was straight business, dark haired in a dark suit. He looked rugged enough to have played football in his heyday, and astute enough to have been the quarterback.

"We're working on it," I told him, referring to my next film deal.

He looked me over and nodded. "I wanted to plug that in, if you had any other offers yet."

"Are you trying to figure out some extra questions to ask me?"

"Well, yeah, you know, just to try a different angle if you had anything. Sometimes the straight interview can be a little flat." He gave me another quick look after his comment. "Then again, maybe *not* with you," he added with a reserved laugh.

I smiled at him and kept my thoughts to myself. Steve was sharp and crafty, and that kept me on my good behavior with him.

"We have another ten, fifteen minutes or so, so if you come up with anything, let me know," he said.

When he went back on the air for the local news, I thought about exploring the angle of the nervous white wives that *Led Astray* had created. However, maybe that would have been too much for the morning news, so I thought better of it. I planned to start plugging ideas about my follow-up book instead. That was safe enough territory. It was new, and it definitely would serve my purpose. So before we went on air, I shared the idea with Steve.

He nodded. "You know we had Omar on the show with the book a few years back."

"Yeah, I just hope that he's not too busy to come back to

my story, you know, with the whole Philadelphia connection and everything."

"I see what you mean. Last I heard he was writing a story about St. Louis."

I nodded. "I have nothing against St. Louis, but I do think that we need a follow up on *me*, if I can say so myself."

He nodded again, agreeing to it. "All right, we can talk about that. That would entail your whole Hollywood story, wouldn't it? I'm sure that plenty of people would be interested in that."

"That's what *I'm* saying," I told him, and it was on.

We walked up to the set to get wired for the microphones and got ready for the countdown.

"Three, two, one," the line producer sounded off. The light from the camera flashed to red, for live, and Steve went straight into his business.

"Good morning again, Philadelphia. Our guest this morning is a local girl turned star, like in Hollywood. The leading actress from the recent hit movie *Led Astray* was born and raised right here in the Germantown area, and graduated from our local Germantown High School. We welcome Tracy Ellison Grant."

The cameras swung on me and went to red.

"Well, is it good to be back home?" Steve asked me.

I smiled real good for the camera and made my opening remarks. "Well, it's good, but I can't say that it's been *all* good. Although it has *definitely* been busy."

"Have you gone down to South Street for a good old-fashioned Philly cheese steak yet?"

I laughed. "Not yet, but it's on my list."

"What about a movie with Will Smith? Have you brainstormed anything like that? That would surely be a hit in these parts with both of *you* guys in it."

I played along with him. "Yeah, and we can hook up with Boyz II Men, Lisa Lopes, Jazzy Jeff and Kurupt, The Roots and Jill Scott, and put them all on the sound track and make it an all-Philadelphia thing, right? That would be a blast!"

Steve said, "It sounds like a plan to me. Now, what many people are just realizing is that you had a book based on your life as a teenager growing up in Germantown, written and published a few years ago by another Philadelphian, Omar Tyree. And I believe that the book, *Flyy Girl*, is still a hot seller. Now how much of that book is actually you?" he asked me with a grin.

I smiled back at him and answered. "All of it. And at first I had a hard time dealing with the responses that some people had to my carefree youth. But now that I've straightened up my act and made it out in Hollywood, I'm actually looking forward to writing a sequel with Omar. I want to give people the full scoop on how a local girl from Philly made it out in Hollywood, wrote her own script, helped to produce it, *and* starred in it."

I was tooting my own horn, *loudly,* but what the hell. That was what I was there to do.

Steve looked with wide eyes, playing it up, and said, "Well, you're not looking to go into the *news* business are you? I'll have to protect my job around here."

I chuckled and said, "Your job is safe, Steve. I don't have any plans for the broadcast news. I just want to finish up on the news about my life for all of the fans who know only *half* of the story right now."

"So, are you negotiating with Omar? Is it a done deal?" he asked me.

"We're still at the table right now, but I'm getting a little anxious about the hesitation, so hopefully we'll sign the agreeable paperwork and get this thing started *real* soon."

"Well, I can't *wait* for that, and I'm sure that I speak for *thousands* of your fans, especially here in the Philadelphia area," Steve added on cue. "Do you have a title for us yet?"

"Ah, not yet, but I'll be sure to let you know when the time comes. I think the most important thing right now is just getting the deal done and letting the people know about it."

"And what about other movie projects?"

"Other movie scripts are in the works as well, and I'll be sure to keep my hometown abreast of everything that I do."

When the lights flashed off from live, Steve said, "That was great! We rolled right on through it!"

"Yeah, that's what I *hoped* would happen with this book contract."

"What exactly is in the way? The money?" he asked me.

I frowned and said, "It's not really the money. Omar just has this thing about the audience. He's trying to go after older readers, and my book, *Flyy Girl,* attracted a lot of younger readers, who have been sharing books instead of buying them."

Steve smiled and said, "Ooohhh, so it *is* the money."

I said, "I don't look at it that way, Steve. Young people have the money for a book. They just have to *want* it, and we never really marketed my book to young people in the first place, because the assumption was that they didn't read."

"I see. Well, *Flyy Girl* proved *that* assumption wrong, huh?"

"Exactly. That's why we have to come back to it. The proof will be in the sequel."

**$ $ $**

I stepped out of the NBC studio and felt like I was walking on air that morning. I couldn't get too carried away with it though. I still had to drive down the street to do WHAT-AM with Mary Mason for an eight o'clock show. Their studio was seven to ten blocks down the road, and right past WDAS-FM. City Line Avenue was media city in Philadelphia!

I arrived at 54th Street at WHAT early as well, and walked up to their second-floor offices. I even had time to stop off for a donut and orange juice, and after having such a good show with Steve Levy that morning, I was no longer nervous about Mary Mason.

I was introduced to her in her office before air time. She looked up at me from her crowded desk, with big hair, full body, and plenty of zest in her eyes. She said, "So, what did your daddy say about you taking your clothes off for that movie, Tracy?" Her young producer broke out laughing and started shaking her head. I guess she was used to Mary Mason's in-your-face candor, and still shocked by it at the same time.

Mary reminded me of an aunt, the one who still smokes, curses, and goes to church every Sunday for forgiveness, just so she can tell everyone *else* what *they're* doing wrong in *their* lives. You couldn't tell Mary Mason that to her face though, because then you'd have a fight on your hands. Nevertheless, the people in Philadelphia loved her, because she had that Philadelphian fire to tell it like it was no matter what. Just like me.

I smiled and said, "You can ask me that on the air I'm sure that everyone else would like to know too."

She didn't budge an inch. She grunted at me and said, "Did you *like* doing it?"

"Not necessarily," I told her. "I wasn't even supposed to play the part."

"What part were you supposed to play?"

"I just wrote the movie, actually. Then things just started to happen in other ways to get the project done."

"Project? Is that what you call it?"

"That's what it's called when it's not done."

"You plan on doing anymore *projects* like that one?"

"Not necessarily."

"You plan on *writing* anymore like that?"

I began to wonder what she would ask me on air with so many rapid-fire questions in her office.

"Hopefully, I can extend my range into other vehicles like Sharon Stone was able to do. Or Julia Roberts and Glenn Close."

"You plan on doing any *black* movies?"

When she asked me that I just stared at her. *This is going to be a long damn interview,* I told myself.

"Black movies, meaning what, an all-black cast?" I asked her.

"A movie that *means* something," she answered.

"You think *any* of these movies *mean* something nowadays?" I asked her back. "Hollywood only makes what the people want to watch. So if we *really* wanted movies that *meant* something, we would *watch* more of them. I don't think Will Smith has made a movie that *meant* something for black people yet, outside of the fact that he makes twenty million dollars a movie now."

She had stepped on *my* fire button, and I was breathing like a dragon. I wasn't afraid of her, and if she wanted a challenge that morning, we could get on the air and go word for word for it!

"Well, when I get Will Smith on my show, I'm gonna ask him the same question."

She seemed to soften up a bit with that, right before her phone rang.

"Excuse me," she said. Her young producer showed me back out and to the studio room.

"Is she always like that?" I asked her.

She chuckled and said, "She can be *worse* than that. And don't believe what she says about Will Smith. She loves him. If you represent yourself well and keep your cool, she'll love you too. I wouldn't even worry about it. You just can't let her scare you or get under your skin. Just stay relaxed and make a joke out of it. Mary likes to laugh, trust me."

It sure didn't *seem* like she liked to laugh, but I had nothing to lose, so if push came to shove, I figured I would make it light. It beat getting into a generational argument. That's all that it would boil down to in the end if we didn't hit it off with each other.

I sat down in my guest chair in front of the microphone at eight o'clock on the nose. The earlier guest and host were both leaving and commercials were still being played. Mary Mason slipped into the room and into the host chair right in time to kick off the show.

"How many of us are sick and tired of these same-old black movies and the stupid roles that some of our people play. I know *I* am. I'm so sick and tired of it that I don't know what to do anymore but keep talking about how sick and tired I am. So I brought on a local actress this morning who played in a recent Hollywood movie called *Led Astray,* where the poor black girl plots to get back at all of these producers and directors who fooled around with her and promised her things that never came true.

"If you happened to see this movie called *Led Astray*, that came out in February, then please call us up this morning at WHAT-AM and let us know what *you* think. We have the young star, Tracy Ellison Grant, in the studio to talk to us about the business of Hollywood."

She looked down at her notes and said, "Tracy Ellison Grant is a graduate of Germantown High School and an English major from Hampton University in Virginia with a *master's* degree.

"Now, Tracy, what I want to know is what do your professors at Hampton think about this movie you starred in? I thought an education was supposed to elevate us *past* the down-on-your-luck whore roles."

"Well, my character spoke good grammar in the movie, so I believe that my instructors would have been fairly pleased with it," I joked. What the hell else could I do?

"Your character spoke good *grammar*? Well, that's about the *only* good thing your character did."

"Well, she didn't allow herself to continue being a victim of falsehoods," I responded. "She did what very few people in Hollywood, or even people at WHAT, are able to do, and that's get even with their bosses."

Mary gave me a look that could kill, but she couldn't deny that I was working it, so she kept right on plugging away at me.

"So what did your daddy say about the naked sex scenes?"

"He said, 'I couldn't look at all of it, but I'm sure proud of your body, girl. You wear it well,'" I lied.

"Your father did *not* say that," Mary snapped at me.

"Okay, he didn't," I admitted. "But what do *mothers* say to their boys when they do *their* things in *their* sex roles? I think it's all hypocritical myself. Humans are humans. Why should it make that much of a difference that the woman is naked if the guy is naked right along with her?"

"Well, in your movie, it wasn't as if the girl was in love with any of these men that she was with."

"Nor were the men in love with her. That's just my point. How come no one ever talks about how terrible it was for the men to do what *they* do? Why is the woman always at fault, when she's no more than the victim?

"I think that a lot of women could relate to the movie in some form or another," I said. "Even you, Mary. Haven't you been led astray by a man before when you were younger? If you haven't, then you happen to be a very lucky woman."

She ignored me with a knowing grin and went to our first caller. That was fast.

"I saw the movie, and I *loved* it," an older sister from West Philadelphia commented.

"What did you love about it?" Mary asked her.

"I loved the fact that she took her life back from these guys."

"How, by sleeping with them and blackmailing them for money?"

"Whatever it takes. Like Tracy said, it wasn't as if these guys were saints. If they were, then the girl wouldn't have been after them in the first place."

Mary took the second caller, an older brother from South Philly.

"I wasn't particularly thrilled with seeing such a beautiful young sister on-screen with these white men, but I did get the point. The only thing that *I'm* concerned about was how she became led astray in the first place."

"Exactly," Mary huffed in agreement with him.

I said, "You're right. I don't know how women fall for men and the American dream either. It must be something in the water that only affects us, the same water that makes so many men want to sleep with every woman they see.

"Like you, sir," I addressed him. "I bet that your wife was the only woman you ever had, and you have never led a woman astray in your thirty-something years of dating."

Mary began to laugh at that one herself. She knew damn well what the truth was. Everybody was led astray, even men.

"Well, I wouldn't say that," the older brother responded. "We all make our mistakes in life, and I have made a few of them."

"Exactly," I mocked them both.

After that, I didn't have a problem with Mary Mason for the rest of that hour-long show. She realized that I could hold my own, so she kept it professional and stopped trying to deliberately set me off.

The young producer said, "See, I told you you could do it. Now she'll have you back again."

"I bet she will," I responded with a grin. I actually enjoyed the show with Mary. She gave me a chance to practice my sharp wit and poise, something I had failed to do with Wendy Williams on Power 99.

I had a huge gap between nine o'clock and two-thirty (the time I planned to pick up my cousin Vanessa from school at Engineering & Science that afternoon), so I drove out to Springfield Mall to try and do some more shopping. Since I arrived there before ten o'clock, I sat inside the car and listened to more of Power 99's Dream Team with

Wendy. This girl was forever trying to get the juicy info on celebrity gossip. I guess we all have to make a living *some* way, but Wendy seemed to take things to the extreme. I guess someone else could say the same thing about me. However, was reporting the sleaze any better than being involved with it? *I* didn't think so. It was all hypocritical, even for the people who loved to listen to it and help spread the damn gossip!

I walked inside Springfield Mall at ten o'clock, right as the doors were opening and strolled past a shoe store. The next thing I knew, a young sister had run out of the store and asked me for my autograph.

"I loved your movie," she said. "I heard you on the *Wendy Williams Show* yesterday and I saw you on the news this morning. Is it tough in Hollywood?"

She was a pretty dark brown sister with a short hairstyle. I don't know why, but it looked as if she could sing. Maybe she reminded me of Anita Baker.

I said, "Everything that's worthwhile is tough. Do you go to school?" I asked her. She looked young and studious. What the hell was she doing working at a shoe store instead of going to college?! She looked roughly around twenty.

"I go to school. I go to Community College. I'm taking media courses right now, but I plan to take courses in computer science soon. I hear there's a lot of job openings in the computer information business to give me something to fall back on."

"Something to fall back on? So what do you *really* want to do?" I asked her.

She said, "I want to be a singer. I'd like to act too, if I had the chance."

Bingo! She *could* sing. I thought about Kiwana.

"Have you ever thought about performing in musical plays?"

"I *have* been in plays before, but not in musicals. I used to perform at the Freedom Theater in North Philly."

I smiled. "I used to go there."

"Oh my God! You performed there, too?!" She seemed really excited by that, as if we were connected in some way. I felt sorry to let her down.

"No, I was just watching back then, but it *did* inspire me," I told her.

"You're a writer too, right?" she asked me. I could see where she was going with that before she even started.

"It's very hard for writers to choose people to play different parts, even when we write things with certain people in mind," I told her. I was assuming that she would ask me if I could get her a small part in a television series or something.

"I meant poetry and books," she corrected me.

"Oh, *that* kind of writing." She caught me off guard.

She said, "I write poetry too, and my own songs. Do you mind if I say one of my poems to you right now? I mean, I know you're busy and all, so if not, then I understand."

"Only if you tell me your name first," I said with a grin.

"Oh, I'm sorry. My name is Staci Madison. Staci with an *i*."

"That's a good name," I told her. "It sounds famous."

"Okay, here's my poem."

She went ahead and did a performance poem right there in the middle of the mall about her "Dark Beauty." I was impressed. Really!

She finished it and said, "I never had a problem with being dark in my life."

"I wouldn't either as pretty as *you* look."

"Thank you."

"Do guys have a problem with it?"

"No." She said that with confidence.

I laughed out loud, imagining how many guys would fall for her.

"But you know what I hate though?" she asked me.

"What?"

"When guys walk up to me and say, 'Damn, you look good to be dark,' as if that's supposed to be a compliment. When they say *that nonsense,* they have no chance at all of getting with me."

"Do you have a boyfriend now?" I was slightly envious of her. I scared a lot of the guys that I met into acting like complete idiots.

"I just broke up with him," she answered. "He started hanging out with the wrong crowd and getting lazy, so I told him that it was time for me to go. And he cried like a big baby, talking about, 'I thought we loved each other.' But I don't have time for anybody who doesn't have a plan for their future."

I was liking this young sister more by the minute. She even reminded me of Kendra a little bit with her can-do spirit.

I said, "Would you like to trade phone numbers? I don't want to get you fired or anything."

"Oh, yeah," she said excitedly. I planned to help her out in any way that I could.

We traded phone numbers and I told the young sister that I would be in touch, and I meant it too. That's the quality I liked about my Philadelphian roots the most. No matter how large we get, we're always down with our people.

"Hey, sis', you passing out phone numbers like that? Can I get one?" this tall, lanky brother wearing FUBU gear asked me. He looked like a college basketball player, and Springfield Mall was Villanova territory.

I asked, "Do I look like one of your groupies to you?"

"No, you look like Tracy Ellison Grant, the big-time movie star." He had sarcastic confidence written all over his face. I could tell that he was used to getting his way with women. If I had nothing better to do, I would string his ass along just to teach him a lesson.

"I'll give you my phone number when you *earn* your degree," I shot at him.

He said, "What are you trying to say?"

"Do you play basketball?" I asked him.

"Yeah."

"Are you passing?"

"Yeah, I'm passing."

"I'm not talking about passing just enough to play, I'm talking about moving on toward *a degree* in something."

He hesitated too long with his answer. "Yeah."

"Sure you are," I told him and headed on my merry way.

There was no way for me to shop in peace that morning. It seemed that too many people recognized me. Since the mall was fairly empty, I guess that gave each person the idea that it was the perfect opportunity to hold my attention longer then they could have hoped for inside of a crowded mall. So I left earlier than I expected and went back home to take a nap and to write another poem, "Prisoners of Fame," because that was what I felt like. No wonder so many celebrities had chosen to become reclusive.

**$  $  $**

When I arrived to pick up my cousin Vanessa (on time) from school, I must have stepped into thirty percent of the student population. They were waiting for me out in front of the school. Girls *and* boys, screaming at me:

"Tracy Ellison Grant!"

"HERE SHE IS, Y'ALL!"

"HEY, TRACY!"

"TRAAAY-SAAAY!"

"Dag! Calm your behind down, boy! You all up in my ear!"

"Can I have an autograph?!"

"Can I have a date?!"

"When is *Flyy Girl* the movie coming out!"

"Can I play a part in the movie?"

"Can you just sign my notebook right quick?!"

"Excuse me, but I *do* believe that I was standing here *first!*"

"Can we go half on a baby?!"

"You got a little sister my age or something?!"

"Older women and younger men are *in* now. Have you seen *How Stella Got Her Groove Back*?!"

"Can you give me a hickey on my neck?!"

"Shut your mouth, boy! God! Y'all are *so* embarrassing!"

"Would you get *off* of my damn *foot,* please?! Stop being so *pressed!*"

"Can I be 'Carmen' in your movie?!"

"Yeah, 'cause you a hoe anyway!"

"Who said that?! *You're* the hoe!"

"DON'T CROWD HER, Y'ALL! GIVE THE LADY SOME BREATHING ROOM!"

"VANESSA'S YOUR COUSIN FOR REAL?! I THOUGHT SHE WAS LYING!"

*I* thought that smart kids were supposed to be more reserved and have better manners. I guess I thought wrong. Those damn E&S kids were acting like lunatics out there! So when I got Vanessa in my father's Buick I just stared at her.

"YOU CAN'T AFFORD A BETTER CAR THAN THAT?!" another silly guy yelled at me as we drove off.

Vanessa chuckled and said, "I did *not* do that. A lot of people saw you on the news this morning, and the rumor got around that you were gonna be up here today to pick me up after school. If you would have come late again, most of the people would have left, but you came right on time."

"Obviously so," I told her. I still couldn't believe all of the attention that they were showing me. "So, I guess that *you'll* be a celebrity in school now," I said.

Vanessa sucked her teeth and responded, "Not really. A lot of people are hating me now, like I'm supposed to be friends with everybody. I wasn't friends with everyone before. I just minded my own business, but now they act like I have a *chip* on my shoulder or something. And it's not even like that."

I smiled at her, knowing exactly what it felt like. I put my hand on her shoulder as I drove and said, "Trust me, I *know* the feeling."

# A Nursery Rhyme

*Hollywood, Hollywood,*
*let me in!*
*Not by the hair of my*
*pink and white skin.*
*Well, I'll huff*
*and I'll puff*
*and I'll blow your house in!*

*Hollywood, Hollywood,*
*let me in!*
*Sorry black girl*
*your résumé is too thin.*
*Well, I'll write*
*and I'll fight*
*and I'll blow your house in!*

*Hollywood, Hollywood,*
*let me in!*
*"Was it you we told no*
*or do you have a damn twin?"*
*I don't have a damn twin,*
*but I'm at the door again,*
*so I took a sledgehammer*
*and I broke the bitch in!*

*But then I got arrested,*
*so I need a lawyer friend.*

# November 1996  $$

When November rolled around, I finally received my share of the advanced payment for *Flyy Girl*, and I could breathe a little deeper, but I still didn't plan on buying any furniture yet. I mailed out a few signed copies of my book to friends and family members, including Raheema, who was soon to be married before me. That smart-ass girl! I still couldn't believe it! Her colors were white and gold, in all-African attire. I had to have my measurements done and send them to her for my dress to be made by a sister from Ghana, who lived close by to Raheema and her fiancé in New Jersey.

Out in California, just like Kendra predicted, when the vote came up for the affirmative action bill, nonwhite Americans lost out *big time!* Latinos and Asians were included in the mix. However, I do not believe that Asians had as much of a problem with it as blacks and Latinos had, because Asians were kicking ass in the books like it was nobody's business! Were we really inferior to them? Were we just lazy? Were we that undereducated? Or was it all of the above? Something was amiss, and Kendra was hurt to her heart over it.

"You watch what happens over the next three years or so out here in California," she warned me over the telephone. "See how many of us get turned away from higher education. This is a *crime,* and nobody seems to care."

"*You* care," I told her.

"Yeah, and like President George Bush used to say, 'I'm just one lonely person out here.'"

I laughed at her and said, "You really *do* need to run for politics. I'm dead serious."

"And who is going to teach my classroom of kids when I do?"

"Someone else," I told her.

"Yeah, someone who doesn't care as much."

When she said that, I felt guilty, thinking about the students that I left back home in Philadelphia. I said, "Girl, I have to stop talking to you. You make me feel like a midget trying to take on a lion sometimes."

"And you're afraid of that? What do you think you're up against out here in Hollywood?"

She had a point. Kendra never let me forget about the odds.

She asked, "So, are you still friends with that New York girl, Juanita?"

I smiled. "Heck no! She went right back to ignoring me. And guess who dug up my phone number and left two messages."

"Reginald?" Kendra guessed.

"Of course he did. I guess he thinks that I'm going to call him back too," I told her. "He called up talking about how he has an East Coast *project* that he thinks I would be interested in."

Kendra laughed and said, "Girl, you asked for it. You should have left his behind alone as soon as you read him at the party that night."

I started daydreaming on the phone. I had one class left at the UCLA Extensions program before I stepped out into the unknown marketplace of Hollywood employment. However, I *did* learn how to write scripts, I just didn't know how acceptable they would be.

"What are you thinking about, Tracy?" Kendra asked me. She knew by then that my silence meant I was thinking something deep.

"I'm just wondering how hard it's gonna be to find a Hollywood job, that's all."

"Have you spoken to Yolanda lately?"

"I'm trying not to bug her too much, you know. I don't want to seem desperate. And *she* hasn't called *me*."

Kendra laughed at me again. "There you go again with that ego of yours. Let me tell you, if you *really* want to make it in Hollywood, you'll have to *eat* a big piece of that humble pie you keep trying to avoid," she advised me. "So if *I* were you, I would get on the phone and call Yolanda Felix up *right now* before you miss out on something. Because from what *I* understand, Hollywood moves fast!"

I hung up the phone with Kendra and thought about calling Yolanda. She was the only real contact that I had out there, but I didn't really know how connected she was in the business. I was still wondering what she thought about my book, if she even had a chance to read it. I was as nervous as I was when I first met her. I was reaching the moment of Hollywood truth (employment), so Kendra was right, I had to call Yolanda regardless.

I dug up her number in my new, relatively empty, Hollywood phone book and took a deep breath. "Here we go," I told myself as I dialed her seven digits.

"Hello, is Yolanda Felix in?"

"Yes, this is Yolanda."

I didn't know if she knew me by first name alone, so I hesitated with my introduction.

"Hi, this is Tracy . . . Ellison."

She got excited and said, "Haaay, girl, just say Tracy! I finished reading your book just last night. You were a *wild* little something. I thought that *I* was bad. Girl, you took the cake and put new icing and decorations on it."

I guess that was a good thing. I was smiling.

I said, "Well, you do realize that I'm older now. I'm not that reckless anymore."

"I know how it is. You were just testing out your new womanhood," she responded. "We all go through that stage sooner or later. You just did yours a lot sooner than most."

I said, "You know, next week is my last week at the UCLA Extensions program for screenwriting and television." I wanted to change the subject away from my juvenile years and get down to the mature business of my present.

"And it's right on time, too," Yolanda told me. "Are you into science fiction at all?"

"Science fiction?" All I could think of was *Star Wars* with Billy Dee Williams playing Lando Calrissian.

Yolanda said, "There's a wrap party that I want you to go to with me this Saturday night. So if you have any other plans, cancel them. You *need* to be there."

*Science fiction?* I was still thinking. "What movie is it for?" I asked her.

"Black Hole Films just finished a project called *They're Here,* slated for release this spring."

"What is it, a Martian movie?" I was smiling again. Did Yolanda really think that I had come all the way out to Hollywood for some science fiction shit? I found that idea comical.

Yolanda said, "Tracy, let me tell you something. The smart people in *this* business, like every other, stay two and three steps ahead of the game." She sounded very serious about it too.

"If you came out here trying to poke your way into this little black stuff, you're gonna end up having a tedious, half-lit career," she told me. "That little black stuff doesn't last, girl. It's all trendy and cute, but you'll be hanging out with the same crowd of people and basically going nowhere.

"What *you* want to do is latch onto something that's going to *be* here," she told me. "As we get closer to the year 2000 and beyond, science fiction is where you want to be. *Mark my words.*"

She paused and gave me a minute to think about it. "Well, you make up your own mind, but if you want to go, make sure you let me know before Saturday," she said.

When we hung up, I sat and thought about science fiction. George Lucas was moving forward with his next series of *Star Wars* movies and re-releasing the old ones. *E.T.* was the biggest hit of the eighties. *Terminator* was Arnold Schwarzenegger's breakout movie which led to *Terminator 2.* The *Batman* movies were big hits in the nineties, just as the *Superman* movies were big hits in the eighties. *Jurassic Park* led to the production of *The Lost World.* Danny Glover played the hero in *Predator 2.* Angela Bassett costarred in *Strange Days,* and Will Smith had just hit pay dirt with *Independence Day.* Not to mention all of the hype about the television series called *The X-Files.*

That was all the thinking I needed to do. I had to at least see what the opportunities would be in science fiction, whether I was interested in it or not. So I nodded my head and said out loud to myself, "Let me go pick out an outfit."

$ $ $

Yolanda picked me up Saturday night around nine-thirty in her silver Jaguar.

She looked at my townhouse from the outside and said, "It looks nice. You're gonna need some rent money, aren't you?"

I smiled as I climbed onto her leather interior.

"I don't plan to be without a job for too long," I told her.

She said, "Good. That's the right attitude to have."

Yolanda was dressed in a black business suit, as sexy as a model, but was strong as a male executive in her demeanor.

"That's a nice suit you're wearing too," she told me.

I was wearing deep blue with tiny gray pinstripes.

I smiled and said, "Thank you."

She said, "When you *want* business, you *dress* business. When you want to schmooze, you dress the part you want to play, but tonight is business for *both* of us, so we look good."

I wondered again how old Yolanda was.

"How long have you been in the business?" I asked her. It was a roundabout way of finding out how old she was without asking.

"About eight, nine years now," she answered. "I actually started off in the music business, but I like film and television a lot better. Let's just say that it's more accessible to me. The music business tends to have too many damn hands in the way."

"So, you're about thirty-six then?" I assumed.

Yolanda chuckled without looking at me. We were on our way north to West Hollywood.

"Tracy, if you want to know how old I am, just ask me."

I smiled and was still hesitant. "How old are you?" I asked her.

"None of your business," Yolanda answered and started laughing. "I'm thirty-four," she told me, "and that's between me and you. I like to use my age to my advantage. If they think young, I let them know that I'm older than what I look. And if they think old . . . then I'll get offended," she added with another laugh. "I keep 'em all off guard that way."

"What about the men out here?" I asked her. It was a roundabout way of asking if she was happily with someone, because every once in a while I got lonely out there in Cali.

Yolanda looked at me and said, "Okay, let me tell you the rules of Hollywood. Number one: You never fuck anyone without protection. *Double* protection if you can, because as you can imagine, these Hollywood types can get around. Number two: If it's business, then make sure they *know* it's business. That means you have to know if your friend is connected the way you need them to be, and that they will *still* help you to get there whether you continue to sleep with them or not. That's important, because if they're going to screw you over and not help you, then you can't sleep with them. Period! Number three: Keep your personal business to yourself. Some people think that Hollywood types like to brag about their partners to make the news, but trust me, there's a lot more fucking going on out here than that couple shit you see on TV and read about in these gossip magazines. So don't believe the hype, and keep it to yourself."

I said, "What about just regular relationships that are not business related?"

Yolanda looked at me and shrugged her shoulders. "You do whatever you want, just keep it to yourself."

I guess that romance wasn't too high on her list of importance, so I made a note to keep *my* mind on more business-related aspects as well. Like Yolanda said, I had *rent* to take care of, and with my *own* money instead of counting on the generosity of some man.

We arrived in the lobby of a ritzy Hollywood hotel where the dress code varied from jeans and sneakers to suits and ties. However, the style of dress did not determine who really had the money and the power in that place. Some of those science fiction people just didn't like to wear suits, or groom for business purposes. As expected with science fiction, there were not a lot of colored faces in the room either. Maybe Yolanda was really onto something, fresh opportunities.

There was a soft piano playing in the background and plenty of private conversations going on. Everyone looked fully into themselves. I was wondering how you even broke in for a word. Yolanda showed me that skill right away.

"Calvin! Good to see you," she said.

A silver-haired white man in his fifties turned and faced us with a smile.

"Yolanda," he responded, taking her hand. His previous conversation seemed to fade away into thin air. I guess it wasn't that important to him.

"Has the buzz been good so far?" she asked him about the upcoming film.

"So far, but we'll see when the time comes."

He looked to me, and Yolanda introduced me on cue.

"This is Tracy . . . Ellison."

I was hardly on first-name terms. Yolanda seemed to forget that herself for a second.

"Nice to meet you," he said, nodding to me.

"Hi," I responded and nodded back with a grin.

"She's an upcoming writer, hot out of UCLA. *And* she moves *fast*," Yolanda filled him in.

He said, "Fast is the only way to move. So you're into science fiction?" he asked me.

Before I answered him, I took in his casual dress code of a dark sports jacket, dress shirt, and no tie. He had the relaxed confidence of big business and not the nervous energy of small business, so I decided that I had better not say no, especially since he was the first person that Yolanda spoke to. I figured that meant something.

"I like to stay abreast of opportunities in *all* fields," I told him. "Besides, growing up as a black girl in the inner city, whenever I saw space movies and no people of color in them, I always wondered if we would even *make it* to the future."

Yolanda and Calvin laughed big-time at that one. It was a good opening line. I could tell right off the bat that Yolanda was proud of me by the way she pulled me into her.

"Tracy's out here to make sure that we add some color to the future," she joked.

"Do you have any ideas developed yet?" Calvin asked.

*Shit!* I was thinking. *They're not lying about how fast Hollywood moves.* I thought fast myself and answered, "Well, I'm looking to knock a few ideas around to see if mine are on point or if I need to redirect them."

Calvin raised his head a touch and smiled at me. Did he know that I was bullshitting? He didn't seem to care. Maybe he just liked my answers.

Yolanda said, "You know how some of these writers are. They're protective of their work right up until they get it green-lighted for production."

"Well, make sure that you stay in touch with me, Tracy. I might want to take a look at what you have. Yolanda has my number."

We moved on, and Yolanda nudged me in my ribs with her elbow.

"That's how you do it, girl! You don't tell these people you're not interested in science fiction. And you always use whatever angle you can to keep them interested."

We approached a group of white women, some old, some young, and all dressed differently, from dresses, to suits, to jeans.

"Yolanda," one of the older women turned and addressed my new mentor.

Yolanda said, "Ladies, this is Tracy Ellison, script doctor extraordinaire, just out from the East Coast."

"Well, we need *more*," one of the other women commented. "These scripts are *horrible!*"

Yolanda was pumping me up, but I didn't feel as confident in a group of women. Women were a lot more sensitive to conversations than men were. I knew I had to be very careful and let Yolanda take the lead.

"I'll be gentle," I told them.

"No-o-o! You *can't* be gentle. They're *used* to gentle," someone said. "You need to take a sharpened *ax* to their work."

"Then she'll be writing a book about how she was run *out* of Hollywood," Yolanda joked.

It was too much for me to focus on any one of them, so I just rolled with the flow.

"That's why I plan to be gentle," I reiterated with a smile. "You're in charge, and you're the creator. I'm only here to make you look *better*. However, if you don't want my help . . ."

The women laughed at my role-playing and added lines of their own.

"I don't need your help, woman! I'm out of grade school now. Go find yourself some other schoolboy to try and educate. I do things *my* way around here!"

"I should just ignore all of the misspelled words then?" I continued with them.

Yolanda decided to jump into the fun. "On second thought, correct the misspelled words before you leave," she concluded.

We all laughed again like civil women, fully understanding that the business of Hollywood, like many others, was a man's playground that could use a woman's touch.

"So what school did you go to?" the first older woman asked me.

I answered proudly, "Hampton in Virginia. It was one of the first Historically Black Colleges and Universities in the country, established after the Civil War." Hampton was much older than many white institutions, particularly those established on the West Coast.

"What part of Virginia?" I was asked.

"Hampton, Virginia," Yolanda answered for me. I'm sure she was as proud of HBCUs as I was, even with the rivalries between Hampton and Howard. We were all family like Sister Sledge.

"Are you from the Los Angeles area?"

"Philadelphia," I answered.

Women often asked a lot more questions too. Did any of it get around to business? Maybe next week sometime. That's why I preferred to talk to men. Men showed you two interests, business and sex, and not necessarily in that order, but at least that gave me a much easier focal point when talking to them. Women, on the other hand, could get really competitive, personal, and petty, so I couldn't wait to get the hell away from them.

Yolanda said, "Girl, you are *workin' it*! You hear me?! If you keep this up, you should have *no problem* in Hollywood."

Shit, I was tired already! Yolanda had no idea how hard I was working to make sure I said the right things. That was a lot of pressure. What ever happened to just being yourself?

Yolanda looked clear across the room and snapped her fingers like a woman possessed.

"Perfect!" she told herself and looked at me. "Have you ever watched the show *The Outer Limits* on Showtime?" she asked me.

I nodded. "Yeah." I was only familiar with *The Outer Limits* because my brother Jason watched the show religiously. They even had marathons on Showtime where they would air two and three of them in a row.

Yolanda said, "Good. I want you to meet Tim Waterman. He's the producer of a knock-off cable show called *Conditions of Mentality*. It's in the same vein as *The Outer Limits* and other psychological, science fiction shows."

*Oh, goody!* I thought to myself with a sly grin. *Now I get to talk to a guy who produces a B- or C-grade science fiction show for cable.*

Nevertheless, Yolanda was pumped about it.

She said, "Tim, are you still looking for new writers to fill out your show?"

Tim was a tall, blond guy with silver, wire-framed glasses. He let his hair grow long to his shoulders. He looked more like a romance show producer than science fiction, but what did *I* know?

"We're just about booked up now. The new season's in full swing and we're rocking and rolling, baby!"

On second thought, he sure *spoke* like a science fiction guy. He was all energy. Two sexy young women were standing by him, creating eye candy for Tim's sexual allure, or maybe I was reading too much into things. They could have been his sister and her girlfriend . . . *Not hardly!*

Yolanda said, "Well, what about assistant writers?"

He grimaced. I don't think he was up for talking business with his candy in the way.

"Writing assistants? Ah—"

Yolanda cut him off. "This is Tracy Ellison, she has a master's degree in English, and she's just about finished her screenwriting courses at UCLA, *and* she has a big interest in science fiction, particularly since there's not many African Americans involved."

Yolanda was practically pushing me down his throat.

Tim looked at me for the first time. He *really* looked at me, if you know what I mean. This guy was a big-time flirt, and I didn't know if I wanted to deal with that on a job. What was the difference between him and Reginald? They both gave me those doggie-style vibes.

Tim opened his mouth and said, "Oh really?"

I opened mine and said, "Don't let my good looks mislead you. I want to be a real creative professional."

He nodded his head and said, "Well, great." He dug into his beige sports jacket and pulled out a business card. "Call me at my office on Monday, and I'll see what I can do."

His two friends smiled at me with snake eyes. *Fuck you too!* I thought. *I don't want your man, I just want a job.*

When Yolanda and I walked away I asked her, "Is he a flirt?"

She didn't miss a beat. "Definitely, but he doesn't try hard. He has women *throwing* themselves at him. So just ignore the flirting and press him for the job."

She said, "He's soft, you can definitely break him. So you get on the job, get yourself some good writing experience, make the right contacts, and pay your rent. Then I can get you in the Writers Guild association for your protection, rights, and benefits."

She made it sound as if it was a done deal. I slid the business card in my purse and planned not to disappoint her *or* myself. Science fiction or not, all I knew was that a writing job was a writing job.

"Mitch," Yolanda called out. We were moving on again, and she sounded real personal with this one. I could tell by the tone of her voice.

Mitch was the first *brown* face that Yolanda and I approached that evening. He was a large and handsome black man in a tailored dark suit with a striking gold tie. He smiled easily with perfect white teeth.

"Excuse me for a minute, Tracy," Yolanda told me, stepping aside with Mitch for privacy. He looked at me, smiled and nodded, and moved on with Yolanda.

I looked and grinned. I was beginning to think that the sister had crossed all the way over until I saw how she acted with Mitch. There was an obvious difference in her closeness to him. Her voice flattened out and her pitch lowered, becoming more humane and less catered. She was definitely still down with the people.

"Tracy Ellison," someone said.

I turned quickly, wondering who knew my name. I was far from being known out there *yet*.

"Susan Raskin," I responded. It was the short, dark-haired girl from the HFI crash course who had snuck a reading of my poetry.

She said, "You know what I was thinking? Are you a relative of the writer *Ralph* Ellison, who published *Invisible Man*?" She had this huge smile and large eyes as if she was really onto something.

I laughed, sorry to have to disappoint her. "People asked

me that in college too, but as far as I know, we're not related."

"Oh, because I was thinking about the whole English
department connection and the fact that you wanted to
write screenplays to add depth to the African-American
story. Then the fact that you are obviously a heck of a poet,
who is trying to be modest about it."

She was flattering me. I smiled and said, "No, I'm just
an ordinary girl trying to make it out here in Hollywood."

"Tell me about it," she said.

"So what are you doing here, Ms. MBA?" I asked her.
She was dressed in a khaki suit. I definitely planned to get
her number that night.

She took a big breath and answered, "Well, as they say,
I'm putting in my dues."

"Same here," I told her. "I'm working my way up from
the bottom, and boy do you have to remember to say the
right things."

"Exactly. Meet the right people. Impress the right people. Blah, blah, blah."

"But do you want to be in the business?" I asked Susan
*and* myself.

In unison we let out a big "Yeah!" and broke up
laughing.

"I didn't know you were into science fiction," Susan
commented.

"I didn't know either," I joked.

We laughed again like old girlfriends or something. I
was really digging this girl. As they said in New York, she
was *mad* cool.

"How old are you, Susan?" I asked her. She couldn't
have been much older than me, and I wasn't afraid to ask

her like I was with Yolanda. I just felt more comfortable around someone who was closer to my age, and who was working her way into the Hollywood arena like I was.

"Twenty-eight," she answered. "How about you?"

I smiled and said, "Actually, I turned twenty-five on the day you met me at the crash course."

"Oh yeah, that was your birthday? Friday, September sixth, right?"

"Yup."

"Mine is August the twelfth."

I said, "You're getting close to the big three-oh."

She shook her head and sighed. "Please don't remind me of that."

I nodded and smiled at her. "Okay."

"Thanks, and let's make sure we keep in touch."

"No problem," I told her. "I was going to ask you that. You beat me to it."

We both wrote our numbers down in phone books.

Yolanda caught us making the trade and waited for us to break.

"Well, I'll catch up to you next go round," Susan said.

"I'll be here," I told her.

Yolanda immediately asked me, "Where did you meet her?"

"At the HFI crash course."

She nodded and didn't say much else about it.

"So, who is Mitch?" I asked her. I noticed that she failed to introduce me to him.

"He was waiting to meet you, but you were talking and we were talking, and then he had to go, so he left."

"Are you good friends?"

Yolanda chuckled and said, "You ask a lot of questions, Tracy," but never answered me.

We left after meeting some of the stars from the movie, and a few more of the Hollywood swingers and players. As we drove back to my townhouse, Yolanda brought up my new friend.

"You know who your friend is, don't you? I was very impressed with you tonight."

I didn't even know who she was talking about at first.

"What friend?"

"Susan."

"Oh, Susan Raskin. What about her?"

"*What about her?* She's the youngest of a very powerful family out here, that's what."

"The Raskins?" It didn't sound like a big-name family to me, but what did *I* know?

"Not really the Raskins, but the Weisners," Yolanda answered. "Edward Weisner is her uncle, a big name in Hollywood, with all of his kids and extended family. Edward's youngest sister, Marla, married into the Raskins, and Susan is *her* youngest kid."

It sounded as if Yolanda had done all kinds of research on them. She knew their entire family tree.

I smiled and asked, "So, that's why you didn't disturb me to introduce me to Mitch?"

"Yeah. I saw you chatting it up with Susan like you went to high school together, and I just decided to leave that kind of chemistry alone."

The Raskin name didn't ring a bell with me, but *Weisner* definitely sounded Jewish. Excuse me for thinking it, but I had heard enough about Hollywood to expect some things.

I asked, "So, is she Jewish?"

Yolanda looked and smiled at me. "They run the show out here," she answered. "You stay friends with Susan, and you should be in *good* shape." She squeezed my arm and was all gassed up about it.

"Tracy, you work *damned* fast! Faster than me," she said.

I didn't even like the sound of that. I didn't go out to Hollywood to deliberately *use* people in order to succeed. You go through that stage in high school, and maybe a little in college, but after you receive a degree and a master's, you would *think* that you know enough and are skilled enough to make it on your own merit.

"Is that how the game works out here?" I asked Yolanda.

I liked Susan as a friend. I didn't have many white friends. I was rarely ever around them, and I damn sure didn't want to use anyone to get ahead. I had grown up from that, or at least I liked to *think* that I had.

Yolanda said, "Tracy, it's nothing personal. Okay? You can be friends and all of that, but business is business."

I guess she could read the heaviness on my voice and the frown on my face.

"Well, let's just put it this way," I said, "I would rather have *not* known who she is than to feel how I feel right now. I mean, we were just talking. I wasn't *plotting* anything."

"Nobody told you to. Just be friends with her and stay in touch. I'm sure she'll stay in touch with *you*. You should even give her one of your books to read."

I looked at Yolanda and said, "Hell no! So she can read how fast I was. That wouldn't look good on my résumé."

"Aw, girl, would you *grow up* from that silly stuff. You've *made it* now. You've gotten *past* the teen stage," Yolanda told me. "If anything, the book will show her how *strong* you are, because a lot of brown girls don't make it *out* of the 'hood."

I thought about my predicament for the rest of that

night. As they say, Real life is stranger than fiction. Who would have thought that I could go out to Hollywood, and the first person I meet and like happens to be a girl whose family is well connected in the business. If I wrote that screenplay, *Dreaming Hollywood,* I would have been laughed out of the classroom for *that* one too. It was like an Orphan-Annie-meets-Daddy-Warbucks script. What the hell could happen to me next?

**$ $ $**

I called up Tim Waterman that Monday morning and caught him in his office. I was determined to do my own dirty work and get my own job without thinking about Cinderella stories. In the long run, Cinderella stories never lasted, but good old-fashioned hard work did, and you gained more respect by it.

Tim answered the phone as if he remembered me. "Hey, Tracy, how's it goin'?" Was he flirting again, or did he realize that I really wanted a job?

"I'll be doing a lot better as soon as I can latch onto someone who wants to utilize my writing talents." I was planning to pour it on thicker than gravy.

He said, "Well, fax over some of your work and let me take a look at it."

I wasn't planning on him saying that. I would have to drive over to Kinko's copy store to fax him.

"Give me a half hour," I told him. I couldn't back down at that point. It was time to put up or shut up.

Tim gave me the fax number and I grabbed some of my assignments together to fax to him. I knew that my writing was crisp with good dialogue, and that was all that I figured I would need for an *assistant* position. Lucky for me,

I knew how to dot all of my i's and cross my t's from grading so many English papers as a middle school teacher. However, for the rest of that morning, I was a nervous wreck.

*What if he doesn't like my writing?* I asked myself as I paced through my empty townhouse. *What if I really can't make it out here? I guess I'll just go back to teaching then,* I contemplated. I was set to throw in the towel already. I started to remake my bed, wash dishes, scrub windows, *anything* that would calm my nerves and release some of my anxiety.

"Shit!" I told myself as the time continued to move forward. I had already called to make sure Tim received my fax, but if he didn't call me back with a response to my work, I was ready to call him again. I wouldn't be able to rest otherwise. I had to have a response.

When Tim called me back later on that afternoon, he said, "You have some good stuff here. And your plots are daring. That's exactly what we emphasize for our scripts, plots with edge. I think you can help us."

I took a big breath, relieved, and asked myself, *Now what? Does this mean I have a job, or am I just being considered?*

Tim added, "I looked into our budget, and we could offer you around two thousand."

I nearly hyperventilated right there while on my kitchen phone. That's how excited I was.

"*Around* two thousand?" I asked him. That sounded like *plenty!*

He chuckled. "Well . . . two thousand," he answered with a pause. He made it sound as if I would complain about it. I didn't plan to.

"Two thousand a show?" I asked, just to make sure I

wasn't dreaming. I would have jumped up and down in the air if I didn't think that I would faint from it.

He said, "Yeah, but we need you to assist, you know, everyone."

It sounded as if he was trying to get over on me, and it was pretty obvious. Yolanda was right, he *was* soft. So even though I was nervous, I wasn't a fool, and asking for more money had always been my thing.

I said, "That sounds like a lot more work than assisting *one* or a *few* writers. Assisting an entire staff sounds more like a *five*-thousand-dollar job, but if we met somewhere in the middle, just to get my feet wet, I couldn't complain about that."

My heart was racing like I stole something. Talking money was what agents were supposed to do, but since I didn't have one yet, and Tim made it seem so obvious that they had more money available, *and* that he could use plenty of assistance, I just *had* to go for broke.

He said, "Well, I'll have to look into it and get back to you on that."

I gave him my full name, my education, my credentials, my availability, *and* let him understand my *urgency* before we concluded our talk. I wanted to make sure that I made my presence felt.

Tim laughed and said, "Okay, I have it all."

"I hope you do," I told him.

When we hung up, I was forced to play the waiting game for a couple of days. The job was officially offered to me on my last day of class at UCLA Extensions. The deal was done for three thousand five hundred dollars per episode. Yolanda looked over the contract for me to make sure everything was legitimate, and the first thing I planned to do was go out and buy the fastest writing computer I could find, a quality fax machine, and start a new account on the Internet. A science fiction writer had to be well connected in the latest of technology.

That following Monday, I signed all of the paperwork, took a photo for ID and security, and showed up for my first day at the job to meet the staff at the studio trailer. I felt immediately self-conscious about my Toyota as I parked it next to the BMWs, Mercedeses, Jags, Lexuses, Cadillacs, and everything else. However, there was nothing I could do about that until I started making some money. I would just have to live with it for a while.

As soon as I walked in (the only brown face in the place, outside of one cameraman), everyone stared at me. Maybe I could have used an official introduction. Obviously, Tim was too busy or absentminded to let everyone know that I had been hired.

Joseph Keaton, the dark-haired head writer with a tense face and a body filled with too much coffee for his own good, asked me the question that everyone else only wondered.

"Who are you?"

I answered, "I'm Tracy Ellison, the assistant writer for the show, and this is my first day on the job, so please be nice to me."

I few of them laughed, a couple of them chuckled, and others only grinned at me, but all I wanted to do was break the ice because I was there to stay. So I took a deep breath and told myself, *This here looks like a tough-ass job, but I know that I can do it!*

# Just Say No!

*To the head games,*
*to the drama,*
*to the pettiness,*
*the peer pressure,*
*the curiosity,*
*the rumors,*
*the liars,*
*the hustlers,*
*the players,*
*the beggars,*
*the cheaters,*
*the whiners,*
*the old girlfriends,*
*the babies' mommas,*
*the older men,*
*the trifling bosses,*
*the social drugs,*
*the alcohol,*
*the cigarettes,*
*and to all of the fucking bullshit*
*(excuse my French)!*

*But without all of that*
*what would a girl have left*
*to live for?*
*Honestly?*

*Shit happens!*
*Just don't be controlled by it.*
*And remember to say YES*
*to self-respect!*

Copyright © 1991 by Tracy Ellison

# April 2000

**$ $**
**$**

I didn't know where to take my cousin Vanessa after picking her up from school because I couldn't really go anywhere without people bothering me. We couldn't just ride around in circles all day either. It was a nice day outside, so I wanted to take a walk and enjoy it. I just didn't know where.

"You want to get something to eat again?" I asked her.

She was wearing a floral wraparound dress that looked sexy and sophisticated. She was even showing off some minor curves.

"I'm not really hungry."

I looked at her and asked, "Would you like to be a star one day, Vanessa?" I had my reasons for asking. Most people wanted to shine in some way or another, they just didn't realize the cost they would have to pay. I wanted to talk to my little cousin about the *cost* of fame.

She smiled, in her introverted way, and didn't say a thing. I took that as a yes.

"Do you know that I can't even go shopping in Philadelphia now?"

She looked at me and asked, "Why not?"

"Because of what just happened at your school," I told her.

Vanessa laughed and said, "They always act like that. You should see them at the basketball games."

"I didn't have to go through that when I used to pick my brother up from that school. But that's when I was still a regular citizen," I told her. "Would you want people going that crazy over you?"

She shrugged her shoulders. "I would just ignore them."

"Lesson number one: You *can't* ignore them. You know why? Because *they* are the people who make you shine, and *they* pay for everything that you do," I told her.

She said, "Well, politicians get our votes, and *they* don't pay us any mind."

I had to laugh. Her comeback line was clever.

"Yeah, well, that's a whole other issue," I told her. "You're not old enough to vote yet anyway."

I headed for Kelly Drive that ran alongside the Schuylkill River. I figured that we could find some peace and quiet out there to talk. I was in a talking mood.

I pulled over in a parking area by the river and climbed out of the car.

Vanessa followed me out. "What are we doing?" she asked me.

"Come on, I wanna talk to you."

There were rowboating teams practicing their strokes, up and down the Schuylkill. I walked over to the edge of the wall that overlooked the river and sat down on it. Vanessa stood there in her pretty dress, watching the boats go by in the sun. She looked beautiful. We both did.

"So, who's your boyfriend?" I decided to ask her. She *had* to have one, unless she was another Raheema, running from boys like a horror movie.

I didn't expect for Vanessa to answer me outright. She

did exactly what I thought she would do. She smiled and tried to ignore what I asked.

"Come on, sit down and tell me about him," I told her.

She looked at the wall, frowned, and shook her head. "Ducks and birds defecate on that wall. *You* should stand up."

"*Defecate?* Oh, I forgot, you go to Engineering and *Science.* A *smart* girl." I laughed and said, "So, you've been down here before."

She nodded. "Yeah. I used to ride my bike down here. It's close to my house."

I had forgotten. I never lived in North Philly.

"Okay, well, let's not get away from the subject. Let's talk about this boyfriend of yours," I pressed her.

"How do you know I have one?"

She was stalling.

I said, "Look, girl, do I look like I was born yesterday." I sounded like my own mother. Funny how things change.

Vanessa looked away and paused. She dug into her brown leather purse and pulled out a wallet-sized picture.

She handed it to me facedown. I flipped it over and looked at it.

"Was that so hard to do?" I asked her.

She just smiled at me.

I looked at the picture again. This light brown, confident brother with dark, almond-shaped eyes, and shiny dark hair stared back up at me.

"Mmmph," I grunted. Little cousin had some *taste!* I said, "He looks like one of Da Youngsta's. What's the youngest one's name? Taj?"

She grinned and said, "Ta*ji,* but they don't call themselves Da Youngsta's anymore."

"Well, is this him?" I asked her.

She shook her head, "No, they just look alike."

"Mmm, hmm," I mumbled. "And how old is this guy?"

"Nineteen."

"Is he a sophomore in college then? You're a sophomore in high school now, right?"

She nodded. "*I am,* but he doesn't go to college."

I looked up at her standing in the sunlight with her eyes shaded by her right hand. Vanessa looked like a video girl herself, the one that the singers chase all through the song.

I asked, "Isn't college where *you* want to be?"

"Yeah."

"Are you protecting yourself?"

She paused, smiled, and shook her head. "I haven't done anything with him. We're just talking. I only met him a couple of weeks ago."

I looked at the picture again. I wondered if this pretty boy was passing out wallet-sizes to *all* of his prospects.

"Does he have a girlfriend?"

"No."

She answered way too fast. I started chuckling to myself, knowing better.

I said, "Don't tell me. He told you that he *just* broke up with his old girlfriend, right, and now he's looking to take things slow? And let me guess. He likes *you* a lot." I knew all of the bullshit games that guys played from A to Z.

"Well, I still haven't done anything with him yet."

Vanessa was slipping. I said, "*Yet?* So you already have *plans?*"

"No, I mean, I think about it, but . . ."

"Oh, I *know* you *think* about it," I said, taking another look at the boy. "Shit, I'm *thinking* about it right now, and this boy is too damn young for me," I joked.

She broke up laughing.

I thought about Staci Madison, who I had just met inside of Springfield Mall that morning, and the boyfriend she had just cut loose.

I said, "Let's look at it this way. This boy is nineteen years old, and he's *not* in college, so what is he doing?"

"Working."

"Working where?"

She didn't even know. "Somewhere," she answered.

"Is he in some kind of trade school?"

"I don't think so."

"And what do you think he's going to be doing in ten years? Hell, in *five* years?"

Vanessa was clueless.

I said, "Now you go to Engineering and Science High School. What's the college enrollment rate at your school, something like ninety-eight percent?"

Germantown High School was probably less than half.

My little cousin smiled, bashfully.

I asked, "Do you know what guys are at age nineteen? *Potential.* That's all they are. Because there's nothing that you can really do at nineteen to raise a family, unless you graduated from high school like Kobe Bryant and went straight to the NBA, *or* you can sing or act or something. And that's *it*! Unless you're a genius who finished college early, and you already have big-time companies calling you to offer you a job.

"Is this guy a genius?" I asked her.

She smiled again. I could tell that she wasn't expecting a lecture from me, and that just made me want to keep going with it. Like I said, I felt like talking that day because I couldn't fucking shop in peace at the malls!

"You know what *you* are at age sixteen?" I asked her.

She just stared at me.

I said, "*Potential,* just like a nineteen-year-old boy. You don't know how to be a homemaker yet, and you can't earn any more than he can. And it's not just a money thing; it's a *family* thing. You have to be ready for it mentally, economically, and everything."

Vanessa said, "Well, *you* went through *your* stage."

I guess she was getting fed up with me.

I said, "I know, right? I can't tell you anything because *I* did everything. But I survived it."

"Are you saying that I won't?"

"I'm saying that you shouldn't *have* to," I told her. "My girl Raheema is happily married now with two kids. She may not have as many stories to tell as I have, but right now, I don't have the happy marriage or the kids."

"Well, maybe everybody doesn't need that," Vanessa responded.

I smiled. "Yeah, that's what we all *say.*" Now I was sounding like my father.

I reminisced on my own teen years in Philly. I said, "I had a nineteen-year-old guy once too, right down here in North Philly."

Vanessa started to smile again. "I know."

"And you know what I was to him?"

She went back to staring at me.

"I was a sweet, tight push in between the legs," I told her. "I was so sweet and tight that he couldn't even control himself when he got me. He was screwing me like a rabbit, two minutes and it was over."

Vanessa broke out laughing and turned away, embarrassed by my candor.

I said, "But that's all that I was to him, a fancy piece of ass, and I'm just being *real* about that, since that's what your generation talks about so much, being so damn *real*. Because we didn't think about being *real* in my day, we just did shit. But now y'all talk about being *real* as if that's supposed to make it all okay.

"I even wrote a poem about that, 'Real Versus Fake,' because which one is which now?" I asked hypothetically. "So you know what *you'll* be to this nineteen-year-old *boy*? A sweet, tight push in between the legs, just like I was to mine. Because if you were to turn around and tell this boy, 'Baby, I love you, I want to have your kids and never leave you,' that motherfucker would run like fire caught to his ass. 'Aw, girl, I just wasn't ready to be *tied down*.' *I know*, because I've already been through it."

Vanessa broke up laughing again. I bet she never had anyone talk to her before like I was, but I couldn't front on her. I *went* through all of that crazy shit.

I stopped and said, "I need to write a poem about *that*. Let me jot that down. 'A Sweet, Tight Push.'"

I asked her, "Did you think that I would get back with Victor when he got out of jail?"

She smiled. She didn't even have to answer me. I knew her answer already. Too many girls believed in that damn fairy tale.

I said, "The truth is, he was still a *boy*, trying his hardest to hold on to his *girl* from jail, but I can't front because he's a *man* now. He just didn't become a man with me. And that's *real*."

I looked out at the water and had nothing left to say. I was all talked the hell out and feeling lonely for some reason. I had a long-ass journey in my life, and for what, to come home to nobody? Something didn't seem right with that, and the money and fame changed nothing.

I took a deep breath and stood up.

Vanessa smiled and said, "You need to wipe off your skirt."

I didn't care about any damn skirt. If I did, I wouldn't have sat there in the first place. I could take the whole damn suit to the Salvation Army and buy a new one. I just couldn't buy it at a mall in my hometown where everybody knew me. However, since I had to drive my father's car, I had to brush off my skirt anyway.

"They have water fountains near the building to wash your hands," Vanessa told me.

I grunted at her. "Okay, Ms. Neat."

I washed my hands and dried them against the front of my skirt. I looked at Vanessa. She looked shell-shocked, as if she didn't know what to say to me, so she looked away.

I chuckled and said, "I'm sorry, little cousin. I shouldn't take my frustrations out on you."

She looked back at me and asked, "Frustrations about what?"

She didn't get it. *No one* seemed to get it! That's why I had to write a new book about it. Fame *was not* all good.

I said, "I can't shop at the damn malls. I almost got carjacked right around the corner from my parents' house. People have a million different opinions about my movie. Some people *think* that I'm Mrs. Santa Claus now with a bunch of presents and goodies for everybody. I just found out yesterday that one of my most positive girlfriends married a white man, and now she tells me that brothers can't handle women like *us*, who have something we would like to do in our lives. Then my *best* girlfriend Raheema, who was *terrified* of guys when we were next-door neighbors, ends up with a smart, handsome brother, and she just invited me up to their house in New Jersey for the weekend, so they can smile all up in my face with their two kids and have a great damn time while I sit there looking like a fool with no damn man, and no damn family of my own.

"And I *need* to put all of this shit in a new book somewhere, but Omar Tyree won't fucking write it, because he's on some other shit now, and my agent feels that if I write it myself, it may not sell as well because too many people wouldn't be able to make the connection between the two. Or I may not write it as well as Omar can, *nor* do I have the *time* to write the shit in the first place."

After all of that, Vanessa just stood there motionless with a grin on her face and didn't know what to do.

I said, "Now can I get a big hug, cousin? Famous people need love, too. *Real* love."

She didn't say a word. She just smiled, stepped over, and hugged me.

I said, "And I'm *not* a lesbian either."

Vanessa leaned back and said, "What?"

"I guess you didn't hear about that on the *Williams Wendy Show* then?"

"The *Wendy Williams Show?*" she corrected me.

"Yeah, whatever. *Her.* You know who I'm talking about."

Vanessa laughed and said, "Nobody believes all that stuff she says."

"Good," I said. We walked back to the car together.

I asked, "Okay, where do you want to go? And if people come up and bother me, I'll just tell them, 'Look, I'm out with my cousin right now, and this is *our time* to be family.'"

Vanessa climbed into the car and shrugged. "I don't know."

I took a deep breath and turned the ignition.

"All right then, we'll just go wherever. I'm okay with

that. As long as you *do* know where you want to go in your life," I told her. I backed out of the parking space and hit Kelly Drive again.

"Age nineteen is *not* the end of the world," I added. "I just want you to realize that before this pretty boy calls you back trying to *promise* the world to you, because he *can't* give it to you. *Nor* will his ass even try."

# When the Sweet Turns Sour

My momma told me
when I was young,
"Don't eat too much of that chocolate."
She said it only tastes good
when it's a bite.

But I was hard headed,
so I bought the whole box
and ate every piece
until the sweet turned sour in my mouth.

Not sour like candy,
but sour like rotten milk.
Lumpy.

And I hurled,
because I was sick
to my stomach,
sick
to my heart.

And I had to wrap it back up,
and throw it away,
even when it still looked good.

# January 1997

$$ \$ \$$$

$$ \$$$

Yolanda was right. *Conditions of Mentality,* a science fiction show, turned out to be a valuable strategy for my future, and once the writing staff realized that I was pretty good at looking over their scripts, I was able to roll along smoothly in my first Hollywood job. I even felt confident enough in my new employment to go out and finally buy some furniture.

Working for an hour-long science fiction show topped employment for a black, half-hour sitcom by a long-shot! It wasn't so much a money thing, but an experience thing. Number one: *Conditions* was not just another funny show, but an intelligent action drama, utilizing scripts that flowed with plenty of edginess to keep you guessing. So I learned the formula of writing intelligent scripts that moved and kept you on edge. Number two: Since we did not use the same actors every week, we worked like a mini movie production team. Number three: A lot of our scripts were actually submitted from outside writers, so I had a chance to see a variety of different styles and who used them. I also had a chance to see plenty of B- and C-list actors, so that I could study what made the difference between them and the higher-paid, more recognized A-list actors. To be honest about that, it looked to me as if a lot of it had to do with better looks, powerful agents, and more confidence in your dramatic delivery. I had the good looks and the confidence to act, but a powerful agent I did *not* have; a strong agent *and* a few acting classes, of course. However, first thing was first, breaking into the *writing* game.

After a while, I started coming up with ideas of my own for the show, but I dared not to bounce them around with the other staff members until I could complete a script that I felt confident enough to have produced. Otherwise, my ideas would have been developed either without me, or as a cowriter. Not on my life would I allow that to happen. I wanted the entire credit like other writers were getting, whether I was an "assistant" to the show or not.

However, before I actually completed anything, I took a couple of days off at the end of January for Raheema's wedding back home in Philadelphia. It turned out that Ernest, her fiancé, had an older cousin who preached at a church in North Philly, right off of Broad Street near downtown. Hotel accommodations were made at the Four Seasons. Very nice!

## $ $ $

After being away from home for five months, and as dry as I was with no love life established in California, I pressed my luck and called my old friend Mike when I got back into town on a Thursday night. We had stayed in touch with each other off and on, but not on any serious note. For all I knew, Mike had a new woman.

"I'm not intruding on anything am I?" I asked him outright over the phone. I guess my girl's wedding occasion made me ask him that question. I wanted to respect the space of a sister who Mike could have been getting serious about.

"Naw, I'm still a free man," he told me with a chuckle.

Typical; even if there *was* another woman, Mike was willing to pick right up where we left off. I guess if *I* were the other woman, I would have been pissed. Since I was not, his freedom was my good fortune.

"Well, I'll try and call you tomorrow night or Saturday to hook up. I have to see how loaded my schedule is first."

"That's cool with me. I look forward to seeing you again."

I repeated his words to myself when we hung up. "I look forward to seeing you again." That didn't sound like much of anything to me. I thought, *Whatever happened to something like,* "*I missed you so much that I can't* wait *to see you!*" I guess that Philadelphian cool can be a blessing *and* a curse sometimes. Sometimes you want a brother to *act* like he really cares.

After talking to Mike, I called my parents.

My mother asked me, "So, how do you feel about this wedding?"

Translation: Are you jealous?

I said, "I'm happy for Raheema, Mom. That's my girl."

"Well, I *know* that, but, you know . . ."

Translation: I still want to know if you're jealous.

I took a deep breath and sighed. "What do you want me to say, Mom, when it will happen for me?"

She got defensive. "I didn't say that."

"Well, you're *thinking* it."

"How are you gonna tell me what I'm thinking, Tracy?"

I didn't hesitate for a second. "Because you're my mother," I told her. Hell, after twenty-five years, if I didn't know what my mother was thinking by then, I needed to be *shot*.

She paused and started laughing.

"Where's Dad?" I asked her. I wanted to push the subject away from the wedding.

"I just sent him out on an ice-cream run. I had a craving."

I *was* jealous about that. When was the last time I could fulfill *my* sweet tooth with a man?

"You sent him out on Wayne Avenue?" I began to think about Victor Hinson again. I couldn't help myself. Wayne Avenue had been one of his stomping grounds, and I had heard through the grapevine that he owned storefront property there.

"Yeah," my mother answered before a pause. She said, "You know your old *friend* has a health food store around there now." She didn't even want to say his name.

I smiled, reminiscing on the eighties and my young love affair with Victor.

My mother took in my silence and said, "I hope you're not still thinking about him. He's married now, right? I thought we went through this already, Tracy."

Although my mother had always considered Victor handsome, how many mothers *do you know* who would openly accept her daughter holding on to a jailbird while she goes away to college? "*You mean to tell me that no nice young man has interested you at* Hampton?! *Get a* grip, *girl!*" my mother had told me during my years of dedication to Victor while he spent time in prison.

"I can't help but think about him every once in a while, Mom," I admitted to her.

"Mmm, hmm," she grunted. She knew that she couldn't say *too* much about it, because she had held on to my father after he walked out on us years ago, where many women would have filed for a divorce. So I guess I got my stand-by-your-man approach from her. Nevertheless, my mother was married to my father and had borne his only children. That's where the similarities stopped. Victor had his *own* family, and I had become an outsider.

"Anyway, is Jason around?" I asked my mom. There was no sense in lingering on about the past, and Victor and I were *definitely* in the past, because there was no getting back together for us. I was wishing on a miracle.

"Yeah, he's home, you want to talk to him?" my mother answered me concerning my brother.

I told her I did, and I had never talked to Jason as much as I *should* have. I felt bad about that. If I had a little sister, I *knew* that I would talk to her a lot more about the birds and the bees and stuff. But with boys . . . you know, it's different. You want to see them sow their wild oats and everything, but at the same time, you want to protect them from the trifling 'hood rats.

"What's up, Tracy. How's Hollywood?" Jason asked me. He sounded pumped up about it like a lot of other people who knew I was trying my luck out there. They just couldn't wait to see my face in the bright lights so they could scream, "I know her! That's my girl!" They damn sure did it with Will Smith during that *Independence Day* movie.

I said, "It's just a job, Jason. It's nothing to really brag about." *Not* yet *anyway,* I thought to myself.

"You meet any stars out there?"

"Plenty of them, and they're *all* regular people," I told him. "*You* look better than a lot of the stars out there," I bragged. Jason *did* look good, too. He was a beautiful chocolate brown with big, bold eyes, long eyelashes, and nearly six foot tall at fifteen. My little brother was always handsome. He reminded me of everything that *I* wanted in a man, just like my daddy, tall, dark, handsome, and slightly rugged. Jason wasn't all that rugged though. He was more of a smart-aleck kid. I guess that was because of dealing with me. My parents also sent him to Engineering & Science, a smart kid's high school. As crazy as it seemed with my master's degree in English and everything, my brother wouldn't have been my type back in the day. I didn't go for smart guys too much. Or at least not *book* smarts.

"Would you like to hang out with your big sister if we have time this weekend?" I asked him. I figured it was the least that I could do to see where my brother's head was.

"When?"

"Tomorrow. We have a wedding rehearsal in the morning, but after that I'm free."

"What are we gonna do, go to a movie or something?"

That was the difference between a little brother and a little sister. I don't believe a little sister would have asked that question unless I was boring, but Jason wanted to know *What do I do with a girl if she's not my girl?* That was a teenage boy for you. Being with a girl had to have a definitive purpose for him.

I chuckled and said, "Yeah, we'll go to a movie then."

"To see what?"

"I don't know. Whatever."

"At what movie theater?"

I sighed, growing tired of his damn pettiness. "Look, would you cut it out already. I just want to hang out with you. Is it okay to do that? God!"

He laughed and said, "Aw'ight. What time are you gonna pick me up?"

"How 'bout I pick you up from school tomorrow?" I

was renting a car to get around in. I even thought about sneaking off to Atlantic City for some recreation after the wedding reception that Saturday night.

Jason sounded hesitant. "Pick me up from school?"

"Yes, pick you up from school. Why, you have something to do after school tomorrow?"

*Does he have any girls?* I thought to myself. *Maybe Jason is faster than what I think.*

He said, "Yeah, we have a basketball game at our school tomorrow. Our varsity only lost one game, to Gratz. We got this boy, Lynn Greer, who's *tough.* He drops like thirty points a game."

*A basketball game. That's more like it,* I thought with a smile.

"How come you don't play? You're tall enough aren't you?"

He laughed and said, "Yeah, but my game is not all that. E&S has some good players."

I couldn't believe it. My own brother sounded like a little punk.

"You mean to tell me that you're scared to go out for the team, at Engineering and *Science?*" I couldn't imagine smart guys being all that good in basketball. I said, "I could see if you went to Dobbins or West Philly." Those were the schools that were good in my day.

My brother said, "Dobbins and West Philly? They're both garbage. Our squad is fifteen and one. I'm telling you, they're good."

"What about Germantown, *my* old high school?" I asked him, smiling.

"*Germantown?*" Jason broke out laughing. "Aw, they're *big-time* garbage. We played them and blew them out by like thirty. I was at that game."

"Anyway, so what time is the game over?" I asked him. You start talking about sports with guys and they'll run their mouths about it all night long.

"You can pick me up around four-thirty, quarter to five. The game'll be over by then."

"Where is your school at again?"

"Nineteenth and Norris."

"Okay, I'll find it. And tell Mom and Dad I'll see them tomorrow night."

When I hung up with my brother I was still filled with energy. I didn't feel like talking to Raheema though, because I didn't want to think about her wedding. On top of that, I was thinking about Victor again and I had to block those thoughts out.

To settle some of my energy, I took a cab and snuck out to South Street to grab a bite to eat at a restaurant, and boy was it cold outside. The California weather never slipped below freezing in January like Philadelphia's did. I wasn't really prepared for the cold climate back home.

"Are you cold?" the Italian host asked me as soon I stepped inside of the restaurant.

I said, "Yeah, so find me a warm spot."

He smiled. "I think I can do that. Are you dining alone?"

"Unfortunately," I answered.

He found me a seat close by the bar that was indeed warm.

"Is this spot warm enough for you?"

"Yeah," I told him. "Thanks."

I sat down and started looking over the Italian food on the menu. It was rather dark in the restaurant, so I had to pull the menu right up to my eyes to see it. I spread it out in front of the candle that sat on the table in front of me and squinted at each entree.

"You see anything you might want on that menu?" another voice asked me. I couldn't see who it was with the menu in front of my face, but the voice sounded familiar.

I said, "Maybe I do, maybe I don't. Would you like to recommend anything?"

I held the menu there between us.

He said, "For dessert, I would recommend the chocolate mousse."

I smiled, and my heart started racing just like it did for him when I was a young girl.

"What if it's off-limits now?" I asked. "I thought I couldn't have that anymore."

He laughed. "You never know unless you ask for it."

I couldn't take it anymore. I pulled that damn menu down from my eyes and stared Victor right into his sexy-ass face. Had I set myself up that night by thinking about him or *what?!* Be careful what you wish for, right?!

Victor and I just stared at each other, with him smiling, and me sweating with fear and nothing to say. A lot of guys were dying their hair and beards jet-black in Philly to look extra sexy like Barry White or Gerald Levert, but Victor didn't need to. His hair was jet-black and sexy naturally, like all of the rest of him.

I just sat there and asked him, "Why? Why did you do that to me? I wanted to *wait* for you."

He knew damn well what I was talking about, and I had never been more serious in my life.

He just shook his head and grinned at me. His hair was cut low enough to show off the perfect mold of his head, and high enough for the small dark curls on top to blend into the waves on the side and down into a perfect Philly fade that connected to his dark beard and goatee. He was wearing all tan, lighter than beige, and I just wanted to reach out across the table and grab him like a damn groupie backstage.

I was so fucking weak for this man, but how could I *not* be attracted to him? Victor had always been extraconfident, bold, sexy, and flyy. He was all-athletic, he could fight, and he was respected by all of his peers. He just had that street flavor that all of the girls wanted, and all of the guys admired. Victor was the shit, a black *god* of a man, and he *knew it!* He needed his own onyx statue somewhere, and since I always wanted to be with the best, I wanted to be with him. The fact that I could never quite have him made me sweat him even more. He would forever be my black butterfly who flew away from my eager love net.

"Answer me," I told him. "Why did you play me like that and go to someone else? I thought that I was the one." I wanted an answer once and for all.

He looked at me for another minute before he opened his mouth. It seemed like a hour.

He said, "You had college to go to. I couldn't come between that. I had to let you go."

"What do you mean, you *'had to let me go'*? I didn't let *you* go."

He shook his head again. "It just wasn't right. You know that. I was writing you like that because I was in jail. Your mind starts playing tricks on you in that place."

"So are you saying that you really didn't care about me like that?" I was *praying* that he wouldn't tell me that. I didn't care if he was married with two sons or not, I just wanted him to tell me that he cared anyway.

He said, "I cared enough about you to let you go. *That's* how much I cared."

I shook my head and said, "That's bullshit! If you *really* cared like that, you would have *kept* me."

"Yeah, kept you away from doing what you needed to do."

"Well, what if I *needed* to be with you?" I asked him. I was saying anything at that point just to keep the heat of the conversation going. You know how it is, you don't want the fire to cool off and blow away, so you add the kerosene.

He stared at me in deep thought. "You were supposed to be doing what you're doing right now, and I was supposed to be doing what *I'm* doing. It was our destiny to be apart," he said.

I was running out of breath. I said, "Victor, don't talk that Muslim stuff to me right now. I don't need that right now."

"This has nothing to do with—"

"Yes it does," I said, cutting him off. "You took the easy way out and got this girl pregnant so you wouldn't have to face *me*."

"Face you for what, to be sucked back into that nonsense? Do you remember how we met, Tracy? Do you remember how I treated you? Is that what you want to remember when you talk to your children? Come on, now. Think about it. We couldn't do that. It was all a fantasy."

"It could have been real," I told him. I didn't know what else to say.

He said, "Yeah, real dumb."

My waiter came. "Are you ready to order?" He looked at me and then to Victor.

"I'm already at a table," Victor told him.

I said, "I'll need a few more minutes, but I'll start off with a house salad and some more water," because Victor was making me thirsty.

When my waiter walked away, Victor said, "I have to get back to my table. I'm down here on a business meeting."

I looked around the restaurant to see where he was sitting.

"What kind of business?" I asked.

"Real estate and storefront property. I own a health food store now on Wayne Avenue. I'm looking to buy a few more stores and a couple of apartments to rent out to college students in North Philly."

Victor was never an unintelligent man, and jail didn't seem to slow down his mind at all. If anything, it had only straightened his mind out for him, and made him see more clearly, which was *not* the case for *most* brothers who went in. That just made me want him more. I would give up everything for him, which was crazy, crazy, infatuated love.

"So how's your wife?" I asked him. Was he still happily married to her? I looked toward his ring finger but missed it when he backed away.

He smiled and never answered me. "I'll see you around," he said.

"See me around where?" I was desperate to stay in touch with him somehow.

He said, "I guess on the big screen, right? I hear you're out in Hollywood now."

"Who told you that?"

"People know you, and I know people," he said and walked away.

I had lost my appetite. Well, not really, I just couldn't concentrate on food, but I was still hungry for it. I just wanted to eat it with Victor still in front of me.

I got up to use the restroom and to spy on him to see where he was sitting and who he was sitting with. I spotted him by the window with an older black man in a dark gray suit. I guess they were able to see me when I first walked in.

All I know was that I wouldn't be able to sleep that night until I found a way to get back in touch with him.

I knew that Victor saw me going to the restroom, but he ignored me while talking to this gray-suit-wearing man as if there was no tomorrow.

I slipped inside the restroom and went straight to the mirror to brainstorm.

*Okay, now what do I say?* I thought. *Do I approach him while he's still talking to this man? What kind of business meeting do you discuss at ten o'clock at night anyway? Does this man know that he has a wife and kids? Of course he does.*

I was full of questions and no real answers.

"Can I speak to you for a minute?" I asked the mirror in a calm businesslike tone. I nodded. "Yeah, that's good," I told myself. "Now I just have to go out there and do it."

I stood there in the mirror and took a couple of deep breaths like yoga or something.

"Well, here goes nothing. Or is it *everything?*" I told myself.

I walked out from the bathroom and over in their direction, only to find two empty seats and dirty dishes at their table.

*No, no, NO! I won't be able to* sleep *tonight!* I pouted to myself. *DAMN! I did* not *need this shit right now!*

I was so weak that I felt like running out in the cold like a lunatic, either that or breaking down and crying. Instead, I composed myself and walked back to my table, a defeated soul of cold, unstirred soup.

The waiter was back with my salad and water. I felt like sending him away again.

He said, "A Mr. Q. told me to give you his card."

I looked and took the light green business card from my waiter's hand. It read "Mr. Q.'s Healthy Treats." It had the name Qadeer Muhammad with an address and a phone number printed at the bottom. I flipped it to the back to see if he had written me a message, but he hadn't. I felt better with the card though. At least I could eat and sleep that night, but what would I do next? Would I hunt him down at his store? For what, so he could embarrass me by showing me his ring and his two sons? I could really make myself look like a fool. I had to fight off the impulse, I just didn't know how. All I could think of for the rest of the night was Victor Hinson giving me another one of his *personal* "treats" in my hotel room at the Four Seasons. However, would that be "healthy" for me? Or would it be more like a poison?

**$  $  $**

Raheema never looked more beautiful or happier in her life than at the wedding rehearsal at church that Friday morning. She was six months pregnant, but she didn't show it much. People call that a boy. Her husband-to-be, Ernest Neumann, was indeed handsome, penny brown with a rounded head and a perfect dimpled smile. He seemed self-assured and happy about marrying my girl.

Raheema's bridesmaids were all of her college friends. I told them plenty of stories about her to keep the mood light.

"So, Raheema was always the studious type?" they asked me.

"No question about it. I thought she would *never* get married unless it was to the books. Now she goes ahead and beats me to the altar, *and* with a baby."

"Would you stop talking about the baby. Everybody doesn't know," Raheema said.

I figured she had to be joking with that. I frowned at her. I said, "Girl, you may not be as big as a cow right now, but you *do* show. So don't even believe that lie that Ernest told you."

"What did *I* do?" Ernest called out, overhearing his name.

"You knocked up my girl, *that's* what you did," I fired back at him.

Everyone laughed, and I felt good while standing right in the middle of things and instigating. I had a few exciting tricks up my sleeve that included seeing Mr. You-Know-Who. I decided that you only live once, so regardless of whether I was embarrassed or not, I wanted to follow my impulse, as long as it didn't kill me. Having another talk with Victor would not kill me. What that talk could lead to, however, was another story.

Raheema's older sister Mercedes showed up before we were finished with the rehearsal, but Raheema didn't seem to have too many words for her. I found my way over to Mercedes just to say hi. She had been through a lot of changes in her life, but she was still my girl.

She said, "How you doin', Tracy? I hear you out in Hollywood now. Have you had any luck out there yet?" Whenever Mercedes asked you something, it always seemed like a loaded question with ulterior motives involved. She thought way too fast to have a normal conversation.

"A little something came my way," I answered her. I asked her on the down low, "How come *you're* not in the wedding?" I didn't want to embarrass Mercedes or make a scene by being too loud about it, but I *did* want to know.

Mercedes grunted, tossed her head back, and laughed. She said, "Shit, Tracy, I wasn't paying no damn hundred and fifty dollars for some African dress that I wasn't going to wear again. To hell with that."

"Watch your mouth in this church, girl," I reminded her.

She looked up toward the brown Jesus with long woolly hair at the front of the church and said, "Forgive me, Lord." She looked again with large eyes. "Damn, when did Jesus turn black? This must be one of them *radical* churches."

I just shook my head at her. Raheema pulled me aside. "What did Mercedes say to you?" she whispered.

"Oh, I just asked her why wasn't she in the wedding."

"She said something about the dresses, right?"

I smiled. "She said she wasn't paying a hundred and fifty dollars for some African dress that she would never wear again." Actually, most bridesmaid dresses were disposable from what I knew, just like with prom dresses. Unless you were old-fashioned and into saving and recycling them.

Raheema sighed and said, "She can be so daggone *petty* sometimes. I would do it for *her* in a heartbeat. This is a once-in-a-lifetime occasion."

I put my hand on Raheema's shoulder and said, "Don't let it get to you, girl. We both know how Mercedes can get sometimes."

While I held my hand on her shoulder, I noticed that Raheema's hair was trimmed into a perfect V at the back of her neck, with big attractive waves that flowed on top. *Damn* my girl looked good in her natural! She even had *me* tempted to try it, but on second thought, my hair was never quite as flowing as Raheema's and Mercedes', I just had the fancy eyes, so I chose to keep *my* hair permed.

Before I stepped out of the door and headed on my way,

my girl's husband-to-be walked over and shook my hand.

"Well, it's good to finally meet the woman behind the book," he said with a knowing smile.

I was tempted to tell him I wasn't that little fast girl anymore, but like Kendra and Yolanda had told me out in Cali, I had to stop sweating it and go on with my life. After all, I *did* agree to publish my life story in a book, so I damn sure couldn't keep complaining about it.

Raheema asked me if I would hang out with her and her bridesmaids later on that night. I didn't make her any promises though. I wanted to make plans of my own.

I took a quick taxi ride to pick up my rental car from downtown, and bought a cheese steak and fries for lunch. By the time I had stuffed my face, it was slightly after four o'clock, so I left to pick up my brother from the basketball game at his school. I figured that finding 19th and Norris Streets would be simple. Maybe if I had remembered to pay attention to the street signs like my girl Kendra had told me, it would have been.

Well, I started on my way, driving through the ruggedness of North Philadelphia, and I kept running into one-way streets, construction, and slow traffic. It seemed like everything that could possibly slow me down and make me late to pick up my brother was happening to me. I got completely turned around and was frustrated. I finally stopped and asked for directions, and this talkative fool that I asked sent me the wrong damn way. I only found that out when I asked for more directions at a quarter to five. When I finally made it to Engineering & Science High School (after five o'clock), I noticed that I had driven right past the school earlier.

"*This* is a high school?" I asked myself out loud. It looked more like a middle school to me. It didn't look as if the building could hold more than five hundred students.

Jason was long gone. I would have to catch up to him at home, and with that being the case, it gave me a perfect opportunity to stop off on Wayne Avenue to investigate Victor's health food store. My heart started racing like a young girl's again to even think about it. I totally forgot about the rush-hour traffic I would have to fight through after five o'clock. So by the time I arrived in Germantown, my energy was all burned out. Nevertheless, I parked the car on Wayne, and went ahead and walked inside of Victor's health food store.

It was a clean place compared to the other stores on that block, and the fresh paint job was all white with green trim and a shiny black tile floor.

"Can I help you with something, sister?" a smooth-looking brother wearing a white headpiece asked me from behind the glass counter.

I don't think they were Nation of Islam Muslims, but regular followers of Islam.

I said, "Let me look around and see what I want first."

"Okay, take your time, sister."

I'll be honest with you: health food never looked too good to me. It didn't have enough color to it. Everything looked brown, green, or white, so the only thing I felt safe with was the vegetable platters. They needed to make health food *look* healthier. Or maybe I was too American-ized with the brainwashing of artificial colors and flavoring, but who was *I* fooling. I was not there for food anyway, I was there for a man.

I stopped the bullshit and just went for broke. "Is Qadeer Muhammad around?"

"Oh, yeah, he's in the back." The brother stopped, stared, snapped his fingers and pointed at me. "I *knew* you looked familiar. You're the one in the book, right? *Flyy Girl.*"

It seemed like all of Philadelphia knew my face. It *was* my hometown, but it wasn't as if I was famous. *Yet.*

"Yeah, that's me," I told him.

He stared at me and smiled.

I said, "And *I've* made changes in *my* life just like the brother *Qadeer* has made changes in his."

The brother nodded to me. "I understand, sister. We all have to take those dark paths before we see the light."

*Okay, well, stop fucking staring at me like you want something and go get your damn boss!* I thought to myself. Muslim or not, that brother was as human and imperfect as the rest of us. I could tell where his mind was, right inside of my damn panties!

"All right, I'll go get the brother," he said, leaving the counter area.

"Thank you," I told him.

He reappeared shortly after. "He'll be right out to see you."

For a second, it all seemed unreal. Victor Hinson, a Muslim with a health food store, the same Victor who drank, smoked, got high, and screwed every pretty girl in the neighborhood who looked at him too hard. It was unbelievable! I had to look away to stop myself from laughing.

"How are you doing today, sister?" Mr. Qadeer Muhammad addressed me.

I turned to face him and looked again for his ring. I found it on his left hand, as plain as day, big, gold, and shiny. He was dressed as casually as any other brother in jeans and a sweater. He didn't even look like a Muslim.

"I'm doing fine. I just stopped in to see what your place looks like," I answered.

Before I could say another word, a little hand pushed me aside.

"Dad-dee?"

"Say excuse me. What did I tell you about pushing through people?" Victor told his son sternly.

I looked at the boy to see if he had his father's looks, and I'll be damned if he didn't! He was a shade or two lighter, but he definitely had the looks, and I was jealous as hell! He could have been *my* son.

"Excuse me," he looked up at me and said. I think he was five years old.

"That's okay," I told him, smiling.

Low and behold, in walked the wife with the second son, looking like twins. They were both walnut brown and small. The second son looked up and smiled, and it lit up the damn room. I was so, so weak, hating *all* of them for stealing *my* family!

Victor, *or* Qadeer, I guess I should say, introduced us right there on the spot.

"Malika, I guess it's time for you two to finally meet each other. This is Tracy Ellison."

His wife nodded her head and extended her small hand to me. She must have been around five foot three, and was very dignified and calm.

She said, "I'm pleased to finally meet you, sister."

I took her hand and was at a loss for words.

"I, ah . . . same here. I'm pleased to meet you."

I wasn't pleased at all! She took my damned husband! Qadeer said, "Malika, give me a minute, okay."

She looked at him and nodded before gathering her sons with authority. "Let's go."

I was just about ready to fall down and die, but Qadeer led me out of his store and into the cold before I had a chance to.

"So, how long are you back in town?" he asked me.

I was daydreaming about rewinding the last twenty minutes of my life and never walking into his store and asking to see him.

"Hunh?" I mumbled.

"How long are you in town?" he asked me again.

"Until Sunday."

He nodded. "You want to talk to me, don't you?"

I looked at him to read his eyes. They were steady and serious.

"What do you mean?" I asked him.

"I mean, we could sit down and talk and clear the air between us. That's what you want, right?"

I was numb, and freezing, but his words were keeping me warm. He would still see me.

"Remember Raheema, my next-door neighbor and Mercedes' little sister? She's getting married tomorrow near downtown," I told him.

He nodded again. "Oh yeah? Well, that's a beautiful thing."

I ignored his comment and said, "We're all staying at the Four Seasons."

"Is that where you want to talk?"

I read his eyes again.

"Ah, we don't have to," I mumbled, "because I don't want any disturbances."

He smiled and said, "I agree with that. It should be just us and our words."

"Can you meet me at the Doubletree on South Broad Street then?"

I could *not* believe what I was saying! *Or* what *he* was saying, right out in front of his store with his wife and kids inside. I was becoming weak again, and the man was married.

"Ten o'clock," he told me.

I finally stopped the craziness and asked, "What about your wife? What will *she* say about this?"

He said, "Tracy, as you mentioned yourself, we have some unfinished business to take care of, right? My wife knows this. It's not a secret. You wrote a book about us."

I smiled. "Yeah, I keep forgetting about that, but other people keep reminding me of it."

He ignored me and said, "Okay, so ten o'clock at the Doubletree."

I was still unsure about it. "Are you serious?" I asked him, glancing inside of his store and feeling like a thief.

"Ten o'clock," he told me. "I'll see you then."

He walked back inside of his store and left me standing there in the cold. I hustled back to my rental car to drive away.

"Okay, so now I have to get a room at the Doubletree," I told myself. I thought, *But what if that's too much? He just wants to talk it all out, so what the hell am I thinking?* In all actuality, I wanted to *sex* it all out. I mean, God, the man hadn't touched me at all in ten years. My body was unfinished business too. I yearned for him. Deeply.

I arrived at my parents' house at six-thirty. The first thing I did was call the hotel to make a reservation.

"You're supposed to be taking Jason to the movies tonight?" my mother asked me in my old room.

Jason was getting himself ready for it, but most of the movies started at close to eight or after eight, which wouldn't give me enough time to get back down to the Doubletree to check in before ten o'clock.

I said, "Actually, I'm gonna have to take him tomorrow because something else came up."

Jason overheard me while out in the hallway. He asked, "What, you got a date with a guy now?"

I paused, feeling guilty about it. I said, "Raheema's getting all of her girls together tonight. She *does* have a wedding tomorrow. This is her last night of the single life."

"You knew that *before* you promised Jason a movie," my mother said, instigating.

Jason said, "Aw, Mom, don't make it sound like I have my feelings all hurt, because I don't. I don't have to go to the movies with her." He was wearing your typical baggy jeans and extra large sports gear with a ski jacket that teenagers of the nineties wore.

"Well, *I* don't think it's right," my mother sulked. "You don't go out of your way to make promises to somebody just to break them."

I sighed and said, "Mom, he'll *live*. Okay? If he would have waited around a little longer for me to pick him up from school today, we could have been at the movies right now."

"I *did* wait. I waited until like five o'clock, and by that time, it was time for me to go, because I'm not just gonna stand around in North Philly all day when I didn't know how long you were gonna be."

"Yeah, you did the right thing," my mother told him. "She should have left earlier to pick you up on time."

I said, "Well, if you feel that strongly about taking Jason to the movies, Mom, then why don't you and Dad take him?" She was really getting under my skin about it.

"Aw, naw, I'm not going out like that," Jason responded.

"That's a good idea. What's so wrong with that, Jason? We could use a good movie outing together."

I started laughing.

Jason said, "Naw, you don't go to the movies with your parents."

"Not as a high schooler you don't," my father walked out from his room and put in.

"Well, do you want to go to the movie with me?" my mother asked him.

I figured it was time for me to sneak away in the chaos. I could check into the Doubletree before eight and have plenty of time to gather some of my more intimate things from my room at the Four Seasons. So I took off from my parents' house to plan the rest of my night.

I made it back to the Four Seasons after getting my room key at the Doubletree, and packed up my sensual clothing to take with me. Even married, Victor did not fail to add excitement to my life, like he had done so many times while we were both still teenagers. No other man could compete with the excitement that he gave me. However, on the way out with my things, I was caught red-handed by Raheema's bridesmaids.

"Where are *you* going, Tracy?"

*Out to mind my own business,* I thought to myself.

I said, "I have to make a last-minute run up to my house in Germantown so my mother can help me sew a few things for tomorrow. I want to make sure I look just right."

"Talk about last-minute alterations," someone said. It was close to nine o'clock by then.

"It's not *that* late, and I don't want to have to do this in the morning," I commented. Imagine that. I was even *lying* to be with Victor again, and I definitely felt guilty about it, but so what? I couldn't stop myself. I was possessed by the dream again, the dream of Victor and I together forever.

Instead of going point for point with Raheema's girls, I just kept stepping. "Tell Raheema I'll see her later on."

Of course I felt bad about not hanging out with my

girl that night, but she *had* her man, and I wanted mine *back*.

I drove over to the Doubletree, parked my rental car in the garage, and went up to my room on the eleventh floor. I had all of the things I had planned for a rendezvous with Mike, but I hadn't even called him back, and I didn't care to.

*He'll get over it,* I told myself. *Life goes on.*

I was screwing over *everyone* just to be with Victor again. Nevertheless, I was jumping the gun. Qadeer only wanted to talk things through. He didn't want to jump my bones or come back to me or anything, I just *wished* that he did. So I kept my things inside of my bag to make sure I didn't embarrass myself. I guess I wanted him to go back to being plain old Victor from around the way, with no wife, no kids, and no Muslim name, if only for one night.

The minutes between nine and ten o'clock seemed like hours. I couldn't stop myself from looking at the clock. Every five minutes I looked. The closer it got to ten, the more anxious I became. At ten of, my crazy behind decided to slip on the electric blue, form-fitting dress that I planned to wear out on a date with Mike. Boy was I desperate for some loving from my old flame. I was just like those silly-behind women in those relationship novels, but I could not stop myself. Like I said, real life was stranger than fiction.

The telephone rang while I adjusted my dress in the mirror, and it shocked the hell out of me. That's just how on edge I was. I walked over and answered it after calming my nerves.

"Hello."

"Sorry, I'm late. I had to find a parking spot."

I looked at the clock. It was eight minutes after ten.

I said, "That's okay, as long as you're here." However, since he had searched for a parking spot instead of using the hotel's garage, I guess he didn't plan to stay long. Of course he didn't, he was married. My heart dropped an inch inside of my chest, weighing low with that final reality. Qadeer only wanted to talk.

I gave him my room number and thought of changing back into something more casual. What difference would it all make?

When he arrived and tapped on the door, I took one last deep breath, while still wearing my sexy blue dress, and let him in. He was wearing the same sweater and blue jeans that I saw him in a few hours earlier. Why should he have changed when he only wanted to talk?

Since it was a last-minute reservation, I had a double occupancy with twin beds instead of a king-size. I walked over and sat down on the bed closest to the window.

He walked in, looked around, and said, "Nice room." He sat on the bed opposite mine in front of me.

I sighed, feeling useless. "Well, where do we start?" I asked. I had all kinds of things running through my mind, and I was a grown-ass woman so I could think whatever the hell I wanted to think!

He looked at me and smiled before ignoring my question.

"That's a nice dress that you're wearing," he said.

"Thank you," I responded. Not that his compliment meant anything.

"That dress could turn on many men."

I stopped and asked, "Does it turn *you* on?"

He said, "Of course it does. That's what you wanted to do, right, turn me on tonight?"

He made me sound like a flirt, but I *was* flirting. How could I deny it? I wanted to do much more than that. After all, he was my man *first, and* he was my first love. I considered his wife secondary. *She* was the thief. Or at least that was what I was willing to tell myself if push came to shove, and I definitely wanted him to push inside of me.

So I answered, "Yes. I *do* want to turn you on."

He nodded, and I paid him my full attention. What would he ask me next?

"You want to make love to me?"

That was my Victor all right. He was straight to the point and confident about it, with no shame to his game. I didn't have any shame in *mine* either.

"Yes I do. Badly."

He looked at me and smiled again. Was he bullshitting, or was he serious? The Victor that *I* knew was not a bull-shit artist. Was Qadeer?

"We can't make love with our clothes on," he said to me.

I looked and read his eyes again, those beautiful dark and steady things that saw so much of so many women.

"Are we really making love at all?" I asked him. I didn't know if I wanted all of the man, or just the sex. I just wanted *something*, something real again, to feel his flesh against mine, and to dig my fingers into him. The rest would come after the satisfaction of the moment. I wanted the moment first. I couldn't even think about the future until the moment had been taken.

"I could no longer touch a woman that I didn't love, Tracy," he told me.

That caught me off guard.

"Are you saying that you love me then?" My heart was

skipping like a happy horse in soft grass. Maybe we *could* have a future together again. I didn't even think about how. I just figured that true love would find a way.

Victor looked into my eyes and said, "Of course I do. But I also love my wife and my sons. Can you understand that?"

How could I not? I nodded to him. "Yeah, I understand." It was just between us, and for the moment we were silent.

"So, you would still make love to me then?" I asked him. He had asked *me* that question, and I was still confused about it. What exactly were we saying to each other? What were we about to do with each other? It was all a crazy predicament.

He said, "Yes, if that's what you want."

"What do *you* want?" I had to know what was on his mind.

"Does it really matter what *I* want? This is *your* hotel room."

"So, what are you saying?"

"I'm saying that this is all on you."

He was still Victor Hinson all right. Mind control. He made it seem as if I was making my own deal with the devil. Was I? . . . Honestly, I was, but that didn't mean I wanted to be *reminded* of that.

"If you love me like you *say* you do, then *you* would want the same thing that *I* want," I rationalized. I was beginning to get defensive.

Victor grinned in response. He said, "That doesn't make it right."

"How could it be *right* at all, Victor? You're married," I snapped at him.

"And you met my wife."

His point was well taken. *I* would be at fault just as much as *he* would.

"So, what do we do then?" I asked, starting back from point A. I really wanted to jump on him, kiss him hard on the lips, and tell him to do me anyway, if just for old-times' sake, so that I could move on with a new lasting memory of him, and of *us* together.

I guess he could still read my mind because he began to smile with those moon white teeth of his.

"Would you be able to live with yourself, Tracy?"

He was teasing me.

"Would *you* be able to live with *yourself*?" I asked him back.

He said, "No question."

"You really don't have any shame about it then."

"Shame about what, making love to a sister who I love?"

"Well, how come I'm not *Mrs.* Muhammad then?" I asked him.

"That's not your world, Tracy. It never *could* be. You know that as well as I do."

He was telling me the truth. I couldn't be a Muslim woman. No way in the world! What more could I say?

"So, do we take our clothes off now?" I asked him. I wanted to see if he would back down from it.

To my surprise, he stood up from the bed and pulled his T-shirt from his pants and began to undo his belt buckle. He pulled his sweater and T-shirt off, dropped his pants to the floor, and started undoing his shoes. When he was done, he stood before me black and naked, and cut like a strong pharaoh.

*Oh my God!* I was ready to faint I wanted him so badly! I slipped out of that dress and my bra and panties faster than a hurricane to join him in nakedness and get on with the boning.

I walked over to him expecting him to push me away. I expected the dream to just stop right in the middle of it, but it didn't. When I tasted his lips and his tongue for the first time in too many damn years, I could already feel the readiness to my private parts as I reached to caress his.

"I missed you so much," I whispered to him. Was I talking to Victor or to his thing? I wasn't so sure.

Victor didn't respond to me. His tongue wet my neck and tickled down to my shoulder. I wanted to feel him inside of me yesterday. Last week. Last year. *Five* years ago! I couldn't wait anymore!

"Do you have any protection?" I asked him.

"No."

I had my own, so I broke away momentarily to go and get it from my bag. It was supposed to be for Mike, just in case he forgot *his* protection or brought some that I didn't like, but when I brought the condoms to Victor, he pushed them away.

"We don't need those," he told me.

I said, "Yes we do," and I meant it. It was my policy as a mature, single woman. No condoms, no sex. Period!

Victor said, "If you really want this like you *think* you do, then you wouldn't *use* protection. You would want to feel everything."

I stared at him for a second to see if he was serious, and he was.

I shook my head and grunted, "Unt unh, that ain't gon' work."

After I said that, he moved toward his clothes on the floor.

"What are you doing?" I asked him, panicking. I was as wet as the ocean.

"I'm protecting us."

I said, "Wait a minute." I was so damn *weak*! I couldn't get *that* close and let him walk away from me again.

He paused with his purple silk boxers in hand. His black behind was shining from his shapely curvature, and I wanted so badly to hold him there while he thrust into my velvet. I could halfway feel it already.

I asked him, "What about your wife? Isn't that, you know . . . kind of foul? I mean, it *all* is really, but going without a condom, that just seems . . . nasty. And then you go back home to your wife and . . ." I couldn't even imagine it. It made me feel queasy.

He smiled. "You don't want me to take anything home to my wife and kids. That's honorable. So why do this in the first place then?"

He had another good point, but I still wanted it. I wanted *him*. I wanted *us*.

I said, "Could you stop playing the head games with me, please. I'm serious." I was whining like a baby. *Damn* I hated him! He was the only man in my *life* who made me whine like that.

He said, "Tracy, this is all *your* head game. You wanted me here, now you deal with it."

I walked over and grabbed onto his waist, afraid to let him go and put his clothes back on. I leaned my head against his chest. "You'll take it out then?" I asked him. I was even willing to break my own rules for him. That's how weak I was.

He said, "Maybe I will, maybe I won't."

I leaned away from him and said, "WHAT?" He couldn't have been serious, but when I searched his eyes again, they remained steady and unnerved. He *meant* that shit!

I broke away from him and said, "That's crazy! What if

I get pregnant? Do you know how ridiculous we would look?"

"That's the price you pay for love," he told me. "Do you love me that much, to look ridiculous with me?"

I shook my head violently. "No. I don't love *no man* that much. Not even my *father.* And if *you* really loved *me,* you wouldn't ask me to *do* no crazy shit like that."

He looked at me and said, "Tracy, I *do* love you. That's why this had to happen this way, because love can't always be bent and twisted out of shape like so many people do with it. That's cheating everyone. So if you *really* want this to happen, then you either act crazy with it, or you grow up and let it go, like I did with you."

"Oh, yeah, that's easy for *you* to say, *you* had somebody else to run to!" I shouted. "*You* wrote those fucking letters from jail talking all that shit, *I* didn't! And I was crazy enough back then to wait for your ass, but *you* weren't crazy enough to wait for me! So don't give me that shit now!"

He began to put his clothes on again.

"What are you doing?" I asked him a second time.

"I'm protecting us," he repeated.

"Oh, so in other words, you were *expecting* all of this to happen?"

Victor ignored me. He was calling my bluff.

I said, "Well, you know what? Don't put your clothes back on then. I want to *be* that crazy! Now you show me that *you* can be that crazy!" I dared him. "You're gonna come up in here and call *my* bluff, well let me see what *you're* willing to do!"

I grabbed his pants and pulled them back down like a lunatic. I was actually tearing up I was so damn angry.

"Come on then, *Qadeer.* Let's do it. Let's make a baby. Let's see how crazy *you* are."

By then, tears were running down my face like a faucet. I didn't even notice it until I felt how wet my neck was. I had waited so long for him just to be bullshitted, and my feelings were hurt.

Victor wiped away my tears with his thumbs and kissed my lips.

"Would you be my second wife?" he asked me. "We can meet with Malika and ask for her permission."

I looked at him and shouted, "WHAT?! HELL NO! *SHE* SHOULD BE THE SECOND WIFE IF ANYTHING! *I* WAS WITH YOU *FIRST!*"

He tried to cuddle me in his arms to calm me down, but I pushed him away from me.

"You got some god-damned nerve coming in here asking me something like that. How dare you?! HOW DARE YOU?!"

He started pulling up his pants again, and I didn't care anymore.

"*Leave* then!" I yelled at him with a shove. If it wasn't for the twin beds, he would have fallen flat on the floor.

He smiled at me and shook his head. It was all a damn game to him.

"I don't see what's so fuckin' funny, *Victor!*" I mocked him.

He finished getting dressed and looked at me with pity in his eyes.

He said, "This is why you're not *Mrs.* Muhammad. You think a sane man wants to go through drama like this? Think about it. I made the right decision, and now I'm going home."

"Well, *stay* your ass home next time, with your little *house mouse!* I don't need her damn *permission!*"

With that, he grabbed my arms before I started to whale on him.

I broke down and screamed, "I fucking hate you! I HATE YOU!" If I was really trifling, I would have spit in his face, but I wasn't, so I didn't, but I thought about it.

Victor held my arms right up until he grabbed the front door handle and slipped out of the room on me. When he was gone, I fell to pieces. I felt so hurt and foolish that it didn't make any sense. I cried and cried and curled up in the bed like a snail.

*He played me like a fool,* I thought to myself. *He knew everything I was gonna do, and he* proved *that I would do it.*

Once I realized his game plan, I broke down and cried some more. Victor was the sharpest man I ever knew. As smart as I *thought* I was, I couldn't do a damn thing with that man but love and hate him. I couldn't even call him a dog, because he was going back home to his wife without penetrating me. I sat up naked and alone in that hotel room and thought about it, coming up with a poem, "When the Sweet Turns Sour." I didn't even have my notepad with me, so I wrote it out on the hotel stationery. And every time I read it, I grew stronger.

As far as Raheema's wedding for the next day was concerned, she was my girl and all, but I was a damn zombie through the entire ceremony. I just couldn't wait to get back out to California and restart my life with full dedication to my new career. Thanks again to Victor, the inspiration for my first poem, "King Victorious," I came up with my first full television script for *Conditions of Mentality* called "The Seduction."

# Everlasting Friendship

*Is like the birds*
*who fly south for the winter*
*only to return each spring*
*and build new nests for their young.*

*Or the setting of the sun,*
*the rising of the moon,*
*and the heavy rains falling*
*to quench the thirst of new flowers.*

*We grow green with progress,*
*radiant in orange and red with passion,*
*blossoming in yellows*
*and then turn blue.*

*With the joy and pain*
*of finding, loving, hurting, and losing*
*humans who you care for,*
*AND who care for you.*

*But as the world turns*
*and the climate changes,*
*we stay down like gravity,*
*together, forever.*
*Friends.*

# April 2000

$$\$ \, \$$$
$$\$$$

Saturday morning, I sat up in my old, twin-size bed in my old room and daydreamed. I needed some peace and quiet time. I was exhausted from everything and thanking God for the weekend.

My agent had sent me three screenplays to look over, so I grabbed them and thumbed through them while I relaxed. To her credit, all three of them were different. She knew that I liked to look at different types of projects, and since I was a writer myself, I knew how to separate the quality scripts from the trash.

The first screenplay I read through was a love story, *Never Let Him Go:* a lovely wife does everything in her power to keep her flirtatious husband from cheating on her. They wanted me to play the lovely wife, but the script was rather boring and typical of a man-pleasing woman. It would be a bit too mundane after my breakout bitch role in *Led Astray. Never Let Him Go* also asked for plenty of hot sex scenes, which I wanted to shy away from. Sharon Stone may have started off with the seduction roles, but she damn sure didn't stay with that shit. I didn't plan on being typecast that way either, so I passed on it.

The second screenplay was a science fiction comedy, *Babes from Space:* a group of beautiful alien women seduce the men from a well-to-do suburban town until the women of the town strike back to reclaim their mates. The script was cute and I laughed through it, but I didn't have much of a role to play. They wanted me to play the lone black girl, and of course, I would match up with the only black man in the town. I figured it would do okay with teenagers at the box office and people who watched the television show *3rd Rock from the Sun,* but it was too juvenile for *my* taste. It was like some video girl script from MTV. They didn't really need actresses, they just needed pretty faces and attractive bodies, and the head alien was a blond chick. I didn't like that idea so much either. Blame it on my ego as a black woman, but I passed on that script too.

The third screenplay was an action-packed thriller called *Road Kill:* a female Special Units agent hunts down a gang of psycho killers who prey on pretty women on U.S. highways and roads. I liked that script immediately. I even liked the title; it sounded edgy and serious. I saw flashes of myself becoming the next Pam Grier, or even Angela Bassett in *Strange Days,* kicking ass for a change instead of just screaming, fucking, and looking pretty. I thought about Geena Davis in *The Long Kiss Goodnight* and Sigourney Weaver in her *Alien* movies. I could become a black woman James Bond and keep it going, but I didn't like the character's name. "Jill" sounded too plain to me, as if they wanted to downplay her fierceness with an average tag. It was also a white woman's role, but my girl had gotten her hands on the script and sent it to me, probably because she knew that I would like it and fight for it. I guess she had saved the best for last.

I looked at my East Coast clock, and it was only after ten, which meant that it was after seven in California, but I couldn't wait to discuss the script, so I jumped up, got the cordless phone, and called my girl at home.

"I was just about to use the phone, Tracy," my mother told me.

"Hold on, Mom, this is business."

I passed her the script to thumb through it herself.

Mom looked at it and said, "*Road Kill?* Hmm, sounds like another controversial movie. You'll have people scared to even drive."

My girl answered the phone and I jammed my excitement down her eardrum.

"What's up with this *Road Kill* movie? They haven't signed anyone for it yet? Did you tell them that I worked on the writing staff of *Conditions of Mentality* for cable? I know *exactly* how to play this role. This is right up my alley. Of course I would *change* that name though. I would be 'Alexis.' That gives the character more edge, don't you think?"

She just laughed, overwhelmed by my excitement for the role.

"I knew you would like that one," she said. She was barely awake, I could hear it in her voice, but not by the time *I* got through with her.

"So what do you think about our chances?" I asked her. "I don't want to get my hopes up for nothing."

She said, "The producer actually likes you."

I said, "But?" She was holding something back from me.

"The director is a pain in the ass, one of those real creative control freaks," she told me. "He wrote the script, and he'll be tough to convince. He wants a blonde."

I said, "Do I get a screen test at least?"

"I'm working on it."

"Well, who the hell do I need to talk to?" I was really desperate for it, and you know how I can get when I really want something.

My girl laughed and said, "Wow! You just read it, didn't you?"

"You know I did," I told her, laughing along with her.

"It's kind of like *La Femme Nikita* redone with a twist," she told me.

"I know, but it's much *smarter* than *Nikita*. And I think that with me in the lead role as Alexis, it would have more of a mass appeal to it, black, white, Latin, Asian; *everybody* would want to see it."

"That's what the producer is counting on. He says you tested very well with white men in *Led Astray*."

"Definitely!" I yelled. "They want me more than black men do."

We broke up laughing again.

"Well, what's their time schedule?" I asked. "Do I need to fly back out there for the screen test? Shit, I'll change my flight plans *today*."

She said, "No, you have time. They still haven't green-lighted the project yet, but I expect them to shortly, and we'll make sure that you're up at the front of the line."

"Fuck that!" I snapped. "I don't even want there to *be* a line! You tell that producer who's on our side that I'm willing to test *immediately*!"

My mother looked at me and frowned, responding to my tart language.

My girl said, "Oh, sure, I'll get right on it," playing her little servant-girl role again.

"Whatever," I told her. "This is a big opportunity and I just don't want it to slip away from me."

"All right, I'll get right on it for you today."

"Thank you. And if I need to fly back out there earlier than planned, then let me know."

I hung up the phone still pumped while my mother continued to thumb through the script.

"This girl is pretty tough, Tracy. You might need to lift some weights to tone up your arms and legs. She has a *mouth* on her too," my mother said with a smile. "You don't *need* any practice with that," she joked.

I smiled and said, "Yeah, but the director wants a blonde. This is just what I needed, a new challenge to get my blood working again. I was just about to get tired."

My mother shook her head and said, "Girl, you need to stop. You better learn to appreciate your slow-down moments. You can't keep running out here chasing these fire trucks to the fire. You're gonna need to learn how to go fishing every once in a while and just relax."

"Yeah, whatever, Mom. When have *you* ever been fishing? Maybe I'll slow down when I'm thirty-five."

My mother grunted and said, "*Forty-five* sounds more like it for *you*."

I said, "Well, like they say, the younger you are in spirit, the longer your life lasts."

My mother grinned and said, "There's breakfast downstairs if you want any."

"What did you cook?"

"Eggs, sausage, and pancakes, and I have some English muffins in the refrigerator if you like those. I don't eat those things myself, but your father seems to like them, so I buy them for him. That and the strawberry jelly." She grimaced and said, "That strawberry stuff is too darn sweet for me. I'll take grape jelly any day."

I smiled and headed downstairs to grab a bite to eat. My father was sitting on the living-room couch reading the newspaper.

"Good morning, Daddy."

He looked up and said, "Hey," and went right back to reading his paper.

I walked into the kitchen and grabbed some sausage. I couldn't eat cold eggs and pancakes. Sausage tasted better hot too, so I tossed a plate of everything into the microwave.

While I waited for the food to heat up, I watched the sunlight shine through the kitchen window and shed light on my mother's plants that hung near the window sill. I began to wonder what my girl Raheema's house looked like. She and Ernest had only moved into their new home in Plainfield a summer ago, and I had yet to see it. With a new energy boost from my next film possibility, I decided that I would take my girl up on her invitation for a visit, so I went and got my phone book and called her up.

"Hey, girl, you still want me up there this weekend? It's Tracy."

"Yeah, we're not doing anything. This is a nice weekend to visit. The sun is out and it's not too hot and not too cool."

"Can I spend the night?" I asked her.

"Yeah, we have a guest room."

"Are you sure you're not having any more kids? Because I don't want to wake up at night to use the bathroom and hear you and Ernest in there going at it," I joked.

Raheema laughed. "No comment," she said. "But we're *definitely* not planning to make any more kids this weekend. A boy and a girl are enough."

"Well, give me some good directions so I can get on my way then," I told her.

I got the directions, took a shower, got my things together for a one-night stay, and told my parents that I'd be back sometime on Sunday.

My mother smiled, looked at my father and then back to me, and said, "Good."

I said, "I wasn't stopping y'all from doing anything, Mom. You damn sure enjoyed Dad's new Infiniti," I hinted with a grin.

My father laughed as I headed for the door.

"You watch what you say to me, girl," Mom huffed at me as I walked out. "I'm not your little girlfriend, I'm your *mother*."

I got on my way to New Jersey in my father's Buick and listened to WDAS-FM, my parents' favorite oldies station. They played Anita Baker's "Angel" and took me all the way back to the eighties, when I was a young girl in love. I turned it up as loud as I could and grooved along with it, like I was still in a slow drag. They followed that up with René and Angela's "My First Love." After that they played Whitney Houston's "Saving All My Love." Boy, I was in *heaven* while I drove! I arrived at Raheema's nice, green area in Plainfield, New Jersey, and wanted to tell her all about those oldies, but first I had to comment on their house.

Raheema and Ernest Neumann lived in a perfect residential area of two-story, brick-built, single-family homes with private driveways, two-car garages, and elaborate walkways from the curb. Some of the houses even had outside sitting rooms for gardens and plants. I was envious all over again. I would trade in my empty house in Marina Del Rey, California, for a husband and family in Plainfield, New Jersey, in a heartbeat! As long as I could still earn my Hollywood paychecks.

I rang the doorbell and Raheema met me at the door with her daughter, Lauryn, named after the singer Lauryn Hill. Her son, Jordan, named after the basketball legend

Michael Jordan, was not far behind them. It was Ernest's idea to name them that way as a testament of African-American greatness in the era that they were born in. Whatever! What happened to letting your children amass their *own* greatness instead of following in someone *else's* footsteps?

"Hi, Lauryn. Hi, Jordan," I said to both of the kids. They seemed happy to see me. I guess Raheema talked about their "Aunt Tracy" a lot.

"You want to play with my Frisbee?" Jordan asked me. Lauryn nearly lunged into my arms from her mother.

"They love visitors," Raheema told me with a smile.

"I guess so, growing up in the suburbs," I joked.

I held Lauryn in my arms and checked her out. She had dimples like her father and was honey brown like me.

"Can you talk yet?" I asked her.

She nodded her head and smiled, but didn't say a word.

Jordan said, "She can say Mommy and Daddy and eat and potty."

"She can say potty?" I asked Raheema.

She nodded. "Yeah. I told you she's ready to start."

"You want to play catch with my Frisbee?" Jordan asked me again.

Raheema said, "Jordan, she has to bring her things in the house first. Okay?"

Jordan was slightly lighter than me, but not as light as Raheema. Their house was a melting pot like thousands of others in the black community, ranging from Ernest's walnut brown to Raheema's light cream. African America was just filled with beautiful "Flavors of Chocolate," another poem by yours truly.

Raheema and the kids walked me back out to the car so I could get my things.

"Where's Ernest?" I asked.

"On his telephone in the study. He should be out soon," Raheema answered.

"The study, hunh?" I asked her with a smile. "I guess that *this* family will spend a whole lot of time in the *study*, with two college professors as parents."

Raheema grinned. "And what's so wrong with that? That idea beats a family that spends a lot of their time in front of the television. That's why we only have *one*, and that's mainly for educational videos."

"Is that right?"

"Yes it is. We have a *reading* family here."

"I know you do, you bookworm," I cracked at her.

When we made it back inside, Ernest walked up and greeted me with pandemonium.

"Oh my God," he said, "we have a celebrity in the house! Honey go get the cameras! Let's get some pictures of her with our kids! This'll inspire *them* to be stars!"

I grinned it off. I said, "I thought that your children's *names* were already supposed to link them to stardom." I couldn't help it, I just had to say something about that.

Raheema looked at me and shook her head.

Ernest said, "If we have another girl, we're gonna name her Tracy."

That caught me off guard. I started cheesing.

"Raheema said that you were not having any more kids," I shot back at him.

"Oh yeah?"

Raheema looked at him and said, "Yeah. Don't let this *celebrity* get you into trouble with your wife."

Ernest just laughed it off. He was nothing like Raheema's father. He had a great sense of humor but he also knew when to cut the bullshit and respect his wife. They were a good couple. I admired that. Raheema chose well.

They gave me a tour of their four-bedroom house that had plenty of African-American art, wooden sculptures, and ornaments. Everything was earth-toned with wooden trim and hardwood floors. It looked as if they wanted their house to seem very classic, and it did seem that way, as if it was a century old.

I helped Raheema to cook a fish and vegetable dinner, and we all sat down at their pinewood dining table by six o'clock to eat. I bet they did everything regulated at their house, like clockwork.

We all held hands to pray, or at least I *thought* that was what we were about to do.

Ernest said, "We want to thank the Creator for giving us the spirit, the hope, and the strength to live each day with a mission for all of humanity, our family, and our dear friends."

"Hotep!" they all shouted, meaning peace. Even little Lauryn knew it.

I smiled. That was very interesting, and cute. I had turned Afrocentric for a second in my late teens, but outside some of my poetic inspiration, my African journey never lasted. It was no more than a phase, like my many other phases. Raheema and Ernest, however, had found a way to incorporate the culture into their daily lives and teach it to their children. I was impressed by that.

I asked, "Do you say the same thing every night?"

Raheema answered, "No, of course not."

"Do you always end it with Hotep?"

Ernest answered, "Yes, of course we do."

We all began to eat with Raheema feeding Lauryn ground-up baby food, until Jordan stood his fish on his plate and began to sing to it and make it dance.

"I'm just ah fiiissh. Yes, I'm only ah fiiissh . . ."

I dropped my fork and broke out laughing. He had the perfect cadence of School House Rock's "I'm Just a Bill."

Raheema and Ernest chuckled at it themselves before Raheema put a stop to it. "Okay, Jordan, stop showing off and eat your food. Would you like your daddy to help you cut the fish?"

Jordan looked and said, "No, Mom, you can't cut the fish. He just wants to be a law."

I had to stand up and walk away I laughed so hard. I choked on my food and my eyes started to run.

Ernest was laughing too, but Raheema only smiled at it. She was obviously not as tickled by it as we were.

"Eat your food, Jordan," she told him.

I enjoyed myself for the rest of the night, and by nine o'clock, Ernest was putting both of the kids to bed while Raheema and I sat alone inside of their peaceful living room.

"How old is Ernest again?" I asked her.

"Thirty-three."

"So he's *four* years older than us?"

"Five. He's turning thirty-four next month."

I nodded. "You two are great together. I'm really happy for you."

She smiled. "Thank you. And I'm happy for you."

I nodded and thanked her back, reminiscing on our younger days.

"Remember Bruce?" I asked her with a grin.

Raheema shook her head and smiled. "I knew you were gonna ask me that. I was just waiting for it."

I laughed. "I mean, he was a nice guy, you know. I wonder what he's up to now."

"Hopefully, *good* things," she commented.

I smiled back and asked, "So, was Ernest your first, you know, *real* boyfriend?"

Raheema shook her head again. She knew what I was getting at. Sex.

She said, "Tracy, I'm not like you. Okay? I don't *have* a *need* to express all of my personal business."

"Yeah, because you were always in *my* business," I told her.

"Well, you had a lot of *business* to be in."

"Come on, girl, tell me. Was he your first?"

She smiled and said, "Don't hold your breath. Tracy. So what did my sister want to talk to you about?" she asked, quickly changing the subject on me.

I said, "You know what she wanted. Money."

"How much?"

"Twelve thousand dollars to put down on a new house in Yeadon," I answered. "And she had the nerve to try and say that she *saved* half of it. I was thinking, 'She probably doesn't even have *two* thousand dollars saved.'"

"So what did you tell her?"

"I told her that I would think about it."

"Are you?"

"Hell no!"

We both laughed.

Raheema shook her head and said, "Mercedes still hasn't learned her lesson about using people."

"Ain't it the truth."

Raheema looked at me and frowned. "Oh, don't try to act like *you* were a saint."

"Raheema, I only had about *two* years of that."

"*Two years!* No, you need to try, *six* or *seven* years."

"Girl, I was *not* like that until your *sister* told me to do it."

"Yes you were. You were using boys all the way back in

elementary school. 'This is my *boyfriend*, y'all,'" she mocked me.

I chuckled at it. "Raheema, everybody does that."

"*I* didn't."

"Bruce."

"Okay, that was real brief," she admitted with a laugh. "But you took it all the way with him, *I* didn't. And I never asked him for anything."

I just smiled, still reminiscing. Ernest popped his head into the room and froze.

"Yup, it looks like girl talk in here. I'll just leave you two alone," he told us and headed back toward the study.

I smiled and said, "Look how far we've come, Raheema, two regular sisters from Philly?"

She smiled back at me. "Well, *I* may have been regular, but *you* sure were not."

I laughed and thought about my follow-up book, and a tell-all book for Raheema.

"You know what?" I asked her.

"What, Tracy?"

I said, "Have you ever thought about writing a book about *your* life? You could call it *The Good Girl.* Because I want to write a sequel about mine, and all I could say about you in *Flyy Girl* were just the things that I knew you and Mercedes were going through with your father. I think a lot of good girls would love to have a full story just about you."

Raheema laughed as if I had just told the funniest joke in the world.

"Are you kidding me? Who would want to read it, Tracy? America loves the drama, not the *good girls.* They want Jerry Springer, not Jan Brady."

"But I'm saying though, people *do* ask me about you."

She ignored me and asked, "So, you're thinking about writing a sequel?"

"Yeah."

"What, *Tracy Goes to Hollywood*?"

I frowned at her title and shook my head.

"No, girl, that sounds like a porno movie: *Debbie Does Dallas* or something. I don't know what I want to call it, but it *will* deal with me going to Hollywood. But I don't have the time to write it. I'm trying to break my way into a new film deal now."

"What's it called?"

I smiled again, imagining how she would respond to it. "*Road Kill*," I told her.

"*Road Kill?*"

Raheema turned up her nose like something reeked, and I broke out laughing.

"It's about this gang of psychos who snatch pretty women off of the highways. I play this Special Units agent named Alexis who goes after them with backup and whatnot."

Raheema said, "What in the world? You mean to tell me that they couldn't come up with something more *sane* than that?"

"Yeah, a bunch of sane, *boring* movies," I answered. "I want to do something wild and crazy. Those are the kind of movies that make you a star, not those *sane* movies. I want to go all out."

"Oh, you're gonna go *all out* all right," Raheema joked with me.

I laughed, and we talked and talked and talked about everything under the sun until we forgot about the time and ended up falling asleep on the couch together. That was me and my girl, just like old times, friends forever.

# Philly Girl

Yeah, that's me,
T-r-a-c-y,
and I USED to be
flyy,
but now I levitate
mentally.

You can't get
into me.
What you get is
NOT
what you see.

Roll your eyes
and cook your lies
if you want,
but you'll need ketchup
'cause I'll be
GONE in the wind.

Now let me be blunt.
Are you my lifetime FOE,
or can you be my friend?
Because where I come from
WE
DON'T
FRONT!

# March 1997

$$ $$

$

"T he Seduction" was about a sister who invites a mysterious and sexy brother into her life because of her yearnings for a special kind of love. This guy wines her, dines her, loves her like a god, and disappears from the face of the earth. My theme was that deep down inside, a lot of women want to be controlled by an uncontrollable man. It's almost as if we are looking for God in a man, but as we all know, God cannot be negotiated with, nor can these playboy men. So sure, we may talk about a sharing, caring, and equal relationship, but in our guts, if a man is not in control (like God), then he is not desirable to us.

I'm sorry for my betrayal, sisters, but I guess I wrote "The Seduction" in my state of depression with Victor, and of course, all of the males at *Conditions of Mentality* jumped up and down at the chance to produce it as my first full script for the show. However, they changed my original brown characters into your apple-pie white couple. At first I was teed off about it, but once I thought it over, I figured it was better to get my point across to America as a whole than to have my script stereotyped as just a black thing. As much as we may like to *think* that humans are humans, and we all go through the same kinds of things in life, white Americans like to throw covers over their minds whenever they see brown faces, because they are so damned used to seeing their *own* faces up on the silver screen. The more Hollywood continued to spoil them, the more they continued to ignore anything with brown faces in it, and that cause and effect became an unbreakable cycle. Nevertheless, I was happy as hell to see my first produced script, *and* be paid the big cheese for it.

Kendra called me up as soon as the show went off of the air. She had taped it, along with ten to twenty of my other friends and relatives that I had informed about my first script. I never told anyone where I got the inspiration to write it though.

"So how do you feel about it?" Kendra asked me. She wasn't excited or anything, just curious. That told me that we had a long conversation on the way.

I said, "It was directed well. They got everything right."

If Kendra wanted an argument over feminism, then I was going to let *her* start it. However, I admit that I *did* feel defensive about the script, especially after the show aired with my name on it.

Kendra asked, "You know why I haven't been out on many dates lately? I don't trust myself to choose the right men. I came right out here to California and got myself involved with some real losers, but you couldn't tell that they were losers from the outside."

I was pleasantly surprised. Kendra wasn't calling me to rant and rave about protecting the sisterhood, she was calling me up to discuss her own truths. I admired her for that, because some sisters let their egos go to their heads sometimes, as if they have never been heartbroken before.

I said, "Yeah, it would be easier for *all of us* if the losers walked around wearing signs around their necks that said 'I'm a loser, don't fuck with me!'"

Kendra laughed. She asked me, "Where did the inspiration come from? Because it seemed to come from the heart."

I paused. Did I really want to tell Kendra about my night in that hotel room with Victor? No, so I passed on it.

"It's a little bit of everything," I told her. "But the only reason they accepted the script is because the guys wanted to see it. They say it reminded them of a movie called *Thief of Hearts*?"

"It reminded *me* of a lot of these black relationship books," Kendra commented. "Except that it starred a white girl."

"Yeah, it reminded me of that too. But is life imitating art, or is art imitating life?"

Kendra didn't miss a beat. "Art is imitating life. No question."

"That's what's so sad about it," I said. "All of these damn broken-heart stories are real. We live them every day."

"Yeah, and now *I'm* afraid to create another one by choosing another *loser*," Kendra reiterated.

"So, what do we do, just say 'Fuck men!' period, and move on?" I asked her.

She chuckled and said, "Move on to what, your career? I've already done that. Does it make you feel better about things? No, it just messes up your groove for your next date, like a basketball player who hasn't played in a while. You're just rusty, but you still want to play."

"In that case, you make it sound like we're supposed to keep going through the garbage anyway," I responded.

She laughed again. "Are you *sure* you haven't been through something recently, because you seem very jaded right now. Usually you have a lot of optimistic energy about you."

"Oh, I still do, just not about guys," I told her. "I'm all

about my work now. I'm brainstorming for my next script as we speak."

"Oh yeah, you have any new ideas?"

"A few, but none of them are really developed yet. I mainly wanted to write something about the consequences of being a player. You know, like, a rubber pops, and the woman tells the man she has AIDS, and then she fakes her own death while he goes crazy thinking he's going to die. *That* would be fun," I said with a laugh.

"So, you all can write a bunch of crazy stuff on that show?"

"That's why it's called *Conditions of Mentality*," I told her. "At first I wasn't really interested, it was just a job, but now I like it. You can do a lot more with your imagination."

"I guess so," she said. "Well, you're on your way to stardom, Tracy. You have your first script produced, and you haven't even been out here for a year yet. I'm impressed!"

I smiled and said, "Thank you. You just have to be willing to work for it, and that's what I'm out here to do. Express myself."

"Well, go 'head, girl! You got *my* vote!" Kendra said excitedly.

When we hung up, I answered phone calls that night from Yolanda, Raheema, Mom, Mercedes, and my little brother Jason. They all called to congratulate me, even Richard Mack from the HFI crash course. We had stayed in touch off and on, but it was nothing continuous.

He said, "That was some good work. I liked it."

"Thank you, but I'm not finished yet. That was just a start," I told him.

He laughed. "Good, because I have a project that I'm working on right now that I might want to hire you for."

"Oh yeah." I was just listening. It could have been just a game, but listening didn't hurt anything.

"Well, I'll stay in touch with you and let you know once I know something definite, because I'm still working out all of the details with the studio and my agent."

I was tempted to ask him what studio he was working with, but I declined. I didn't want to show too much interest in case it was all bullshit. I still needed an agent to represent my own work. However, Yolanda was still in my camp as a good lawyer who knew the ropes, so at least I was safe.

I said, "Okay, well, stay in touch, and I'll see what's what when it all happens."

"You got it. And keep up the good work."

Later on in the week, I got a call from Juanita's man, Reginald. He caught me at home for a change, because I had been avoiding the guy. I was sitting in bed eating coffee ice cream of all things—Yolanda had turned me on to it—when he called me.

"I saw your work, Tracy. People are buzzing all over about it."

"Really? There are a hundred new shows a week. I didn't know that writers could get that popular," I told him.

He laughed and said, "Well, the insiders know who you are. You always have to keep your eyes on new talent."

"I bet you do a heck of a job at that," I said. I didn't really feel like talking to him. He represented what *all* women needed to get themselves the hell away from: the wrong kind of man.

I asked, "So what has Juanita been up to?" just for the hell of it.

He paused and said, "I think she went back to New York. I haven't seen her in a while."

*Yeah right,* I thought to myself.

"Look, if you need a mentor or anyone to take you around and introduce you to important people, just let me know," he told me.

I asked, "Are you a lawyer?"

"No."

"My mentor is," I told him, referring to Yolanda.

"Oh, so you have somebody already."

"How do you think I got *this* job?" I asked.

He chuckled. "Tim Waterman is the boss over there isn't he?"

"I didn't get the job *that* way," I snapped, irritated by his insinuation.

"What?" he responded to me, playing the innocent role.

I said, "You know what, you are a sad excuse for a brother. I just want you to know that." I had no time to bullshit with him, and my tolerance level was at zero. He had *Victor's* narrow ass to thank for that!

Reginald paused a long time. I think I got to him. I wanted to see how he would respond to it. He said, "You don't really know me to be saying things like that. I've helped out a lot of people in the business."

"It seems to me like you're more concerned with helping out yourself," I responded.

He said, "I don't know how people are in Philadelphia, but out here, you definitely want to make more *friends* than enemies."

"Oh, yeah? Well maybe you should learn to play by your own rules for a change. How many enemies do *you* have?"

That skinny-ass man was getting on my *last* nerve that night. He couldn't do a damn thing for me, not even lick my fucking toes!

He said, "Have it your way then," and hung up.

Three minutes later, he called me back.

He said, "You know what? You are really starting to irritate me. I'm trying to go out of my way to help *you* out, and you treat me as if I'm trying to harm you."

I said, "Look, what the hell do you want from me?"

"What do I *want* from you?"

"Yeah, what the hell do you want? I never asked for your help."

"Sister, don't even go there," he whined.

"Don't give me that *sister* shit, *brother!* All that is is a front. If you *acted* presentably, then I would *treat* you that way!" I told him.

"Why do you think I'm trying to hurt you so much?" he whined again. He sounded like a big punk.

I said, "Look, I was enjoying my night, sitting up in bed and eating ice cream. Okay? I don't need this shit. So don't call here no fuckin' more!"

It was *my* turn to hang up.

CLICK!

I went back to eating my ice cream and thought nothing of it.

# $ $ $

At the trailer that week, on the job for *Conditions,* we all had a visit from Tim.

"How's everybody loving the show so far?" he asked us. "*I'm* sure loving it."

The head writer, Joseph Keaton, mumbled something about a raise and laughed it off.

Tim looked at him and said, "That'll come, Joe, but right now we have to focus more on our consistency, and we did pretty well in our market share last week due to Tracy's first script."

I heard my name and froze. He was singling me out.

"Oh, thank you," I said.

"Yeah, it seems that we had a lot more *women* who tuned in for last week's show, *and* we didn't lose any men. You got any *more* scripts for us, Tracy?"

I froze again. I was supposed to be an *assistant* writer. I don't think the other writers took too kindly to me stepping on their toes with a superior script. Nevertheless, I was not planning on backing down from a challenge.

I said, "Not yet, but I'm working on it."

Joseph Keaton shot an ugly look at me that I caught before he could smile it off. I knew what he was thinking: my scripts would turn *Conditions* into a girl show.

Tim said, "Well, these next couple of months are very important to see if we'll be picked up for next year. Everything looks promising so far, but let's not lose our edge on anything."

"That's right. Let's keep it edgy and fresh," Joe commented. It sounded to me as if he was sending a clear message to stay away from "girl" scripts, but I didn't plan to write any. As I had already informed Kendra, I wanted my next script to be more from the male perspective.

It's funny how things can change when other people feel that you're moving up in the world. Elizabeth Finley, one of only two women staff writers (outside of myself and another assistant) on the show, began to ask me things that she didn't seem to care about before.

"Hey, Tracy, so what's it like in Philadelphia? Is it pretty rough?"

Liz was a flaming redheaded California girl. I guess she got into the science fiction thing just to take on something new, because she didn't appear to be too successful in her scripts. They were manly enough, but far-out. I think most people just didn't get it. Maybe Liz was ahead of her time.

I thought about my book and answered, "It's only as rough as you make it. If you hang around with the wrong crowds, it can be *very* rough, just like it is in different parts of California."

She nodded, in deep thought about it. She asked me if I had ever been to the Watts housing projects in South Central Los Angeles.

"For what?" I asked her.

She shrugged and said, "I don't know, just to visit I guess."

*Why, because I'm BLACK?!* I wanted to yell at her. I kept my cool instead.

I shook my head and said, "I have no reason to go over there."

"Would you want to go out there with me? You know, maybe we could come up with some script ideas together."

I looked at her and smiled, venomously. "Like a safari trip to the 'hood, hunh?" I was being sarcastic, but Liz didn't even get it.

She smiled and said, "Yeah, exactly."

I said, "Would we take a couple of wide-lens cameras too?" *This white chick is crazy!* I thought to myself.

Liz finally stopped herself and frowned at the idea. "Well, I don't know about that. I mean, do you think that we could get away with cameras? You know, I don't think they would like us taking their pictures."

"Oh, no, they wouldn't mind. We could just line them up with their blue and red scarves on their heads and start snapping away. You know, because gang members love to take pictures."

Liz looked at me and caught on to my sarcastic drift.

"You're wild," she told me. "But I'm seriously thinking about going out there."

"I know you are, but I'm not the person to take you there," I told her. I could see it in her eyes. She was excited even to mention the name Watts. I wasn't. I had seen all of that hard life shit before. It wasn't any news to me.

After Liz was finished with me, Joe walked over to add his two cents for the day.

"So, are you working on any new scripts for real, or you just didn't want Tim to think that you were done for the year."

He was insulting me, and being rather blunt about it.

I said, "Well, I signed on to *Conditions* as an assistant because I wanted to break into the writing game, not because I wanted to help others to write *their* ideas. Of course I'm working on new scripts."

I was thinking that maybe I had come off a little too strongly for him, but he responded with a nod.

"Well, let me see it as soon as you have something, okay?"

I looked at him hesitantly. I didn't trust him. Maybe he wanted to have a quick opportunity to shoot my script down. Well, I had news for him: I was not planning on rushing anything.

"When it's ready, it's ready," I told him. "I had ideas since I walked on the job, but I didn't present 'The Seduction' until I felt good about it. That's just the way I work."

He wasn't going to rip apart *my* script ideas. I was way ahead of him.

He said, "Well, when you become a regular staff writer one day, you won't have the *luxury* of popping scripts out of your *lab* whenever you get *ready* to."

"I guess that being an *assistant* has its advantages then," I commented like a smart aleck.

He got me right back when he said, "In everything but the pay. Are you sure you don't have another script ready?" he asked me again.

I guess he figured that my three-thousand-five-hundred-dollar pay was an insult, but I had news for him again: most people would *kill* to make that much money in one week. I paid Joe no mind. I would hand in another damn script when I was good and ready to, because I was *far* from starving!

That same night, Tim Waterman called me at home. He said, "It was the smartest idea ever to hire you on as an assistant, Tracy. What do *you* think about that? Have you learned a lot with us?"

"Of course I have," I told him. He knew *that* already. He was getting at something else, so I waited for the hook and bait.

"How hard will it be for us to hire you on for next season as a full writer? You seem like the type of woman who has bigger and better things on her mind. Are we just a stepping stone?"

First he was pumping up my head. I spoke very carefully.

I said, "*Stepping stone?* Is that all you think of *Conditions of Mentality*? I thought it was your baby."

"Oh, it is, but babies grow up and then you find *new* hobbies."

"Is that right? New hobbies like what?"

"Well, feature films, of course. Some people have it, some people don't. And *you*, Tracy, I can tell, *you* have it."

There it was. Tim Waterman wanted to be my mentor in the same way that Reginald was trying, with a little bit of

S-E-X on the side. I could feel the vibes from him. I already knew that Tim was a big-time flirt, and with the feature film talk, he had bigger bait, but I was smart enough to know that I was nowhere near feature film material. One damn script wasn't worth all of the attention that I was getting. Or maybe I was underestimating myself, particularly since "The Seduction" was written while in a state of minor depression. However, writing for feature films *was* my goal for the near future.

I played the starstruck role and asked, "You really think I have what it takes?"

"Sure you do. I give you a year and a half, and you'll have something piping hot for the studios to fight over."

I chuckled to myself. Tim took the terms *bullshit* and *game* to another level. I guess he really thought that I was a damn fool.

I said, "Well, I thank you for having so much confidence in me."

"No, you've *earned* it. You came right on board with your ideas and made our entire staff better. Some of the writers won't admit to it, but they know that it's the truth, Tracy. You're the *bomb*, baby!"

*Oh my God!* I thought to myself. I couldn't believe he had used the word *bomb* on me. I had to stop myself from laughing in his ear.

He said, "Oh, I'm not pulling your leg here at all, even though they're sexy."

When he said that, I stopped smiling. He was scaring me. I didn't want to be in an awkward position with my boss. My job was just beginning to get interesting. I didn't need any complications surrounding it. So I thought of making up a lie to get off of the phone and recuperate.

I let out a fake yawn and said, "Oh my God, I need to

get some rest, I've been up since early this morning. I'm sorry, Tim. Maybe we can finish this discussion tomorrow or something. I'm just too tired right now. I'm sorry."

I know it was corny as hell, but I was desperate to get the hell off of the phone.

My boss went for the kill anyway. "Well, how about you just say that we'll do dinner together one of these days, just to talk about where you would like to go in your career. Maybe I could point you in a few directions."

I got nervous and faked another yawn. "I'm just so tired, I can't even think right now. I'm sorry." I was hating myself for the weak bullshit, but I just didn't want to deal with my boss's invitations to me until I had a minute to think about it.

He said, "Well, you get some rest, Tracy, and think it over. Lunch, dinner, breakfast, whatever. As long as I can sit down and go a few rounds with you," he said.

"Go a few *rounds*?" I questioned.

"Oh, that's just guy talk for the ropes. You know, boxing ropes, and the ropes of the business."

"Oh, yeah," I said. At first, I thought he was talking about getting drunk with rounds of alcohol. "Well, we'll see," I told him, noncommittal. I definitely didn't want to make any promises to him.

"Great!" he responded as if I had promised him a date anyway.

I hung up the phone with my boss and panicked. I felt trapped. Would he find a way to fire me if I didn't play ball with him? I was a nervous wreck again. My mother was killing me with all of her predictions. How could I get from under her damn spell?

"Shit! These motherfuckin' *men*!" I shouted. "I didn't come out here to sleep around. Fuck that! And fuck that *job* too if *that's* how it's gonna be," I told myself. However, giving up a nice income was not going to be that easy. I was already getting used to the money. Nevertheless, I was *not* planning on fucking my boss to keep my job.

Soon after hanging up with Tim, I got another call from Richard Mack. He was inviting me out to a party in Venice that Saturday. I must have been as popular as a beauty queen all of a sudden. I couldn't keep playing the scary role though. I would just have to face the Hollywood music and be strong about it. Just because I went out with a man didn't mean that he would get an automatic key to my panties. I was overreacting, so I planned to loosen up and keep my head.

"Okay," I told Rich. I couldn't keep turning *every* offer down. Rich was cool anyway, and I *needed* to unwind.

$ $ $

I found my courage and went ahead to meet my boss for brunch at a nice beachside restaurant in Santa Monica that Saturday afternoon. However, I had a surprise for his ass. I showed up on time and wearing a gray business suit to send him a clear message: I was there strictly for business.

Tim looked at me and asked, "Tracy, can I ask you a question? Who wears business suits on Saturday? Christ, man, loosen up over here! This is California!"

I just smiled at it and kept my cool. Tim was dressed in dark slacks and a long-sleeved, yellow cotton shirt with a wide collar. His top buttons were open so his flawless neck could breathe.

"Where are you from again?" he asked, half smiling himself.

"Philadelphia."

He nodded and said, "Philly, Will Smith's hometown. Is everyone so uptight over there? Will Smith seems like a great guy."

"I'm not Will Smith," I told him, "but if I ever get as big as *he* is, then maybe I *will* loosen up."

"So, how long have you known Yolanda?" he asked me.

"Since I moved out here last September. I guess I first met her last July."

He nodded again and took a sip of his drink in a tall glass with a small blue umbrella.

"She's good company," he said with a grin.

I didn't want to touch that. That was *their* business. I moved on.

"So, is *Conditions of Mentality* a stepping stone for *you*? How many people over there know that you're looking into feature films?" I asked him.

"Everybody looks for feature films during the summertime. It's our hiatus out here. It beats jerking off the whole summer," he said with another sip of his drink and a grin.

I asked the waiter for a glass of water and a house salad to start off. I was afraid to even drink any alcohol.

"So, you're not leaving the show then?"

He shook his head and frowned at me. "No, of course not. It's a good gig, and it's paying my phone bills."

Just as he said that, his cellular phone went off. He had it attached to his belt.

"Yeah," he answered. "I'm on a lunch date. How about"—he looked at me and then to his watch, a gold Rolex—"five o'clock sometime?" It was nearly twenty after one. "Okay," he said, "I'll see you then," and hung up.

"These damn things are a pain in the ass sometimes," he told me, referring to his cellular phone. "But like they say with men, 'You can't live *with* them' . . . and blah, blah, blah."

I planned to get back down to business. I didn't even own a cellular phone yet.

I asked, "So, what's the percentage of women writers who get feature film deals?"

Tim looked at me and grimaced. I guess he wasn't there to talk business like I was. He said, "You have to be as tough as nails with your script, and I'm sure that you can do it, because you're showing me your shark's skin right now. Jesus!"

I smiled. "Well, you said you wanted to go a few *rounds* and talk about the ropes of the business with me."

"Yeah, and you're out here kicking my ass in the first round," he whined. "At least give the people their money's worth and get your KO in the ninth. Don't be such a *Mike Tyson* over here."

Our conversation kept being interrupted by Tim's phone calls, but he continued to answer them. I wondered what he would have done about that phone had I been more open to his advances, because the calls didn't sound that important. They sounded more personal than business related. Maybe he had them all set up to make me believe that he was a busy man with so many connections that they were bothersome, but I still hadn't fallen for it.

Before we separated, with not much progress made (or at least the kind of progress that *he* wanted because *I* had learned a lot), Tim leveled with me and said, "Tracy, you're not going to get as far as you would like in this business unless you loosen up a bit. All right? Even your homeboy Will Smith had to play a gay role to get into the feature film world. You just remember that."

In my opinion, it was low for Tim to even bring that up,

but that was a shot-down man for you, black *or* white, they could *all* act like *assholes* when they wanted to.

I did take Tim's advice to loosen up, I just wasn't planning on loosening up with him. So I drove back home and picked out something more revealing for Rich's party in Venice that night.

I had been to quite a few California parties by then, but most of the time I showed my face and left early. They were not my kind of parties. No one even *danced* half of the time; there was just a bunch of bullshit talk about upcoming projects and Hollywood deals. However, for Rich's party that Saturday night, I planned to stay until the cows came home just to see what the difference would be.

I walked into this huge, glass beach house, wearing a light blue summer dress, cut high above the knees and held up by spaghetti straps, and I was impressed! This place was nice and roomy, and it had a full balcony where you could look down on the crowd. I had no idea that Rich was handling things that well. I planned to give him a big hug and tell him how impressed I was. The place was jam-packed, too, with a young and hip mixed crowd of MTV types. It was right up my alley. People were even dancing. I spotted Juanita from New York on the balcony, and it soured my mood for a second. I figured that maybe Reginald would be there too, and I didn't particularly care for either one of them.

Juanita spotted me and began to speak to a couple of girlfriends who she was with.

I shook my head and moved through the crowd in search of Rich. Maybe I *wouldn't* be staying long if I had any drama to dodge.

I found Rich and he immediately gave me love.

"Tracy Ellison! You didn't tell me you had a *book* out!"

he said, loud enough for plenty of people to hear him. It wasn't as if I had spent much time promoting the fact; I was too busy working out the events of my *present* life.

I said, "How did you find out?"

"Somebody read it and told somebody, and then the word just got out. You know how Hollywood is," he answered.

"Is this your place?" I asked, changing the subject.

"I wish! I'm renting it out for the night, and the owner is selling the alcohol to make up the difference. I told him, 'Fine, all I want to do is have a big bad party here. But if anyone dies in a drunken car crash afterward, then that's on *you.*'

"Most of these people here are friends that *he* knows," he said, "but they'll be *my* friends after tonight. So have a ball!"

You know how it is when you're the host of a big party, you can't really talk too long to one person, so Rich introduced me to a couple of people and worked his way through the crowd. I didn't mind. The place was lively, and I planned to find my own fun.

This muscular chocolate brother asked me to dance, and I nodded and started grooving to an Ice Cube and Mack 10 song.

"What's your name?" he asked me.

"Tracy."

I smiled, reminiscing on old-school house parties back home in Philly, with the cuties inside of the stuffy basements asking you for your name and your phone number.

"Where are you from? Everybody's from somewhere in here. This reminds me of Florida during spring break," he told me. He sounded suburban and young. Maybe he had just come out of college, or didn't finish.

"Philly," I answered him.

"Oh, Will Smith's town."

I shook my head. Will Smith had really blown up out there because of the *The Fresh Prince of Bel-Air* television show and his blockbuster movie, *Independence Day.* He also had another science fiction movie coming out that summer, *Men in Black.* Boy was Yolanda right about blacks in science fiction. Will seemed *perfect* for that part.

I said, "He's not the only person from Philly, you know."

"Yeah, Kurupt's from Philly too."

This guy was definitely young. His points of reference were all in hip-hop. I bet he didn't even think about Bill Cosby, Sherman Hemsley, or Patti LaBelle. They were all pretty big in their *own* right, and so was Boyz II Men. Yet, all of a sudden, Philly had become "Will Smith's Town."

The next thing I knew, one of Juanita's girlfriends was dancing right beside us with no partner. She looked over at me and asked, "Are you Tracy Ellison, from *Flyy Girl*?"

I said, "Yeah," expecting some drama, and playing it down.

My chocolate friend looked puzzled. "You were in a movie already?" he asked me.

I shook my head.

"*Flyy Girl* is a book," the sister filled in, overhearing him. "I'll have to pick that up and see what it's like," she said to me.

"You wrote a book?" my partner asked. He looked stunned, all wide-eyed and shit.

I said, "I gave my life story to a writer, and *he* wrote it."

"Oh."

"I heard it's some wild shit in that book too," the sister commented with a grin. I immediately thought about Juanita and wondered what she had said about me. With

*Flyy Girl* and my nasty screenplay of *Crenshaw*, where the female lead screws both brothers, I felt that maybe Juanita had told her girls that I was a freak body.

I felt like fighting for my honor.

I turned to the sister and asked, "Juanita told you she read it?"

She looked shocked. I guess she didn't figure I would take the direct approach.

"Yeah, she read it."

What else could she say? She couldn't lie about it, she had already put her foot in her mouth.

I asked, "Where is Juanita now?" I was ready to handle my business just like old times, and by myself too!

"She's, ah, somewhere around here."

"Excuse me," I said to my dance partner. I went to look for Sister New York, because I had a bone to pick with her. Juanita wasn't far from the dance floor either. She was standing alone and searching the crowd, probably looking for Reginald. It was perfect.

I said, "Hey, Juanita, Reginald told me you had gone back to New York. Did you get back in town recently?"

She looked at me and said, "I never left town," with attitude.

"That's what I figured," I told her. "It didn't make any sense to me. I didn't think that you would give up so easily and leave town. You seem as determined as I am to make it out here."

She didn't have anything to say, so I kept going with my setup.

"So, I guess that you and Reginald aren't talking anymore then," I baited her.

She went for it just like a fool.

"Why, *you* want him? You can *have* him."

"Too skinny," I said, shaking my head. "I like athletic guys myself. Reginald seems like he trips and falls over his own feet a lot. Don't you think?"

She just looked at me, still trying to figure out my angle.

"But I guess he was okay for you," I added to the pot.

Juanita looked at me and finally asked, "What are you trying to say?"

I let her ass have it. "I'm saying that you don't represent New York *or* black intelligence too well, sister, if you're gonna come out here and act petty over some damn guy who's only out to get his *thing* wet. I could see his behind *ten* blocks away! And I'm a grown fuckin' woman now, so I *dare* you to raise your voice or your hands at me with some dumb shit, because that's exactly how you're acting. Dumb!

"Now if you have some issues you want to settle with me, instead of talking foul shit behind my back, you say it to my face, so we can squash that shit right here, right now, or however you want to do it!"

I had Victor on my mind, and pure violence in heart. I hadn't had a good fight in *years*, and I was still hurt from that crazy night in the hotel room, so I was just about ready to open up a can of whup-ass on anybody who wanted some just to make me feel better.

As it turned out, Juanita didn't want a damn thing, nor did her girlfriends. They looked at me as if I was a crazy woman and backed off. I guess they thought that I was a pure ghetto sister, but I was just under a bad moon and they came up against my full howl. Nevertheless, the drama was ready to ruin my night. I didn't feel so friendly anymore, and if I didn't feel friendly there was no sense in staying there.

To top things off, I bumped into Susan Raskin again.

She said, "Tracy, I thought that was you. Is everything all right?"

She looked timid. I guess she saw me in action and was afraid of me. That was all that I needed, my new white friend thinking that I was straight black and ghetto.

I sighed and said, "It's been a long day, Susan. What can I tell you?"

"I guess that this is a poetry moment," she responded with a smile.

I looked at her and asked, "What do you mean?"

"Well, sometimes you just sit down and write a poem when you can't do anything else to change things."

She was right on point. I asked her, "Are you a poet too?" I didn't put it past her.

She smiled and shook her head, "No, but I know the inspiration. *All* artists have it. They have a way of taking regular everyday things and shedding light on them with their deep introspection."

I nodded, thinking, *Damn! This white girl is just too cool.* I said, "So you think that I'm an artist?"

She grinned at me. "Of course you are. You have the words *passionate artist* written all over you. It's in your veins. I know enough gifted people to be able to tell."

*I'm sure you do,* I thought to myself, referring again to her family ties. Although I didn't want to use Susan to make my way in Hollywood, I still figured that we could kick it because we clicked. So we hung out for the rest of the night until close to three o'clock in the morning.

# The Queen

My drummers would beat
an urgent rhythm
on golden paved streets,
while big voices
attached to little feet
yell out, "SHE'S COMING!"
The strong
armed, brown men keep drumming.

As I approach, the drums grow
louder, deafening
with blaring horns.
BA-DURRNN!
BA-DURRNN!
For miles they hear
my clearing path, while
my pounding drums pop ears.

They fear me,
the fabulous, BLACK
and pretty, inner-city
'hood girl, with
ambitions and visions
to rule the world, while
my drummers keep drumming
in loincloths and sweat.

I announce myself
to the masses,
"HEAR ME!"
and my voice echoes
in the distance,

*bringing silence*
*as I continue, "WHO HERE*
*OPPOSES MY RULE?"*

*And the silence*
*was infinite!*

*Copyright © 1989 by Tracy Ellison*

# April 2000

$ $

$

When I was ready to leave Raheema's beautiful family on Sunday afternoon, they all lined up outside to see me off, Ernest, Raheema, Jordan, and Lauryn, and I hugged each one of them.

Ernest said, "Whenever you want to wind down with a good family, Tracy, you call on us and we'll receive you with open arms."

I smiled, and I knew that they all meant it. My girl Raheema had done real well. I hated to leave, but that was her life, and I had to go back to my own.

"Call me when you get in," Raheema told me.

"Call *me* too," Jordan piped with a chuckle.

I laughed myself and told them that I would.

On my way home from Plainfield, I began to think about family and what it meant to me. I wasn't planning on grabbing onto the first man who presented himself to me, but I figured there was another way for me to stay rooted to family and loved ones.

I made it back to my parents' house and immediately called up my little cousin Vanessa with a plan.

"Vanessa, it's Tracy," I said, recognizing her voice.

She got excited and said, "Hi."

"I have a big idea for you," I told her.

She hesitated. I guess she figured I had more big-girl

advice for her, but I didn't. Or at least not at *that* moment.

She asked me, "What big idea?"

I said, "How would you like to spend the summer out in California with me?"

"Oh, yeah, I'll do that!"

"First I have to talk to your mother though."

She calmed way down and said, "Oh."

"Why'd you say it like that?" I asked her.

"You'll see. She already says that I think I'm special."

"You *are* special," I told her.

"Well, tell *her* that. She's not home right now though."

"When will she be back in?"

"Any minute. She only went to the grocery store around the corner, and she could *use* the exercise too."

I chuckled and stopped myself. "Don't talk about your mother like that, Vanessa, that's not right."

"She doesn't do anything that's right. She's always hollering at somebody, as if *she's* all perfect."

I didn't get along with my mother as a teenager myself, but I was still made to show respect. I told Vanessa about my problems coming up, and how it was all behind me now. My mother and I had a solid relationship as two respecting adults, and that's what Vanessa needed to think about.

"So, you didn't hang out with my mother at all?" she asked me.

"Nope," I told her. "Patricia was four years older than me, she lived in North Philly, and we hung with totally different crowds, but I heard about when she got pregnant with you though."

"Was she in trouble with my Grandmom Marsha?"

I thought back and said, "Shit, girl, *everybody* was in trouble with Aunt Marsha. She hated *my* mom."

Vanessa laughed and said, "I know. She's still mean like that 'til this day." She sighed and said, "Sometimes I just feel like I was born into the wrong side of the family. Grandmom says that I remind her a lot of *your* mother."

"I can see that. All that red bone," I told her. "God gave *me* a little bit of honey in my tone." I stopped myself and said, "Damn, that sounds like a good line for a poem. Let me write that down."

Vanessa broke up laughing and said, "You got a poem for everything."

I asked her, "What did you think about my movie *Led Astray*?" I had never bothered to ask for her opinion on it.

"I thought it was deep. She was very cunning, the way she set everybody up like that."

I laughed and said, "I know. Thanks. So if your grades are still good, I'll reward you with a trip to California every summer."

"If my *grades* are still good?" She sounded offended. "That's easy."

"Let me see you prove it to me in June. Then I can try and get you in UCLA."

"For real?! UCLA?!"

"For real," I told her.

"All right then."

"Vanessa!" someone shouted in the background. "Why are you always on that damn telephone? I *swear* I don't know how you get good grades, because you're always running your damn mouth on that *phone*!"

"That's your mother?" I asked Vanessa with a grin.

"Mmm hmm," she mumbled. She whispered, "You see what I mean?"

I figured that if Vanessa didn't get a chance to express herself, she could very well be a problem soon, especially with her introverted ways. A hyperactive mother pressing her all of the time didn't make matters any better. Mercedes and Raheema went through hell with that with their father. However, on the flip side, *I* took my mother through hell.

I said, "Let me talk to her," referring to my first cousin.

"Mom, the phone is for you," Vanessa told her mother.

"Who is it?!"

"It's your cousin Tracy."

". . . Oh." Patricia came to the phone and said, "How are you doing, Tracy?"

"I'm doing fine. How are you doing?"

"I'm doing what I'm doing," she told me.

I didn't get into that. I said, "Well, I was wondering if I could give Vanessa a gift for getting good grades all these years."

"A gift? A gift like what?"

"A summer in California."

There was a long pause. Patricia said, "I don't think it's good for her to separate from her little sisters like that. They may think that she's getting special treatment."

"Well, she *is* the oldest."

"And she *thinks* that she's the *cutest* too," my cousin snapped. "No, I don't think that's a good idea."

"Mom—"

"I'm *talking,* Vanessa!"

I didn't know what else to say, but I had to say *something* because I had gotten Vanessa's hopes all up. *Shit, I should have asked Patricia about this first!* I told myself. *What the hell was I thinking?*

I said, "I was thinking about trying to get her into school out here at UCLA."

"Temple is good enough for her. That way she can help

me out around the house with her younger sisters," Patricia countered. "Temple's a good school. Your brother goes there."

I said, "Well, maybe she wants to do something for herself." As soon as those words slipped out of my big mouth, I knew that it was a mistake.

"You know what, Tracy?" Patricia started, "I didn't ask you for your fuckin' money. I didn't ask you for your fuckin' time. I didn't ask you for your advice, and I *damn* sure didn't ask you to come around here putting that Hollywood *shit* in my daughter's head *either!*

"For what?! So she can be another big-screen hoe?!" my cousin screamed at me. "You better check yourself, Tracy, because you *will* get *wrecked*!"

She went ahead and slammed the phone on my damn ear.

When I put the phone down, my mother caught me staring into empty space in my old room.

She said, "I didn't mean to eavesdrop, but were you just talking about Vanessa in California or something?" I had my door open the whole time.

I didn't even want to talk about it. My brother walked in next, and I guess he had caught the tail end of my mother's question.

"You taking Vanessa out to California?" By then, Jason was six foot two (an inch taller than my father), and was sticking his chest out because he had his own apartment at nineteen, a golden number it seemed for men. They even had an antidraft song about being nineteen back in the eighties.

I shook my head and said, "Vanessa could use a break. I can feel it."

"You can feel what, Tracy?" my mother asked me. She had that mother-knows-best look in her eyes again.

"I can just tell that she needs a change of pace. A getaway."

"Oh yeah, well, I could use one of those too," my brother told me. "I'll go out to California with you. Can you set me up with a summer job out there?"

My mom said, "I thought that was what you were trying to do, and it's wrong."

"What's so wrong about it?" I asked her.

"Do *you* have a child, Tracy?" she asked me back. "I didn't *think* so. You can't impose yourself on people's lives like that. That was wrong."

I knew she was right, and I couldn't really argue with her, but that didn't change the fact that I had already opened up the can of beans.

"So, what do I do now?" I asked. "Vanessa was willing to go."

"You can take me instead. You can impose yourself on *my* life all you want," my brother interrupted again.

My mother just looked at him and didn't say a word.

"What, Mom?" he whined. "I could *use* a vacation. I didn't even go away to school."

"That's because you wanted to follow your little friends to Temple," she shot at him.

"Her mother's just going to ruin her life, Mom," I said, referring to Vanessa and my cousin Trish.

"Who are you to say that? Are you an authority on parenting all of a sudden? Do you even know how to *raise* a child?" my mother asked me. "What master's degree do you have on that?"

I frowned and said, "Come on, Mom, you know Trish isn't the best mother to those girls. She was pregnant at sixteen, and she still hasn't learned her lesson about making the right decisions in her life."

"But *you* have?"

"Yes, I have," I snapped.

My brother read the intensity inside of the room and said, "I think that's my cue to go," and walked back out.

My mother said, "Tracy, regardless of what you, me, or the rest of the *world* for that matter, *thinks* about Vanessa's welfare, it's only *our* opinion, because Trish is her mother. Now when the girl turns eighteen and graduates from high school, if she wants to break out and do her own thing, then that's *her* prerogative to do so. Until then, she's still in high school and under her mother's roof, so you leave her the hell alone."

I shook my head defiantly. "I hope nothing happens to her before then."

That only made my mother curious. "Why are you so concerned about her all of a sudden. Did you find out something?"

"No, I'm just saying."

"You're just saying that you want her in California with you for the summer because she's your little cousin. And what about when you start working on this next movie? Then what?"

"I take her on the set with me as my assistant and pay her. Vanessa would *love* that!"

My mother shook her head and started to walk out from the room. "It sounds like the same old Tracy to me. *My* daughter, as selfish and conniving as she wants to be."

*Mother knows best* indeed. I was breaking my neck just to have family for company out in California. Just because I knew that I was being selfish, however, didn't mean that I would stop.

I left my room and went to find my brother before he

disappeared. He was downstairs on the couch with Dad, watching the Los Angeles Lakers play the Minnesota Timberwolves for a late NBC basketball game.

I looked at my brother and said, "It's beautiful weather out there in California. We have palm trees, beaches . . ." *Pretty girls,* I thought to myself but dared not to say in front of my father. I was being terrible, but what was so bad about having family over for the summer?

Jason asked, "Yeah, so you're gonna let me stay out there with you this summer?" just like I knew he would.

I said, "I don't know. Dad, you think your son's mature enough to come out to California with me?"

My father didn't even look at me. "Don't get me involved in this," he commented.

*"Mature enough?"* Jason asked me. He was offended, just like I figured he would be. Boy was he easy to pull by the nose!

I said, "Jason, they have a lot of crazy turf wars out there that I wouldn't want you to get involved in."

"What, Bloods and Crips?"

"Exactly."

"They're not where *you* live, are they? I'll just hang around where you live."

He had a point. To my knowledge, there were no Crips or Bloods in the Marina Del Rey area.

I said, "What do you think, Dad? You think I should invite him?"

My father smiled, while watching the basketball game. He said, "Tracy, I think you need to stop the bullshit, because you wanted this boy to go to California with you from the minute you walked down those stairs. So stop bothering me while I watch this game in peace.

"If you want a *real* argument about it," he said, "then

you go on back upstairs and ask your *mother* if Jason can go."

"Wait a minute, I have to *ask* for permission?" my brother asked rhetorically. "I'm in college now?"

"And?" my father asked him.

Jason looked at me and grimaced. "You see what you started, Tracy? You should have just asked me."

I knew that I would have no problem getting my brother out to California with me, but Vanessa's situation was more tricky and urgent. I brainstormed for the rest of that night how to release her from the imprisonment of her mother, because that was all that it was, imprisonment, just because Patricia had given birth to her.

However, with the new law banning affirmative action programs at the university level, Vanessa would have to compete academically against thousands of white students who had more facilities than she had. *Ain't that a bitch!* I thought to myself. *My girl Kendra was right all along; that shit is an outright* crime, *and nobody fought against it!* So if you could not dunk a basketball, run a touchdown, or long jump, and your family didn't have any money, you would basically have to be a black or Mexican genius, or leave the state of California in order to receive a higher education.

I went to sleep with that thought on my mind, as pissed off about it as Kendra was *years* ago. I guess you really have to see how a new law can immediately affect *you* and *your* family before you really give a damn.

# Nasty Girl Talk

*Girl,*
*I called up my MAN last night*
*and told him, "Baby,*
*why don't you take a slow cruise*
*downtown for me.*
*And once you get there,*
*you gon' come up to this gate*
*with bushes in front of it.*
*And what you need to do, right,*
*is dip down real low*
*and push your way through the bushes,*
*but not too fast*
*because the gate is sensitive*
*and you might set off my alarm system.*
*But if you slip through the bushes*
*just right,*
*and inch your way across the lawn,*
*I can let you come up to my room*
*inside the house.*
*And please,*
*when we get good and busy,*
*don't tease me when I moan*
*because*
*I don't particularly care for that*
*disrespectful, macho shit!*
*Jus' like YOU wouldn't like it*
*if I slipped and got your name*
*mixed up*
*with the burglar who snuck in here last weekend."*

*Girl,*
*my MAN said, "WHAT?!"*
*Then I said, "Si-i-i-ke.*
*You know you my only playa',*
*Boo."*
*Then*
*me and my girl broke up laughing*
*on the telephone*
*all night,*
*talkin' 'bout guys*
*'n shit.*

# July 1997

$ $

$

**B**y the summertime, I just couldn't take it anymore! I had to have some sex! I had gone nearly a full year out in California without having any. I think the guilt that I felt about new people reading my book and how fast I was back in the day, along with the sleaziness of Hollywood, had really turned me off from getting down and dirty. However, when those California brothers started getting suntans and shit, with the new summertime heat kicking in, I had to have myself some more chocolate, and I was a grown damn woman, so I could have a piece of chocolate if I wanted to, as long as it still came in the wrapper.

I wrote my second full script for *Conditions of Mentality* called "Bad Karma," about a playboy who finds that all of his usual moves with the ladies were going sour on him, so he seeks out a spiritualist for answers. A decision was made to make my script the season's finale, and the catch was that I had to extend the plot with a part two to begin the next season. I was getting plenty out of my first Hollywood job; I even had a one-page profile in *Take 1* magazine, a Hollywood biweekly. I didn't sweat any of that stuff, though. I *really* wanted to sweat a man, or sweat *with* a man, to tell you the truth. I felt how guys did when *they* craved intimate companionship. Desperate!

Yolanda, however, was more concerned about my writing success.

"Shit, girl, you're gonna become a legend out here," she told me. "Do you know how hard it is for a new writer to get a season's finale? You're not even a full staff writer yet. That's unheard of!"

It was a simple business decision to me.

I said, "Yolanda, they only used my script like that because they knew I could pull in more women viewers, and if we could hook them to wait for next season, we would have a better chance at getting picked up for another year.

"And I can tell you right now," I added, "the head writer, Joseph Keaton, *hated* the idea, but I have to give credit to Tim, because he was probably the one who fought for it."

Yolanda asked, "By chance, did you, ah—"

I cut her off and said, "Sleep with him?"

She chuckled like a witch.

I said, "No," and didn't have to hesitate. I didn't get down like that. Business was business and sex was *not* included, or at least not with *me.*

It was funny how Yolanda was asking me about *my* business after not discussing her own, but I didn't say anything about it. I didn't ask her anything else about meeting men in LA either, because her vibes were not the kind that I wanted to follow. It seemed to me (and I really didn't know because she never told me and I had stopped asking) that she fucked people more so for business, and I wanted mine purely for pleasure. The last thing in the world that I wanted was someone to believe that I made my way through Hollywood while on my back, because I was working *too hard* to come up with solid script ideas to make a name for myself. So I didn't hang out with Yolanda much, and when Kendra's mom got sick in Baltimore,

Kendra went back home for the summer and I ended up hanging out with Susan Raskin. However, I didn't expect for Susan to be able to help me in my mission to hook up with a black man, so when push came to shove with meeting brothers, I had to go solo.

I visited Venice Beach with the sole purpose of meeting a chocolate brother to chill with. I still didn't want to attract any knuckleheads though, so I dressed conservatively with my nose up in the air to avoid the weaklings, because only the strong could survive, and I had no time to waste on underlings.

Venice Beach was jam-packed, but what did I expect on a hot Saturday afternoon? You had the bikers, in-line skaters, skateboarders, T-shirt vendors, fruit stand owners, lovebirds, the wanna-be basketball players, bodybuilders, blacks, Mexicans, stray whites, and plenty of competitive women showing their thighs, stomachs, and shoulders to anyone with their eyes open. Venice Beach may as well have been an outside singles' club with all of the posturing going on.

I thought, *Shit, this may be too much action for me. This place seems like a damn carnival! I can't hope to meet a serious man out here.*

"Watch it!" a skateboarder warned me, zipping past on one of those giant, colorful skateboards.

"*You* watch it," I mumbled to myself. He was long gone already.

I began to stroll up the beach while keeping my eyes open for anything that looked like fresh chocolate, but my view was mostly filled with Mexican men. Plenty of them were looking good too, but you know, I wasn't there for any caramel, I wanted chocolate brown. Every now and then a brother would pop out, but they were usually not my type, and when they were, they were already with a woman. So by the time I began to make my way back toward the basketball courts, I figured that Venice Beach would have been a better place to *take* a man to have a good time with than to *meet* one. I stopped at the basketball courts and watched plenty of out-of-shape men trying to run ball.

*This looks like the place where Wesley Snipes and Woody Harrelson filmed* White Men Can't Jump, I told myself. I just stood there and daydreamed for a second trying to remember my favorite scenes in the movie.

"I can't even play basketball," someone said to me.

I expected to spot some loser when I turned to match the voice with a face, but I was pleasantly surprised. The brother looked like he had never needed to shave a day in his life. His brown face was baby smooth. He was wearing a gray shorts outfit, with a white wave cap, the kind with the wraparound strings attached, and for what? It didn't look as if he had much hair under the thing for waves. That turned me off, and I let him know about it.

"Why do you have that *thing* on your head?" I asked him like his mother.

He smiled and answered, "I don't want my head to sweat." He was not flustered by my forwardness. For that I gave him a plus; the brother was confident.

"Do you have a bald head under there?" I asked him. He nodded. "Yeah."

He seemed like he was showing off too, a definite California thing, or at least from what *I* had picked up while over there. Kendra had told me about that from day one; everybody wanted to be a star in California.

I said, "So is that your come-on line, telling women that you can't play basketball? Because I don't recall asking." He *looked* tall and athletic enough to play. Maybe he was bull-shitting.

He shook his head and said, "No, I can't play. I broke my ankle trying to play when I was a kid, and I haven't played since."

"Are you a quitter?" I asked him.

He looked at me and frowned. "I don't quit, I'm just not a basketball player."

"Nobody said that you were. That was *your* line," I told him with a chuckle. I wonder where he really expected to go with that.

He asked me, "Why are you watching basketball then?"

"Because there's nothing else to do."

He looked toward the water and smiled. "We could go swimming, walk on the beach, get something to eat, or whatever you want."

I smiled back at him. "*We?*"

"You said you didn't have anything else to do."

He caught me slipping. I laughed it off.

"All right, I did say that," I admitted. I was tempted to ask him how old he was, because he didn't seem over twenty-five. Nevertheless, I didn't want to bust his groove with the particulars. I guess I was living out my own television script and being *seduced* myself because of my yearnings for male attention. If you stare at a dog long enough, it *will* bark at you.

I thought about that and laughed again.

"What's so funny?"

"What is your name?" I asked him instead of answering his question.

He said, "Co," like in cobalt.

I looked at him and frowned. "*Co?*"

"Short for Colby, but once Kobe Bryant signed with the

Lakers, I just started calling myself Co with an *e* at the end," he explained.

"So, you let Kobe Bryant make you change your name. What, are you an actor, a model, or something?" I could see if it was a business decision for name recognition.

The baby-faced brother smiled with a mouthful of pearly white teeth and asked, "How'd you guess?"

He was so vain that I just started laughing again. His entire approach was obviously to lead a woman into asking him what he did, so that he could spring the whole model business on you.

"So, what's your full model name?" I asked him.

"Coe Anawabi."

"Ah-na-wa-bee," I pronounced correctly.

"Yes, my father's from Sierra Leone, Africa."

That explained his baby face. African skin was the smoothest in the world, and Coe seemed to be bragging about his roots too. I couldn't blame him, though. I bragged about Philly, and everyone else bragged about where they were from.

I went ahead and teased him. "I guess that I'm supposed to be all over you now, right? Is that how you operate?" I was pumping his head up and having a good time with it whether it went anywhere or not. At least he was interesting.

He laughed and said, "I only want to know if you'll walk with me."

I thought about it. "Why not?" I told him, grinning.

"Because you may fall for my charm," he answered.

I said, "I already have," and we started walking.

"What is your name?" he asked.

"Tracy Ellison from Philadelphia."

"Oh, Philly . . ."

"Will Smith's town," I added for him.

He smiled and said, "Yeah. So what do you do?"

"I write." That's all I told him. I wanted to go question for question just to stretch out the conversation while we walked.

"You write what, articles for a magazine or something?"

I smiled. "No, but that's a good idea."

"What do you write then?"

"Poetry, and a couple of scripts."

"Scripts? For what, television?"

"Yeah, I write for a small-time cable show."

"What's the name of the show?"

"You probably never heard of it."

"What's the name of it anyway?"

*"Conditions of Mentality."*

He looked at me and said, "I watch that show. It comes on the New Millennium Channel, NMC."

I said, "Yeah, that's the one." I knew he was younger than me then. I just didn't know *how* young he was.

"You write for that show? That's one of my favorite shows."

I was suddenly embarrassed. I wasn't expecting that. I smiled, nodded, and said nothing. I wanted to change the subject.

"What kind of modeling work have you gotten?" I asked him.

He shrugged his shoulders and blew it off. "You know, basically sports stuff. So, how do you guys pick the actors over there, because you have, like, new actors for every episode, right?"

I could see where he was going. He was beginning to lean away from the personal and get into a business talk. He wanted to act. I cut that shit short, quick!

"I don't have any control whatsoever over the actors, and most of them have agents who call us up for auditions."

Coe said, "Oh," and nodded. "Sometimes, when you model, you want to do more than just sit there and take pictures, you know. That gets boring. You want to do something extra with your energy."

I said, "I heard that modeling is *very* tiring, though, like you use up *a lot* of energy."

He frowned at the idea. "Yeah, because you get tired of just standing around."

I noticed that we were just standing around ourselves and had stopped walking. We had walked over to an area where cars were parked.

Coe said, "Wait right here," as if I had somewhere to go. He beeped off an alarm system for a cream-colored Porsche that was two cars away from us and walked back over with a pager and a cellular phone with him.

I smiled and turned away momentarily to hide it. The boy was going into extra show-off mode, so I played my part for him.

"That's your car?"

"Yeah." He attached his pager to his gray shorts, and strapped on a gun holder around his shoulder that fit his cellular phone.

I said, "Let me see what your car looks like."

He grinned and walked me over to it. He had COLBY on his California license plates.

He saw me looking and said, "I still have to change that."

Inside of his car he had tan leather interior. Nice. *Very* nice! I sat inside and started daydreaming about cruising down the highway.

Coe leaned into the driver seat and took his wave cap off. His bald head had the same baby's-ass smoothness as his face. I had to stop myself from grabbing it right then and there. I shook my head and climbed out of the boy's car. He was too young for me, and there was nowhere for me to go with that brother but to the bedroom. His entire approach was a set up to get him plenty of California punnany. If you asked me, I would say that he had bent over backward to buy that car, and was probably still paying for it.

He said, "You don't want to go for a ride?"

"I still have my car here," I told him.

"We can come back to it."

I said, "I thought we were walking on the beach."

He nodded, seeing that I was not budging. "Okay, we can finish our walk."

*Finish our walk,* I repeated to myself. I think the young brother was a bit teed off at me. Coe Anawabi was used to getting his damn way; that's what I read into it, and he didn't know who the hell he was dealing with. I may not have been a match for Victor, but I could eat most brothers alive, especially young, *rookie* players like Coe.

"I'm through walking anyway," I told him. "I came out here to meet a man, and now I've met one."

He just stood there and smiled at me, speechless.

I said, "So give me your number and we'll just hook up at another time."

He nodded and said, "All right. I like that; a woman who knows what she wants."

"Yeah, and I *don't* want your damn pager *or* your cell phone number. I want a *house* number. And if I call and find out that it's not a house number, then I'm throwing it away."

He looked at me to see if I was serious. "Damn, it's like that?"

"Yes it is. My time is precious, and so are my phone calls."

"Well, can I have your house number too?"

I said, "When I call you I'll give it to you then."

He stared at me for another minute and said, "Man, is that how the sisters are in Philly?" and handed his phone number to me.

I said, "Why don't you go ask Will Smith? He seems to be the authority on Philadelphia out here. I'm just a pretty face." I stepped away from him, but that didn't mean I didn't like him, nor did it mean that I wouldn't give him a call. I just had to let his young behind know that if we ever hooked up, it would be on *my* terms, and *my* terms alone!

**$ $ $**

Later on that week, I met a brother at the grocery store who was a dentist with his own office. He was thirty-one and had less reason to show off. However, we didn't talk too long when we first met, so I set up a weekend dinner with him to find out more about him. He suggested seafood at a place in Marina Del Rey. I told him I'd meet him there at seven. Eight would have been pushing it. Most times you don't actually eat until an hour after arrival, so I didn't want to lead the brother on by going too close to midnight on a first date with him. It was just a fact-finding mission.

Susan called me right as I got ready to go out.

"Hey, what'cha doin'?" she asked me.

She was so comfortable with me that she began to break the language down into real girlfriend talk: commonspeak.

I said, "Getting ready for a date."

"Oh, that must be nice," she responded.

"What are you doing tonight?" I asked her.

"Sitting here reading your book *Flyy Girl.*"

I froze on the phone. I still hadn't talked about it with her, nor had I given her a copy.

She said, "I can't believe that you didn't tell me you had a book out. As soon as someone told me, I went right out and bought it."

I was still speechless. I didn't know what to say.

I finally said, "Well, I didn't know that you would be interested in a black book."

"Really," Susan responded. She sounded sarcastic.

I said, "Well, you know, they have the black sections in the bookstores for the black readers." My explanation was so ridiculous that I began to laugh.

Susan said, "So the African-American section is off-limits to me because I'm Jewish, right, and I wouldn't understand? So I guess that *I'm* supposed to read in only the Jewish section."

I stopped laughing and felt like I was in hot water for some reason. Did I offend Susan by not telling her about my book? I had to ask her to make sure.

"You're not offended that I didn't tell you about it, are you?"

Susan paused. I took that to mean that she *was* offended.

"I wouldn't really say that I was offended by it, I just felt distant, like you had a part of you that you wanted to keep to yourself. However, you've published it now, so they're selling it. It's no longer private. So I didn't understand why you wouldn't tell me about it, that's all.

"I said, 'Wow, we've been hanging out together and

Tracy has told me *nothing* about it. What else hasn't she told me?'" she said.

"Well, now that you're reading it, what do you think?" I asked her.

She started to chuckle. I didn't take that too well but I had to wait for her to answer before I could jump to conclusions.

"It's good. I mean, you were quite an adventurous girl, curious and spirited, just like a lot of artists are. You wanted to find everything out on your own."

"Does it make you think that I'm extra hardcore?" I asked her. I thought back to the night at the beach party in Venice, and my confrontation with Juanita.

"Everyone goes through that stage, Tracy. Punk rock, hip-hop, sports jocks, bad boys, sexuality; you name it, we all have those issues," she answered. "This is an excellent coming-of-age book for the eighties generation, dealing with the fast life and all of the materialism. I think it's great that you had the courage to put this out there. It reminds me of *Bright Lights, Big City.* Have you ever read that?"

I laughed and said, "Not unless I had to read it for school."

Susan said, "See, so maybe you need to visit the *other* sections."

"You mean the rest of the *store*? Let's not get it twisted, Susan," I said. "Just because *you* picked up my book, basically because you know me, that does *not* mean that other Jews and whites will. And I'm not mad about it, that's just the way that America is, just like with movies and television shows."

"Okay, so what about *The Cosby Show*?"

"I *knew* you were going to say that," I told her. "And that's typical. You find *one* black show to relate to, and that's it. You get *one* black author to read—Maya Angelou—and that's it.

"And we can have this discussion all night long, but I have a date to make," I said. "I'm sorry for not bringing up my book before, but now that you have one, enjoy it, and I'll sign it for you the next time we see each other."

Susan laughed and said, "You promise?"

"I promise."

That girl made me late for my date, and when I arrived at the seafood restaurant in Marina Del Rey, the hostess there was waiting for me.

"Excuse me, are you looking for Mr. Squire?" the college-aged girl asked me, wearing all white. I was wearing a nice burnt orange dress. I felt like dressing sexy for a change.

"Yes, Arturo Squire," I told the hostess. I wanted to make myself sound professional and not just another hot date.

"He's right this way."

She led me to a seat in a back corner next to the window. It was a secluded table, a good place to talk privately.

"What is this, your favorite spot?" I joked to Artis. He told me that his friends called him Artis and never Arturo, but since Arturo was his given name, he made people aware of it.

He stood up to pull out my chair. He was dressed in black and tan, *GQ* style. I was impressed.

He said, "How did you guess this was my favorite table?" He was smiling when he asked me, and of course a dentist *would* have perfect teeth, but was he pulling my leg about the table or was he serious?

I asked, "How often do you come here?"

Artis was bronzed brown like Yolanda with clear Native

American blood. I could tell from the dark smallish eyes, the long straight nose, and the thick wavy hair. He had sex appeal oozing all over him. Yet, I was skeptical about his love life. A man so fine with a sure income like the dentistry profession should have been married by age thirty, or at least *I* thought so.

He answered, "I dine at my favorite table here with a new fine woman just about every week."

I couldn't figure him out just yet, but he didn't appear to be so bold about his "skills" when I first met him. Maybe dark restaurants were his place to get jiggy with it and let it all hang out, so I threw the game back in his lap.

"Well, tell me something then, how do I rate against the other women?" I asked him.

He grinned and said, "*Very* well."

"Meaning what? Am I at the bottom of the curve, the middle, or at the top?"

He smiled even wider. A real player wouldn't have been flattered so easily. *I know,* I had been with the best. I guess more California men would have to find out who I was, because *obviously* they didn't know.

"I would say that you're somewhere around the top. No doubt in my mind."

I thought, *How does a dentist come off as a player anyway?* Maybe I was stereotyping the dental profession, but I couldn't see a man who worked inside of people's mouths all day as a sweet talker. You just give them a big needle in their mouth, and go on about your business. I didn't see any social skills there myself. However, my father was a pharmacist, and *he* sure put a whammy on my mother. I didn't see many social skills in filling out medical prescriptions either.

I ordered a seafood combo, and Artis ordered a lobster

dinner. I didn't know if he had something to prove with his order, but I never really liked lobster. The big deal over lobster was overrated if you asked me. It never tasted that good. It was damn chewy, like eating white rubber.

After a while, I began to understand how Artis could still be single at age thirty-one. He was boring. I mean, after w got past the initial bullshit stage of how many women was supposed to have dated (either real or fake), our co versation wasn't really stimulating. He started talking ab black art and jazz as if that was supposed to turn me something, but maybe I was just too hip to new-scho forms like hip-hop and videos to really get into h school talk of jazz improvisations and the love Coltrane.

I was more familiar with Miles Davis myself, cause he was always changing for the new age holding on to that old-time shit. Or maybe know enough about jazz to follow Artis in tion, so I led him back to what *I* was mor with, poetry and film.

"Do you read poetry at all?" I asked hi

He wiped his mouth with the red mou "Funny that you asked. I was just liste Heron the other night. I think poetry popularity. Have you seen that *love j*

Now *that* was my kind of conve solutely *loved* that movie. We nee down, talk-to-your-soul movies."

He smiled and said, "So, I gue then."

I nodded, "It was all right. Mekhi Phifer. We need to pu love movie, a hot and steam

I caught myself, but it was too late. Artis was already grinning and sizing up his competition.

"So, you like the bald-headed, roughneck variety?"

I had put my foot in my mouth, so I had to cover up my tracks. I said, "Bald heads don't look so hot on everyone. And it shouldn't always be related to roughneck street culture either. I think the most *famous* bald-headed black man on the planet is Michael Jordan, is it not? And he is not *hardly* some street-walking roughneck."

"He could have been if it wasn't for basketball," Artis responded.

Damn that was low! I was shocked, and it left me speechless, because if I would have responded to it instinctively, I might have cursed his ass out. Who's side was *his* brother on? That was a major turnoff. I understood the whole deal with male competition and all, but a brother dissing Michael Jordan like that was unheard of. I mean, Jordan may not have been the most politically active brother in the world, but I thought that *everyone* agreed that he displayed the ultimate representation of black class and manhood.

I opened my mouth and said, "My best girlfriend back home in Philadelphia named her first son, Michael, after Michael. He was born this past April. She made me his godmother." That's all I planned to say about it.

I guess that *Ar-tu-ro* got my message. He said, "Well, I can't say how his life would have turned out if it wasn't for basketball. I hear that he comes from a close-knit southern family."

I didn't like how that sounded either, with that "Southern family." He made it sound more obedient and less respected. I was just about ready to get up and leave. That

man had soured my mood. I guess he felt that his professional status gave him the right to talk down on other brothers and sisters. It was a classic house-nigger, field-nigger move, and *Ar-tu-ro* was obviously very happy to be in the house.

I said, "When are we gonna stop all of this classism stuff? This North and South stuff? This East Coast, West Coast stuff? That shit is all nonsense. And now Biggie Smalls is another brother dead because of it. However, *you* don't even know who he is, because he was just another *street* nigga to you.

"Well, you can pay for the bill, because you got it like that, right? You're a professional." I stood up to leave, but before I walked out, I lied to the brother for a grand exit and a reminder for his weak state of consciousness.

"And you see this dress I have on?" I asked him. "I stole this shit from Macy's department store this morning. I just wanted to impress you."

I guess that he would never find out that I had a master's degree in English from Hampton. What difference did it make? If education was only to be used to allow you to look down on your people instead of trying to uplift them, then *fuck* education!

## $ $ $

I was still pissed off about my date when I got back to my townhouse in Baldwin Hills that night. I couldn't even write a poem about it I was so mad. I got this crazy-behind thought in my mind. I wondered what Coe Anawabi was doing. He wasn't necessarily a street brother, but he *had* bought into the mysticism of black bald heads, and he was a lot more interesting to be with than Mr. *Ar-tu-ro* Squire any day of the week, even in Coe's show-off immaturity. At least he wasn't snobbish.

I dug up his phone number and called him for the first time at a quarter after ten that Saturday night only to get his message machine. He had a smooth jazz instrumental in the background of all things:

"This is Coe, the man you've been looking for, but I'm not in right now, so leave a message and I'll make your dream come true when I get back in. So peace out for now, but make sure you leave that number for later."

I felt like a silly-ass groupie leaving him a message on that machine, but the brother actually sounded poetic against the jazz track, and that turned me on, so I left him a message to call me anyway:

"This is Tracy Ellison from Philly, the sister you wanna know better. So if you get in tonight at a decent hour, give me a ring on this thing . . ." and I left him my phone number.

After I hung up, I thought of the many poems that I had written on black-on-black sexuality, and I began to dig them up on my old notepads to read. I didn't expect for Coe to get my message until the next morning sometime (it was a Saturday night—party time), but in the meantime I figured that I could use my own poetic words, written over many lonely nights, to love me down.

I started reading and laughing out loud while enjoying my own shit and forgot about the time. When the phone rang, it was eleven thirty-seven. Who could it be?

"Hello," I answered.

"I just happened to call my message machine before I walked into this party, and found out you called me."

It was you-know-who, the man in demand, with the cream-colored Porsche.

I had no time to waste. I said, "Are you going into that party, or are you coming over here to see me?"

He started laughing as if it were a joke.

"I'm dead serious," I told him.

"I know you are, but my man Jonathan was expecting me to be there tonight at his Bistro 880 Club in Carson," he responded. "He has a special party for distinguished brothers going on, and I'm one of the distinguished brothers."

I wondered if I could talk him out of going, but I couldn't whine like an amateur. I had to use reverse psychology on his young behind.

I said, "Well, you have a good time down there in Carson, and I'll find a way to have a good time up here in Baldwin Hills."

"I can come by later on," he said.

"No you can't."

"Why not?"

"I don't take cold orders. If I can't have it right now, then I just can't have it, because I like it hot."

He broke up laughing again. "Girl, you trippin'."

"Okay, well, have a good time."

"Wait a minute. I haven't made up my mind yet," he told me in a hurry. I guess I sounded pretty convincing to him. I took it to the next level.

"Look, it's already a quarter to twelve, and I want long-term company tonight, so don't make me wait for it."

"*Long-term company?*" he asked.

I said, "If you come over here tonight, you can't leave until ten o'clock in the morning. That's what I mean by 'long-term company.' I don't want no quickies."

"Oh, it's like that."

For a second, I believe that I told him too much information. He could have taken me for granted, so I had to cover my tracks.

"*If* I'm still in the mood at all by the time you get here. I might just change my damn mind about the whole thing," I teased him. "In fact, I'm tired of talking about it now. I mean, *I* know what I wanna do, *you* just don't."

He said, "All right, all right, I'm coming. I'm not even in Carson yet. I can make it back up to Baldwin Hills in ten minutes."

"Ten minutes? Don't kill yourself, just get here. And please . . ." I paused for effect, "don't play with me. If you wanna come . . . then come."

When he laughed again, like he was high on weed or something with the giggles, I knew that I had him, so I gave him directions. I hung up the phone and said, "Damn, how come none of my shit works on Victor, while everything *he* does works so well on me?"

I pulled out a thick purple candle and lit it in my room. I got ready for company with the right body scents and slippery clothes: purple for royalty. Coe was just plain lucky that night. I even bought myself a thirty-six pack of condoms that week to make sure that I never broke my rules. If it wasn't for Mr. *Ar-tu-ro* acting like an asshole that night, then maybe I could have fallen to sleep without needing to release so much pent-up energy. As it was, I had a love jones of my own, and it needed to be satisfied.

Coe rang my doorbell in good time, and I answered it with nothing on but a long purple nightshirt of satin. He was dressed in all cream like his car, looking one hundred percent like a fine-ass model, and I was glad as hell that I had called him. However, it *still* had to be on *my* terms.

I stopped him at the door before he entered. "Now what

did I tell you you had to agree to do before you came in here?" I asked him.

He laughed again. Maybe he *was* high. I don't remember him being that silly at Venice Beach, but his eyes were clear, and he smelled like sweet cologne.

I pressed him for an answer. "What did I tell you?"

"You told me I can't leave."

"Until what time?"

"Ten o'clock."

"Okay, as long as you know." I backed up and let him in.

He walked inside and finally stopped laughing. I locked the door behind him.

"What kind of cologne do you have on?" I asked.

"Jean Paul Gaultier."

I nodded. "It smells good. You want something to drink?"

"Yeah, something fruity," he answered.

I pulled out the Hi-C fruit punch from the refrigerator and poured us both a small glass.

"That's all you're gonna give me?" he said, looking at the small glass.

I answered, "Yes and no."

"What?"

I explained, "Yes, this is all of the *juice* that you're getting, and no, this is *not* all that I'm gonna give you."

He started laughing again. "Are all the women in Philadelphia like you?"

I noticed a bulge in his pants.

I smiled and said, "There's only one me, but we *do* know what we want in Philadelphia, and we're not afraid to say it."

"Yeah, that's what I know."

I led him to the stairway and said, "Come on."

He nearly tripped over his feet to follow me.

"Are you okay?" I asked, smiling.

"Yeah, I'm all right."

"You weren't drinking and driving were you?"

"Naw."

"Good."

When we got up to my bedroom, I told him to sit on the floor at the foot of my bed.

"Why?" he asked me.

I gave him a no-nonsense look and said, "Just do it."

"For what?"

"I want to read something to you. Are you into poetry?"

He said, "Good poetry, but I don't like that twisted stuff that I can't understand. What the hell is that?"

I laughed. "Me neither. I never write that kind. My poetry is straightforward."

"Oh yeah. I wrote a few poems, not that many though, and I don't know them by heart, so don't ask me to say them."

I smiled. "I wasn't. Sit down and turn around so I can put my legs on you."

He looked at me and started laughing again. The bulge in his pants was still visible. I hoped that he knew how to use it.

He finally sat on the floor and I flipped to the poem that I wanted to read to him, and tossed my bare legs across his broad shoulders. The candlelight was on the dresser where I could see.

I said, "This is called 'A Homemade Twinkie.'"

He turned around and started laughing to see if I was serious.

"Why do you keep laughing so much? God! Am I blowing your mind, or *what*?" I asked him.

To my surprise, he said, "Yeah, you are. I mean, you just . . . you just . . ."

"I just say what the hell is on my mind, right?"

"Yeah. I'm not used to that. I mean, I'm used to it, but not like you."

"Anyway," I told him, getting back to my poem. Since he was honest about things, I leaned over and kissed him on the lips, good and wet, with a tiny bite to let him feel it. I wanted him in a sexy mood when I read to him, and not that silly shit. After I kissed him, his mood was right.

I said, "Listen to me in silence, and I'll let you know when you can move. Okay?"

He nodded. "Okay."

"'A Homemade Twinkie,'" I read to him:

> "I was made from priceless flour
> grounded from the sweetest grains
> and mixed with collected honey
> from swarms of African bees
> who protected my nectar
> with STINGS
> that were fatal.
>
> "I was stirred with milk
> so filled with nutrients
> that it fed entire plantations
> of children
> because the Master loved
> his sons and daughters
> and Mary Sue's milk
> was NEVER as nurturing.
>
> "I was thickened with eggs
> that began the world
> and produced the seeds

*who built the Pyramids*
*who built the Great Wall of China*
*who civilized America*
*BEFORE it was discovered*
*AND who landed on the moon*
*seeds from MY eggs*
*EVE*
*in case you caught worldwide amnesia.*

*"I was flavored with sugar*
*straight from the cane*
*cut down by Abel men*
*cut down by Cain*
*cut down in sin*
*then Nations came*
*Nations addicted to sugar*
*that ROBBED their brains*
*of sanity.*

*"I was sprinkled with natural oils*
*that allowed my hair*
*to stand at attention*
*unwashed*
*and still clean*
*nappy*
*and still breathe*
*kinky*
*and still grow*
*short*
*and still sexy*
*LONG*
*and braided.*

*"Then I was baked ALIVE*
*and molded in the heat*
*of slavery*
*in the heat*
*of dehumanization*
*in the heat*
*of bigotry*
*in the heat*
*of poverty*
*sexism*
*racism*
*classism.*

*"Until I was finally left alone*
*a cold*
*loveless*
*hollow shell*
*of my past greatness*
*needing YOU*
*with your cream*
*to fill me up*
*and start the world again*
*with a treat*
*of our sweet*
*and completed*
*love."*

When I was finished, I leaned over and kissed Coe on the lips and told him, "Now you can move," before I pulled him onto my bed with me.

# when it's vacation time

i dream of peace and quiet
i see beaches and ocean water
i hear laughter and bare feet
running
sisters wear bikinis and
brothers bare their chests
while i just chill
drinking strawberry coolers
or piña coladas under colorful umbrellas
drunk with the feeling of relaxation
finally
with no one knocking at my door
no one ringing on my phone
no one yanking down my skirt
my hands are no longer writing or typing
or ironing or cooking
my mind no longer pressed for thought
or at least not in urgent organized patterns
because now i can think of anything
on my own time
like
what if i were a mermaid?
stranded upon shore
would a black fisherman rescue me?
would he freak out and scream and run away?
or would he take me home with him?
to hide me and love me in fresh salt water
see?

when it's vacation time
i can think of anything
with no commas or periods or capitals in my way
only thoughts and questions
like
what if i were a moon woman?
whose skin glowed like 100 watt light bulbs
would a black man astronaut find me there?
on my moon
could he be able to handle my glow?
or would he always wear moon shades?
and lie
that i do not hurt his eyes with my illumination
maybe i need a vacation from thinking
about black men
now that would be a vacation
but when would i go back home to him?
if i went back home at all
and if i had a real him to return to
then why did i vacation alone?
like he does
he is always on vacation
or saying that he needs one
so that he can think to himself
he says
but when will he come back home to me?
see?
when it's vacation time i can think
of anything
and i like it
my freedom thought
maybe i should vacation more

*maybe we all should*
*vacation*
*so we can think of anything*
*to take us away from bondage*
*to everything*

# April 2000

$$\text{\$ \$}$$
$$\text{\$}$$

*T*racy, the telephone is for you," my mother told me in my old room. I looked over at the clock. It read quarter to eight in the morning. I had nowhere to go that day, and it couldn't have been my agent, because it was only a quarter to five out in California.

My mother read my confusion and said, "It's Vanessa."

"Oh."

My little cousin was calling me, probably on her way to school that Monday morning.

I cleared my throat and answered the phone. "Hello."

"I told you how my mother was," Vanessa announced to me.

"Are you at school?"

"I'm on my way."

"Well, we'll talk about it," I told her.

"Did I wake you up?"

I paused. "Well—"

Vanessa started laughing. "I'm sorry then. I'll call you when I get back home today."

"Yeah, you do that."

I hung up the phone, and my mother was still standing there waiting for me.

She said, "You see that, you've started something."

I sighed and said, "Mom, I can't be a mentor to my little cousin? What's so wrong with that; she's blood, ain't she?"

"Okay, well, get prepared to bleed then. You asked for it."

"I asked for what? Vanessa's not bad at all."

My mother nodded, knowingly. "Tracy, when people start to depend on you and hold you accountable for their welfare, things can get very hairy, but I guess you wouldn't know that; you don't have any children yet, nor do you have—" She stopped herself and said, "I'm not even going to say it," before she walked out to finish getting ready for work.

I caught on quickly and hollered, "I don't *need* no man, Mom! I'm making it just fine without one!"

"That's what they *all* say!" she yelled back at me.

I remained in bed that morning and relaxed. Sometimes you need relaxation. I had been home for a full week, and all I did was run, run, run. I was exhausted, obviously, but I was also used to a hectic schedule. If you're *not* running in the business of entertainment, you miss things; that's just the way it goes. I went out to California with my track shoes on, expecting to run and run far, and I had. I wanted to run farther too; that's just the way that *I* was, always pushing forward with something new.

Before I went to bed that Sunday night, I had tossed my mother's *Ebony* on the floor to read. She said I was quoted in an article for their May issue discussing the black actress and the new millennium. I remembered the interview. I was very open with them. I wondered how much of my openness they had captured in the article, or bothered to print. That was what I hated about the media. They asked you questions, but they only wanted to print what they wanted to hear, so they wait for you to say it, and ignore everything else that you say. In feature stories, they focused only on the external things: what you're wearing, who you're dating, where you live, how much money you're making; all gossip information. What about discovering the artist within, the *internal*? I guess no one was really interested in what artists *think*. That's why I needed to continue my story for those who *would* like to know, but maybe since I had become a star, even my *Flyy Girl* fans would want to ignore me. I no longer "represented" a reckless teenager for them. I no longer had my roughneck man in Victor. I no longer ran the streets of Philadelphia. I was highly educated at that, with a master's degree in English (of all things, with my yuck mouth as a teenager, right?) and no man. Higher education and no man was like poison to a black woman, and my parents wouldn't let me forget that. So what was a girl supposed to do, finish high school and get married at age eighteen, like they did in 1952? I don't *think* so!

The comedian Chris Rock said that the black intelligentsia was no longer valued in our community, only athletes, actors, musicians, and comedians like himself. I saved the *Notorious* magazine issue in 1999 that quoted him. He called the black intelligentsia "wack." I even wrote a poem about it, "Wacky Intelligence." Was Chris being sarcastic when he said that? Was he misquoted? *He* was labeled intelligent for his award-winning concert *Bring the Pain*. Intelligent humor was what put him on the map, but he seemed to be caught between his intelligence and his fear of not representing for the 'hood: *Bigger & Blacker*. He was caught up in the great Black American contradiction, just like I was, the flyy girl who grew up and expanded her mind, only to return to the bullshit of Hollywood before anyone noticed her again. No one paid any attention to me as a schoolteacher. Maybe Raheema was right. Who wants to hear an intelligent story of success when we love to struggle so much? Crabs in a barrel. *Happy* crabs, dancing around and snapping at each other for wanting to jump out of the barrel and explore.

I was thinking so much in my relaxation that I didn't open the *Ebony* magazine for another thirty minutes or so. When I did, I found that they had interviewed ten black actresses for the article, including Cicely Tyson and myself. Cicely Tyson spoke on our need to find more vehicles that expressed a balance of our culture. She felt that in the year 2000 and beyond, we *owed* ourselves that mission, not just to star in films, but to star in films that meant something for the younger black girls who watched us.

Of course, Cicely Tyson was right, and she had starred in plenty of smaller films to prove her dedication and commitment to black culture. She presented another contradiction for me: How could I complain about the media not taking me seriously while I starred in a movie like *Led Astray*? As expected, my quotes in the article were marginal. I talked about how surprised I was to be offered the starring role in my first green-lighted screenplay. The article went on to discuss more sisters, like myself, writing our own scripts as new vehicles. I felt good about that. *Ebony* captured the fact that I was a pioneer. I closed the magazine with a smile on my face, but I still wanted to tell more of my story, and I wanted that damn book contract signed and sealed before the summer was out. So I planned to call my agent again and ask her what the progress was on the book deal, and to begin exploring new options.

I thought about Raheema's older sister Mercedes, my second idol. Of course, my mother was my first. Anyway, I had written a poem called "Mercedes" that related her to the car that she was named after, expensive, hard to keep, hard to repair, but forever valuable and always noticed on the road. I guess that *I* was more like a BMW myself (even though I owned a Mercedes). I was faster to accelerate, technologically hip, and I didn't cost as much, so I never paid the price of my flashiness like Mercedes had paid. Nevertheless, even though I had gotten much farther than her with my education and drive, Mercedes would always be more complicated than I was, and more expensive. Would I turn down her plea for twelve thousand dollars like I told Raheema I would? . . . In reality, I didn't know. Maybe if I got the starring role in *Road Kill*, I would give Mercedes the down payment on her house anyway, as long as she understood that she would have to keep up her own mortgage and maintenance to keep it, because I would *not* bail her out of anything, and I meant that!

I relaxed and thought, and relaxed some more, being as lazy as I wanted to be that morning until I fell back asleep again and didn't wake up until after one o'clock that afternoon. I thought of calling my girl for a progress report.

*Should I wait another hour before I call her?* I asked myself. *It's only after ten in California. Maybe she could use another hour or so to get things done before I call.*

Right as I hovered near the phone, still indecisive about the timing of my phone call, the phone rang and startled me.

"Hello," I answered.

"Hey, Tracy."

I smiled. "I was just about to call you. I was sitting over here stalling to give you more time."

"Well, I don't need it," she told me. "You got what you want. The producer said that *Road Kill* is not yet green-lighted, but if they could decide immediately on the lead, it would push things ahead much faster. So he wants to meet with us for lunch on Thursday."

I said, "Okay, so I have to get out of here by Wednesday to prepare for this meeting. Good job, girl!"

"You didn't doubt me, did you?"

"No, of course not, but while we're on the subject of getting things done, what's up with the book deal?" I asked her.

"I came up with an idea," she said. "Since we both know that we want to use some of your poetry, and I've let *them* know, I need you to print out, I guess, twenty-five or so selected poems that you would use in the book, so that I could send them out and let them see what we're trying to do. Last time you guys just sat down and did it, but this time you're both moving forward with your careers and everything, and you really need to agree ahead of time on how everything is going to be executed.

"I would also look at other books that use text and poetry to figure out the best way to integrate the two without destroying the flow that you guys created with *Flyy Girl*," she advised. "I would say that this book should definitely be a little different too, because sequels are very hard to do. You can't give your fan base the exact same thing, even though they may ask for it, because they'll become dissatisfied. You have to take it up a level."

I nodded. "Yeah, I know what you mean. People are quick to say, 'It wasn't as good as the first one.' So I think that the first thing for me to do would be to use my own voice instead of third person, so that they can really feel me."

"Well, that will take away from the minor characters involved, but I do agree with you," she said. "A first-person narrative would be a major change."

I was impressed! My girl was really stepping up the game plan, and she was absolutely right; we had not approached it in a business-plan format like we needed to.

I said, "I'll get on that right away, and pick out the poems that would relate the most to what I would like to cover in the book."

"Do your parents have a computer at home?" she asked me.

"Yeah, but I didn't bring my notepads out here with me."

"Oh, yeah. Well, I guess you'll have to get started on that when you get back out to LA."

"No problem. My girl Raheema was just telling me this weekend that I should start typing out my poetry and storing them on disk anyway."

"Yeah, she's right. But tell me again how you came across the first book deal with Omar. I never really asked you the details about that. I may be able to use some of that information for this new book deal."

"I met him at a poetry event in Philly," I told her. "I had performed this poem about the materialism that I got caught up in during the eighties, and we got to talking about it and reminiscing on how flyy the initial hip-hop generation was, you know, with the gold and fancy clothes and hairstyles and all of that.

"Well, one thing led to another, and he started saying that my life story might make a good book. And at first, I thought he was joking," I added. "So when I agreed to do it, I wanted to make up a name, but he convinced me to write it straight up and keep it real. And that's how it happened."

My girl said, "Okay, that's good to know. Now we have to convince *him* to keep it real again and produce a sequel, because your fans want to know the rest of the story."

"Yeah, so let's get to it," I commented. "And I'll start thinking about what poems to use."

"All right, well, I'll talk to you as soon as you get back out to LA."

I hung up that phone and went right back to my bed. It wasn't as if I couldn't think from my bed. I was relaxing. I hadn't even put on any clothes that day. I stretched out across my bed and thought about all of the things I wanted to say in my sequel, what poems to use, when to start it, how to finish it, the whole shebang. The next thing I knew it was three o'clock and the phone was ringing again. I didn't even feel like answering it, but I did.

"Hello."

"It's Vanessa."

"Hey, Vanessa. You weren't kidding when you said that you would call after school today, hunh?" I joked.

She said, "No."

"So how was your school day?"

"The same-old same-old. Nothing new."

I knew what she wanted to get around to, and both of us were stalling, so I decided to come right out with it.

"Okay, so we have to figure out a way to get you out to LA this summer," I said.

"I know," she agreed. "My mom is so shortsighted. I told her this could really expand my horizons for the future."

I mocked her mother and asked, "Expand your horizons for what, so you can be another Hollywood hoe?"

Vanessa laughed and said, "Yup, that's what she said, and I told her, I don't have to be *in* movies, just behind the scenes with it. A lot of people make good livings behind the scenes."

"Not as many black people do," I leveled with her.

"But that's why it would be so wide open for people like me."

I sat there on the phone with my cousin and got a little

nervous. My mother was right, I *had* started something. I was just asking Vanessa to come out to California for the summer in the essence of family love, not to get her started in the business of Hollywood. She was jumping *way* ahead of me!

"You were thinking about this all day long, weren't you?" I asked her.

She laughed and said, "I couldn't even sleep last night."

*SHIT!* I thought to myself. *Momma knows best! This is crazy!*

I had to cool Vanessa down a bit. I said, "Hollywood isn't for everybody, Vanessa, and it's just not that easy. I don't want it to seem like anybody can just jump right in."

"But if you know the right people and you get schooled on the business side early, then you can make it. I'm smart enough to make it. I *know* I am," she insisted.

With one quick conversation I had created a monster, but my little cousin *was* smart enough, I just didn't know what kind of *stamina* she had. A lot of people had that start-out energy, but not many of them had the energy to *finish* what they started.

"Well, like I said, the first thing for you to do is to keep your grades up in school, and I'll work on your mother little by little, if she'll even *talk* to me," I joked. "Maybe I'll sit down and write her a couple of letters or something.

"In fact," I said, "that's a good way for me and you to stay in touch, because I have to head back out to LA on Wednesday now."

Vanessa said, "For real? I thought that you were staying until Sunday." She sounded disappointed.

"I was initially, but now I have a meeting for a lead role this Thursday."

"Oh. Well, what's the name of the movie?"

Boy did she sound deflated already.

"*Road Kill.* It's a female action flick. A thriller."

"It's coming out next year?"

"Hopefully."

"Okay."

I said, "Look, we'll stay in touch, Vanessa, it's not like it's the end of the world or anything. You're my little cousin, right?"

"Yeah, I know."

"So stop sounding like your boyfriend dumped you. *God!* How is that guy doing, anyway? Mr. Nineteen? Have you talked to him lately?"

Vanessa sucked her teeth and said, "He's mad at me now."

"Why, you wouldn't go over to his house this weekend?" I assumed.

"No, he wanted me to let him in *my* house."

I chuckled and said, "Oh, so he's a *bold* one. And you see how they get, right? Ain't nothin' changed, girl. Not a *thing,*" I broke it down to her.

She said, "I know."

"So, I'll give you my address and phone number to call me collect, and we'll just stay in touch and see what we can work out for the future."

"Okay then."

I gave my cousin all of my information over the phone and hung up feeling relieved. Vanessa could prove to be high-maintenance just like I was, whether she was introverted or not. In fact, with her introverted personality it was hard to know *all* that she really wanted until she made up her mind to verbalize it. So I decided right then and there, that if I had to deal with Vanessa on a daily basis at any time in the near future, I would have to stick it to her ass to get all of the answers *right away*.

I slid into bed and went right back to relaxing, daydreaming, and thinking about any- and everything that crossed my mind.

"Damn!" I told myself after a while. "I have to call the airport and change my flight plans. Back to Hollywood I go. Hollywood, Hollywood."

# That's on Everything

*My good looks,*
*I put that on my parents.*
*Because with Mom,*
*as pretty as she is,*
*and Dad,*
*as handsome as he is,*
*I just couldn't miss.*

*My hard head,*
*I put that on my father*
*alone.*
*Because just like*
*he wanted to do*
*his thing,*
*I wanted to do*
*mine.*

*My poise,*
*I put that on my momma.*
*Because whenever I got*
*too hot,*
*she made sure*
*to cool my ass*
*back down.*

*My determination,*
*I put that on my race.*
*Because who else*
*has struggled*
*as much as we have,*

*pushing, striving,*
*and surviving?*

*My greediness,*
*I put that on America.*
*Because the good, old,*
*red, white, and blue*
*damn sure*
*makes you want it.*

*My craftiness,*
*I put that on the streets*
*of Philadelphia,*
*slippin', slidin', and hidin'*
*to put my thing down.*

*My confidence,*
*I put that on myself.*
*Because*
*I just think that*
*I was*
*born with it.*

*And my success,*
*I put that on everything.*
*Because everything I've done,*
*seen,*
*or been through*
*prepared me for*
*who I am today*
*and all that I do*
*for tomorrow.*

# July 1997

$$ $

$

I made it through my first full year of Hollywood, and after the summer of 1997, California had grown on me. Before the new television season got under way, I signed with the Writers Guild association, completed my continuation script to the season's finale of *Conditions of Mentality, and* I had plenty of other television producers wanting me to write for *their* shows. I was "the flavor of the month" in hot demand and absolutely *loving* it! I even had a young stud with his nose wide open for me. However, Yolanda and I had grown farther apart.

In August, when I decided to freelance with my scriptwriting for the new television season instead of signing on full time with *Conditions of Mentality,* Yolanda snapped at me as if I were her daughter.

"I can't *believe* that you didn't sign on with *Conditions* so you can write spec scripts for these little *black* shows," she said. "Do you understand what you're about to do? You're cutting yourself *out* of the loop with the real players out here."

I said, "They all offered me the same amount of money, so I would rather have my freedom to write whatever I want, and for whatever show." It was that simple to me. Besides, Tim Waterman had left as the producer of *Conditions,* with Joseph Keaton still there as the head writer, and

I damn sure didn't want to deal with that man every day. Tim had hired me and protected me (regardless of whether I gave him some of my pudding or not), and without him there, I didn't feel comfortable about going back.

Yolanda said, "I keep telling you, Tracy, you want to look at the *long term*, and not the *short term*."

Frankly, I was tired of hearing her mouth. Every time I turned around, Yolanda had something to suggest to me rather strongly. I never denied that she had hooked me up with my first Hollywood job, but I wasn't *indebted* to her for that. It wasn't as if she was my manager or anything, and I always paid her fee to review my contracts, so it wasn't as if she had given me anything for free.

I said, "Well, I'm moving on," and that was the end of it.

Yolanda stopped her horses from running and asked me, "Are you still hanging out with Susan Rockin?"

I didn't like her question because I knew where she was going with it. I was even tempted to lie and tell her no, but I didn't.

"Yeah, we're still friends," I answered.

"Okay, because you're gonna *need* some allies, especially if you plan to make your own way instead of establishing yourself somewhere stable."

"Somewhere *stable?*" I responded. "*Conditions* was not stable. We didn't even know if we would have another season until the last minute."

"And it was *your* shows that pushed them over the top, Tracy," she reminded me. "So if you would have *stayed* there, you could have increased your name recognition for the bigger shows: *dramas* on NBC, ABC, and CBS."

"Well, who said that I wanted to stay in television anyway?" I snapped back at her. "I'm just having fun right now writing these scripts." My real mission was to write feature films, but I kept that to myself.

Yolanda got real quiet over the phone. She said, "All right. You're gonna go right ahead and fuck up your career messing around with these little *cliques*."

"They're *all* cliques out here," I told her, "and everywhere else. So which one are *you* connected to?"

I was tempted to ask her if she really went to Howard University in Washington, D.C., because she damn sure wasn't down with Black Hollywood. I wonder if Kendra knew how anti–black business Yolanda was. I don't believe that she did know, because they didn't really talk about business like we did. Kendra wasn't in the business.

I planned to spend my twenty-sixth birthday hanging out with my two main girls on the West Side, Kendra and Susan. They got along together, too. At first I was a little nervous about mixing a Hollywood Jew with a Baltimore "sistah," but we all related on a human level, and Susan liked how "real" Kendra and I both were as opposed to the "fake" Hollywood girls (her words, not mine) she grew up with in California. I guess you could say that Susan was "crossing over" to us, but after a while, I began to wonder if she had a man, or was even interested in men, because she never talked about them like Kendra and I. Susan never seemed to have any opposite-sex dates either.

"Hold on, it's the telephone. Turn the stereo down for a minute," I told them. We were all at my place getting ready to go out while listening to the Roots, the Philadelphia hip-hop band, on CD.

"Hello," I answered.

"It's Coe. Happy birthday, Tracy! Do you need me for anything?"

"Not tonight, but I'll let you know."

"I know you will," he said with a chuckle. I hated to admit it, but I had to turn Coe Anawabi into my little sex slave. It was better than sleeping with new men that I didn't particularly like just to satisfy my intimate needs. The only problem was Coe's age. The boy turned out to be twenty-one. I found that out in a past photo shoot he had taken for *Vibe* magazine earlier that year.

Kendra looked toward the phone and got suspicious. She had witnessed my woman power over Coe when she arrived back in California in mid August. Susan met him too, but I don't know if she suspected anything. I just introduced him as a friend. Maybe Susan did suspect, but I didn't really care. Coe was still fine, young, and mine, or at least for the meantime, because I couldn't delude myself into keeping a younger man.

I said, "I'll be calling you soon. Just stay on standby."

*"On standby?"*

"That's what I said," I snapped at him. Coe still tried to assert himself every once in a while, but it wasn't working. I had him firmly under my spell.

When I hung up the phone, Kendra stepped near me and whispered, "What did you do to that boy, Tracy?"

I played innocent and asked her, "What?"

"You know what I'm talking about."

I don't think Kendra thought that Susan knew from the way that she was talking in code, or maybe it was a black thing to keep the brother talk to ourselves.

"No I *don't* know," I told her.

She looked at me sternly and said, "We're gonna talk. *Later.*"

I looked over to Susan and watched her dancing to the

Roots. She had this stiff shoulder move with her fingers snapping to the snare drum with no body or leg movement to the bass. I shook my head and started to laugh at her.

"Susan, what's up with the legs, man, move your body."

She tried to move her body and legs and it only made the situation worse.

"Oh, my God! I'm gonna have to give you dance lessons," I joked with her.

Kendra started to laugh too.

Susan said, "Kendra doesn't move all that much either."

Kendra stopped and said, "Don't go there, okay? *I* can dance when the music is right."

"No you can't. You think too much to dance," I teased her.

"Whatever," Kendra responded to me. "Who made *you* the dance expert?"

"The rhythm," I said to both of them, "I know how to follow it." I rocked it for them, real smooth and whatnot to show them how it's done.

"Well, isn't this a Philadelphia group?" Susan asked. "She has an advantage over us," she said to Kendra.

"That doesn't mean anything. I can dance to Dru Hill better than Kendra, and they're from Baltimore, and I can dance to Snoop Doggy Dogg better than you, Susan, and he's from Long Beach."

"I'm not from Long Beach," Susan responded with a chuckle.

"It's close enough," I told her.

"Are we just about ready to go now?" Kendra asked me. I said, "Yeah."

"Well, let me use the bathroom before we leave then." Kendra went to use the bathroom, and I had this crazy thought on my mind to get the scoop on Susan and her love life.

"Susan, do you have a boyfriend or anything who you never talk about?"

She smiled at me and shook her head as if I had caught her off guard.

"I'm serious," I told her. "You never even talk about guys. You don't like girls, do you?"

Sometimes my damn mouth needed a zipper on it, I swear!

Susan looked at me and said, "*No,* I don't like women like that! I just keep my personal life to myself. Besides, I'm not serious about anyone right now anyways."

I tried to joke it off with her.

I said, "Okay, because I know I look good, but I like *brothers* to tell you the truth, Susan."

Susan was stunned with this big old smile on her face that she couldn't seem to erase.

"You can be very vain sometimes, okay, Tracy. *Very* vain," she told me.

I smiled and said, "Well, thank you. Do I measure up to the other Hollywood girls you know?" I was referring mainly to white girls with loads of A-list money, and I was still far from it. Even Susan had a BMW to my Toyota, and despite my moderate success in scriptwriting, I had still not gone crazy with my income.

Susan shook her head and answered, "Not quite. You may be vain, but you're still very practical. The girls who I know, they're vain *and* impractical, and those are two *very* bad combinations to have."

I said, "Yeah, because I can't *afford* to be impractical. *Yet,*" I added with a grin.

Kendra stepped out of the bathroom, and we all made

our way to a club off of Beverly Boulevard in Susan's midnight blue Beamer. Who the hell wanted to ride in Toyotas? We wanted to show up in style.

The party was jam-packed that night with a mixed crowd and a New York DJ who must have been really popular, because the crowd was loving him!

"Wow!" Kendra said. "I haven't been to *anything* like this over here." She was referring to California parties.

I said, "Me either," because the whole place was dancing for a change, and that represented the power of the DJ to pick quality songs that made you move. He couldn't miss with Lauryn Hill and the Fugees.

"Have you been to a party like this before, Susan?" Kendra asked.

Susan smiled and said, "Yeah."

I looked through the crowd and spotted rappers Yo Yo and Mack 10, with a posse of other West Coast rappers in the house that I didn't recognize as readily. I wonder what they all thought about the New York DJ playing the New Jersey–based Fugees for a California crowd. I guess it was all love, though. Everybody wasn't mixed up into the East Coast–West Coast feud.

Kendra spotted Yo Yo and said, "I remember girls at Hampton back in the day who used to *love* themselves some Yo Yo. That 'Pass It On' song was their *anthem*."

I laughed and said, "I know just who you're talking about. Those girls got high like every other day. I wonder if they ever graduated."

Kendra said, "Yeah, they graduated. It just took them an extra couple of years."

She asked Susan what school she had attended.

"Stanford."

Kendra nodded. "Pretty good school, and good sports teams."

"Yeah," Susan said with a pumped fist and a smile. "Go Cardinal!"

I smiled myself.

"Hey, you wanna dance?" someone asked Kendra.

She looked and smiled at me before going to get her groove on.

"It's me and you next, Susan," I said. "Don't get nervous now."

"Hey, Tracy," someone called me, tapping me from behind. I turned and met eyes with Richard Mack.

"Hey, Rich."

"Let me talk to you for a minute," he said.

I looked at Susan. Before I could open my mouth to her, she said, "Go ahead, I'm fine."

I stepped aside with Rich. He said, "Remember I was telling you about that project in the spring?"

I nodded. "Yeah."

"Well, I just sold a pilot to UPN for thirteen episodes in mid-season. I was wondering if you wanted to write a couple of the scripts. I wrote four of them myself already. And do you know Juanita Perez?"

I grinned. I didn't hold a grudge against the sister or anything.

I said, "Yeah, I know her."

"Well, she's working on a couple of scripts too."

"So, what's the pilot about?" I asked.

"It's called *Brothers and Sisters*, about a group of Hollywood blacks all from different walks of life who rent a house in Beverly Hills, while they all try to make it in the business."

I smiled. "That's pretty clever. Why didn't you tell me about that before, you were afraid that I might steal your idea?"

He chuckled and said, "I trust no one until I have the paperwork signed, and now I have it."

"So, what is it, three guys and three girls, a black version of *Friends*?" I was only guessing. *Friends* and *Seinfeld* were the talks of television that season. *Friends* was coming in and *Seinfeld* was going out.

Rich smiled at me again. "You know how Hollywood works by now, Tracy; copying a successful show is *always* the bomb."

I said, "Well, yeah, you can count me in on that." A few extra dollars and more script credits wouldn't hurt me at all. That was what I was out there to do, to put my thing down.

"You're not signed with *Conditions* for the season?"

I frowned. "No, they have a new producer so I didn't feel it was comfortable for me. But they'll still look at my spec scripts, and my continuation from last season kicks off the show, so they'll be calling me; they just don't have me under contract."

"Have you ever thought about developing your own show?"

All of a sudden, the party became secondary. Rich and I were talking business in that place like nothing else mattered.

I said, "I haven't even thought about a show idea, but thanks for asking me. Maybe I *should* think about that."

Rich nodded with a big grin. "It pays well. You become the show creator, and you just sit tight, write a few scripts here and there, and start working on creating another show."

He said, "I read about writers who make their living that way, whether the shows are successful or not."

"Black writers too?" I asked him. I couldn't see that idea working so well for a black writer. The success rate of every show was too important to us.

"If you're good enough, they'll pay you to do next to nothing just to keep you away from the competition," Rich told me with a greedy grin.

Once I thought about it, I didn't know if I liked the idea of developing shows just to make a quick buck and then dropping everyone who put their hard work and effort into it. That's what had so many Hollywood types scrambling on their last dollar to make the ends meet as it was, especially in *Black* Hollywood.

"Do you think that's right?" I asked Rich candidly. "I mean, we both know how hard it is for black people to keep a show on the air. Developing new shows just for the money seems really irresponsible to me."

I just had to tell Rich like it was because I didn't agree with it.

He said, "Tracy, it's not like these people are going to run out of money. They'll get over it, and they'll find some new black show to exploit next year. It's all about the money out here."

"I'm not talking about the shows themselves, Rich, I'm talking about the people who play a part in making the show happen; the actors, directors, writers, extras, wardrobe people, and the fans who watch."

I was beginning to think that Hollywood had already gotten the best of Rich. He was still cool and everything, but the money seemed to be pulling him by the nose.

He nodded and said, "I see what you mean." After that he smiled at me. "I had no idea that you would be that type."

"What type?" I asked.

He said, "I finished reading your book *Flyy Girl*, and I thought that *you* would be the *first* one to chase the money."

I just shook my head, but I wasn't that upset about it anymore. I had to get over it. I said, "Rich, my flyy girl days are over with, okay? I'm a grown, responsible black woman now, who cares about the images of her people. Now if *you* don't, then that's *your* problem."

"So are you still interested in writing for the show?"

I paused, not wanting to commit to something that I may have regretted later on. "Only if it's good," I answered. I grinned to let him know there were no hard feelings between us.

He said, "That's fine with me, and if we get to keep the show, then that's even better."

"That's the way to sound about it," I told him. "Have some faith in your own creativity whether Hollywood has faith in black shows or not."

"All right, well, let me get back to my girl before she thinks I'm over here trying to sleep with you."

I laughed and said, "She'd probably be right."

He chuckled and said, "I'll be in touch."

By the time I made it back to my girls, Susan was dancing with some cute white guy, and Kendra was nowhere to be found.

"Have you seen Kendra?" I asked Susan.

She shrugged her shoulders. "She's in here somewhere."

I searched through the crowds just to be nosy and found Kendra with the same guy who had asked her to dance earlier. They were having a drink by the bar. I smiled and decided to leave them alone. Love was in the air.

I spotted Juanita's boy Reginald getting his freak on

with a long-haired, light-skinned video girl. I hated to stereotype, but the light-skinned sisters allowed it to happen by agreeing to do so many of them damn videos. Realistically, how many of them would say no, just for the sake of changing the imagery? All production had to do was ask the next light-skinned, long-haired girl. So I guess I had to blame the imagery more on the producers.

Reginald caught me daydreaming in his direction, and I turned away. I had a feeling that he would approach me that night, and I was right. Before the night was over, he did approach me.

"I hope you still don't see me as some kind of slimeball," he said to me.

I shook my head and grinned. "Your words, not mine," I told him.

He said, "You know a lot of people wouldn't mind you writing for them over at Warner. They say you have that realism thing going on, with believable characters."

"Because I take my time and get it right," I bragged. "I know I'm in demand. I got a call from your boss, Harold Wiggins, last week."

Reginald smiled real wide like he knew something. "And who do you think gave him your number?" he asked me. He said, "See, I'm not your enemy. Just remember that the next time you try to tell somebody off out here, because Hollywood is a small town. Trust me."

*That motherfucker!* I thought to myself. *He doesn't deserve any cool points for that. He would have been stupid not to give his boss my number! It wasn't like he was really hooking me up or anything. Harold probably asked him if he had it. Reginald would have looked unconnected if he had lied and said no.*

That was Hollywood for you; people were always trying

to take credit for the smallest damn things. Would I do the same if *I* was pressed? . . . Honestly, I didn't know. However, Reginald was right about one thing: Hollywood was small as hell, like a fishbowl, and everyone was swimming in the same dirty water, hungrily searching for morsels of food.

"So, what's his name?" I asked Kendra. We were back on our way to my place after three o'clock in the morning.

Kendra smiled and didn't say a word, bitten hard by the love bug.

"That's *your* business, Kendra," Susan warned her. "Tracy only wants to write her next script based on your love life. That's why I keep *my* personal affairs to myself."

"I wouldn't do that to y'all, unless it was a really *good* story," I admitted with a laugh.

"Yeah, that's what you *say;* that's what they *all* say, until you see characters who are very similar to yourself up on the big screen," Susan said.

Kendra just laughed, and I had a funny feeling that she wouldn't be around me as much anymore. I just felt it in my gut. Kendra had found a man. That made me page Coe at close to four o'clock in the morning, and the boy had a nerve to be wide awake and energetic.

"What are you doing, Coe?" I asked him. I was suspicious of his liveliness at such a late hour.

He sounded nervous about it. "What?"

I asked him again, "What are you *doing?* Or should I ask, What are you *about* to do, or have *just* done?"

He got real quiet on me and tried to run some weak-ass game. "I'm just getting in the house, and my pager went off, so I called you back. What are you talking about?"

I said, "Coe, listen to me closely, okay? You're *not* my man, and you're *not* in trouble, so don't fuckin' lie to me."

"I'm not lying—"

I cut him off and said, "The next time you're with company, do me a favor and call me back when you're free to tell the truth, okay? That would be *much better* than calling me back and sounding like an asshole."

When he got quiet again, I knew that my strong hunch was right; he was with a woman.

He asked, "Do you need me over there or something?"

I guess she wasn't a *strong* woman either, because he was seriously playing her.

I was tempted to say yes, just to pull my strings on his behind, but I figured, *What's the use, the boy is too young for me anyway.*

"No, you go ahead and finish what you started," I told him, "just don't do anything stupid to jeopardize your future. Okay? Be smart, and protect yourself."

". . . All right," he responded with a delay.

I hung up the phone with Coe and squeezed my pillow tightly to my chest. Sometimes you just have to grow up and let go. Victor had taught me that lesson rather painfully. I just hoped that he hadn't given me so much of a reality check that I would lose all faith in ever loving someone again.

# Family Ties

*They are like shoe laces,*
*they come undone.*
*When you are young,*
*you don't know how to tie them;*
*your mom and dad do it*
*for you.*
*But as you grow older*
*you learn,*
*otherwise*
*walking forward becomes dangerous.*
*And when you trip and fall*
*on your face,*
*outsiders will laugh at you*
*and say that you are clumsy*
*and not capable*
*of starting a family of your own.*
*However, you do it anyway*
*with untied shoes,*
*and you trip and fall*
*again,*
*and again,*
*and again*
*until*
*no one offers to help you up anymore.*

# April 2000

$ $
$

When I told my parents that I would have to return to California sooner than expected, my mother said she wanted to cook a big family dinner that Tuesday night before I left on Wednesday afternoon.

By seven o'clock that Tuesday evening, my mother had finished cooking a ten-pound turkey, candied yams, greens, wild rice, macaroni and cheese, and cranberry sauce, as if it were Thanksgiving.

I joked, "Mom, isn't Thanksgiving in November?"

She looked at me and said, "No, Thanksgiving is today, because *we* need to give thanks for your success and *our* success as a family. A lot of families are not making it anymore."

I couldn't argue with her on that. I sat at the dinner table and looked at my father. He just grinned and stared into empty space. Did he still feel guilty about his absentee years? Suddenly I had all the respect in the world for my mother *and* my father for finding a way to keep it together despite the struggles that they had early on. Jason, however, was holding us up, because he was late.

My brother walked in at a quarter after seven, smiling, and sat down at the table with us without washing his hands.

Mom said, "Jason, first of all, if you have a job starting

at nine o'clock in the morning, what time do you get there?"

He smiled even wider. "A quarter to nine," he answered.

My mother looked at her watch and asked, "Do you know what time it is right now?"

My father started to chuckle.

"Mom—" Jason uttered.

"I don't want to hear it," my mother cut him off. "If you *start* early, you get there *on* time or *ahead* of time. If you *start* late, you'll *be* late.

"Second of all," she added, "do you have a dish of soap and water in that car? Because I *know* that your hands are not clean." I had given Jason my Toyota Camry a year ago, when I moved on to bigger and better things.

Jason stood up from the table and said, "My fault."

"Mmm hmm," my mother grumbled, looking at my father.

It was obvious where I got *my* sass from. I began to laugh.

My father looked at me briefly but did not say a word. He didn't have to because I knew what he was thinking already. *Don't believe your mother's hype, Tracy. I'm still the boss around here!* That made me laugh even harder.

My mother turned her hard eyes on me, the same almond-shaped eyes that Jason and I both had, and said, "What's so funny, Tracy?"

I shook my head and answered, "Nothing. I don't even want to get involved. I have one more night here."

"You don't want to get involved in what?"

I just shook my head and stayed out of it.

Jason sat back down at the table with clean hands.

I asked, "Can I lead the thanks for dinner?"

My mother nodded. "Sure, this is *your* night."

"Okay, let's all hold hands then."

Jason looked and frowned, all macho about it, a typical testosterone fiend.

He said, "*Hold hands?*"

My mother snapped, "Do what your sister says, boy, you're the baby."

My brother was still hesitant until my father spoke.

"Jason," and that was all he needed to say. My brother stepped right in line and held hands with us around the table. I admit, sometimes I envied the hell out of manhood! I wanted the authority that my father had.

I said, "I want to thank the Creator for giving us each other, our friends, and our extended family a chance to live, love, and learn during the short time that we all have on this earth."

I raised our hands up high and said, "Hotep!"

They all followed my lead, curiously.

"Hotep!"

I smiled, and I was satisfied with all of us, the Ellison family.

My mother grinned and asked, "How long have you been doing that? And what does 'Hotep' mean, anyway?"

My father jumped in and said, "It means peace."

I looked and asked, "Dad, how do *you* know?" My family was not exactly the most Afrocentric in the world. We were your typical nonpracticing Christians.

My father answered, "I know a thing or two about our culture."

"Well, excuse *me* for *not* knowing," my mother said.

I smiled back at her. "Actually, I just got it from Raheema's nice little family in New Jersey. They have it all together."

My father nodded and asked, "Have you said hello to Beth and Keith next door since you've been home?"

"Yeah, I spoke to them, but I guess I should see them again before I leave, hunh? I'll go over there once we're finished eating."

"Are you all packed up already?" my mother asked.

"Almost."

"Jason can help you take your things out to the car," my father said. "I'll take an early lunch and drive you to the airport tomorrow in my birthday present."

I smiled and asked, "Are you sure you don't want to trade it in for a Cadillac Escalade?"

He looked and said, "Don't tempt me, Tracy."

I shook my head and paid him no mind.

Jason was busy stuffing his face already. I packed my plate and stuffed mine.

"What new movie are you going to be in?" my brother asked me once he had calmed down with his food. By that time I was in the middle of eating mine.

I gave him a raised index finger, then I decided to point to Mom; she knew what I was hoping on for my next role.

"She's trying out for some crazy, special-agent movie where she's chasing down some psychos. It's called *Road Slaughter* or something."

"*Road* Kill," I mumbled through my food.

"*Road Kill?*" my father questioned. "That sounds pretty physical."

My mother said, "It is. I told her she's gonna have to pump some weights to play the role, fighting crazy men and carrying on."

"Fighting men?" Jason responded. He broke out laughing. "That sounds like one of those cornball movies."

I stopped eating and asked, "So what are you trying to say, Jason? I can't fight a man?"

He had never been the physical type himself. If I were

mad enough, I believed that I could give Jason a run for his money in a fight.

He said, "You're too pretty to be fighting men. The audience would never believe it. Those pretty-girl movies are always corny. You need to stay in those roles where you outsmart the guys."

My father started laughing through his mouthful. I was still speechless. Jason had caught me off guard with his candid response. He was giving me a dose of urban realism, so I listened. I had been away from the hard streets of Philly for a while, and I had written for a bunch of comedy and science fiction shows. Maybe I didn't know what was real anymore.

Mom said, "Now wait a minute, are you saying that she can only play a certain kind of role?"

"Not if she was ugly. If she was ugly she could play a lot of different roles." Jason added, "Just not *leading* roles." He was dead serious, too.

That made my father laugh even harder.

"What the hell is so funny, Dave? Our son is a chauvinist, and you think that's funny?"

"*Chauvinist?* I'm just telling her what time it is," Jason argued.

I shrugged my shoulders. "He might be right though, Mom. I mean, he *is* the perfect age for this movie, *and* the right gender. So if he thinks it's corny, then maybe it is."

"What are you gonna do then, Tracy? Are you telling me that you're changing your mind because of what your *brother* says?"

I thought about it and looked at Jason. "How do I make it believable?" I asked him.

He broke out laughing again. "You're asking *me?* I'm not the movie writer."

"So what? You brought it up," I snapped at him. "I'm serious. How do I make it better?"

Jason hadn't even seen the script, but I was willing to listen to him anyway.

He said, "Aw'ight, this is how inner-city guys think. First of all, are these psychos white or black?"

I said, "White, and I'm not even supposed to be in this movie myself. I'm trying to *steal* the role," I told him with a laugh.

"Okay, well, white guys can't fight, but they're still stronger than pretty women, and they're *wild* too. So what you need to do is have fast reflexes and attack with knives, or stun guns, or just shoot them as soon as you get a chance.

"Now *that's* believable," he said.

"I don't believe you're even asking him this," my mother told me.

I listened anyway. Jason had everyone's full attention. I wasn't even hungry anymore.

I asked, "What about when they catch me off guard or something?"

Jason shrugged his shoulders. "After they rough you up, I guess you play dead, like you would if a bear was after you, and then pull out another weapon on them."

We all started laughing.

"That's ridiculous," my mother commented.

My father said, "Go 'head, Jason, then what?" I think he was enjoying it.

Jason said, "I'm saying, psychos like seeing people dead, right? Or at least in most of the movies that *I* saw. They kill you, and then they sit there and stare at you like it's a painting or something. So you play dead and surprise them. It makes perfect sense."

I said, "But I can't do that every time."

"No, but you use a different weapon every time. And we can't see it beforehand, because then we would know what's gonna happen. You have to surprise us with it, like a thin, black wire to strangle one of them with, brass knuckles on both hands, a long needle inside your hair; you know, like those Ninja movies."

I laughed again. "You're making this movie sound *extra* brutal."

Jason said, "Wait a minute, you said *psychos,* right? Are they killing people nicely in this movie?" He had a point. "All right then," he told me, "you get as brutal as *they* get. Now *that's* believable!

"And after the movie, guys'll be a little paranoid of pretty girls. 'You not like that girl in *Road Kill* are you?' *That's* believable!" he insisted. "You gotta make guys think about it *outside* of the movie, like when they go back out on the street."

"Well, how come Will Smith gets to do all of these crazy *alien* movies then? Is *that* believable?" Mom asked him.

"I'm saying, Will Smith is still a guy though. He's like my height, he started pumping weights, *and* he plays in those science fiction action movies with humor in it. That's different. This is a *mean* cop flick, with a girl, so it should *feel* like it."

My father looked at me and nodded. "He's right," he said. "If you really want to play this role, you have to play it like you *mean* it. It has more action in it than *Silence of the Lambs?*"

I said, "Yeah, *much* more action."

"Well, that's what you have to do then."

Jason nodded his head and said, "Yeah, and I would go to see that."

I smiled and said, "Yeah, I bet you would." I was damn sure glad that I had talked to my little brother about my next film though, because I had some major changes to make.

$ $ $

When I went next door to say my farewells to Raheema's parents, it was close to ten o'clock, and I was thinking about Mercedes again. I had to at least call her up and tell her what I planned to do about that house in Yeadon. Hopefully, there *was* a house and she wasn't scheming twelve grand out of me.

Her mother, Beth, greeted me at the door. I had called them to make sure they were home before I visited.

"Here she is! Everybody knew you would be a star," she told me. I gave her a hug.

"Either that or in a crazy house for *trying*," I joked with a laugh. As soon as I said that, I wanted to take my words back because of the hell that Mercedes went through, but it was too late.

Beth ignored my comment and asked me what time my plane left the next day.

"After one o'clock," I told her.

Mr. Keith walked out from the kitchen with a Pepsi in his hand, a thicker and calmer man than he had been when we were all growing up.

He smiled and said, "I hope they pay you well for those roles."

I guess some things never change. I said, "You mean to tell me that you wouldn't look forward to seeing Raheema in a Hollywood role like mine?"

He laughed. The younger, leaner and meaner Keith wouldn't have.

He said, "You'd get Mercedes in one of those roles before you'd get Raheema in one."

"Stop riding Mercedes. You don't even know if she can act," Beth responded to him.

Damn, things had changed! Beth was the biggest house mouse in the *world* when I was younger. She *rarely* spoke back to her husband then. I smiled. It was good to see both of them loosen up and sound like a normal man and woman who bickered. They had found a way to hold their family together too.

I said, "Do you guys mind if we called Mercedes up while I'm over here? I want to speak to her before I leave tomorrow."

Beth went right for the cordless phone.

"So did Mercedes ask you for any money yet?" Mr. Keith asked me. He was as calm about it as if he was asking about the weather.

"Why, did she talk about it?" I asked him.

He started laughing again. "As soon as you came home, she started talking about getting a house all of a sudden."

"She hadn't been looking for one before?" I figured I would milk her father for all the information I could get, since we were already on the subject.

He said, "Yeah, but she wasn't all that excited about it. Then she kept coming over here to see us every other day. I knew that something was up then. I guess she figured she would bump into you."

I smiled and said, "Well, she sure did."

We quieted down when we heard Beth on the phone with her.

"Yeah, Tracy's right here with us. She's leaving out for California tomorrow afternoon."

I waited to be handed the phone.

"Hey, Mercedes," I answered.

She whispered, "You see how they get along all peacefully now? She even talks back to him. My mom acted more like his *third daughter* instead of his *wife* when *I* still lived there."

I held in my laugh. Mercedes was a social genius if you asked me. She could read people through *one word* or with *one look*. I just wished that she could use her talent more constructively.

I said, "I'll call you up within a week, okay?" If I got the *Road Kill* lead, I planned to send Mercedes fifteen thousand dollars with a tough-love warning to spend it well. What can I say, I still had a warm heart for her.

"A week? I sure hope that house is still for sale by then," she responded.

I continued to smile and shook my head, thinking about Mercedes' father. Keith knew exactly what she was asking me, in code or not. Maybe she had gotten a lot of her social genius from him; I just hadn't bothered to see how cunning he could be.

I said, "I'll be calling you. I still have to pack tonight."

"So, when will you invite me out to visit you?" she asked.

"So you can snatch up my acting roles for yourself?" I joked.

"I'm not any damn actress," she commented.

*Ain't that the truth!* I told myself. You couldn't *get* any more street realism than Mercedes!

I said, "I'll let you know. And I love you, girl."

When I said that, it seemed like everything just stopped for a second.

Mercedes said, "Thank you. I love you too." I knew that she meant it, whether she was twisted or not, because she was still human, and she was like family to me. Even through all of the bullshit Mercedes had been through and was still going through, I just couldn't shake my love for her. So I called her up again once I had packed my things that night.

"Hello," she answered the phone, scratchy-voiced.

"Were you sleeping?" I asked her.

"Tracy? Girl, aren't you going back to Hollywood tomorrow? Get your damn rest, girl . . . just don't forget to hook me up," she added with a tired laugh.

I shook my head and smiled again. That damn Mercedes was a *trip!* I said, "I just wanted to talk to you again before I left, that's all."

She got quiet on me. "Thanks," she responded. "I'm glad you still feel for me like that."

"What, you thought that I *wouldn't*?"

"Well, when people go Hollywood on you . . . shit changes."

"And sometimes the people around you change," I reminded her.

"Yeah, that too," she admitted. "But, you know, you gots to do your thing and make that money, right? That's what it's all about."

I stopped her and said, "That's *not* what it's all about. I mean, sure, you make good money and everything, but you have to love what you're doing *first* to become any good at it. That's where you were always wrong, Mercedes. You can't love money, and things, and people who idolize money, because all of that stuff will eventually fade away."

"Not if you make enough of it and you know what to do with it," she argued.

"And how much is enough?"

She paused. "Give me about twenty-five million, and I'd be aw'ight *for life!*"

"And what will you do to *get* that twenty-five million?"

"Whatever you *have* to do."

"And you've started on your plan already?" I was playing her bluff, because I knew that Mercedes didn't have a clue. I hated to think it, but *her* way of getting twenty-five million would be more like seducing a basketball player. Or seducing *me* if I let her; seducing me through our life-long sisterhood.

She said, "Tracy, I'm just saying what time it is in the world right now, that's all."

"And that's why the world is so fucked up!" I snapped at her. I was calling Mercedes back for a peace talk, but she was getting under my skin with the ignorance. I had worked my ass off to get paid, not because I wanted to be paid alone, but because I wanted to be good at what I did, *and* gain recognition for my work, but all that anyone ever counted was the fucking dollar signs and the facade of fame, and that shit was really beginning to piss me off!

Mercedes only laughed at my temper tantrum. "Calm down, girl. It's too late at night for that hyper shit. And I'm just gonna tell you like this: If you don't have any money, nobody gives a fuck about you. And even the people who *do* care about you, they can't do much for you *without* money. And I'm just being *real* about that."

I said, "In other words, if *I* didn't have any money, then telling you that I love you wouldn't mean shit? Is that what you're saying?" I asked her.

"I'm not saying that it wouldn't mean shit. The thought of it is nice. But if you're on your deathbed, Tracy, and you need an operation to survive, *a thought* ain't gon' save your ass from dying. That's all that *I'm* saying."

I could see that Mercedes and I would end up on the phone all night, and I still wouldn't get my point across to her. She was nearly middle-aged and *definitely* set in her ways, so I just decided to end our conservation.

I said, "Well, you know what, Mercedes, I *do* love you . . . and maybe that's all I should leave you with. I just hope that you're not on your deathbed right now, because I'm sorry to tell you, but money alone is *not* going to save your life." Before she could respond, I simply hung up the phone on her, because I didn't have anything else to say on the subject.

**$ $ $**

"So, when will you be making your way back home again?" my father asked me. We were on our way to the airport on I-76 East.

I yawned. It had been a long night for me. I planned to get at least three hours of sleep on the plane.

"I don't know, Dad. Why, you want me to move back in?"

He smiled. "Your mother and I were thinking that *we* could move in with *you*."

I read his face to see if he was serious. My father was still hard to read. His entire personality was filled with misdirection, always three steps ahead.

He said, "You're thinking too much, Tracy. It was only a joke."

"I can't tell when you're joking or when you're serious half of the time," I told him.

"That's because I don't want you to tell."

"Why not?"

"Because then your daddy would be boring to you."

"But I would still love you."

He said, "Yeah, you just wouldn't admire me."

I laughed. "Who said that I admire you now?" I did admire my father, I just wanted him to explain himself to me again.

"Nobody has to tell me."

"You just know, hunh?"

"Just like you know that I admire you."

My eyes lit up and I felt all excited about it. "You do?"

"Yeah, I admire you. You remember how nervous your mother was when you first started talking about Hollywood?"

I thought back and said, "Yeah."

"Well, I had to convince her every other night that you would be fine out there. If you would have called home more often, it would have helped me out a bit, but I guess you were busy taking care of business."

"Yeah, I was, plus we have that three-hour time difference, so I didn't know when to call a lot of the time."

My father looked at me as if I were crazy. "Now you know damn well we didn't care what time you would have called, as long as we heard from you."

I turned away, feeling guilty about it. "I'm sorry. I won't let that happen again. I'll make sure I call home once a week now."

He started laughing and said, "Don't promise me something you can't keep, just call us when you can."

When we pulled up to the airport, a few of the baggage checkers noticed me, but they tried to stay calm about it because of my father. I could tell.

"Give me a big hug, girl," my father told me as they ticketed my luggage for the flight.

I hugged my father and squeezed him like a giant teddy bear. "I'll call as soon as I get in."

He nodded. "All right then. I'll tell your mother."

"Bye," I told him, while I headed inside backward.

"Bye now, baby."

If it wasn't for my father being with me, I would have been asked to sign at least five autographs for the baggage claim guys, because they were still sneaking peeks at me as I slipped away toward the escalators.

I carried on my black leather briefcase with the *Road Kill* script to fall asleep while reading on the plane. I planned to begin jotting down ideas for changes on a notepad.

Luckily, I was able to walk through the airport with only a few looks and no big commotion. Everyday citizens had no idea how tiring notoriety could be sometimes. You just never know when you'll be asked to share your time with twenty people who you have never seen in your life before. Nevertheless, I had asked for it, and I was getting it, the good parts *and* the bad parts.

I boarded the airplane, first class, thinking, *Great, this is pretty painless!* However, a sister in her late thirties noticed me after I had been seated.

"Tracy Ellison Grant! You go, girl! When is your next movie coming out?!"

I smiled, embarrassed by her enthusiasm in front of a bunch of white passengers who didn't seem to know who I was, which was a peaceful thing.

I answered, "Hopefully next year."

"What's it about?" The older sister was holding up the aisle.

"It's an action movie," I told her. "I'll talk to you about it when we land," I said, just to keep her moving along.

"Okay."

I settled back down in my window-view seat, with a gray-haired white man sitting next to me. He was minding his own business, so I began to read my script as we took off down the runway. Before I could reach page five, my minding-his-own-business white man turned to me and asked, "So you're an actress? What movies have you been in?"

*Here we go again,* I thought to myself before I responded to him. *I need to start flying in a damn private jet!*

"I starred in a recent film called *Led Astray,* about a woman who gets revenge and a big payday after dealing with some greedy Hollywood men who had misled her career interests and used her. It was my first starring role." I figured I would get it all out of the way so he would have less questions to ask me about it.

He nodded his head and said, "Oh. That's sounds interesting."

I was so tired of giving my résumé to strangers that I wanted to hand out a sheet of paper sometimes, or post it across my damn chest. However, was I irritated enough to give it all up and become an around-the-way girl again? . . . No way! I *wanted* to be special. So I had to learn to deal with it.

# Sub Conscious

*I had a dream*
*that I was sinking*
*and watching the earth*
*turn darker*
*as I went down*
*in slow-sand,*
*because there was nothing quick*
*about it.*

*My voice*
*only echoed upward,*
*sounding weak*
*and panicky*
*as I cried for help,*
*with no rope,*
*or rescue*
*to save me.*

*And when I awoke,*
*I realized*
*that my future*
*was ALL on me,*
*a solo arrangement.*
*That's when I sang*
*at center stage*
*like ARETHA!*

# Spring 1998

$$\$\$$
$$\$$$

*B*efore 1997 was over, eleven out of fifteen of my scripts were produced for television on various networks, and I assisted on five other produced scripts. I even got Coe some acting work in a couple of sitcoms. (When I said I had to let him go, I didn't mean completely, I just meant that I had to unleash him from my grip and treat him more like a young man instead of as my plaything.)

What I *didn't* like about my writing progress was how many of my scripts were changed in production. It wasn't as if I could hold any creative direction with my work through spec writing. Everything was produced at random. There also were not enough black drama series in Hollywood to write for. Everything had to be a damn comedy! Nevertheless, for the fall of '97, I was *still* "the flavor of the month" in Black Hollywood for my writing skills, which led me to meet more of the movers and shakers. I got to know a lot more of the actors out there too, and if they were not connected to a stable show, they were mostly scrambling to find work and passively complaining about the lack of roles being offered to blacks in either television, commercial advertisements, or film. I say complaining "passively," because many of them didn't have a clue as to how to change anything. I felt for them, I really did, so I tried to write as many new actors into my scripts as possible. I was getting a lot of these actors jobs, and I became a very cool person to know. Go figure! *Writers* were supposedly the *last* people to make things happen, but as fast as things heat up in Hollywood, they can cool off just as fast.

By 1998, rumors were everywhere that the big boom of black television shows was about to come to an end, and a lot of it was more than just rumors. *Living Single* and *New York Undercover* were the biggest shows on the way out. Everyone was nervous about a big domino effect on *all* black shows. However, *Moesha* was still hanging tough.

By February, Richard Mack's creation, *Brothers and Sisters*, was well under way, but the writing for the show was horrible. No wonder Rich was thinking of only creating show ideas instead of sticking with them; he couldn't write a lick. I was embarrassed to even tell him that, but I had to.

"A lot of shows start off in the basement and then they get better," he told me over the phone.

"Not black shows," I argued. I had just finished watching the third episode of his show. I was developing my own ideas for scripts, but so far *Brothers and Sisters* was nowhere close to what I had envisioned.

Rich said, "*The Cosby Show* wasn't that good when it first started, nor was *A Different World,* or *The Fresh Prince of Bel-Air.*"

"Yeah, but they all had major stars attached to them," I reminded him. "Besides, just because *they* ended up doing well, that doesn't mean that *we're* going to be afforded the same opportunity to stick around long enough to be good. We both can name a hundred other shows that didn't go on to be winners in the ratings game, black *or* white."

He said, "I wouldn't worry about it this soon. After week *seven, then* I would start to worry."

I began to think that the network would put Rich out of

his misery after only *six* episodes, but he laughed at the idea as if it were a joke. I could hear Yolanda's mouth somewhere in the back of my mind. *I told you about that black shit. You're gonna be running around in circles chasing your cheese like a sewer rat.* I could damn near *see her* in my mind!

I broke out laughing.

Rich said, "What's so funny?"

"You don't even seem as if you *care* about this show," I responded.

"This is all business, Tracy, you *can't* care."

That was what I was afraid of; the Hollywood pessimism had gotten to him. Rich was throwing in the creative towel for money. It was a decision that everyone would have to juggle with in Hollywood; you either sell out or starve *(Hollywood Shuffle)*, unless you were plain gifted or lucky. I had been mostly lucky, because I didn't want to think of myself as gifted until I succeeded at the next level and had an original screenplay produced.

Just to change the subject, I said, "You know, I talk to a lot of the actors out here now, and it just amazes me how so many of them have no clue where their next role is coming from. And I keep asking myself, 'How can they live like that?' I just don't get it."

Richard said, "That's why I'm not an actor," and laughed. "I'm no damn fool."

"Yeah, but when they hit it big, they can hit it for *a lot* more than us," I argued.

"Yeah, and it's a thousand of them looking to strike it rich at only two or three slot machines."

He was still laughing about it, but it was true. Black actors in a predominantly white country was a tough bag to be in. Oh, sure, everyone dreamed about the few starring roles, the magazine covers, and the television interviews, but I got a chance to see the paranoia of not knowing where your next meal ticket was coming from. Nevertheless, if I hadn't lucked up and gotten a chance to show off my writing skills, I wouldn't have been able to count on my meal ticket either. Thank God that wasn't the case!

"So, what's gonna happen to the actors on your show?" I asked Rich.

"They get over it and move on, but the show is not over yet, Tracy."

In *my* book it was. *Brothers and Sisters* couldn't even get a serious look from the small black market that the studio was trying to attract. The show aired on Tuesday night when a bunch of basketball games were on cable, so it attracted virtually *no* males. I didn't tell Rich what I was thinking though. The brother simply needed to do more homework.

"You're not backing down on me are you?" Rich asked me.

I hadn't signed any paperwork or anything, and I was glad that I hadn't, because I actually *was* thinking about ditching his show. It wasn't a money thing for me; I wasn't starving, so I didn't want to ruin my good track record with some bullshit show, friends or not. I was even beginning to think of creating my own show idea.

I said, "What has Juanita come up with?" I didn't want to answer him.

"Oh, she's all right. Her stuff is just a little too hardcore. I told her to tone down some of that New York stuff. These shows need to play nationwide. It shouldn't be a coastal thing."

"Well, in that case, what do you think of *my* stuff?" It wasn't as if I was writing girly stuff, especially for *Conditions of Mentality*. I even agreed to cowrite a Watts gang story with redheaded Liz.

Rich said, "You got all the right stuff, Tracy. Your writing is realistic, smart, funny, in-your-face, and subtle, all at the same time. It just works."

I smiled. *Just like my poetry,* I thought to myself, *it just works!*

I said, "Well, thank you for the compliment, but remember, you still can't sleep with me. You have a woman."

He laughed it off. "All right, well, get back to me as soon as you have something."

"Do I have a deadline?"

He paused. "I'll need something finished in another week."

I nodded, thinking of a million different ways to get out of it. "Okay," I told him, but I had to admit it to myself: I was not planning on touching that pilot show. I had other plans, which included creating a pilot of my own. I had told Rich in the beginning that I would write for his show only if it was *good,* and I *meant* that!

## $ $ $

I had a lunch meeting later on that week with a young actress who I was interested in creating a show around. Her name was Reba Combs, from Decatur, Georgia. She was a cute brown-toned sister with a perfect build, nice height, good attitude, and commendable acting skills. However, she represented exactly what was wrong with so many of the actors out in Hollywood, black *and* white: they had no faith in developing their own ideas. Not saying that they all needed to be full-fledged writers or anything, but at least have an idea of what kind of project you would like to be in.

Reba Combs was twenty-three years old and had finished only a semester at Clark Atlanta University before traveling to California for her big break in Hollywood. So far she had played a bunch of minor roles and as an extra before I came along and helped her to get some quality work with my scripts.

"So, you mean to tell me that you've been living off and on with different people out here since you stepped foot in California?" I asked her. She had lived out in LA *twice* as long as I had, and she had just gotten her first small apartment on account of the paychecks that she had received from performing in my scripts.

"Well, it wasn't as if I was leeching or anything, because *they* weren't doing that well themselves a lot of the time," she answered with a chuckle.

I just stared at her. "And it never bothered you that you didn't have any stability?" I couldn't imagine it myself. I *always* had stability, whether I was chasing the fast life out in the streets or not. I knew I always had somewhere safe to return home to, even if I had no furniture.

Reba said, "It's all a part of putting in your dues."

At least she had the right attitude about it.

"So, what things are you working on in the future?" she asked me, bright-eyed and interested.

I said, "Have you seen that new *Brothers and Sisters* show yet?"

She shook her head. "No. What about it?"

"Do you stay up on the new shows at all?" I asked her.

She said, "I used to, but after a while it got depressing. A lot of those roles I wasn't able to get, so now I try to focus only on what I'm up for."

"Is your agent doing a good job trying to place you?"

She grimaced. That meant no, but she tried to give her agent the benefit of the doubt.

She said, "You know the truth about agents: they can only take you as far as you can take yourself, really. Because if nobody wants you, then it's very hard for an agent to *make* them want you. But if *everybody* wants you, then it's easy."

I nodded. "That's true," I told her. "Agents can't create the work, all they can do is pump you up and talk about it." I still didn't have an agent myself, but I figured that I would need one as soon as I stepped it up a notch and started creating my own pilot shows and original screenplays.

"What kind of productions do you imagine yourself starring in?" I asked Reba.

"Any- and everything," she answered.

"Do you have any preferences?"

"If I did when I first came out here, I sure don't now," she said with a laugh.

I figured that Reba would do very well in emotional roles. Her face was a magnet for emotional depth. Some people had faces that could look a million different ways with just a twitch of a muscle, and Reba had it. Of course, if no one bothered to use it, then what difference did it make?

I said, "I know you're not a writer, Reba, but if you *could* write a script for yourself, what would you write about?" That was a question that *all* actors should ask themselves, really. However, my question caught Reba totally off guard.

She smiled and said, "Oh, good question." She had to think about it for a minute. "You know what we haven't had much of? Black Southern stories. So I would write something about growing up in Georgia."

Granted, Reba had no Southern accent from what I could tell.

"Did you have an accent when you first moved out here?" I asked her.

She smiled. "A tiny one, and that was the first thing that I got rid of."

"But now you're telling me that we need more Southern stories."

I took a sip of my water and let her think about the hypocrisy. She smiled again.

"I see what you're saying, but you know how Hollywood is: they can typecast you into playing only Southern roles if you have an accent."

"So you turn it off and on when you need to," I told her. She took a bite of her grilled cheese sandwich.

"You're saying all of this because you're a writer; you get to create things. I want to bring those creations to life with my acting."

"But what I'm trying to tell you is that if you have *nothing* to bring to life, then you have *nothing* to offer anyone. You can't see that?" I asked her. "There are thousands of white writers writing for white people, and in order for me to be able to write for you, as my sister, you have to at least *guide* me on what kind of things you would want to be in.

"And not just *anything*, but something that you would like to star in with a passion," I told her. "Now, since I don't know much about the South, what would be the most logical thing for me to do if I wanted to write about it?"

Reba shrugged her shoulders. "I guess you make a visit and do research, right?"

I looked at her and asked, "*Make a visit*? For what? You're sitting right here in front of me. You can't tell me anything about Georgia? You think one of these white writers is going to take a trip to Georgia to write for you?

"Forget about it," I told her. "Better yet, if someone wanted to write a script about Philadelphia, do you think I would tell them to take a trip to Philadelphia? Hell no! I'd tell them, 'If you want to write about Philadelphia, then talk to me, and I'll tell you all about it.'"

"Yeah, because you're a writer," Reba responded. "And you get *paid* to do that."

She still wasn't getting my point. I said, "So what? You're *more* than just an actress, Reba. That's where your problem is. You're a human *first;* a black woman from the South, and you need to *validate* that perspective wherever you have to. You're not some faceless person."

"You remember *Boston Commons*?" she asked me.

"Yeah, I liked that show," I told her. "It was young, hip, and different."

"Well, what happened to that?"

"They didn't give it enough time. But it happened, so their perspective was validated."

Reba smiled at me as if she knew better and went back to eating her grilled cheese sandwich. I guess we just had two different perspectives about the business.

### $ $ $

I wasn't hanging out much with Kendra or Susan anymore, so we had a girls' get-together at my place just to catch up on things. Kendra was busy teaching California kids and entertaining her new man, I was busy developing new script ideas, and Susan was good and happy about *something* that I had no idea about.

I joked, "What, you found a new man too, Susan?" I was picking with Kendra. She was still with the guy she had met at the club that night in September. She was keeping it to herself because she said she didn't want to ruin it by counting her chickens before they hatched.

"No, it's not a man," Susan answered. "I just got bonded in the state of California to be an agent. All of my dues are paid, I have plenty of references, and now it's time for me to start going after talent and getting them deals."

I nearly swallowed my tongue. In all of the time that I had spent with Susan, I had no idea that she was putting in dues to be an agent. The truth was, I didn't really want to investigate what she did.

"Well, congratulations!" Kendra told her from my living-room sofa.

I was still speechless.

Susan looked at me, and I looked at her and wondered if she wanted to ask me what I was *thinking* she would, to represent me, even jokingly.

"Oh, well," I mumbled, just to fill the empty space. It was an awkward moment for both of us.

"So, are you gonna represent Tracy now?" Kendra asked Susan. Kendra seemed to be the only person in the room with the courage to pop the question.

Susan chuckled nervously. She said, "Well, I don't know. I was thinking of starting at the bottom somewhere, not at the top." She was flattering me.

I smiled and still didn't say a word. Had Susan been playing me all along, while I tried my hardest *not* to play her? I was confused about the whole thing.

"So, what agency do you work for?" I asked her for the very first time.

"You didn't know that?" Kendra asked me. She looked at Susan and said, "The California Entertainment Agency, right? CEA?"

Susan nodded and said, "Yeah."

I explained to Kendra that Susan and I never really talked about our professional careers with each other. Kendra frowned at that too.

"Why not?" she asked, still confused by it. "I thought it was obvious that Susan was going to represent you. I thought you two were both waiting for her to be able to do her thing."

Obviously, Kendra had asked Susan *plenty,* and the entire revelation presented thick air that we needed to cut through. Susan started cutting the air first.

"Well, I didn't really want to impose myself on our friendship like that," she said. "If it happened it happened, but I felt comfortable with Tracy because she never once bothered me about it. Other friends of mine were constantly asking me, and that made me feel uncomfortable, as if they wanted to use me in that way.

"On the other hand, I never really brought it up to Tracy because I didn't want *her* to feel the same way about *me,* that I was using her friendship so that I could represent her in the future."

Kendra nodded. "I can see that," she said, "but business is business, right? And Tracy needs an agent."

I guess it was all on me after that. I stopped and said, "-I'll have to think about all of this, you know, because this really caught me off guard."

Susan held up her hands in surrender and said, "Wait a minute, I didn't say that I was asking to represent you, Tracy. You're under no obligations from me. I'm still your friend."

I couldn't think straight for the rest of that night. I called Kendra at her home at one o'clock in the morning, and she had to teach the next day.

Kendra said, "What's the problem, Tracy?" She knew I

wouldn't have called her so late on a weeknight unless something was disturbing me.

I said, "You know why I never asked Susan what she did? Yolanda Felix told me she was the niece of a big-time Jewish movie mogul out here named Edward Weisner, and I didn't want to make it seem like I was getting next to her to use her connections."

Kendra burst out laughing, even in her sleepiness. "I *knew* you were thinking something like that. I just *knew* it! You're always trying to gain your own credit for everything."

"That's a *good* thing," I told her. "Yolanda made me seem villainous for even *talking* to Susan, and the girl was just cool. You see how Susan is, we *both* get along well with her."

Kendra said, "Well, I got news for you, Tracy. Grow up! Business is business. But if you ask me, Susan seems a little *too* cool to be a good agent. I mean, *Yolanda* seems more like the agent type to me. Susan may not even be able to get you any good deals. You've been doing fine so far by yourself."

"Yeah, *so far,* but I'm about to start creating my own show ideas and getting back into writing screenplays soon, so I'll *need* an agent for the real numbers game," I responded.

Kendra paused and grew quiet on the phone. "Well, it's your call, girl. *I'm* not in Hollywood."

I hung up with Kendra and thought to myself that night for a few more hours. I had been doing just fine by myself with negotiating television scripts, but there wasn't much to negotiate. The going rate was ten thousand dollars a script, and a split fee for a cowrite. It wasn't as if I was writing for any major shows where I needed an agent to push for higher pay, or at least not yet. So I guess that Susan had come along at just the right time for me. However, I didn't want to give her ten percent of my pay for work that I knew I could already get for myself. That was part of the reason why I didn't have an agent; I was already pulling my own strings with a strong Rolodex. If I agreed to give Susan a try as my agent, it would be only for new work that she was able to get me, if we could actually do something like that. Maybe the people at CEA would not allow her to work that way, with a partial contract on me.

I called Susan at her Santa Monica apartment that next morning to discuss my plans with her. First I asked her officially if she even wanted to represent me.

"Yeah," she said convincingly enough. She knew how much work I had gotten for myself, she knew that I could write, *and* she knew that I had been working hard and would *continue* to work hard. I just had that kind of workaholic drive in me. Blame it on my Virgo sign, because I never knew how to sit around and do nothing.

I said, "Okay, well, here's the deal: if I sign with you, it's only going to be for new work and higher pay than what I'm getting now. I don't think it would be fair for you to get ten percent of what I already established for myself, but for the things that you get that I haven't been able to, it's yours."

Susan said, "Traditionally, the work of an agent would be to continue to service old, present, and new contacts so that *you* wouldn't have to, but I understand your predicament. So what we'll do is make a short list of the contacts that you would like to keep on your own, and then we'll go from there so that we're not bumping heads. However, when and if you decide to renegotiate any old or present relationships with a new business understanding, then I'll be capable of stepping in for you."

I don't know what Kendra was talking about, but Susan sure sounded like a seasoned agent to *me*. I like how she used the term *short list of contacts*. She almost made it seem as if my Rolodex of working business relationships amounted to next to nothing.

I asked, "So, when will we be able to sit down with some paperwork where I can see what we're talking about?"

I sounded real pushy, but Susan had to understand that she was moving into a business relationship with me, and I was always pushy in business. Blame it on my Virgo sign again for always wanting to be on top of my game plan.

Susan said, "We can sit down and discuss it this weekend. You want me to swing by your house?"

She was still taking it light. I admired that. It looked as if we *could* work together.

I smiled, pleased with the idea of Susan Raskin representing me. I said, "Yeah, swing past my house when you get a chance and we'll talk about it."

## $ $ $

To make a long story short, I signed with Susan and by the end of March she had sold two of my spec scripts to NBC and ABC respectively, for twenty-five thousand dollars each. Both scripts were produced for mid-season pilot shows. Susan was outright *earning* her money, but like Reba Combs had said about agents, it was easy for Susan to walk me through the doors with my talent and track record. Nevertheless, she still had to have the *keys* to open the door.

Yolanda looked over the paperwork and said, "*This* is

where you need to be, at the *big* networks. And don't you *dare* think about going back to that small-time shit either! But you have to *fight* to stay up there!"

Kendra called me and said, "Well, I guess you made the right decision with Susan."

Coe called and asked, "Can you get me on one of those NBC shows?"

Tim Waterman called and said, "Keep up the good work, Tracy. You got me in your corner all of the way."

Reginald called and said, "I guess you're untouchable now, hunh? Watch your back up there, Tracy. I hear it's treacherous."

My mother called me from home and said, "I guess you've proven *me* wrong. *Again!* Your father and I are very proud of what you're doing out there, Tracy. Keep up the good work."

Raheema called and said, "As they say, you're '*blowing* up the spot' in Hollywood. Now tell me something that I *didn't* know would happen."

Reba called and said, "What do you think about the chances of our own pilot show being picked up now?"

I told her that I was working on it.

I got a call from Rich, and all of the praise stopped there.

"So, you ditched *my* show for NBC and ABC, hunh?"

It was a no-brainer. *Brothers and Sisters* was headed for a fast exit on a smaller station, and he actually expected me *not* to write for an NBC or an ABC pilot. He had to be out of his *mind,* but I still felt guilty about it.

I said, "It wasn't in my plans for things to happen this way, Rich. Honestly."

He paused over the phone for a minute before he laughed. He said, "Yeah, I knew you were the money type.

You tried to play it off like you were not, but it all comes out in the end."

"*You* were the one chasing the money," I snapped at him defensively. "All *I* want is good opportunities, and your show was *not* one of them. I'm sorry." I had to be real with him.

Rich said, "You think those NBC and ABC pilots you wrote for are gonna last? Hell no! They only did those shows to appease black people while they get ready for next season. At least UPN sticks to the audience."

I was speechless. Rich was right. None of the major three networks had much patience for black television shows. Even FOX, the new upstart, was beginning to get stingy with black audiences as they moved their way up the ratings chart.

"What do you want me to say?" I asked him.

He said, "Well, I really can't blame you. I was just pissed off when it first hit me, you know, because I felt like second fiddle. My show wasn't good enough for you, *and* you got better pay over there.

"I guess that anybody would have done the same thing," he admitted with a chuckle. "And I guess I'm a little jealous about it, but that's cool. Just remember to hook *me* up like I tried to hook *you* up."

I paused. It was a setup. I said, "Rich, to be perfectly honest with you, your writing has to get a lot better. I mean, your ideas are great, you just have to focus more on developing those ideas."

Rich laughed out loud and right in my ear. "Oh my God!" he responded. "You get a couple of writing credits with the big boys, and all of a sudden you become an *expert.*"

"I didn't call myself an *expert,*" I said, "but we *both* know that scriptwriting is not really your forte. And to be honest, if *I* were you, I'd put more of my energy into creating and producing shows and leave the writing to other people."

He said, "That's what I told *you* last year."

"And then you went ahead and tried to write the first four episodes of *Brothers and Sisters* and you ruined a great idea," I told him.

He chuckled. "You think my writing is that bad, hunh?"

I didn't even respond to that. He knew that his writing was bad.

"Well, thanks a lot, Ms. Expert. I'll take your advice, and the next time I create a show, I'll let *you* write the first four episodes."

I didn't make him any promises, and when I hung up the phone with him I felt hollow for some reason. All that response to my moving up in the industry made me feel as if I was hungry, but I wasn't. I just felt eerie. It was as if I didn't know what to do with myself, so I called my girl Raheema in New Jersey to talk about it.

I said, "Raheema, it feels like things are moving too fast for me or something. I don't know how I'm supposed to feel yet."

"Success anxiety," she told me. "Everybody feels that way when they get there. Now you just have to keep going."

"But what if I can't make it at the next level?" I asked her. I didn't want to verbalize it, but I was afraid of failure. People's expectations of me were rising, including my own.

Raheema chuckled. She said, "Fear has never stopped you before, so why should it stop you now? If I know *you*, you're already thinking about creating your own show ideas, writing screenplays for the big screen, and everything else."

I broke out laughing. Raheema knew me *back, forth,*

and *sideways!* I said, "But people out here are already saying that I'm moving fast enough. I guess I should feel content."

"*Content?* What is your name again? Tracy Ellison from Diamond Lane in Philadelphia? The *Flyy Girl?* *Content?* Girl, please! You better *do* what you went out there to do. *I* know you, Tracy. Those people out there don't know you. They can read your book and *still* don't know you.

"You're on your *own* pace, Tracy, not theirs," Raheema told me. "You've *always* done things fast, because you plot out your plan, and then you do whatever you have to do to get what you want, while other people just sit around and talk about it. *You* know that. *They* just don't know it. So keep working right along to get to where *you* want to be.

"That's why you don't know how to feel right now," she added. "*You* know that you're not really there yet. And you're in your *zone* whenever you're working *toward* something and not when you're being praised for things that you've already done."

When I hung up with Raheema, I smiled and felt at peace again. "That's my girl!" I told myself, and I was inspired to write another poem, called "Volcano," before I went to bed.

# Volcano

Hot, creative
lava
boils in my brain,
searching for an orifice
to erupt on nature,
violently
burning the old soil,
and terrifying the settled creatures
who have gotten used to things
as they were,
so they run, shriek, and squeal
as my lava rolls
quickly down on them
from up high.

But when it is over,
I cool off in fresh ashes,
raising those old things
to higher levels,
so that the creatures can return,
enlightened,
and start again,
while the earth awaits
my next
eruption.

# April 2000

$ $
$

As soon as I arrived back in LA, I went out to the video store by my house in Marina Del Rey, and rented *Barb Wire*, starring Pamela Anderson Lee, to do some research. I figured that I would hate the thing because the movie didn't really create any positive buzz outside of her breast size, her reckless rock-star husband, and her pregnancy. However, after watching *Barb Wire* for the first time, I liked the movie, and I could see exactly what my brother was talking about by making a pretty woman believable with fast reflexes, violence, and plenty of weaponry. I didn't particularly like the flashbacks though. Flashbacks tended to slow movies down. I didn't particularly care for character narration either; it tends to get in the way, unless you really like the sound of the narrator's voice.

I had a million things I wanted to do, including shopping for something to wear to the meeting that would fit the character Alexis; something sexy enough to turn a man on, but sane enough not to alert him to a setup. I also wanted to begin picking out and typing up twenty-five or so poems for my sequel book deal.

I went out to a thrift store to buy some inexpensive clothing for my character. I bought a couple of denim skirts and shorts with bright and colorful halter tops. I went to a nearby adult store and bought some of that freaky, black leather lace to give Alexis some of the edge that her name implied. When I arrived back at home, I hooked up a complete outfit for the meeting, planning to show up in character and seal the role as quickly as possible.

I decided to wear the pair of black leather strapped sandals that I had bought from the adult store with a pair of baggy denim shorts that would allow room to keep a small gun on my hip underneath. A pair of silk pink panties would do the trick to give me that extra feminine appeal. I could wear the red halter top so that I could keep a knife in the back where my bra clip would be. Around my neck, I'd wear more black leather straps that crisscrossed like a bra and matched the sandals. I'd put my hair up, or in a ponytail to keep it out of my way, like a woman on the go, a jogger or workout nut or something.

I put on all of my props and looked at myself in a full mirror, absolutely *loving* it! However, my mother was right, my arms and legs needed toning, but the look was *working*, so I told the mirror, "My name is Alexis, and I'm one tough bitch, but don't call me black; I know *what* I am, and *who* I am. Okay? Now let me go find some psychos. I want to give them a taste of how it feels to die."

While still wearing my gear to feel out my character, I read the *Road Kill* script again with a red pen in hand, making all of the changes that were needed.

**$ $ $**

I met my agent at twenty of eleven, up the street from the studio lot, so that we could do a final game plan before going into our meeting with the producer at his office. He was a forty-something guy named Donald Hollis, who liked to refer to himself as "The Don." My girl told me when she briefed me about him over the phone that morning.

As soon as she saw me stepping out of my black Mercedes convertible, *in character,* she smiled and said, "Good idea." She was dressed in a dark gray suit with a hot pink silk shirt, and looked hip herself.

"What statement are you trying to make with *that* color?" I asked Susan out of curiosity.

"That we're *hot* chicks here to take care of business, man."

I laughed at her.

"So, we drive in together in my car and leave yours parked out here?" I asked.

"Yeah, let's show some solidarity," she answered, moving quickly to my passenger's side. I hadn't told Susan any of my plans of execution to get the role, but I had *plenty.*

"Well, here we go again," she said. "And this time, we'll be ready to shoot for a three film deal if they're offering us enough money."

I hadn't even been thinking about the money, just about getting the part and tailoring the script to meet my needs, but that was what agents were for, the money talk.

I asked, "How much do you think we could get for a three-film deal?"

"Actually, I was thinking about negotiating some kind of an elevator clause, starting at two to four million for the first film, and rising at least two million for each additional film, depending on the box office gross for each *prior* film."

I did my calculations and came up with a minimum of twelve million dollars for three films, but it could end up being *more.*

I looked at Susan and asked, "You really think we can *ask* for that much so soon?"

She gave me this long lingering smile. "*That,* my dear, depends on *you,* and a million other things at the box office," she added with a chuckle. "However, *Led Astray* did twenty-eight million, which earns *you* a check of one point four million and some change, from the five percent gross that we negotiated on the first deal. That check should arrive at the office any day now."

I thought about that and said, "Shit! We're about to roll in some *serious* money, Susan."

"You better believe it," my girl said.

I responded, "Twenty-eight million ain't bad for a movie that released in less than a thousand theaters. We almost made *four times* our budget. You think they'll give us ten percent gross now?" I asked Susan.

She grinned. "That's what we still want," she answered. "That's why a lot of the studios don't like to give up those gross points, because if it pays off for the talent, they know that you're going to want more of the same. And we do," she commented with a laugh.

Ten percent gross sounded damn good to me. Ten percent of a blockbuster movie, pulling in a hundred million dollars, equaled ten million dollars *after* my initial payoff. That sounded like gravy over the potatoes and rice, but first we had to get more theater releases for my films. Distribution was a real bitch, especially for black movies! However, Latino and Asian films were not doing *half* as well as black films were.

I thought about all of that and nodded my head before starting up my engine. "Well, let's go do it then," I told my girl. I was determined to move my way up in the industry.

We drove up to the security gate and gave our names and who we were there to see before we drove in amongst the cars of the people who made deals with the stars.

We parked in the visitors' section and headed right into the luxurious office building to make sure that we were there on time at eleven o'clock sharp. The office building had three levels and was full of open light for the many plants and small palm trees. It was like an inside safari. We were really moving up the ladder.

"Can I help you?" we were asked by a sister receptionist.

I gave her that black people nod and a smile. She smiled back at me and kept it cool.

Susan said, "We have an eleven o'clock meeting with The Don," and smiled herself.

"Your names please?"

"Susan Raskin and Tracy Ellison Grant."

The sister smiled even wider and made the call. "Susan and Tracy are here." She buzzed us into his office. "By the way, Tracy," she added before I left, "I loved *Led Astray.*"

"Thank you," I told her. I guess she didn't want to *assume* who I was before she praised my work. That was smart, because stars have *huge* egos, and they damn sure don't like having their names *or* their work confused with that of others.

We walked into the office of The Don, who was dressed in all white and still talking on the telephone. He looked up as we were walking in.

"Ah, I have to take a meeting right now, so I'll get back to you after lunch. Okay? Ciao."

I had to read him as fast as I could to see how to play him. So far he seemed supercool, so I planned to be cool myself.

Susan said, "Don, this is Tracy Ellison Grant," and left

me alone. She knew that I knew how to work it. An introduction was all that I needed.

He stood up and took my hand lightly in his. "Is this your rendition of the character?" he asked me of my outfit. He was moving faster than what I had planned.

I said, "You know, there are a lot of different weapons that a girl could hide in an outfit like this, but I still look normal, almost like a sweet-and-sour thing going on. It's definitely attractive to a man who's looking for a good time."

Don smiled and said, "Yeah, I can see that. Have a seat."

Susan and I sat down in the tall, comfortable brown leather chairs that flanked his huge desk. He sat down behind his desk, with his chair evenly spaced between us.

"So, what do you think about the script?" he asked me.

Perfect question. The Don was straight to the point. I guess he had a busy day ahead of him, but I had practiced myself silly with the pitch, so it was no problem with me; the sooner the better.

I said, "You know, I don't see this character as a woman who doesn't talk much. I mean, what are we trying to do here, create a female Clint Eastwood?"

He chuckled, but I had no time to waste, so I kept going with it.

"If anything, a woman who doesn't talk much would send all kinds of alarms to a man," I told him. "Talkative women are easy, right? Everyone knows that. Or everyone *assumes*. So we give her an advantage of playing the easy, talk-to-anyone-about-anything role, and then her violence will catch the audience *and* the bad guys totally by surprise."

He nodded, in deep thought about it.

"And this hand-to-hand combat thing will be a *real*

turnoff for the mostly male audience that we're going to attract with this movie," I added. I slapped my black sandal on his desk to illustrate my point. "I could slide a couple of thin black knives in these straps, and you would hardly notice them." I stood up and undid the thick black leather belt that held up my baggy denim shorts. "Inside of *these* big things, I could hide up to four guns. I could have one in the front, one in the back, and two on the sides, but one gun on the right hip would do just fine, preferably nickel-plated. And who knows what I could do with this big-ass black leather belt in my hand.

"By the way," I told him, "I know you noticed my pink panties, Don. Do you like what you see?"

He leaned back in his chair and broke out laughing. Susan laughed at my performance herself.

"And my hair? Oh, I could stick all kinds of surprises up in a bun or in a ponytail. And don't let the size of a weapon fool you either," I said. "Because if you stick them in the right places, they can hurt *really* bad."

"So, she's like a Ninja woman now?" Don asked me.

I shook my head. "Ninjas are too secretive. Alexis is just a tough bitch from the streets of Chicago, but I wouldn't use any flashbacks to explain her. That just slows down a good movie. Let the audience make up their *own* stories about her past."

Don said, "Wait a minute; *Alexis* from *Chicago*?" He was intrigued by the change of the script, but he was definitely not sold on it. *Yet!*

"You damn right!" I responded in character. "This is the year *2000!* If a honey brown girl named Alexis from Chi-Town can get the job done with confident authority, then who needs a damn Jill?" I smiled and got sweet on him. "But I can understand if you still don't want to use me, baby. You got the blonde and blue eyes on your mind. That's fine, I just figured you might want to fuck something else for a change."

Don was beside himself with laughter. He was obviously blown away. "Oh my God!" he said. He looked at Susan for an explanation to my method, but all that she could do was shrug her shoulders and smile. She had no idea what I had planned, she just knew that it would be good.

"So, what other changes would you make?" Don asked me.

I stopped the acting and went into business mode. "I could have a full script of changes ready for you by next Monday."

He nodded. "You're a hyphen, right, an actor-writer?"

I smiled and corrected him. "Writer-actor. I wrote for a year and a half for *Conditions of Mentality*. We specialized in psychological stories that *moved*. So *Road Kill* is right up my alley."

"Would you, ah, be wanting screenplay credit?"

I looked at my girl Susan. That was *her* job.

She smiled and said, "Of course."

Don shook his head and grinned. He said, "Well, my *writer-director* is just going to *love* this." He was being sarcastic of course. No one liked their creations being messed with. He joked and said, "How about just calling it *Alexis*?"

Susan's eyes popped as wide as a pie, but I declined the idea.

"That would be too much. We want to introduce them to the character first, and when and *if* it does well enough for a sequel, we can call it *Alexis* on the next deal."

I put my belt back on and proceeded to toot my own horn a bit. I said, "By the way, after reading the script a few more times, your guy seems more like a *director-writer* to me."

Don said, "And you really think you can pull this off?" He wanted my assurance.

I asked, "Do you have a hard-on behind that desk right now, or at *least* on your mind?"

He laughed again. "Are you sure you don't want to do a comedy instead. You're hilarious!"

I told him, "One flick at a time, Don. Now as soon as you call us up on this role, I can begin toning up my arms and legs and taking lessons to kick ass."

He looked me over and said, "I see. Well, you're tall enough to be a threat to a man, and you're crafty. *Very* crafty."

"Well, thank you," I told him. "That's how *all* women vigilantes have to be. This is a *man's* world, right?" I asked him with a smile.

Susan got in *her* last words before we left. "We'll talk about the figures," she told him. "And my Uncle Eddie *loved* your production of *The Gypsy Lover.* He said it was *splendid.*"

Don looked and said, "Oh yeah? Well, tell Edward I said hi, wouldja?"

"Sure."

When we walked out, I mocked Susan and said, "Uncle Eddie, hunh?"

She grinned and shook her head. "I *hated* to do that, but I had to protect you somehow. I felt desperate."

"Why?" I asked her. "You didn't think that I did a good job to convince him?"

"Oh, you did a *hell* of a job. *Too* good! That's why I became so nervous," my girl admitted. "You gave him a lot of new ideas before signing, so now we *have* to get you that role, or they'll figure out a way to use your ideas with someone else. Then I'll have to find a way to take them to court about it, and it would just create a big mess."

I laughed at the idea. Susan sounded borderline paranoid. Call me cocky, but I figured that the role would be signed and sealed as soon as I turned in the revised script on Monday morning. They may not have agreed to everything, but they *would* agree that my vision would enhance the picture *threefold*.

As we climbed back into the car, I said, "I wanted that role, Susan," and started up my engine.

Susan laughed on our way out and said, "Well, you got it now. I'll make *sure* of that, and I'll be going for the *jugular* with the money."

"You do that," I told her. "So, where to now? You have a busy schedule today?"

"No, I'm free until this afternoon, and I'm hungry. Let's do lunch."

I smiled and asked, "Did your uncle really like that *Gypsy Lover* film?"

Susan smiled back at me. "Actually he did, but I wanted to *save* that line for a rainy day."

"So, I must have made it rain in there, hunh?" I asked her.

She answered. "Yeah, but you always seem to make it rain, or shine, or *something*. That's just your way with things: the Tracy Ellison Grant mystique."

# Love/Money

I never wrote a line
in my life
strictly
to get paid.

I did it as expressions
of all of the beautiful
sides
of me.

And maybe I will never
even
publish
my poetry.

But if I ever do,
I guarantee
that it won't come
cheaply.

Nevertheless,
is the price you pay
for creativity
the only thing that people see?

Validated
success, that
torturous
irony.

# Summer 1998

$ $
$

Susan and I tried our hardest for three straight months to sell my show idea, *Georgia on My Mind*, pitched as a Southern *Moesha*, featuring Reba Combs as the leader of a local R&B group called Peaches, to a network and had no success. We played with the title a bit, changing it to *A Touch of Georgia* and *Georgia Peaches*, but to no avail. We also had the location argument: Would we shoot the show in Georgia, or develop a Southern-looking set? We were thinking about developing a Southern set, of course. I even toyed with the idea of a Southern family moving north to Philadelphia called *Up from Georgia*. Kendra put in her two cents and said, "Make them move to Baltimore," but I didn't consider Baltimore northern enough. Of course, Kendra just figured that I wanted to use *my* home city instead of hers, and she was correct.

I guess Reba was right, no one particularly cared (or at least not in Hollywood) about the perspective of the black South, because we couldn't get anyone interested. Reba even joked and said, "Sometimes I think of spreading the rumor that I'm Sean 'Puff Daddy' Combs's cousin from down south, and maybe that would get us a show." I even thought about that idea, but ultimately, I didn't want my show being accredited to a planted rumor. Call me a square, but I didn't feel that route would be worthy of my hard work.

Susan thought that it was just a matter of timing. "I still think that it's a good idea," she said. "We just may have to wait another season for the creative cycle to swing in our favor."

I didn't know *what* to think. I was just stressed about it, so I kept tweaking the show with different ideas to try and make it acceptable to a studio.

Finally, during that summer of '98, Susan stopped by my place on a Friday evening with some good or bad news, depending on how I would take it.

She put her hands together like a prayer and said, "Okay, Tracy, here's the deal. I have a production company who are interested in the Southern show idea, but they wanted to make it a biracial project to attract a larger audience, similar to *Clueless*, but with Reba Combs in the lead as Peaches."

In other words, Susan had found a production company who wanted to water down my idea for the ratings. I just stared at her for a minute. "And who would they use for the other role?" I asked, just out of curiosity.

Susan took a seat on my sofa. "They have a young girl from the Florida area named Becky Summer. She's done some modeling work, and they're looking for a vehicle to get her into television. And get this: She sings."

I got it all right. Even if Reba *was* the lead, the white girl (a majority draw) would be the marketing focus of the show, and they would probably use it as a springboard for bigger and better things, while Reba (a minority draw) would eventually get the shaft, unless she flat-out kicked ass on the show. It was too risky. I could see disaster coming a mile away.

"So what do *you* think about this?" I asked Susan, taking a seat beside her.

She thought before speaking, I guess to be diplomatic about it. "It's not everything that you want, but it *does* establish the Southern perspective, and it gives you a vehicle to do a lot of different things with it."

"Yeah, but for how long before they take it over?" I said, assuming things. It just didn't seem like a secure development for Reba and myself, especially if this production company had this young white girl's best interest in mind. Everyone in Black Hollywood knew too well about FOX's network takeover of the Wayans brothers' show *In Living Color,* where they began to make changes for a "crossover audience." That ultimately killed the original flavor of the show, and I was *not* trying to go through that in *my* career. I had to deal with enough changes to my spec scripts as it was.

"Tracy, you'll still be the creator," Susan argued. "And since young-women shows are so hot right now with *Buffy, Moesha,* and the *Scream* movies and everything, I figured we could get a good seventy-five thousand or more up front, and a healthy percentage of each show. This deal would set you up for bigger and better things, Tracy.

"Like Kendra said," she added, "business is business. I mean, come on. Get with the program."

I wasn't even thinking about the money at that point. I was only thinking about the integrity of my work and the realism of my perspective: *Reba's* perspective, and the perspective of the black South. How in the hell could you mix that with a white girl?! I didn't know and I didn't care. However, I *did know* that "the program" involved a lot of compromising of your ideas, and I was getting tired of that shit.

I stood back up and said, "So is that it, Susan? Is it all about the money game for you? You want me to sell out my show and my people for the money? I thought that we were cooler than that." I felt as if Susan was showing me her true colors, right then and there, a Jewish girl tempting the talent of an inner-city sister. However, I *knew* better than to fall for that. I was educated, pro-black, and I was *not* desperate and starving while trying to get paid by any means necessary. I considered myself a true artist who believed in the integrity of my work.

Susan looked at me and froze. She was obviously caught off guard by my strong remarks. She stood up beside me and responded, "Tracy, this is ridiculous, and I don't appreciate your assumptions. How could I be your friend and represent you if I didn't respect who you are as a person and who you represent as a people?"

"You tell me," I asked her. I was just being me. I wasn't going to change because she was Jewish, my friend, and my agent. Whenever I had any kind of a beef, I had to settle it. Straight up! So was she asking me to sell out or what?

Susan said, "I can see that you're reading me wrong here, Tracy."

"Well, how *should* I read you then? You *or* your family," I snapped. I didn't mean to say that. I was throwing low blows, but I had followed through on the swing already.

"Do you even *know* my family to judge us like that?" she asked me. She still hadn't backed down from me, giving up six inches and nearly twenty pounds.

I responded, "No, but I can imagine."

We didn't have to explain it to each other. We knew all about the politics of America, and we had discussed them: education and poverty, racism and opportunity, the inner city and the suburbs.

Susan looked ready to lose her mind for a minute. I didn't know if we were ready to fight or what, but I prepared myself for anything. She ended up taking out her cellular phone from her bag and made a call.

"Hi, it's Susan. Are you busy?"

I was wondering who the hell she was calling. Was she putting out a hit on me right there in my living room? My heart started racing.

"Can I bring a friend over to meet you, or is it too late?" Susan asked over the phone.

It was just after eight. The sun was not even down yet.

"Okay, thanks," she said. "We'll be there in less than an hour," and she hung up.

"We'll be *where* in less than an hour?" I asked her. I was *not* stupid. If Susan had a beef to settle with me, then I wanted to do it on *my* turf.

"What, you don't trust me?"

She was calling my bluff, all five foot two of her.

I thought about it after my heart rate had settled a bit. Was I overreacting again? How much power did Jewish people really have? Was I afraid to find out? . . . Hell no! So I turned off the television set and grabbed my things. "Let's go," I told her. I wasn't afraid of her, *or* whoever she had called. However, when we began to head north on Route 405 and ended up driving around the mountains behind Hollywood, I got anxious as hell, not only at Susan's driving on mountain roads, but about just how far she was taking me. I couldn't take it anymore.

"Okay, where the hell are we going?" I asked her.

She grinned, but *I* wasn't joking.

"To meet my uncle," she answered.

I thought about that and smiled to myself. I wondered if Susan would have driven me out there to meet her uncle had we not had a heated discussion regarding business and racism. Did she have something to prove? I guess I would soon find out.

**$ $ $**

We arrived at this huge, brown brick house with various shapes, windows, and outside decks that was situated low in the mountainside.

"Here we are," Susan said as we drove up to a multiple-car garage and parked in front of it. There was a black Bentley parked there. I made note of it and kept my thoughts to myself.

When we climbed out of the car I asked Susan, "Does he know that you're bringing a *black friend* to meet him?" I could imagine the embarrassment that ridiculous wealth could bring when faced with outsiders, and I was a *serious* outsider.

"Are you assuming that you're the only black friend I've ever had in my life, or should I use African-American?"

She was getting cute on me. I smiled it off. We were let in the door by a Mexican woman in a royal blue dress, who looked more like a regal grandmother than a housekeeper. I *did* assume that she was a housekeeper though, and I was right.

She said, "Oh, Susan, it's so very nice to see you," with an accent.

They hugged and Susan introduced me.

"This is my friend Tracy. She's a writer from back east in Philadelphia."

"Ooohh, Philadelphia. It is very cold there?"

"In the wintertime, but it's probably hot right now," I told her.

She nodded, "Yeah, right, it is the summertime now."

"So, how have *you* been Mrs. Sanchez?" Susan asked her.

The housekeeper frowned and said, "I told you to call me Maria."

Susan just smiled at her.

Maria said, "All of my kids are doing great. And Miguel just got his law degree from San Jose. He'll be coming home to visit us soon."

"That's great, but how are *you* doing?" Susan asked her again.

"Oh, I'm doing fine. I look fine, don't I?" She stepped back and showed off her blue dress. She looked fine to me, like I said, a regal grandmother with money, and she carried herself with plenty of pride. I chuckled.

Maria looked at me again and said, "You have very pretty eyes, Tracy. I *love* them! They shine so bright."

I chuckled again and said, "Thank you. I try to use my bright eyes as much as I can."

"Well, use them well, and never abuse them."

The elders, no matter what the race, were the wisest people on earth. Maria was poetic without even trying, and she had a beautiful spirit. She turned back to Susan and said, "Your uncle is waiting for you in his study."

She led us through the large house of fine wood, crafted brick, fancy glass, plush carpet, and black steel (I guess to fortify the house from earthquakes), and into a tiny study toward the back. She gave Susan and me both another hug before she left us.

"Call me if you need anything. Okay?"

"Okay," Susan told her.

I took a deep breath as we walked into this tiny study, which was no bigger than my old room back at home in

Philly. I couldn't imagine such a big-time man having an office in such a small room of his large house. Was there an irony going on there, the biggest ideas from the smallest room?

Her uncle stood up from the black leather comfort chair behind his desk to greet us. He was a medium-sized man with low cut gray hair, a trimmed gray mustache, and thick gray eyebrows. He was wearing a brown cotton sweater of fine quality with black pants and black shoes.

He held Susan's face in his hands and kissed her forehead before he hugged her.

She said, "Uncle Eddie, this is Tracy Ellison from Philadelphia, one of the best upcoming screenwriters in the business."

He looked at me, surprised. "You're tall," he said, as if my height were about to knock him over. I stood almost eye to eye with him.

"Yeah, the height is in my genes," I told him.

He hugged me and asked us both to sit in the chairs before his desk, while he sat on top of it between us. Three of the walls in the small study were stacked with fine wooden shelves that were filled with books. Behind his desk was a huge window with a clear view of the mountainside, the moon, and the stars.

Mr. Edward Weisner looked at me again. "Did you say your surname was Ellison?"

I nodded and said, "I don't know if I'm related to *Ralph* Ellison though. My father doesn't know the whole family history, so maybe I'll do some research on it one day."

He nodded back to me. "Ralph Ellison was a great man, a man of dignity and character."

I nodded again, not really knowing what to expect from him.

He nodded back to me. It was a rather awkward meeting.

Suddenly he asked, "So, Tracy, what is your dream film idea? Do you have one yet?"

First I looked to Susan, who only smiled at me. Payback is a bitch! She had me on the spot.

I answered, "Honestly, I don't know."

"Find out," he said, "because if *you* don't know, then *no one* knows."

I figured it was an ambiguous question. A "dream film" could change every year. Maybe it was his test question to all new hopefuls in the business, and it looked as if I had failed.

As if he were reading my mind, Mr. Weisner said, "Tracy, *every* film that you do *should be* a dream film."

I smiled, agreeing with his point.

He went on and said, "You write every film as if it's your *last*, because you never want to save anything when the *inspiration* of your people is at stake."

Did Susan set my ass up for a lecture, or did her uncle always spit out advice like a professor? Nevertheless, the man had my full attention.

He said, "You have to *believe* that *you* can somehow make a difference. Maria Sanchez had *eight* children, and a husband who passed away before her oldest son was fourteen. And *today, all eight* of Maria's children have earned college degrees."

He paused a moment to make sure that I understood his point before he started back up again. Susan didn't say another word.

"We all get opportunities in life, Tracy, no matter how big or how small. But the question we all have to ask ourselves is this: Am I going to *take* that opportunity, and *if* I do, then *what* am I going to do with it?"

He was a dramatic speaker using emphasis for clarity. All I did was nod and continue to listen to him.

"You have to have a *passion* for whatever it is that you decide to do with your life. And to live your life *without* passion," he said, "is like not really living at all."

Susan smiled and said, "Tracy has plenty of that. She'll speak her mind on anything. She even has her own book out, and she writes some *fabulous* poetry too."

I guess that Susan wasn't that mad at me because she was damn sure pumping me up.

Her uncle looked and asked, "Oh really?"

"It's sort of a novelized memoir book based on her coming-of-age in Philadelphia during the 1980s called *Flyy Girl*," she told him.

I didn't consider *Flyy Girl* as the kind of book that he would be interested in, but my poetry could stand up against *anyone's*.

Her uncle nodded. "A fly in the buttermilk, to stand out against the mundane, the exceptional against the average," he commented. He said, "And the great Jewish American poet Allen Ginsberg said the poem itself was his way of speaking out and telling the truth."

I nodded and finally decided to speak up myself. "I like Ginsberg's poetry. He makes it exciting to read," I commented. *Just like* I *do,* I thought to myself.

"Of course he does; he was passionate about the art," Mr. Weisner responded. "And what you always want to remember, Tracy, is this: Those who create for the love of the *art,* are *consistently* getting better, but those who create for the love of *money, those guys* are forever getting worse."

**$ $ $**

"So, what do you think about my uncle?" Susan asked me on the way back to my townhouse in Baldwin Hills that night.

I smiled and said, "He wasn't what I expected." I had some apologizing to do.

Susan said, "You expected to meet some snobbish old man who barely spoke a word to you, right? A man who would judge you every second that you're there, and talk about you as soon as you leave?"

I hesitated to admit it, but I had to.

"Go ahead, Tracy, say it. That's what you expected, right?" Susan coerced me.

"You've made your point, Susan," I finally responded to her.

"I've made my point about what?"

She wanted a full confession out of me. I grinned and said, "I apologize for the assumptions. Your uncle seems like a nice guy. He understands things."

Susan shook her head and smiled to herself. I knew not to read her wrong anymore. She was indeed good people, rich or not.

"And I'm sorry about my assumptions with you," I added. "But you *heard* what your uncle said, right? All of your ideas should *mean* something to you. And you can't compromise that. Just like *I'm* not going to compromise my show."

Susan grinned, understanding my point. "You're right," she said. "I jumped too far ahead of myself on that. So I apologize to you as well. And we'll just keep shopping your original idea until we find a place for it."

She had learned her first big lesson as an agent, and she knew not to take my ideas too lightly, because I was *not* a sellout. However, her uncle had inspired me. I wasn't even thinking about television shows anymore. I was thinking about writing my first "dream film."

I chuckled about it. I asked, "Does he always give lectures like that, or did you set me up?"

Susan laughed out loud. She said, "He taught film studies courses at USC, nearly a half century ago, before he got into the film business himself. Now he has these flashbacks of his teaching days whenever he gets around young people. I guess that I'm a little used to that by now."

"Mmm hmm," I responded. "So you *did* set me up for that."

**$ $ $**

When I sat at home by myself that night, I couldn't sleep. I thought about the whole money game verses art, in film, music, sports, *everything*. It was very easy for a person who never had anything to be led astray by the money. The hunger does it to you; the American hunger for excessiveness. You just want it all because they *tell you* that you can *have it*. Some people will even kill for it. So I wrote two poems that night, "Blood Money" and "Love/Money." After that, I came up with a screenplay idea dealing with a sister who comes out to Hollywood, gets caught up in the confusion of it all, and is basically led astray herself. I wrote a poem about that subject as well, "Led Astray," and I figured that the title would also work well for the screenplay, *Led Astray*, the feature film. Before I went to bed that night, I wrote down the beginning and the ending of the script.

The beginning: A jaded, twenty-something black woman makes several phone calls to Hollywood agents, directors, and producers from her drab apartment in East

Hollywood. On all of her phone calls she gets the same runaround: "We'll get back to you."

She sits next to the phone, lights up a cigarette, and takes a small drink, plotting: "I'm gonna find out a way to get these motherfuckers. *All* of them!"

The end: The same black woman smiles, looking healthy and uplifted as she leans over a piece of white legal paper with a pen in hand. She signs over the rights of her Hollywood story to a film company for two and a half million dollars.

Afterward, the media asks her, "So how does it feel to be a brand-new millionaire?"

She stops and thinks to herself, holding their attention for a long television close-up. Five different stations all push and shove, desperate to capture her first words for their own network ratings. She smiles and answers, "No comment," and slips on designer sunshades to walk away from it all in the bright afternoon sunshine.

# A Declaration

*Us*
*black*
*WOMEN*
*have to realize*
*when we KNOWS our shit!*

*Us*
*black*
*WOMEN*
*have to realize*
*that NOBODY can TAKE IT away!*

*So, these*
*black*
*MEN*
*have to realize*
*that we DESERVE our respect!*

*And these*
*black*
*MEN*
*have to realize*
*to PROTECT their pearls!*

*Need I say more?*
*I THOUGHT not!*
*So let it be written,*
*and PUBLISH IT!*

# April 2000

$ $

$

*I* sat down with the screenplay to *Road Kill* in front of my computer that Thursday evening and began to re-tool the entire script. First, I had to give my girl Alexis a lot more lines, with cool, sharp, urban wit. I had to rewrite the action scenes to add more weapons, fast reflexes, surprises, and street smarts to replace the wrestling, kicking, crawling, and all of the obvious setups. I think we've all seen enough of the bad guys falling through windows, or up against broken broomsticks and sharp hooks, and carrying on. Those tricks were as old as bloody panties, and they *all* needed to be soaked, scrubbed, dried, and sometimes thrown the hell away! So I tossed that stuff out of the script completely. I also tossed all of the flashbacks to explain my character. I would let her words do it.

For example, to explain why she's so damn tough, I'd have her say something like, "Actually, I should have been born a boy, but that doesn't mean I eat pussy. *I* like to be the one being pleased. *Deeply.* But if I *was* a man, then *I'd* be the one *doing* the pleasing." That way, there would be no confusion about her sexual orientation. She's straight.

To explain how she became a Special Units agent, she'll just say, "I was qualified." After you see her kicking ass, who's going to doubt her? I did away with my character showing extra sympathy for the abused women. Leave it to a *man* to write some ignorant shit like that! Feeling a connection to the horror of sexual abuse is a *given*. Alexis could reveal that empathy with one long stare and a nod. So I deleted all of that sympathy shit too. *My* version of *Road Kill* would be a hard-core, psychological, *action* movie, driven by a *black* woman! I wanted the screenplay to be off the hook, off the chain, and off the damn *pole* when I was finished with it!

I added an inch-long scar to the left side of my character's neck that would run from behind her ear and stop at her jawline to add a little depth. She hides it with makeup when she's undercover. I added a scar right below her panty line on the right side of her abdomen. To explain the scars, she simply says, "I survived it." I also wrote in a black man and a club scene to the script. I figured that Alexis is still a woman, so she would want to get her groove on like any other woman. I would have her meet a brother at a club, and he takes her back to his place and tries to get a little rougher than what she wants. So she kicks his ass and nearly kills him, just to send a message out to all of those brothers who are used to getting away with that date rape shit!

It took me until Sunday afternoon to make the script perfect, or as perfect as I could make it. I printed it out from my disk and took it to a nearby Kinko's to have five copies printed and bound.

"Hey, aren't you Tracy Ellison Grant from *Led Astray*?" the copy guy asked me. He was an early twenties heartthrob for white girls, tall, dark-haired, and handsome. I bet that he wanted to be in pictures too.

I smiled at him and said, "Yup, that's me."

He nodded and smiled back at me. "I loved your performance. You're a heck of a talent."

"Thank you," I told him.

He started my print job and asked me if *Road Kill* was my next big film project. I told him that it was.

"It sounds pretty interesting. I'm just going by the title."

"Well, you're the audience. You, your gang of buddies, and all of your girlfriends; the early twenties crowd who like edge and plenty of surprises," I said. "*The Blair Witch Project* crowd."

He grinned and nodded. "Cool."

When I left, I stopped off at a carryout for some Chinese food, and even they noticed me.

"Hey, you're, ah, Tracy Ellison Grant," the cashier said to me. She was a young woman in her early twenties as well. Maybe she was a college student.

I smiled and gave myself away. The young woman turned and said something in her native tongue to an older woman, probably her mother, who approached me at the counter and nodded with a smile.

"I like ya' movie," she told me with a fixed smile.

I couldn't help it; I felt *great* when I drove back home that Sunday evening! Stardom wasn't *all* bad, especially when people appreciated your work. I arrived at home and checked my answering machine before I ate my hot and spicy chicken and shrimp platter. My girl Kendra had called me and left a message. She and her new husband, Louis, were expecting their first child in October. I was happy for her.

I called her back before I ate.

"Hey, fat belly, I'm back in town. What's going on?"

Kendra laughed and said, "I am *hardly* fat."

"You're *gonna* be," I told her, "especially if you're having a girl."

"You believe that stuff?"

"Yeah. My mother said that she was much fatter with me than she was with my brother," I told her. "And my girl Raheema was heavier with *her* daughter."

"Whatever," Kendra said. "So how was your trip back home?" she asked.

I took a deep breath and sighed. "It was full of ups and downs, girl. *Full* of 'em. I even found out that one of my best girlfriends from college married a white man."

"Get out of here! From Hampton? Do I know her?"

"No, she went to Cheyney State, outside of Philadelphia, when I was back in high school."

"Oh. Well, what did you say about it, because I *know* you had something to say," she assumed.

"Actually, I was kind of in shock. I didn't know *what* to say."

"Get out of here! You *always* have something to say."

"Well, I tried to let her know that nothing is perfect with *any* man, especially those on the other side of the color line, but she said that she was happy with hers and showed me pictures of her two daughters. They even have African names. So what could I really say? I just have to get over it.

"I'll call her up soon and talk to her," I added. "She told me that I shouldn't expect to treat her any differently, so I'll call her up and see if that's true."

"I know you will," Kendra said with a laugh.

"Well, I just wanted to call you back, girl, because I'm about to eat over here."

"What are you having?"

"Hot and spicy chicken and shrimp."

"Chinese food?"

"Yup."

"Hmm, it *sounds* good, but I don't know *what* I can eat

nowadays. Sometimes I smell stuff that I *used* to like, and I feel like throwing up on the spot."

I laughed and said, "Well, that's all a part of pregnancy, so I *hear,* because I've never *been* pregnant."

Kendra didn't respond to that. She said, "Well, let me go and let you eat, and I'll talk to you later on in the week."

Before she hung up I told her that I was up for a big lead in a psychological action film.

Kendra stopped and said, "I'm really proud of you, Tracy. You just didn't come out here to squeeze your way onto a couple of sets, you came out here to *run* the show!"

"Well, you know how we do it in Philly. We *always* go for the gold," I bragged.

Kendra sucked her Baltimore teeth and said, "Here we go with that again."

I chuckled and said, "All right then, I'll talk to you later."

I hung up the phone, got out a big plate to eat my food, and sat down in front of the thirteen-inch television set in my kitchen to watch the entertainment channel. They were interviewing Halle Berry. She was still doing her thing in Hollywood, and she was still up and down with her love for the brothers. I couldn't feel sorry for her, because she was working her career like a charm. I did think about myself though. I was on my way to turning twenty-nine, one year away from thirty, with no permanent man.

Suddenly, a chill ran up the back of my spine and struck my brain.

"Damn! *Thirty,* with no family!" I mumbled to myself with food in my mouth. I couldn't talk the bullshit that there were no available brothers out there either, because I had close friends who were happily married.

I tried to keep eating and block it out of my mind. I thought about Kiwana again. Halle Berry had tried out the other side of the color line too, to get her Dorothy Dandridge role. Plenty of sisters were crossing the line. Could it happen to me in two or three more desperate years? I doubted it. It wasn't that I didn't *have* any men, I just had a hard time telling myself to stay with them while being committed to doing my own thing. Was it my fault for being a woman heavily into her own career? If it was, then that was too damn bad. The *real* brothers were into *their* careers, and no one seemed to have a problem with that. Thirty years old wasn't the end of the world anyway, so I finally *did* succeed in blocking it out. I had a script to turn in.

**$ $ $**

After turning in three copies of my completed script for *Road Kill* to The Don at his office that Monday morning, Susan took her copy, and I kept two for myself, including the original printout.

Susan called me at home that afternoon and said, "It looks like you had a field day on this thing. I might have to ask for a million for the script alone now," she joked.

I said, "Well, what will the other guy get, you know, the director-writer?"

"I guess whatever his agent can get for him."

I didn't like the sound of that. It didn't seem fair. It *was* the other guy's original screenplay, and I was still a practical woman. I didn't think that they would give us *both* a million.

I said, "Maybe we should split it down the middle, that way it would be fair."

Susan said, "The only thing about that is, they may not be offering him that much money. You're a much bigger draw than he is, and that's just the way it goes in the business."

I said, "Well, let's be creative. You tell them that if they give us the four million for the role, and a million for the script, we would be willing to split the script fee and pay the director his share, and then let his people negotiate whatever he's going to get for directing the film."

Susan chuckled and said, "You're a saint, Tracy, you know that, right? Most people wouldn't care."

It was very easy to understand how Hollywood movies began to cost so much. Money always became a major issue out there to fill up the ballooned egos of the stars, who seemed insatiable sometimes.

I said, "I just want to be able to live with myself. And if we get our ten percent gross in the deal, I *will* be."

"Yeah, that check should be here any day now for *Led Astray*," she told me again.

I didn't sweat it though. I knew what was coming to me, and I had earned it, so I didn't feel a bit of guilt about it.

## $ $ $

For the rest of that week, I began to pick out and type up the possible poems that I would use in my sequel to *Flyy Girl*. I didn't pick out the deepest or necessarily my best poems, but just the ones that would fit the book. There was no worse decision that could destroy art than to add things that shouldn't really be there. However, artistic precedents are sometimes set by the unusual, where everyone else begins to follow, leading to a new norm. I liked being special and ahead of my time anyway. I was used to it.

I began to search through other books that I could use

as an example of how to piece my own book together with prose, narration, and poetry, and make it all work. However, I didn't want to make it too simple. Complications can make things a little harder to follow sometimes, and I wanted to be without peers, to stand out again, a fly in the buttermilk, the exceptional instead of the average. I didn't want anyone to be able to follow me, and if they did, it would be so obvious that they would only make it harder for themselves to gain any respectable recognition for it.

Susan called me Friday morning and asked me to meet her for lunch at Spago's, one of the hottest Hollywood meeting places, so I knew she had good news for me. When I arrived, she already had a table for us. As soon as I sat down, she passed me a white agency envelope with my name typed on it.

"Don't spend it all in one place," she told me with a grin.

I opened it up and read the check in my name for $1,256,155, minus Susan's ten percent. I nearly stopped breathing.

"Shit!" I responded to Susan with shaky hands. "My *Flyy Girl* fans will *hate me* for this. I'll have to leave *this* part out of the sequel."

Susan laughed and said, "Why? Everybody wants to be rich, and you've *earned* it."

I said, "Yeah, I thought so too, but actually seeing the check with your *name* on it is enough to make you have doubts." I felt as if someone would rob me before I even made it to the bank with the check. I had a sack of African diamonds in my hands with a gang of international smugglers after me. I was thinking of all kinds of crazy things with that much money in my hands.

Susan, however, got right back to business. She said,

"Okay, well, here's the deal on the new film. We got two million for the role, a million for the script, and half of the script is split with the director-writer, *plus* they gave you the ten percent gross, *and* they're willing to give us the escalator clause for the next two films."

"So, this is a three-film deal?" I asked her to make sure.

"With a minimum of two million dollars per film," she responded. "They wouldn't give us the four million yet."

I could not *believe it!* That was a guaranteed *six* million dollars, *plus* ten percent gross!

"I also negotiated a deal for any script that you work on, including films that you don't star in, with a five percent gross on the *unstarred* films," Susan added. It was all business to her, but I was sitting at the table in shock. I didn't even notice the waiter standing there to take our orders. I just told him to bring me more water before I fainted.

I joked, "Susan, before I walk out of here, can you call up a bodyguard service for me please?" I was having flashbacks of the many stickups that occurred in the streets of Philadelphia during my teen years. What would they do to me as a millionaire?! I was already paranoid.

Susan only laughed at me, but I was halfway serious. No wonder so many stars could not remain at ease in residential areas. You had a hell of a lot more to lose, so it became imperative to move to more secluded property. Even the home insurance people would advise that. I was thinking of relocating again, and I *liked* Marina Del Rey; it was very scenic and wide open.

After a few moments of my hushed silence and introspection, Susan asked me, "Do you really want me to get in touch with a bodyguard service for you? I can do that."

I didn't answer her right away. Did I really want to give up my freedom to walk around?

I asked, "Are people going to publish how much money I'm making now?"

Susan read the concern in my eyes, and nodded slowly. "That's another catch-22 of Hollywood," she told me. "If they give you that much money, it's automatic that they're going to talk about it to increase the buzz for your projects, because they have too much riding on you now. Once you sign this contract, you're a made woman, and they're going to want everyone to know that."

I was in a coma. I really needed to get away and think to myself.

Susan said, "Tracy, I know that this puts a lot of pressure on you, but you're brave enough to deal with it, I *know* you are. It's just the initial shock that you're going through."

I wasn't so sure if I could deal with it at all. I could barely deal with the *entry* level of stardom, let alone move up to the high B-list. I just kept staring into empty space while Susan's food arrived. The waiter asked me again if I was ready to order, and I told him to just bring me out some mild-flavored Buffalo wings or something.

Susan smiled and said, "Well, look at it all this way: they really liked your retooled script for *Road Kill,* so you should have a great time with the direction. And you'll know more on the set than anyone. It was because of *you* that they got the green light.

"You're really building up a track record as a go person," she told me with a grin and a light slap on my arm.

With that, I was finally able to smile again, but just a little bit.

When I calmed down at home that evening, I called my

little brother Jason three times before I finally caught him. He was rushing to make some party. He was nineteen and it was Friday night.

I said, "Pick out a nice car for yourself, but not your dream car. I'll get that for you when you graduate."

"You got the role?! Did you make the changes I was talking about?!" he shouted at me.

I answered, "Yeah, *all* of them, and they *loved* it! You got us the green light, Jason. Thank you, baby! MMMM-MAA!" I kissed the phone.

He laughed and said, "You buggin'. So how much do I get for this?"

I paused and screamed, "GREEE-DEEE!"

My brother laughed again. We were both acting like kids at the circus.

"All right, well, I want a Lexus."

"After you graduate," I told him. "I don't want to spoil you."

"Well, I got you the role, didn't I?"

I sighed. "Here we go," I responded to him. "If you're gonna act like this, then forget that I even told you about it."

"I would have found out when the movie came out anyway," he said. "When are they gonna release it?"

"Next summer, after the spring and July blockbusters."

"So like, in early August?"

"Exactly, if all goes well."

"That's a good month."

"I know. Maybe one day I can move up to July, and then June, and then May, the *real* blockbuster month!"

"GREEE-DEEE!" my brother mocked me.

I laughed, slowly getting over my initial shock of millionaire status.

"So, what can I get then?" he asked me about the new car.

I thought about it. "How about I get you a Ford Explorer, the two-door Sport in black?"

"Yeah, aw'ight, that's cool with me."

I liked the Sport for my brother more than the four-door, because I wanted to try and limit how many friends he would pack in the car. Too many young black men in one car still spelled too much trouble in America. In fact, the color black was too intimidating. Maybe Jason would be better off in a green or gray vehicle, the less attention-getting colors.

When I hung up the phone with him, I felt like calling everyone else who loved me, just to ground myself in reality again, starting with my parents. I wouldn't tell them how much money I was going to make though. If the publications were going to announce it through the grapevine, then I'd just let everyone speculate and find out on their own. I planned to shoot the number down with complaints of taxes, overdo bills, run-up credit lines, bad stock investments, and anything else I could say to lessen the amount.

Like I said, I just needed a little more time to think, and I would work everything out. As far as the bodyguards were concerned . . . I think it was time for me to get some.

# Led Astray

*Hollywood called my name*
*from black limousines,*
*wearing designer dresses*
*and flirting with*
*pretty-skinned men,*
*while puffing on long,*
*exotic cigarettes*
*from under straw beach hats*
*to hide*
*the glare of stardom.*

*Hollywood called my name*
*with twenty million*
*dollars*
*per film*
*from Los Angeles, California,*
*New York, New York,*
*Paris, France,*
*and Tokyo, Japan.*

*Hollywood called my name*
*from 1915,*
*birthing babies*
*in Massa's house,*
*with Harlem's Jazz*
*and Billie's Blues,*
*for* A Raisin in the Sun
*on* Superfly *Street,*
*drinking* Coffy,
*and watching* The Color Purple
*in* Star Wars

'cause She's Gotta Have It,
the Hollywood Shuffle
and the Glory
for Boyz N the Hood,
who satisfy my love jones.

Hollywood called my name
and got me high,
and had me wet,
nuked,
and begging
for the fuck,
and then left me there
squirming like a nasty,
stepped-on snail
against the sidewalk.

Hollywood called my name
and made me walk
on Sunset Boulevard
after dark,
with no condoms,
no sense,
and no gun.

# Fall 1998

$$\$\,\$$
$$\$$

When the premiere television season rolled around in September, Susan and I had no new takers on the Southern-flavored pilot show, and the production company that we had turned down got desperate and contacted Reba. The shit hit the fan after that. Reba called me up and was pissed as hell about us not taking up the offer.

"Why the hell did you do that?" she asked me over the phone. To tell you the truth, I had left my girl hanging, thinking that someone else would give us a better offer. Meanwhile, I stopped working on her show altogether and was well into writing my own screenplay.

I said, "Reba, they weren't giving us a good deal, so we were still trying to shop it."

"What do you mean 'they weren't giving us a good deal'? Were they gonna *pay me*?"

Reba was talking the bottom line: money.

I said, "Girl, they were trying to set us up to use the show as a springboard for this young white girl."

"So what? As long as *I* get paid, they can do what they wanna do. It could have been a *springboard* for me too," she snapped.

"*Or,* they could have picked another black girl to replace you," I argued. "We had nothing set in stone yet, Reba."

"Well, why would they call my agent then, if they were gonna use someone else?"

"Because we had already turned them down. They're just trying to get *you* to agree to it. That's not even professional. That just shows you how slimy they are," I told her. "You don't do that. They're already showing their colors."

"You're showing *your* colors too; you gon' turn it down without even telling me about it," she said. "How are you gonna make a decision for me? I can't *afford* to turn anything down, but *you* can," she added. "It was *my* idea in the first place. You're not even from the South."

"Yeah, but *I* was the one doing all of the work to develop it, *and* pitching it," I told her.

"Oh, so *that's* how you are? I guess I *do* need to learn how to write then with people like *you* around. Fuckin' *backstabbers!*"

"Reba, I did *not* stab you in the back. If *anything*, I was trying to protect you."

"Protect me from what? From getting paid?"

"It's not all about the money," I said rather weakly.

"Hmmph. It ain't? You could have *fooled* me," Reba huffed. "Why don't you give me *your* money then, if it's not about the money?"

She had a point, and I was caught speechless for a change. I didn't know what to say.

"That's what I *thought!*" Reba snapped at me. "Well, thanks a lot, *Tracy!* You got *your* fuckin' money, now you gon' try and hold *me* back from getting *mine.*"

I took a deep breath and asked her, "Are they still willing to work with you?" I hoped that they were. I had to admit, I felt bad about it. A starring role *did* represent a big step up for Reba, whether she would have been selling out or not.

She answered, "Wouldn't *you* like to know," and hung up on me.

I was dazed and confused. I must have sat there silently for a good half hour, thinking about everything. I honestly didn't believe it was realistic for everyone in Black Hollywood to turn down bad ideas. However, if more of us did, then maybe we could have more of the *better* ideas developed. Was I wrong for standing my ground? I didn't think so. Nevertheless, Reba was right; I had no business trying to make her decisions for her.

The next thing I knew, the word got around that I thought I was the shit and was out to make my own moves in spite of my friendships. People were calling me a backstabber. It's funny how quickly things change. I went from being the flavor of the month to a backstabber in just one year. At first, I wanted to step up to Reba about it, but then I just decided to ignore it. I knew that I wasn't like that, so I blocked it all out, kept my focus, and continued to work on my screenplay.

Reginald called me up and tried to pour salt into my wounds because I hadn't had anything produced on television in a while. He asked, "It's not so easy to get a credit with the *big* networks during premiere season, hunh? Are you sure you don't want to come back down to us? We'll forgive you. And now you know who your *real* friends are."

I guess he assumed, like others, that television writing was my ultimate goal, but it was not. I just blew him off, basically. Reginald had no effect on me, and my name was not Juanita.

Rich called and said, "I heard about what happened." He was laughing at it. I guess it was all a big joke to him.

He said, "I can't believe you actually turned that down. Well, I hope you don't starve out here while trying to be a big shot.

"You better learn how to take the money when you can get it," he added. "*Seriously!*"

Yolanda called me with her usual. "I told you about that Black Hollywood shit, Tracy. They are *real* petty. I learned my lesson about that years ago. But you *still* should have taken that deal."

I was just about fed up with everyone's opinions about my actions. So I leveled with Yolanda. I asked her, "You know why I keep coming back to you for business?"

She answered, "Because I'm black."

"Exactly," I said. "Otherwise, I would have stepped off from you a *while* ago. But you're also good at what you do, and I respect that. But your damn mouth . . ." I didn't even finish my sentence. She got the point.

"Tracy, whenever you're ready to leave, I have other clients to take care of. Okay?"

That shocked me. I never imagined Yolanda Felix as a quitter. Maybe I was wrong. She had quit Black Hollywood, and she was ready to quit me.

"Is that how you feel about it?" I asked her. I was actually hurt by it. She couldn't take me telling her the truth? I felt that was petty on *her* part. *Susan* was strong enough to deal with my candor. I mean, it wasn't as if I was overbearing or anything, I just stayed on top of my business and spoke my mind about it.

Yolanda said, "The world keeps turning, Tracy."

I couldn't even breathe straight I was so damn mad. I felt that I could always count on Yolanda, whether she ran her mouth at me or not.

I said, "You know what, if your ego is that fucking *inflated* where you can't handle me telling you the truth, then *fuck you too!*" and *I* hung up on *her* ass!

My heart was beating fast, my head was hurting, and I felt miserable. There I was sticking my neck out for the black community, and all I was receiving in return was flak, and from my *own* people. I guess it was just me against the world then. I always worked well when I had something to prove anyway. So I used all of that negative *bullshit* to fuel my determination, and by October, I had finished the first draft of *Led Astray* to add to my beginning and ending:

ACT I: Cynthia Moore prepares for her intricate plot of payback to several Hollywood businessmen who have led her astray for three years of her acting career. She jots down their names for the last entry in her diary and puts it in an envelope to be sent to Detroit, Michigan. She calls her mother long distance in Detroit to let her know that she'll be sending home an important package which is to be left unopened, regarding legal film matters. She orders an open, one-way plane ticket to Detroit. Then she calls Peter Dalvin, a sleazy wanna-be Hollywood player, and sets a date.

CYNTHIA: (over the phone) I need to get high.

PETER: (smiling) Me too. Where do you want to meet?

PLOT POINT I: Cynthia's date with Peter is all about gathering information on the real players of Hollywood. Peter knows it all, and he likes to talk, especially when under the influence. However, at the end of the night, he gets no love, while Cynthia leaves to begin her next level of the plot. She meets with a young and hungry screenwriter, David Bassenger.

CYNTHIA: (grinning) I have a blockbuster story for you.

DAVID: (cynical) Oh yeah, well, so does everybody else.

CYNTHIA: (confident) Trust me. And make sure you stay in touch.

ACT II: Every Hollywood player is into something that they need to hide, shady deal ings and extra lives, and Hollywood is a small town. One by one, Cynthia wields her plot up the ladder, exposing the dirty laundry of each player, and causing them paranoia, while they lose out on big-money deals, have family problems, suffer public embarrassment, and ultimately deteriorate in their loss of omnipotence.

PLAYER #1: (to his wife) Honey, it's a lie. I love only you.

PLAYER #3: (to Player #2) Did you tell the media about my therapy?

PLAYER #2: (responding) Why would I do that? I'm not perfect either.

PLAYER #4: (hysterical) What the hell is going on around here?!

PLOT POINT II: Peter, still pissed off that Cynthia didn't give him any, catches on to her plot, and threatens to inform everyone involved unless she cuts him in on the deal.

CYNTHIA: (playing innocent) What are you talking about?

PETER: You *know* that I know, and I want a piece of this deal.

CYNTHIA: What deal? Are you high again? I think you need some help.

PETER: Don't fucking bullshit me! I want in, or I'm talking!

ACT III: Player #1 and Player #2 both confront Cynthia after Peter gives them the scoop. Peter then threatens to go up the ladder to Player #3 and Player #4, the much bigger prizes, unless she cooperates with him. Player #2 is also interested in her ultimate scheme. However, Cynthia won't be denied her revenge, nor her payday.

CYNTHIA: (to Player #1) I could call your wife and straighten everything out if I could afford the phone call.

PLAYER #1: (eager) How much will it cost me?

CYNTHIA: Fifty thousand.

PLAYER #1: That's a hell of a phone bill.

CYNTHIA: How much is your marriage worth, less or more?

Player #2 confronts her with subtle threats of violence:

PLAYER #2: (as calm as a killer) It's a very dangerous game to play with people's lives, Cynthia. Very harmful things could happen to you.

CYNTHIA: Harmful things have *always* happened to me in Hollywood. Sometimes you need to write them down just to keep your sanity. I sure hope my mother doesn't open my diaries at home. It's still personal. And I wouldn't want her thinking the wrong things about our business.

PLAYER #2: (thinking) *Shit! She's untouch-able!*

RESOLUTION: Peter needs to be eliminated to protect Cynthia's plans. With the money that she's paid to save the marriage of Player #1, she buys the services of a transvestite hooker from Detroit (who loves to get high), and hires a local cameraman to catch Peter in an embarrassing act of sleaziness to shut Peter's damn mouth. Cynthia then cuts a hush deal with Player #1 and Player #2, the lower end of the pecking order, to sell a screenplay based on the secret lives of the big boys, Player #3 and Player #4, to be written by David Bassenger. All of the little guys, except for Peter, get a healthy payday from a big, insatiable film company. The media falls in love with Cynthia Moore and her award-winning chutzpah, but she has all intentions of using her plane ticket for home. Bye-bye Hollywood.

I read my screenplay through and absolutely *loved* it, but writing a first draft was only a first draft. I had to do research on other produced films that had similar plots to my own to figure out how to create an exotic spin and have my story stand out from the rest. I also began to think about black women stars to play the role. In the meantime, I sent a copy of the draft to Susan to see what she would think about it. She called me back close to midnight on the same day that she received it.

"Tracy, I *swear it,* if I *can't* sell this screenplay, I will *quit* the business!" she told me. "This is *great!* Oh my God! It wouldn't let me go to sleep. I can't *wait* to shop it!"

I was excited that she liked it, but I was also a perfectionist, so I had to slow Susan down.

I said, "Wait a minute, I'm not really finished with it yet. I want to make sure that it has a spin that's different from other screenplays."

Susan said, "It reminds me of *The Player,* starring Tim Robbins, but it's three times the fun; it's got more action, twists, and players involved. And I just *adore* Cynthia's last line, 'No comment.' It's like a cool way of saying, '*Screw you,* I'm rich now!'

"The audience will *love* that," she said. "Now we just have to think of a black woman lead to attach it to. What do you think? Halle Berry?"

"No," I told her immediately. "She's already starred in *The Rich Man's Wife,* and I didn't particularly care for that movie."

Susan said, "Yeah, I know what you mean; it just didn't roll over well. It was kind of flat and laboring, but that's not the case with *your* script."

I said, "Well, still, let me do some research before you start to shop it. I have to think everything through first."

She agreed to it. "Okay, but *please* don't make any major changes. It reads *great* as it is!"

I hung up with Susan, and then *I* couldn't sleep. She was really excited about my screenplay. It felt good to still have *someone* in my corner. However, writing the script was only the beginning. Pitching it was a whole separate ball game, and getting the actual green light was another. So the big question was: How long could I hold on to my artistic integrity?

$ $ $

I needed to get some outside opinions on my screenplay, but I couldn't trust anyone in the business anymore, so I asked Kendra to read a copy of my script and tell me what *she* thought. In the meantime, I rented at least two female-led movies of seduction a night, doing comparisons and contrasts to *my* script. The first thing I noticed was that the other female leads were mostly murder mysteries or cop thrillers. In fact, I really couldn't call *Led Astray* a seduction movie at all, because I didn't have any sex in it. The sex had happened in the back story *before* the plot.

When Kendra got back to me after reading the script, she broke it down with the quickness.

She said, "Tracy, this is an *excellent* screenplay, but Hollywood isn't going to make this. This is more like an independent film. You know why? Because they're not going to allow a black woman to make a fool out of them like this, and then put it out as a movie."

She said, "This exposes all of their own dirt, and it's *not* a comedy."

She had a point. I didn't even think of it that way, I was just writing from the heart.

"They're gonna ask you to turn it into a comedy, you mark my words," Kendra told me.

I laughed at the idea. "Kendra, there is *no way* in the *world* that I could turn this script into a comedy."

"Okay," she said. "Watch."

I joked, "Here you go with your radical stuff again."

Kendra said, "Tracy, *Led Astray* is radical. Trust me! White people are only used to black movies that they can ignore, *or* black stars acting like *clowns* in action comedies."

I was speechless. Kendra was telling me the truth. White people just didn't get it.

She joked and said, "You better go talk to Spike Lee about *this* script. He's about the only one who would produce it. It's like a Girl 6 gets her revenge."

I snapped my fingers. "Yeah, it is, isn't it? I didn't even think about that movie. I guess because *Girl 6* was in New York."

"She came out to Hollywood at the end."

"And she still wouldn't take her clothes off for the camera," I remembered.

"Well, how about using *her* for the role? Theresa Randle, right? That would be a natural for her," Kendra suggested.

"Yeah, but how many people even *saw Girl 6*?" I argued. "It didn't do that well at the box office."

"And, I'm sorry to tell you, but *Led Astray* won't do that well either. It's an independent film," she insisted.

I told her, "Susan read it and said that if she can't sell it, she'll quit the business."

Kendra broke out laughing. "Poor Susan. She was off to such a good start."

I didn't like the sound of that. I asked, "Wait a minute, are you saying that it's no way we can get this film made?"

Kendra backed down from it. "You know what, Tracy, I wish you the best of luck on it, because I would *love* to see a movie like this. It reminds me of Pam Grier's movies from back in the seventies."

"What about *Jackie Brown*?" I asked her.

"Yeah, your script reminds me of that one too. But that Tarantino guy can produce anything he wants. His films have an independent feel to them too."

"So, maybe I need to pitch mine that way, using *Jackie Brown* and *The Player* as my hook films. You're supposed to connect your movie to others that did well at the box office."

"Yeah, well, in *Jackie Brown*, Pam Grier had a white boy to help her out."

"But *she* led him into it. Cynthia has people to help her too," I commented of my protagonist.

"Yeah, I guess you're right. Well, we'll see then."

I asked, "Okay, enough about me, what's been going on with you and Louis?" I had finally gotten the guy's name out of her. He was an architect from Suitland, Maryland, and a graduate from Bowie State University. No wonder they clicked so fast; they had that Maryland state connection. Kendra wouldn't tell me much more than that though.

She answered, "Like your girl in the script said, 'No comment.'"

She was getting a little ridiculous with her no-talk, no-jinx rule.

I said, "Are we that bad in black relationships where we can't even speak openly about our satisfaction with a brother? You're obviously satisfied with *Lou*, as you call him."

"Hold on to your love, girl, that's all *I* can say," she responded to me with a chuckle. "I'm not gonna sit over here and brag about anything."

"I didn't ask you to brag, just to talk about it."

"For what? I know what I'm doing."

I laughed it off and said, "All right then, be that way."

She was right. I was just being nosy for my *own* satisfaction, but Kendra's love life was none of my business. So when I hung up, I felt like having some male company over. I called up Coe again. I trusted him the most, and he wasn't as complicated as other California brothers and the Hollywood types that I had dealt with.

"Hello," a familiar voice answered his phone, but it wasn't *Coe's* voice.

"Reba?" I asked. I was shocked, but I kept my cool about it.

She took a deep breath and said, "What are you calling Coe for, so you can come up with a show idea for him too?" She handed the phone over to him before I could respond.

*Shit!* I cursed to myself. Reba and Coe had been around each other, but I was so damn busy trying to make movies that I had hardly noticed any chemistry between them. If she was answering his damn phone, then obviously they had found some. A single man doesn't let just *any* woman answer his telephone.

Coe came on the line and asked, "What's going on? You have another role for me?" I guess that he didn't care about the rumors of me being a backstabber, and I had obviously become all business to him.

"No, no new roles," I answered. "I was just calling you to see how you were doing."

"I'm doing all right. I have a few model shoots coming up for Pelle Pelle and FUBU."

"That's good. Those designers are really getting out there."

However, our conversation was stale. Coe Anawabi had moved on from me for good, and with *Reba* of all people. I guess I was being made to pay for doing her wrong. I took a deep breath myself and decided to ask him about her.

"So, are you and Reba a couple now?"

He paused and didn't want to say it. "Well, you know . . ."

*Fuck!* That was all that I needed to hear. Damn, it hurt to lose him to *Reba* like that! Why was I still sweating a younger guy anyway? I doubted if he had told her anything about us. It would have been too much of an awkward situation for *all* of us. Reba just figured that I was cool with Coe like I was cool with a lot of other brothers in Hollywood, or at least before she started spreading rumors about me.

When I finished my short conversation and hung up the phone with Coe, I had a long thought about my lack of a love life, or lust life as the case may be. If push came to shove, I was sexy enough to go out and get the best dick on the market, but that wasn't what I wanted to do. I had already gone through that in my younger years, and it didn't do anything for me then, so why would it do anything for me at age twenty-seven? Nevertheless, sex was a part of mental and spiritual health, it really was.

I sat there in my townhouse and flipped through my notepads of poetry, looking for a pick-me-up, and found a gem called "Life" that I had written in my graduate school years at Hampton:

> *"There's no sense in*
> *fussin' 'bout no rotten milk*
> *when you still got a cow.*
>
> *"And you can never freeze*
> *in no shabby house*
> *whenever you got strong lovin' inside.*
>
> *"And even if*
> *you ain't got no man*
> *you still got what they want.*
>
> *"All you have to do is*
> *open up your front door and*
> *them niggas'll zoom right in*
> *like flies*
> *sniffin' the apple pie.*

> *"That's real, girl.*
> *That's life."*

I smiled and read the poem a couple of extra times, deciding to get right back to what I came out to California to do, not to find a man, but to become a star. My man had left me for another woman anyway . . . and then he asked me to be his number two.

**$  $  $**

I had no real reason to change anything in my first draft of *Led Astray,* because there were not that many screenplays like it, so I went ahead and had it registered with the Writers Guild association. However, my girl Kendra was right on the mark when she talked about the difficulties of trying to get it produced. Susan and I attempted to pitch my screenplay for the next couple of months, and everyone liked it, but the studios didn't know what to do with it. To hell if we were going to sell it to anyone without any guarantees on it being made. Sometimes a studio can buy or option a film project only to bury it, and then you'll never see a green light.

We had the creative vision wars with everything that Kendra predicted. I won't name any film company names, but the meetings went like this:

Studio A asked, "Can you make it into a comedy? You know, like a *Hollywood Shuffle* kind of thing? That was a fun movie. Maybe even Whoopi Goldberg would like this. We could sell it as *The Get Back.* What do you guys think about that? It could be Whoopi's next big hit. That would really put you on the map as an A-list writer."

Studio B asked, "How about you team her up with a

mentor or something, a white girlfriend who can really walk her through the doors of power? I mean, how is she going to even get close to these people? She's cunning, but not *that* cunning. You need to mix up the plot more to make it realistic. And while you're at it, she could use a few sex scenes, at least three. These kind of films don't work well without any sex involved."

Studio C said, "This is a *great* script! We love it! But let me ask you something. Why does she have to be black? This happens to every woman in Hollywood. I don't see this as a black vehicle. Let's sell it to a larger audience. We could get Demi Moore in it. This seems like her kind of movie. If we got Demi Moore involved, we could make it happen for you. I mean, really, who's gonna compete with Demi Moore from the black community? You have to think about your career, and not the racial politics."

Susan sure got a new education after that. She could see my point about race and integrity clear as day. She said, "I can't *believe* this crap! A *Whoopi Goldberg* comedy? And a black woman can *no way* be this intelligent, right? Hell-lo, a black woman wrote the screenplay. I guess she's supposed to *fuck* her way to the top, like every other woman. That's realistic, right? Yeah! And how come a white person always has to show up and save the day? This is such *bullshit!*"

She was learning just how powerful racism was in America. I don't even believe I had ever heard her curse before. I was pissed off about it at first myself, but after a while it became comical to me. I had heard about the horror stories of script changes and Hollywood simply not getting black movies, but *damn!* When you come face-to-face with it, it's enough to spin your head in a full three hundred and sixty degrees like *The Exorcist.* It was really *wild!*

I told Susan to calm down and just keep hunting. We knew that we were onto something. A lot of the producers and studio people actually like me. They were shocked to see a young, unknown black girl with such a hot script. They just wanted to see how quickly we would bend. In the meantime, I had two out of six of my spec scripts produced for television, both on ABC for thirty thousand each. I mean, I still had to pay my damn bills, right?

Like Kendra had predicted, Susan and I finally struck gold with Studio D, a small, up-and-coming production company called Wide Vision Films. They asked us about the lack of sex in the screenplay as well. We pitched the film to a thirty-something producer named Jonathan Abner, who had moved up and over from music video production.

He said, "I love the script. I think it really has potential, but let's face it, sex sells. If you're not going to have any sex in it, you guys might as well take it to network television. I mean, we're talking about attracting an audience of maybe seventeen to thirty-five on this film, right?"

Susan nodded. "That's about right."

"Well, it'll work. I can see that. And we wouldn't have to put much money into it," he said. "It could do great as a low-budget film with a high profit margin. We could even cast an R&B singer in the lead."

I was just listening. Sometimes when you listen, you can really hear how interested producers are in your pure script. If they start talking too much off the mark, then you know it's time to walk. Jonathan Abner sounded pretty reasonable, just cheap. However, what did I expect from a smaller film company?

"What do you think, Tracy?" Susan asked me.

I looked at Jonathan. He was brown-haired and tall. He looked younger than his actual age. He didn't even look right in his dark gray suit. He was probably more comfortable wearing grab-and-go clothes, like a true beatnik. I had to stop myself from laughing at him.

I asked him, "What singer would you have in mind?" just out of curiosity.

He shrugged his shoulders. "I don't know, whichever one can act the best for the role, I guess. We could have a regular lineup of singers," he joked.

I thought back to what Yolanda had told me concerning Tim Waterman at *Conditions of Mentality*. *He's weak. Press him for the job.* I smiled and felt comfortable that I could have my way with Jonathan Abner as well. He was already eyeing me.

"So, if I added a few sex scenes, and we decided on the lead, there would be a good chance to have *Led Astray* green-lighted at Wide Vision?" I asked him with a lingering stare. My eyes never failed me with flirtatious men. Jonathan had most likely scored with a bunch of video honeys, and he was willing to try out different flavors. I could see it in his eyes.

He nodded and said, "Pretty much, yeah. I mean, I really like what you're doing with the script. It moves well, it's extra smart, and we could really do a lot of fun things with this. We feel like a little guy as a film production company, so we would love a chance to fuck the big guys," he added with a boyish grin.

He was game. He had even gotten the script on his read. I looked at Susan and nodded.

"Okay," I told Jonathan. "I'll add the sex scenes, and then we can have another meeting."

Susan looked thrilled. I guess she got to keep her job.

"So, we'll be back in touch then. And thanks for your time," she told him.

When we left their offices, Susan said, "Tracy, we don't have to go with these guys if you don't want to. I know you didn't expect a small-budget film with your screenplay, and if you want to try another crack at a larger film company, then I say we hold out and go for the gold."

I had already made up my mind. I just had a feeling. I said, "If they follow through on letting my vision stand as I write it, *and* let me add as much input along the way, then I'd rather try it with them than to go with a bigger company that could run all kinds of game on us. I mean, Kendra was right."

Susan asked, "Kendra was right about what?"

I smiled, forgetting that I hadn't talked to Susan about my chat with Kendra on black cinema in white America.

"Kendra said that *Led Astray* would be perceived as a radical black movie because it cuts too close to the truth and it's not a comedy."

Susan smiled. "Well, like Jonathan said, they would love a chance to screw the big guys, so maybe this could be another strike of small gold that lights up the bank. Hollywood is full of small stories that went big. We could probably get a much better deal here, too. The bigger guys are pretty structured on how they like to do things, but smaller studios are willing to give you a lot more contractual leeway."

She said, "But I would watch those sex scenes, Tracy. Just write in that they were climbing out of bed or something simple, because if you get too detailed and they like it, the producers will look for more of the same from you in the future."

**$ $ $**

When I went back to the lab to retool my script, I ignored Susan's warning about the sex scenes. I definitely knew how to write them. I had early training in seduction and I knew *exactly* how to turn guys on, black, white, or otherwise. However, when I went to turn in the script and talk it over, Susan told me that she wouldn't be able to make it with me. I was a big girl about it. I didn't need her there with me per se, I just felt that something else must have been more important to her.

So I walked into Jonathan's office by myself to hand over the new script, and he had a softback copy of *Flyy Girl* in his hands. I damn near fell out on the floor, I was so shocked.

He smiled at me and said, "You're pretty modest. I didn't know you had a book out based on your life."

"Susan sent you that?" I asked him. She had set me up again. No wonder she didn't come.

"Yeah, she said that I might want to look into this, and that you were really a passionate person who was playing it cool and incognito as a writer."

I sat down and laughed it off.

Jonathan couldn't stop grinning. I could just imagine what he thought of me after reading *Flyy Girl*, *if* he had a chance to even read it, as flighty as many Hollywood producers were.

I said, "We all grow up, you know," just in case he *had* read it.

"Yeah, but the raw passion; you don't grow up from that, it's always with you," he responded. "After I flipped through your book, I saw a lot of similarities in you as a teenager and your character Cynthia as an adult. You're both very crafty, cool under pressure, and driven to get what you want. I think I love the script even more now. This book is a great back story," he said.

"That means that you're interested in making this movie then," I commented to make sure.

"Oh, definitely! We want it. The only question I have to ask you now is: Can you act?"

I just stared at him and smiled with my mouth open. "I'm gonna kill Susan," I told him.

"I mean, let's look at it this way, who's gonna know how to play this character better than you?" he asked me. "Come on, Cynthia *Moore*? Tracy always wants *more*, right? Are you happy with just being a writer? Of course not."

He was reading me like a champ. I hadn't even allowed myself a chance to think about acting much, I was just thinking about the power to create. However, Jonathan was right, starring in the film was the ultimate! No one remembers who wrote the script unless you also directed the film.

I asked, "So, you would throw out the popularity of a singer for an unknown writer from Philly?" I was trying to back my way out of the immediate pressure, but I damn sure was willing to try it.

He said, "Are you kidding me? A lot of these singers need tons of makeup to look good. They can't necessarily hold the camera without movement or singing either, but when I look at you . . ." He stopped and shook his head. "Wow! You're just a natural beauty," he said.

*Watch yourself with this white boy, Tracy!* I told myself. He was really pouring it on.

I said, "Okay, cut the bullshit. Now I retooled the crip . . . I mean *script*," I corrected myself with a chuckle.

Jonathan broke out laughing. "See that, you can't even think straight now. You know you want the part. Go ahead and say it."

I said, "I haven't even taken any acting lessons."

"Well, take some. But a natural is a natural. You just go with what you feel. And I know you know what Cynthia feels, because you wrote the script. Most writers just don't look like you do to be able to play the part."

"So, when would we be ready to start shooting the film?" I asked him, to see how much time I would have to prepare.

He answered, "No later than April of next year. That way we can make it an early 2000 release."

It was late November 1998, and he was dead serious. I nodded my head, almost in a trance. It was really happening for me, at light speed, as if it was a fast-paced dream.

I said, "Okay, but if I stink, be gentle with me and whisper it in my ear."

He laughed and said, "Deal," and reached out to shake my hand.

As soon as I left and reached a telephone, I called Susan and caught her at the office.

"I am going to *kill* you!"

"For what?" she asked, halfway laughing.

"You set me up."

"You mean I got you an opportunity."

"An opportunity to look like a damn fool," I told her.

"Well, he was open to the idea, and I know that you're not some nerdy bookworm, because I've seen you get *heated* plenty of times, even with me. You just have it in you, Tracy. So I told myself, 'Let's just try this out,' and decided to send him a copy of your book."

I shook my head with the pay phone in hand and

said, "Girl, I sure hope you know what the hell you're doing."

Susan turned on this little-girl voice and said, "Oh, I'm so sorry, I didn't know that you were afraid of anything. I didn't mean to do it. Honest! I just wanted to be your friend. Please forgive me."

I broke up laughing and couldn't even talk back to her. She had caught me off guard with everything, including the reverse psychology. Finally I mumbled, "I'll tell you one thing, you're *earning* your ten percent. Damn straight!"

Susan went back to her normal voice and said, "That's because I really like you. And I have a rule that I plan to stick to: Never represent *anyone* who you could not consider as a friend."

I said, "That's an honest enough rule when you're first starting out, but we'll see if you stick to that when the big-money clients start calling and they happen to be real pains in the ass."

Susan said, "They'll be a pain in the ass somewhere else, because I don't like pain. And *you're* a big-money client to me."

I laughed and said, "Okay, well, we have to go out and eat or something tonight to celebrate now. *My* treat."

"We can't celebrate yet, the work is just beginning," she told me. "And if you can pull this off as an actress, I'm gonna get you the sweetest deal that I can get."

I grinned and said, "Okay. I can't complain about that, as long as we get the creative direction that we want."

Susan said, "Exactly. I'm with you on that."

I hung up the phone and smiled. Susan was really impressive. I nodded my head and said, "That's my girl. I'm *glad* that I made her my agent. She really has my back."

# Prisoners of Fame

I have a vault filled with gold
and thousands of Benjamins
that belong to my tribe.
And when I get horny at night,
if I wanted a man
to even lick the crack of my ass,
he would pay me to do it.
And I wake up every morning and step on
every little nobody
who wouldn't give me the time of day
yesterday,
but now them same motherfuckers beg
to see me for tomorrow.
And I have never worn a damn
red and white Santa Claus suit,
so why is every day Christmas?
Then I become the Grinch
who stole it
whenever I say no.

Would you like to join my tribe?
It's fun!
But once you join us
and the vault door closes,
you can't get back out
unless you fall out
and end up strung out
and begging
to get back in.

# May 2000     $ $
                    $

*R*oad Kill was to begin shooting in the Nevada desert on Wednesday, May 31, 2000. The budget for the film was capped at about twenty million dollars. That was a big jump from the eight million that we used to make Led Astray. It also meant that I would have to break the forty-million-dollar mark at the box office in order to keep moving up. We were scheduled to shoot up until early August. So much for having family over for the summer. I wrote my cousin Vanessa a letter to inform her.

During my down time before our first location shoot, I began to work out twice a day on body strength, stamina, speed, and drills with Tae-Bo. I also attended a Beverly Hills weight room facility to work with personal trainers to bulk up for the role. Since I hadn't been much of an athlete, my muscles got sore as hell, but the results were immediate. I felt stronger, faster, in shape, and I was toning up my little-used muscles.

On another note, for my sequel book idea to *Flyy Girl*, I selected the final poetry that I would use, as well as the style in which I would want the book written. The poem count came out closer to *forty* than the twenty-five that Susan suggested, but they were all relevant poems, and I didn't know how many chapters I would have yet.

When I found the time, I sat down and had a long thought about sending Mercedes money in Philadelphia. In a way, I owed her because of the emotions that I had borrowed from her life to play the role of Cynthia in *Led Astray*. On the other hand, I didn't want to spoil Mercedes. She needed to catch the fire from *somewhere* and keep it lit on her own. So I decided to write her a letter asking to let me sign for the house that she wanted. Once she paid off the rest of the mortgage, I would turn the ownership over to her. However, if she didn't pay the mortgage, and she started acting up . . . then I would sell it. Actually, I didn't believe that Mercedes would agree to that, and it would only make things more complicated between us. I just wanted to see how serious she would be. It was my challenge to her to get her priorities back in order with her life.

**$ $ $**

I called Susan over to the house on Thursday morning to catch up on all of our business. I had to get used to not being able to go out as much. I had two interviews set up at my house for that afternoon, one with *Movie Life* magazine and the other with *Fade In:*.

Susan walked in and said, "So, are you still thinking about leaving this place?"

I loved my Marina Del Rey home, and I had been there for less than a year. I hadn't even bought a lot of furniture yet, because I was busy half of the time. It wasn't as if I had a family or anything. However, all of a sudden, I was worth four times the property value where I lived.

I shook my head and said, "I just may have to deal with whatever, Susan, because I don't really feel like moving. I just *moved in* here."

"I know," my girl said with a chuckle, "but that's how fast you're moving up."

"So, what am I supposed to do, move to a two-million-dollar estate now?"

"Or at least one million," she joked.

I shook my head again. "I think I'm gonna stay right here until something *forces* me to move, like an earthquake or a burglary."

Susan said, "That's what *I* would do. I'd stay put and save my money for other things."

I said, "Okay, well, I've typed out the poetry, and it's more like forty poems than twenty-five, plus I have the style that I want to write it in." I handed her a copy of the poems and a one-page proposal on the style.

She took a seat on my sofa (in the middle of my wide-open family room) and looked through it. She began to smile and nod, liking what she read.

"This is going to blow people away," she told me. "When most actors and Hollywood people try to write books, it's so"—she stuck her finger in her mouth for a gag gesture—"but this is serious material here."

I smiled, raising my hand. "I'm the English teacher with the master's degree, remember?"

Susan broke up laughing. "Yeah, you're a ringer, I almost forgot." She stopped and asked, "Okay, so tell me now, Tracy, how much should we offer Mr. Tyree to ghost-write this book before we move on to someone else? I hear that Eric Jerome Dickey is hot, and he lives in the area. We could get this proposal over to him in a day or two and see what *he* says."

I smiled. My girl was ready to move the hell on from my Philadelphia connection. I said, "Well, let's try it with the poetry and the proposal *first*, and see what Omar says before we move on. And if push comes to shove, *we will* move on."

"Okay, so what's the offer?"

I thought about it. "A half of a million dollars, and half of the royalty rights like before. And if he doesn't jump at that, then fuck 'im; we go somewhere else."

Susan smiled at me, but she also looked concerned.

"*Half* of the royalty rights?" she asked me. She turned to serious in a hurry and said, "No way! This is *your* poetry, *your* life, *your* proposal, and we're having to practically *beg* him to do it.

"When you guys got together on *Flyy Girl*, I could see giving him half, because it was a real risk involved," she said. "Neither of you really knew if it would sell, but to his credit, it did, mainly because of his ability to piece together your story in a very entertaining, fast-paced style that worked out very well for you. But *this* book is different. You'll be a lot more involved this time. And with five hundred thousand dollars to write it, Mr. Tyree will already be making a *killing* off of you.

"I would offer him no more than fifteen percent, the limit on a literary agency fee," she advised me. Susan *knew* her damn numbers!

I began to smile and couldn't hold my tongue. I said, "You know my people would say that you're being a little bit greedy right now, just like a J-E-W."

Susan looked at me dead-eyed and said, "Tracy, this is business, and if I'm going to represent you as a friend and agent, I'm going to do my job."

I broke out laughing and said, "I know, I know. You're not offended by me saying that are you?"

She smiled. "No, I think I know how you are by now, Tracy, and you'll say anything that comes to your mind, but I *will* give you a serious warning: Do not even *joke* like that to the press."

I looked at Susan and said, "Shit, I wasn't born yesterday. In fact, my people need to think more in regards to their *own* money issues instead of complaining about other people. You know how many black celebrities died penniless? *Too* many! And it was all because of their *own* lack of good money habits."

"Well, that won't be you. If *you* die broke, then *I'll* die broke. And I *mean* that."

I looked into Susan's eyes and she was dead serious. I knew her well enough to know it too. Besides, it wasn't as if I was depositing my money in her bank account. My finances were all up to me anyway, and I was sure that Susan would say something to me if I began to spend money on Mike Tyson–like shopping sprees.

I said, "Okay, you're right; he gets fifteen percent. Now what about the five hundred thousand? Do you think that's too much?"

Susan grinned and said, "Well, since I don't want to sound *greedy* like a J-E-W, we can offer him your two million."

I broke out laughing again. "Two million of *your* money," I snapped.

She said, "Well, you know, I was just being a stereotypical B-L-A-C-K. I just *love* throwing money away. Take me to the nearest clothing or jewelry store," she cracked.

"O-o-o-kaaay," I responded. I smiled it off and chuckled, but I sure felt the burn.

Susan asked, "You're not offended that I said that are you?"

What the hell could I say? "No, I'm not offended," I whimpered.

"Good, because if you're gonna dish it out, then be prepared to take it back."

I smiled and nodded. "That's why I like you, Susan, you tell it like it is, just like *I* do."

She stood up and said, "Well, I've had good lessons from you. Boldness is growing on me now. So, I'll send this proposal and offer out right away and see what happens."

**$ $ $**

When my first reporter arrived from *Movie Life* magazine, a dark-haired Italian woman named Jackie Perrotta, I showed her in and planned to be as lighthearted as possible. Who really cared about cultural and political views of an actress anyway? I planned to give the people just what they wanted, the hype. I was sure that Jackie already knew the figures on my new contract from reading *The Hollywood Reporter* or the *Daily Variety*. So I just went wild with the interview.

She said, "So, Tracy, you're obviously beautiful. You could make tons of money by just being pretty on the screen. But now you're going to do a big-time action movie. Is that what you want to do, or are you just trying something different?"

I answered, "Are you kidding me? I've wanted to kick a guy's ass real good all of my life. Haven't you? They're such assholes!"

Jackie laughed her behind off. I guess I caught her off guard with it.

"Yeah, I've had a few," she admitted.

"I know you have. Have you dated exclusively Italians?" I asked her.

She shook her head and said, "No."

"Well, so far, I've only gone for brothers with the gusto, you know," I said, grabbing at my crotch, à la Foxy Brown. "But if these white men keep offering me these Robert Redford deals, I don't know how many more I can turn down before I break out and say, 'SHOW ME THE MONEY!'"

Jackie could barely ask her questions because she was laughing so hard. "Well, is it true that it's increasingly difficult for a black woman of your stature to find a suitable man?"

I looked around in my big, beautiful, and relatively empty California home and asked, "Do you see one? What is he, invisible? TY-RONE!" I stood up and screamed for affect. "DAR-NELL!" I yelled up my stairs. "POOO-KAAAY!" I hollered toward the back porch.

"Oh my God!" Jackie commented. "You're an absolute *riot*!"

I didn't think much at all of that interview, and that's not because I didn't like Jackie or *Movie Life* magazine. It was their job to give the people what they want, and the people didn't want education, they wanted entertainment.

When my second reporter arrived, a young East Indian woman named Pascha Shiam, I was pleasantly surprised. She was darker than me with long, straight, jet black hair that black American men would damn-near *kill* for on a sister! Since I was already in a silly-behind mood, I went straight for the jugular.

"So, Pascha, have you ever slept with a black man?"

"Excuse me?" Her eyes nearly popped out of her head.

I asked, "You know, have you ever jumped bones with a black man before, like Denzel Washington in *Mississippi Masala*? What do y'all call boning in India anyway?"

She was too embarrassed to answer me.

"I'm supposed to interview *you*," she said with a laugh.

"Well, I haven't boned an East Indian man. Are they fairly large downstairs?"

Pascha laughed some more before she pulled out her tape recorder.

"Can we get you on record too? Tell me about the size," I pressed her, "when the tape is on."

She said, "I'd rather not, but the size is normal."

"And what does normal mean?"

She put her face in her hands, still embarrassed by me. She said, "I guess around six inches."

"You actually measured them?" I asked her.

"No, I read that somewhere."

"Are you sure you don't have a little nine-inch ruler in your bag, Pascha?"

"I swear to you. I don't."

Pascha told me that the interview for *Fade In:* was a straight Q&A. That caught me by surprise as well. Once she told me that, I got rid of my silliness *real* quick.

"This is a straight Q&A?" I asked her just to make sure.

"Yeah."

"With all of the background information up front?" She nodded. "Yes."

"Well, shit, is this a cover story?" *Fade In:* usually used the Q&A format for their cover subjects.

Pascha said, "They haven't really made up their minds yet, but I heard the editor asking about seeing if we could get some photos of you on the set, so maybe they are."

"But this is *far* too early for that. *Road Kill* doesn't come out until next summer."

She shrugged her shoulders. "I don't know until it happens."

I was getting excited for nothing, because it *couldn't*

have been a cover story. You would know that well in advance. Nevertheless, there was no way in the world that I would allow myself to sound like an idiot for a straight Q&A interview, so I changed my entire tone.

"Okay, let's do it then."

She clicked on her tape.

Q: "You had an unusual start as an actress where you were actually a television writer first. Was that the way that you planned it, to move into screenplays and then acting?"

A: "No, I actually had no plans on that at all. I knew I wanted to write screenplays eventually, but the acting thing just sort of happened for me. I was told that most writers don't look like I do. But this whole Hollywood merry-go-round, for me, all began with my lack of fulfillment teaching English in Philadelphia. So I figured that it would be natural for me to start with the writing, and then one thing led to the next."

Q: "Did you find that your educational background made it easier for you to succeed, or was it something that had very little to do with the creative process?"

A: "Oh, I like that question. Thank you for asking. A lot of people assume, particularly in the African-American community, that education and creativity don't necessarily mix. But the more you know, the more you have to be creative about. For instance, I write poetry, and I've written poetry since my senior year of high school. And as I received more education, my poetry became more complicated, and more inspiring. I look at screenplays the same way. You can't write what you don't know. That's why creative people tend to stand out, because they know more and they use what they know to their advantage. And I'm not saying that a person who never went to college cannot succeed in this business, I'm just saying that it was a

straight arc of success for me because I did have that educational experience to know what work needs to be done
to get there."

Q: "However, plenty of young people in Hollywood
have education from various film schools, and their arc is
still not as fast as your arc was. In your opinion, what made
your talents stand out, or was it as simple as luck?"

A: "Well, luck is never that simple, because you can luck
up and destroy your career if you're not prepared for it.
When I first arrived out here in California, every young
writer I knew was talking about the famous Shane Black
story of success too fast. And it can ruin you just like that.
But I think that my special talent is just plain hard work.
I'm always thinking about new ideas, and I follow my
heart, just like with my poetry. So when other people say,
'You can't do that' I ask, 'Why not?' and do it anyway. I'm
bold like that, and I've always been that way."

Q: "How different is the acting from the writing?"

A: "It's very different, and very similar. The difference, of
course, is the feeling. You have to feel the role and almost
become possessed by it. In writing, you have to think the
role. What would this person say? What would this person
do? But then there's some feeling in the writing as well,
feeling out the entire rhythm of the activities involved, and
in acting there is some thinking involved, particularly
when the feeling tells you that something is wrong in the
script. And you have to be confident enough to speak up
about it. So with *Road Kill,* I made a lot of changes to the
original screenplay as an actor and as a writer."

Q: "Will you write more of your own vehicles to star in
in the future, or will you read other scripts and tailor them
to fit your specific needs?"

A: "Both. Because I know there will be stories, specifically as an African-American woman, that Hollywood will not write. So I will have to write those stories myself. Then there will be roles like this one in *Road Kill*, where an African-American woman will not be a consideration for the part, and I'll have to force my way in, but it will not always be about tailoring the script, because if someone writes a strong generic role that does not need to be touched, then I will feel the honesty in that and play the role as it was originally written."

On the last question for the *Fade In:* Q&A, Pascha asked me to give any final words of advice or encouragement to aspiring writers and actresses of color.

I said, "I wrote a poem while teaching in the Philadelphia public school system called 'Ignorance Is Bliss' to explain the commonality of people who don't seek out information. And it's a short poem where I wrote: 'Ignorance is bliss / because real knowledge / is painful. And who really wants to wake up / and do nine to five / when lazy dreams can be so / pleasant?' And it basically means that answers make you work. So as long as you can say, 'I didn't know,' you have an excuse not to do anything. And in the business of Hollywood, of course, many people would love to be stars, but then when you tell them that they have to take step one, two, and three, a, b, and c, dot your i's, cross your t's, and remember your commas, they say, 'Well, what's the other way to become a star?' And there is no other way. Because pure luck, like I said earlier, will lead you astray and have you strung out for the Hollywood fame with no real skills to survive in it. So I would say to always seek out information and be prepared to accept the workload involved."

**$ $ $**

I felt uplifted after the *Fade In:* interview. I must have thanked Pascha four or five times for her great questions, and I apologized to her for my ignorance from when she had first walked in. However, once I sat down and thought about it, I asked myself, "Now how many black people are going to even read *Fade In:?* I need to have a great interview like that in a black magazine." Problem was, many black magazines seemed more concerned with the entertainment value or the money aspect and not the educational value. The *Fade In:* Q&A spoiled me to the possibilities of my own voice. So I nodded to myself and made a decision. "From now on, if it's not a Q&A, then I'm not doing the interview. Because I have no time to waste for other people's editorials determining who I am and what I stand for."

# Lucky Like Me

*You step up.*
*I step up.*
*You choose your number,*
*and I choose mine.*
*Then we both become*
*blind*
*as our numbers*
*bounce, bounce, bounce,*
*smack, slap, POP*
*in the box.*

*Then*
*SSSOUP!*
*My number shoots up,*
*and I win the prize*
*that you still*
*hope for.*

*Sistah,*
*my life,*
*and yours*
*should be much more*
*secure*
*than a*
*damn*
*lottery!*

*Educate*
*yourself*

*and your number,*
*like mine,*
*shall rise*
*regardless!*

# Early 1999

$$\$$

When Black Hollywood found out that I had a movie deal in the frying pan, and that I was about to take acting classes to prepare for the lead role, the shit hit the fan again. I guess that I was just the girl who everyone loved to hate out there.

Reba Combs called me up first, and we weren't even on speaking terms anymore. I had heard through the grapevine that our Southern pilot show idea had turned into something called *Peaches and Cream,* about a black girl and her white friend who ends up moving in after her parents are killed in an airplane crash. That was exactly the kind of *transformation* that I was afraid of. They had turned a realistic, Southern perspective into something wholly unimaginable. You mean to tell me that a Southern white girl wouldn't have any other family members to take her in. Child, *please!* However, that was Hollywood for you, banking on a fish-out-of-water story.

Reba asked me, "You wrote a role for yourself? You can't even act. Are you even a member of the Actors Guild? Why would you do something like that? You are really a *trip,*" she huffed at me.

I said, "Reba, I don't have the part yet, but they asked me to try it, so I'm going to try it. It's as simple as that."

The girl went ahead and hung up on me again. I couldn't believe it!

I called her ass right back, and she either wouldn't answer the phone, or she hadn't called me from her apartment, the apartment that *I* helped her to get. In fact, she was still working off and on for the smaller network shows because of *me*. Even the new pilot show that she was still in development for was all because of *me* trying to help her ass out! Boy, she had something *coming* when I finally caught up with her! She had gotten on my last damn nerve!

I called Coe's apartment to see if she was over there.

"Hello," he answered.

"Is Reba over there with you?"

"Yup."

"Let me speak to her."

"Hold on."

I waited for only Coe to return to the line. "She doesn't want to talk right now."

"Well, tell her to grow the hell up!" I snapped. "And I plan to be out here making movies in Hollywood for a while, so she should be *very* careful about making enemies on account of pettiness."

Coe said, "All right, I'll tell her."

I was tempted to ask him how *he* felt about it, because I knew she had told him. However, I was too pissed off to stay on the phone, and that was just the beginning of it. The bad buzz about me was even beginning to travel to family and friends back at home.

My mother called me up and said, "Tracy, what's going on out there? We've heard that you've been in fights over shows and carrying on."

"I wasn't fighting over no damn show, Mom," I responded rather tartly. "People need to get the facts straight."

"Well, what *are* the facts?"

"The fact is, we got a lot of *petty-ass* people out here!"

I heard that people were saying I would continue to set everyone back if I played a role that was damaging to "professional black actresses." They hadn't even given me a chance. They *all* needed to grow the hell up! Of course, there *were* some sisters who called me up and said, "Go for it!" It wasn't *all* bad. Nevertheless, you had others who were only trying to stay close to me in case I didn't work out in the role. Jonathan Abner must have received thirty-something phone calls with sisters trying to sabotage me and push their way into the role, which was highly embarrassing. We looked like a bunch of slaves *begging* to be sold at the auction.

You would think that I would be at one of the happiest points in my life, but that wasn't the case. I was only human, so I was getting tired of fighting all of the nonsense out there. So I called my girl Raheema, long distance in New Jersey, with tears in my eyes, tears of anger, hurt, and disappointment in my people. All I had tried to do was push ahead with my creativity, and I hadn't stepped on any toes to do so. I had done nothing but try to help people, yet I was being called a traitor because I had an *opportunity* to play a lead. That's all that it was, an opportunity. I thought that opportunity was supposed to be the American way and the American dream, but I guess it was not, because quotas were in full effect, and they were driving my people crazy!

I asked, "Raheema, are you busy? You're not, umm, breast-feeding or anything right now are you?" She had just had her daughter, Lauryn. Time was really flying by on me.

She paused. "No, I'm not breast-feeeding. What's going on? Is everything all right?"

I guess she could hear the instability in my voice.

I said, "I haven't told anyone at home about it because nothing has been finalized yet, but I completed a screenplay called *Led Astray* that we have on the table, and they're giving me an opportunity to play the lead role."

"So what's the problem?" Raheema asked me calmly. She knew that there was one from reading my solemn tone of voice.

"Well, I have to take some acting classes this month, and in the meantime, a lot of the sister actresses out here are stirring up the bullcrap about me being selfish, and ruining things for all of them."

Raheema chuckled. "Stick to the writing, right?" she asked me.

"I guess *so.*"

"Do you remember how many girls couldn't stand you when we were younger?" she asked me.

I smiled. "Yeah, I remember."

"'That cat-eyed so-and-so thinks she's all that,'" Raheema mocked.

I smiled and wiped my tears.

She said, "But you know what, Tracy? They never stopped you from being you, no matter what they said."

I said, "I remember when I used to give *you* advice, but now it seems like *I'm* always the one looking for strength."

Raheema laughed. "That's the way of the world; things go around and keep turning. In the next ten years, I may be calling on *you* again."

"So, I guess I just go ahead with my plans to take acting classes and get this role then."

Raheema paused for a second time. "I know you don't need *me* to tell you."

I laughed while loosening up.

She said, "I knew this day would come. You're revolutionary, Tracy, and you don't even know it. I keep telling you that you're doing *exactly* what you're supposed to be doing. And when you're finished, you'll have another story to tell."

I asked Raheema how her family was doing with the new baby girl and everything, and when I hung up with her, I thought for the first time about writing a sequel to *Flyy Girl*. However, first I had to take care of business and succeed at what I was doing in Hollywood. Because if I did not succeed, there was no way in the world that I would write a book about my failure. Who wants to read that? We had *enough* sob stories in our history.

**$ $ $**

I was right back in the UCLA Extensions program to take two separate classes on acting, one focusing on the fundamental techniques, and the other focusing on performances for the camera. They both began in late January and went up until April, so obviously I would have to do a screen test for *Led Astray* in the middle of my training in order to stay on schedule to begin shooting the film in April.

The fundamentals of acting had to do with relaxing nervous energies, concentrating on your performance, using your memory of events, your emotional recall of how those events made you feel, then improvising with the character's tasks, text, and delivery. I thought about all of that and smiled my ass off. I had already done all of that stuff in my poetry performances. Shit, I could basically *teach* the fundamentals of acting myself. The best poetry performances were all about confident delivery and controlling your audience with a complete range of different emotions, charm, anger, fear, victimization, seduction, inspiration, and everything else. So I felt totally at ease in that class. The movie *Slam* had won the Cannes Film Festival award and was a winner in the Sundance Film Festival, smoking up the screen from coast to coast on the strength of poetic delivery and improvisation.

After learning what the fundamentals of acting entailed, I felt that the role of Cynthia was in the bag for me. The second acting class, dealing with the camera skills, became my main focus. How could I control the camera, knowing that it was there, and pull it into me and away from everyone else? I wanted to seize the lens and hold it hostage like a prisoner of war. In the meantime, I went ahead and bought Spike Lee's *Girl 6*, starring Theresa Randle, from the video store, to study her delusional solos with the camera. *Girl 6* was a tremendously underrated film. I guess only performers who understood the passion involved in art and life could actually get it and love it as much as I had learned to.

Nevertheless, my character, Cynthia Moore, in *Led Astray*, would push her way *past* the delusions of revenge, and put real plans into action. I could not *perform* for the camera, I had to *possess* the camera and make it *believe* in me and want to follow me wherever I go. So I stayed up for most of the night before my first performance, a grocery scene skit at the small Los Angeles theater where we met for three hours of class.

$ $ $

I was up third for my performance with the camera that day, which was good, because I had a chance to watch at least two performances before mine.

The setup was that a man bumps into a woman at a grocery store, she tells him to say excuse me, he apologizes, and then they strike up a conversation while walking through the aisles.

The first man-and-woman team interpreted their skit with humor. They were both young and white, and a romantic comedy fit them, so it was a good performance that was believable. Our instructor said so himself. They did it a couple of times and were dead-on with each performance.

The second man-and-woman team was a young sister and another young white guy. The sister interpreted her skit, first with irritation, and then with intrigue, which was corny as shit, and that made the white guy look bad too. If a man irritates you, you're not going to turn around and become interested in him in the next three seconds. The sister obviously didn't know what the hell she was doing. She had no consistency.

Our instructor said, "Work on it!" and they did it three more times.

As I waited for my turn, with another white guy who appeared to be nervous while watching the mixed couple ahead of us that was fucking up, I decided that I was not participating in the skit for the class, but for Cynthia and *Led Astray*. If my partner couldn't follow me, then to hell with him; I had ulterior motives.

When it was our turn, I took a deep breath, located the camera, and went into my approach.

"ACTION!"

I walk forward with deep thoughts on my mind, like a

daydreamer. The guy bumps into me. I stop and raise my hands with my ten fingertips meeting in a pyramid.

"Excuse me . . ." I pause in the middle of my sentence and work with my hands, trying to keep my concentration on deep thoughts and not on the person in front of me, because I have shit to do. "Could you please watch where you're going." I'm not irritated, I'm just busy.

"Oh, I'm sorry about that," he says.

I walk ahead, dropping my hands slowly as I respond, "Of course you are," but I never look at him. He is not at all important to me.

He follows me up the imaginary aisle. I know he's coming, but so what?

"Look, ah, would you happen to know where any great parties are around here?"

I finally look him in the face and read his smile, but *I'm* not smiling; I'm trying to figure out what to do with him. *Can I use him in some way? Maybe, maybe not.* I decide not and keep walking.

"You're asking the wrong person," I tell him.

He follows me around the invisible corner of the aisle. "You mean a fox like you never parties?"

I take in his words and grimace with just a hint of a smile, while shaking my head. I'm thinking, *This fool doesn't know me.* So I keep walking ahead, but now he has my attention so I move slower. He has broken my train of thought. One more word wins him a short conversation.

"Okay, well, I guess you don't party then," he says.

Now I nod my head and stop, turning to face him again. "What kind of parties are you into?" I may know something after all, depending on what his answer is.

He smiles at me again and says, "Any kind."

I finally smile back at him with my own thoughts on the matter. *I might be able to use him after all.*

I point with my right index finger, low at my stomach and nonthreatening, to motion with as I speak. "I'll tell you what? You give me a contact number, and when I find out something, I'll let you know."

He nods his head, pleased with it. "Well, all right! That's what *I'm* talking about!" He writes his number down while I think about a million other things on my mind, paying him no damn attention. I'm thinking, *Why am I wasting my time with this guy? I can't use him for anything. Who does he even know? He's asking* me *shit!*

He snaps me back to attention when he finishes writing. "So, you'll call me, right?"

I take the number and tell him, "Sure," while on my way out.

He says, "Don't forget."

I walk out of the imaginary door and make a move to toss his phone number in an imaginary trash can, but then I stop myself, thinking, *Hollywood is a small town. Maybe he* does *know someone.* So I take another look at his name and phone number before I slip it into my purse and walk away.

"CUT!"

Our instructor said, "*Excellent* interpretation! And I don't know who you are, lady, but you definitely have something on your mind. You're planning to use him for something. You just have a whole lot going on there. You have so much on your mind that you never bothered to buy anything."

I laughed it off and said, "Actually, I forgot."

He said, "But that's okay, it worked. You sure had *me* interested."

He addressed my partner and said, "And you hung right in there with her. 'You mean a fox like you never parties?' That was good. You may have some ulterior motives yourself. This one looks like a good murder mystery to me.

"And 'What kind of parties are you into?' I *loved* that line! Now *that's* improvisation! Let's see if you two can do it that well again," he told us.

"By the way, what is your character's name?" he asked me.

I kept a straight face and answered, "Cynthia. Cynthia Moore."

"And what are you thinking about up there, Cynthia?" I smiled and answered, "Just some things."

He laughed and said, "Yeah, well, just remember to buy something this time."

From that moment on, *Led Astray* was money in the bank.

**$ $ $**

Susan and I called Jonathan Abner at his office in late February to tell him that it was time for our screen test. He agreed to it, and we all met at a small studio lot in Culver City where Jonathan introduced us to Danny Greene, a forty-something, hands-on kind of guy who was just starting to gray around the edges of his dark hair. He looked like a real player to me. He wore a Giorgio Armani suit, expensive shoes, an attractive silk tie, and he looked confident and secure, a wife and three kids secure.

He extended his hand to mine and said, "Pleased to met you, Tracy. I'm Danny. I'm very interested in this screenplay that you've written. You know why?"

"Why?" I asked him.

He spoke with his hands like an Italian. "Well, I'm a little new in the business of Hollywood like you are, and I'd like to fuck the big guys too, but if we're gonna fuck 'em, we have to fuck 'em right. So show me how."

Everyone broke out laughing but me. I had already begun to slip into character. I did it off of instincts. After all, Cynthia hated the players, so she had no time to be flattered by them.

I said, "If you take your time, then the fucking comes naturally."

Danny felt my words. "Okay, okay," he said with a grin. "You're gonna read with her for the camera, right Johnny?"

Jonathan nodded and handed me the side sheets that he had chosen from my screenplay. One was the dinner scene with Peter Dalvin, and the other was a later scene with Player #2. Both scenes were sitting down, so a couple of production assistants gathered a table and two chairs. I handed the side sheets back to Jonathan and nodded as I sat down in the chair.

Danny laughed and said, "She doesn't need the lines, she *wrote 'em!* We need to hire *more* writers who can act. Maybe that'll be our thing. Especially if they look like you do, honey."

I turned and smiled at him, a controlled smile from Cynthia.

We had two cameras, one in my face behind Jonathan, and one behind me that was pointed in Jonathan's face.

"All right, ACTION!" Danny yelled himself from in front of a video monitor.

Jonathan glanced down at his side sheets and did his lines.

"So, you decided to stick around in Hollywood a little longer?"

I smile and lean back, slow enough for the cameras to follow my lead.

"Yeah, maybe I just haven't spent enough time with the right people out here." I stare momentarily with my eyes so that "Peter" could read me.

He nods. "Now we're talking. What took you so long to figure that out?"

I lean against the table on my left elbow, placing my chin between my left thumb and index finger, while making sure not to cover my face from the camera behind me. My eyes wander blankly through the room, reminiscing as I speak.

"I guess it finally hit me when that asshole over at Agency One screwed me over."

Peter laughs and pulls out a pack of cigarettes, offering one to me. "Yeah, Player #1 is a real come fiend. He fucks everybody. Then he brags out in public how much he loves his wife."

I smile, mischievously, as we light up our cigarettes. "Well, he isn't any good at it. Now Player #2 at Studio One, he knows how to make a woman feel the burn." (I hadn't filled in all of the details on names yet. I figured we would do that in production with the actors.)

Peter frowns. "You screwed that asshole?! He's such a fucking brownnoser. He has his nose so far up Player #3's ass, I don't see how he can even breathe."

Peter accidentally puts his cigarette out in his water. "Shit!" He lights up a new one.

I grin, continuing with my web of deception as I take a deep puff and blow out the smoke.

"He talks about Player #3 as if he hates him."

Peter says, "Yeah, he hates him and loves him like a wife. 'Honey, don't fuck me so hard, please!'" he jokes with a laugh.

I chuckle and add more kerosene to the fire. "From what I hear, Player #3 is married to Player #4 from Studio Two in that way, two old and freaky guys."

Peter laughs hard. "You've been getting around out here." He puts out his second cigarette and says, "Look, enough about these other fucks. Let's just talk about me and you, back at ground zero. Now you still want to get high?"

Peter's dick is hard for sex and drugs right as the food reaches our table.

I smile at the waiter and wait for him to leave.

"I thought that you were high already," I comment to Peter.

He smiles and says, "Just a little, but you're not." He tosses a Benjamin on the hot, untouched food. "Let's go."

Peter stands up.

I sit still and stroke my plate with my right index finger, sucking the food from it with a nod. "Mmm, that tastes great."

Peter smiles, ready to come in his pants while he waits for me.

Danny Greene yelled, "CUT! Jesus Christ, Johnny! Do you want to play this part or what? You're beautiful! And Tracy . . ." He lost his words and just stared at me. "You were *born* for this part! She's a natural, a black Linda Fiorentino. What do you guys think?" he asked the two cameramen.

They both nodded. "Yeah, that was great stuff."

"And great eyes."

"Great everything!" Danny told them. He said, "Johnny, I think we have a movie to make."

Susan sat there and beamed at me, sucking it all in. When we walked out and chatted amongst ourselves, she took a deep breath and said, "You're amazing! You're absolutely *amazing!* I've been with *ten-year professionals* who have never blown producers away like that!"

I just smiled. I asked, "So what about the business side?"

Susan paused. "I'll have to sit down and come up with something really creative. This is your first film, and you don't want to walk into it too cheaply, but since we're all thinking low-budget here, we can't ask for the cow either."

"As long as we get more than a pig," I joked.

Susan smiled. "Oh, we won't get a pig, I can assure you of that. We want at least a big, clean turkey, with plenty of leftovers. That's the key to *this* deal, leftovers."

I asked, "Leftovers meaning what?"

"Back-end residuals. Don't you get a royalty payment on your books?"

I nodded. "Yeah."

"Well, that's what we want to focus on here," she told me, "gross points from the studio. So if the movie does well at the box office, even if they only paid you five hundred thousand to star in it, you can make some real money through the back-end points. That's the advantage of going with smaller studios. They have to bend over backward sometimes to stay in the hunt for good projects."

I nodded. Residuals sounded rather complicated and legal to me, and I didn't have Yolanda on my side anymore to look over the paperwork.

"Do you have a lawyer to make sure that we don't get screwed here," I asked Susan jokingly.

She looked at me and asked, "I thought you had a lawyer already?"

"I did, but now I don't."

Susan said, "I don't really secure contracts on my own, that's what the agency is for, to make sure we cover each other's backs. We have plenty of lawyers who go through the contract before you even see it."

I looked and said, "So, in other words, I was paying my lawyer for nothing."

Susan paused. "Well, I wouldn't say that, because it's pretty smart to have checks and balances wherever you can. Not saying that I would do anything to harm you, but we could *both* miss something. And I'm just being honest with that."

I nodded. In other words, I needed to get another damn lawyer just in case.

## $ $ $

Susan came up with a deal that would split a million dollars between my screenplay and my starring in the film, but the butter on the biscuit was the gross points. She was going to ask for ten percent on the strength of how much I would be involved in production. Included in that were rights for cable, network, and video sales, as well as foreign rights if we were ever able to cross overseas with the film. So if we made a measly ten million dollars alone, I would have another million coming *before* we even went to cable, network, or video. As long as the movie continued to sell, in *any* capacity, I would have checks written out in my name for it.

I thought about all of that and said, "Damn!" I still hadn't hooked up with a new lawyer yet. I was itching to call Yolanda back to tell you the truth, but I didn't want to be the one who took the first step to mending our soiled relationship, because I was not the one with the big ego who had ended it. So I got Kendra in on the deal to call Yolanda up as a peacemaker and let her know how disappointed I was that we had split, because it was still a black sister thing that we needed to work out and keep together.

In the meantime, Jonathan Abner called me with ideas for directors. He mentioned a young Latin guy named Poncho Morales, who he had been interested in for a while, and several other young, and relatively cheap directors. I had watched a couple of music videos directed by Poncho myself, and I liked the images that he brought across the camera. His pacing was right on, and he never went overboard with close-ups or color filters. His camera work looked lively, but still human, and very easy on the eyes. Other directors with music video history got too caught up with the tricks of the camera and ended up creating long flashy videos instead of stable films. I didn't want that tricky camera shit in *my* movie. *I* wanted to be the one doing the tricks!

However, Jonathan hadn't made up his mind on who to go with, and I was getting tired of all the damn talk and no action, so I tracked down Poncho Morales myself. He was shooting on a set at Redondo Beach for a five-member, white-boy pop group. It seemed like white-boy singing groups were popping up everywhere, New Kids on the Block all over again.

"Excuse me, this is a restricted area," I was told by a blonde production assistant. I had already slipped by the security men.

I put on my little Puerto Rican accent and said, "Jus' tell Eddie his cousin is hea' to see 'im from New Yawk." (I had done some research on Poncho. He was from Spanish Harlem and his first name was Eduardo. He was inspired as a kid to pursue a career in Hollywood because of the television show *CHiPs.*)

Since the production assistant was white, I felt safe with my Puerto Rican accent, but had she been a Latina, I wouldn't even have tried that shit. Some fast Spanish would have busted my groove with the quickness, but this white girl didn't know what the hell was going on.

"Oh, well, what's your name?" she asked me.

"Nina."

"Okay, well, I'll get his attention for you as soon as I can."

I was close enough to see Poncho, but I didn't want to yell anything out at him on account that he didn't know who the hell I was. I had to get close enough to him to hand him a fresh copy of my script and explain my game plan to him.

Poncho began to make a move toward his small trailer with no security surrounding him, and I stepped right past the PA and made my move.

"Wait a minute," she complained, trying to block me.

I pushed her out of my way and said real fast, "Look, I don't have any time for this. He know's I'm hea' already." I actually made it to the director's trailer and let myself in. Talk about being *pressed*!

Poncho looked at me while zipping up his pants from his private restroom and said, "Who the hell are you?" He was olive-toned, with deep, dark eyes, dark hair, and built like a swimmer, slim but muscular. He was gorgeous!

I said, "I'm your best opportunity to make a name for yourself in Hollywood films," and handed him a copy of my screenplay.

He looked at the title and nodded. He said, "This is pretty good, I've read some of it."

"Why not direct it then?" I asked him.

He shook his head and said, "Not enough money. If they're only offering me three hundred thousand, I'll just keep doing videos; they're a lot less work for about the same amount of money." He was already heading back out the door.

"What if I could get you more?"

The PA barged in and said, "I tried to stop her."

Poncho waved her off and showed her back out. He asked me, "Who's starring in it?"

I smiled at him. "I am."

He paused, and studied me as if he was sizing me up for the camera. He asked, "How much more could you get me?"

I blurted out, "How about five hundred thousand?" I was willing to pay him the extra two hundred thousand myself if I had to. I just wanted to get the film rolling.

He said, "They're not gonna give me that. I've already talked to those people. I don't think they respect me that much. That's why I can't do your movie."

"Who's your agent?"

He looked at me and frowned. "Why?" He was interested, he just needed me to convince him and show him the money. He was standing his professional ground, and I respected that.

I said, "Sometimes your agent can be in the way. You get a more respected agent, and you get to push things through."

"What if I don't have an agent?" he asked me.

The PA stuck her head back in the trailer and said, "Poncho, everyone is ready and waiting for you."

He waved her off a second time for me. "I'll be there."

I said, "If you don't have an agent, then that's your problem. You can end up doing videos for the rest of your life unless you get one." I was bluffing, but it sounded good. Agents were getting more powerful as the Hollywood stakes continued to increase. I couldn't have gotten the bigger and better deals myself without Susan.

"Who is your agent?" Poncho asked me.

I smiled. "Now we're talking. You're reading my mind. Let's trade phone numbers and talk about it."

He nodded and gave me one of his cards. I wrote my number down on the title page of the script.

"Poncho, this is gold. Don't lose it," I told him of the screenplay *and* of my home phone number.

He smiled at me and said, "We'll see," and we walked out together.

The PA looked at me with the nasty names all over her face. I just smiled at her.

"Thank you," I told her.

"Yeah," she said with a huff and rolled her eyes.

Poncho said, "We'll talk," as he headed back to work.

"We sure will," I told him.

I got back to my car and called Susan at her office from my brand-new cell phone. Once business started to get too hot and heavy, a cell phone became a necessity.

"Hey, what's going on?" she asked me. "I have a meeting with Wide Vision for early next week to go over the deal."

I asked, "Have you ever heard of Eduardo 'Poncho' Morales, the music video director?"

"Yeah, I've heard of him, but I don't know that much about him. I hear he's good."

"And he's also without an agent."

Susan paused. "Okay."

"And Wide Vision wants to sign him."

"All right."

"But they're not offering him enough money."

"Which is?"

"He wants five hundred thousand, but they're only offering him three hundred, and *I* want him."

"*Three hundred thousand?*" Susan responded. "Oh, they can do *much* better than that. They're not *that* small."

"So, you'll do his deal then?" I asked her.

"I can't just take him on as a client, but I can try to include him as a package deal and see how that goes."

"Whatever," I told her, "and then you can see if you'll take him on after that."

"I can't promise anything."

*But I can,* I told myself. If Susan couldn't get the deal done, I would just have to count eight hundred thousand for my purse instead of a million, so that I could pay Poncho and get the green light rolling forward.

Next I called Jonathan at his office to let *him* know what my plans were.

"Jonathan, this is Tracy."

He was excited to hear from me. "Hey, Tracy, hold on a minute. Let me shake this other line."

Who would have thought that I could have Hollywood players sweating me as hard as the boys in the 'hood. I smiled about that before Jonathan came back on the line.

"Yeah, Tracy, what can I do for you?"

I asked, "Once we get the deal signed and the director on board, we'll finally have the green light for this movie?"

"Hopefully, yeah," he told me.

"Okay, well, I would like to work with Poncho Morales on this."

"I would too, but he turned us down already."

I said, "He didn't turn *me* down."

"Oh, so, you know him?"

"I know him now."

Jonathan paused. "Oh, really."

I smiled and said, "I don't know him like that, so don't even think about it. I just dropped by his trailer a few minutes ago where he's shooting a video at Redondo Beach."

"Good move. So, what did he say?"

I cut straight through the chase. "He said he wasn't offered enough."

Jonathan responded, "Well, we *are* trying to keep this budget pretty low."

"How low is low?"

"Under ten million."

I said, "We can do that. You can get the writer, the lead star, *and* the director for under *two* million."

He laughed and said, "And what are we going to pay everyone else?"

I joked, "They can eat cake," and laughed. "No, I'm sure we can work it all out, I'm just ready to get this damn thing going, and Poncho is a good guy, he just doesn't want to come out naked on this deal. He already told me he likes the script."

Jonathan chuckled and said, "Well, you're just trying to do everything. Now you're jumping in on *my* job. I better get you this go-ahead before you end up replacing me."

I said, "That's what I'm gonna have to do next, if you're planning on keeping me waiting. April is right around the corner, and I'd like to get this done *on time*. I'm a Virgo," I tossed in there just for the hell of it.

"Oh yeah, well guess what other *Virgo* likes to stay on schedule?" he asked me.

"When's your birthday?"

"August twenty-seventh."

"Get out of here! I'm September sixth."

We just laughed with each other being silly.

Jonathan finally asked, "So, Tracy, when are we gonna go ahead and do lunch?"

I looked at the phone and shook my head. Those white producers wanted to fuck me something *bad!*

I said, "Jonathan, the only thing that I'm hungry for right now is to make my damn film *Led Astray.* Now are we on the same page or what? Because I'm not fucking *anybody* until I can fuck the camera."

Jonathan laughed and said, "Okay, okay. If you bring Poncho in and he agrees to everything, then we'll work out the deal. Now is there anything else that you want? Wow!"

I took a deep breath and answered, "A new damn car." I was still driving my Toyota.

"Oh, you'll be able to take care of that," he told me. "If you keep up this kind of urgency throughout your career, you'll end up driving red Lamborghinis."

I said, "That's not my style. I don't want a car that's sexier than me. That would be overkill."

He laughed again. "Boy, is it gonna be fun making a movie with you."

I said, "Yeah, just don't bullshit me. Because you *know* how us Virgos can get when we've been fucked over."

"Ain't it the truth?" he commented. "Well, don't worry, Tracy. I'm on your side, and we'll get this thing done."

It was well after three o'clock, so I hung up with Jonathan and called Kendra at home.

"Hey, girl, it's Tracy."

Kendra said, "Oh, I talked to Yolanda and she said that maybe she *did* go a bit overboard with you, but that you didn't have to say 'F her' either."

I smiled. Kendra didn't curse. She said she wanted to be as clean-mouthed as she could because she didn't want anything to slip out in the heat of the moment with her students.

I asked, "Did she say she would apologize to me?"

Kendra said, "You know what, *both* of you need to apologize, because you're *both* acting childish."

"Well, *she's* older than us," I commented.

"So what? You two just need to sit down somewhere and work out your differences."

"At your house?" I asked her.

"Wherever."

"Well, let's make it at your house then for this Friday."

Kendra paused and asked, "*Why* did I let you drag *me* into this? What if I have something to do on Friday?"

"Come on, Kendra, it'll only take a half an hour."

"A half hour that could be done on your *own* time."

"Pleeease," I begged her.

Kendra broke out laughing. "Now you're going back to your *Flyy Girl* days, always expecting to get what you want."

"I don't get everything I want," I told her.

"Yeah, well, I'll call Yolanda up again and see. But if she can't make it, or she wants me to convince her to do it, then you're on your own, because this is *not* my business."

"Thank you so much," I told her, grinning.

"Yeah, whatever."

I hung up the phone with Kendra and took a breath. I told myself, "I'm gonna *make* this movie! These people don't know who the hell they're dealing with. You don't *fuck* with me like that! Only Victor can do that and get away with it . . . until I find out a way to get *his* ass back too!"

**$ $ $**

When Yolanda and I met at Kendra's house that Friday, we were both walking on eggshells.

She said, "Tracy, I don't appreciate being cursed out, because all I've been trying to do is give you good advice."

I said, "Yolanda, I don't mind your advice, but I *do* mind how you choose to give it to me. I believe I deserve more respect than some little girl off the street."

She nodded and said, "I agree. You've proven that you know what you're doing."

I said, "Whether I know what I'm doing or not, Yolanda, there are certain ways in which we talk to people, especially while you're in business together."

She said, "And that includes not cursing people out and hanging up on them."

I nodded, "I agree with that as well."

However, we *both* stopped short of apologizing. Kendra caught on to that and started laughing.

"You two need to quit," she told us. "Are *both* of your egos that big? My God!"

We laughed it off, but we still hesitated to say the words.

Finally, I said, "Okay, okay, I'll say it."

Yolanda said, "No, I'll go first."

Kendra said, "Who *cares* who goes first, just get it over with."

Yolanda said, "Tracy . . . I apologize," as if it was killing her.

We all broke out laughing before I did my part.

"I apologize for cursing you out and hanging up the phone on you."

Kendra said, "Thank you! Gosh!"

After that, we gradually began to talk about my new movie *Led Astray,* and every other sister film, or the lack thereof, until late at night. I guess Kendra didn't have any plans for that Friday night after all.

**$ $ $**

By mid March, the miracle finally happened. Wide Vision Films had given us the green light to begin production for *Led Astray,* beginning on Monday, April 5th, 1999. They also began to cast the other actors, who were mostly white. However, that was the reality of the power structure of Hollywood. I wasn't blind to that fact, and I planned to present an honest picture.

I signed for a one-million-dollar split between my screenplay and my leading role, and five percent of the gross profits, including rights for cable, network, video, and overseas. They wouldn't give us the ten percent, so we compromised. Susan also worked Poncho's deal, getting his five hundred thousand to direct. We maintained a budget of eight million dollars, and I had no more mouth when I showed the paperwork to Yolanda. She was just happy to be my lawyer again.

I called my girl Raheema in New Jersey to give her the news, but she wasn't in, so I left her a message on her answering service:

"This is Tracy, and I'm smiling right now because I finally got my movie deal done. *Led Astray.* We start shooting early next month, and we're looking for an early release for year 2000. I just *love* how that sounds, and I didn't have to *screw* anybody to get it, but I *do* have to do some of that in the movie. But it won't be real, you know, just camera angles.

"Anyway, I'll tell you all about it when we catch up to each other," I said.

I hung up the phone and began talking to myself. I said, "Here I am trying to sit and write a poem about how I'm feeling right now, but I'm too damn happy to write anything. Ain't that a blizzard? When I'm mad or sad, I can think of a million things to write, almost immediately, but now that I'm happy, all I can do is sit here, smile, and look silly."

# Genesis

*In the Old Testament*
*God said,*
*"Let there be light,"*
*and there was light.*
*Not saying that I'm God,*
*but He did*
*make us in His image,*
*so why not we,*
*in the New Testament,*
*make light*
*in images of our own?*

# May 2000

$$

The writer-director (or director-writer, as *I* called him) for *Road Kill*, was a curly-haired Greek American named Paully Silarus, and he was obviously pissed off that I had tampered with his project and got the green light on my revised screenplay instead of his original. I don't believe he wanted a black woman in the role either, but tough cookie; I was a bigger draw than he was. Deal with it! If he was *that* pissed off about it, then he should have taken his check and walked. I wouldn't have walked away if the same thing had happened to my vision in *Led Astray*, so I felt for the guy, I really did. Nevertheless, he wasn't trying to get along with me. He had a mean streak from hell and he was making the set miserable for everyone. It was already as hot as an oven out there in Nevada. He needed to gather his emotions somewhere and cool his hot behind down!

"CUT! We need more *anger*, Alexis! You want to *kill* this guy, remember!" he screamed at me.

I don't know if Paully liked the name "Alexis" either, but he sure said it enough. I believe he was boycotting my real name. We also had a difference in opinion as to how my character would deal with the killing. *He* wanted violent rage, like a horror movie, and *I* wanted controlled calculation, like a Mel Gibson character. To make Paully feel better, I was trying my best to interpret things *his* way, and it had my body sore as hell by the second day of shooting.

At that moment, we were shooting a car scene where Alexis and one of the psychos swerve to a stop and go at it on a deserted roadside.

We backed up the scene and did it again, and I ended up bruising my chin in a kick move.

"Fuck!" I yelled out in pain.

Paully said, "Yeah, let's get some of that pain on camera."

I gave him an evil look, but I kept my thoughts to myself. They were paying me two million dollars, so I couldn't complain.

"Let's do it again. That was *much* better."

We backed up and did it a fifth time, but after the kick move, I pulled out my hidden gun that was filled with blanks, and let off four unexpected shots into the bad guy.

Paully said, "What the hell was that? You weren't supposed to shoot him yet. What happens to the build up?"

I looked at him and said, "It just felt right. I'm tired of kicking this motherfucker."

Everyone laughed but Paully.

"It's not in the script that way," he complained.

"Well, let's change the damn script," I told him. "That was a good take. It was natural. You see how surprised he was when I shot him? He can't act that well if he tried."

Everyone was agreeing with me. It was very obvious that my reflex instincts had worked much better than a worn-out fight scene. It would also save us time.

"I think you've done enough *changing* of the script as it is," Paully responded.

Our producer, The Don, had not made the trip out to Nevada with us. He sent an assistant producer named

Catherine Belle instead. It was her job to step in as the peacemaker and make sure everything moved along as planned, and she was very efficient at her job.

"Paully, let's just work with that," Catherine stepped in and said. "It's very hot out here, and we have too many stunt scenes to shoot today as it is."

She didn't say it outright to save Paully's ego and everything, but Catherine agreed with my take as well. I could see it in her face when I did it.

Paully looked at her as if he wanted to curse her out. Many directors wouldn't stand for a producer upstaging them, but again, Paully wasn't an A-list guy, so he had to ride it out or be replaced on his own project.

He said, "Fine! Any-fucking-thing goes! Okay, let's put the effects in on the kill."

When I got a chance, I stepped aside with Catherine. "I'm gonna have to have a talk with him, or he's gonna make this film a nightmare for *all* of us," I told her.

"Good idea," she said with a smile, "because I don't want to keep stepping in."

I said, "I know what you mean. I don't think he likes either one of us."

Once we had a long enough break and Paully made it back to his trailer, I went and knocked on his door.

"Yes!" He even answered his door irritated. He didn't even know who it was yet.

I walked inside instead of telling him. He saw me and frowned. "Okay, what do you want to change now?" he asked me.

I took a seat and said, "Your attitude. Do you want to finish making this movie or what?"

He answered, "*I* wanted to make this movie *years* ago, before you ever *heard* of it."

"So, what's supposed to happen now? You want to fuck it up, and say, 'I told you so; the black bitch wouldn't work.'"

He actually grinned at it, as if those same thoughts were really on his mind.

I said, "Well, I have news for you. *I'm staying,* and I'm not gonna let myself look bad. So, if *I* were you, I'd try to make the best movie I can make out of this thing and move on to the next deal, unless you want to end up looking like a big baby being overruled on everything and ruin your chances on future projects."

"Yeah, that's easy for *you* to say," he huffed at me, pulling out a cigarette.

"Well, next time, hold on to your film rights and push to have your vision made as is. That's how *I* got here," I responded to him.

"Yeah, yeah, everybody heard about your story."

I looked at him and shook my head. I wasn't doing too good of a job of making peace.

I said, "*My* breakout project *could have been* a Whoopi Goldberg or Demi Moore vehicle if I didn't fight for *my* vision."

He said, "Oh, yeah, well, why don't you give me that rabbit's foot that you slept with?"

I stood back up and finally said, "If you make this one look good, I've already been offered a sequel idea. But if you want to act like an asshole about it, we'll just move on to someone else."

I walked out of his trailer still uncertain about him. Some damn peacemaker *I* was. It sounded more like I was rubbing the whole deal in his face more than settling him down. However, my talk seemed to work. Pauly became more relaxed over the next couple of days about his methods and overall vision. That only made me work harder for him, because I wanted to get along and make another good film. After all, I wasn't satisfied with the twenty-eight million and change that *Led Astray* had pulled in. With *Road Kill*, I wanted to shoot for *seventy* million!

## $ $ $

By our fifth day of shooting in Nevada, I was physically exhausted. We shot most of the other scenes that day so that I could rest. In the meantime, I had an interview with *The Black American* magazine.

A young sister reporter approached me in front of my trailer with a tape recorder and a cameraman, who wanted to snap pictures of me in my action gear. I had forgotten that I had agreed to do the interview. That's just how tired I was.

The young sister commented, "These are the kind of American films that turn into blockbusters, one black star in the middle of Vanillaville." She and her dreadlock-wearing cameraman were laughing about it.

I must admit, I was getting used to being around white people, and I was starting to understand how human they were along with everyone else. It wasn't *always* a black and white thing.

I said, "If it's not a good film, it won't matter." I didn't even remember getting the sister's name (I guess I forgot it in the heat), but the cameraman was named Jabari.

He said, "You have to admit though, this is how black stars are made, because you'll stand out in this movie, like Eddie, Will, Whoopi, you name it. Chris Tucker. Even Richard Pryor made his mark in Vanillaville."

They shared another laugh between them.

I'm sorry, but I didn't even feel like talking that radical shit at the time. I had a movie to complete for two million dollars that I had already been paid half of.

I asked, "Is this a straight Q&A or what?" I was ready to get it over with.

The sister answered, "No, this is a feature story."

I didn't trust those two to write a damn feature on me. I could tell already, they had come to write a militant piece on blacks in Hollywood. They didn't necessarily want to hear what *I* had to say. I would become a sound bite for their trite opinions. That was exactly why I had a new policy.

I said, "I don't do feature stories anymore. Call your editors back and tell them I want a Q&A, and I want to see their okay in writing. We have a fax machine that you could use in the production trailer."

The sister looked at me as if I had lost my mind, but so what? If she wanted to talk that militant shit, then write a commentary, don't mix me up in it. Not saying that I had crossed over or anything, but I didn't appreciate being a damn *pawn* either.

She said, "Well, we weren't really prepared for a Q&A."

"What, you don't have any questions to ask me?" Of course she didn't, they just wanted me to respond to shit so that they could play me like a fool. I knew the damn game, and I was tired of it.

"Well, I had questions, you know, but not like a Q&A kind of thing."

I said, "Well, you have time to come up with some. I'll be here all day and all night. In the meantime, call and get that okay in writing from your editors."

I know the sister wanted to call me all kind of names. I had just ruined her militant Hollywood story. I even chuckled at it. I liked my new policy. If they wanted to write a story that said I wasn't available for comment, then fine. At least they wouldn't have any quotes of mine that they could *misuse*. I didn't mean to single out a black magazine, because my policy would stand with every one of them, as if I was the president of the United States.

The sister asked, "Well, how about we just hang around and get some action quotes while you're shooting on the set?"

I shook it off. "Not with this movie," I answered. "We have too many stunt scenes to shoot for you to be in the way. You could get hurt or something, and we don't have any insurance on you." I was saying any-damn-thing that came to mind to let the sister know that it would be *my way* or *no way*.

She sighed and finally went ahead to get the Q&A agreement in writing. When she returned with it, I signed it and told her to fax a copy back.

She stopped and asked me, "What's the deal on this? You don't trust me with a feature story, sister?"

I looked her dead in her brown eyes and answered, "No, and it has *nothing* to do with color. I would do the same thing if you were a white girl from *People* magazine. That's just my new policy."

She took a deep breath and went to fax the copy back. By that time, Jabari was laughing and shaking his head at the whole scene. I guess he figured that I was ego-tripping, but I wasn't. I was simply protecting my intelligence for the story.

The sister made it back to me again, and was ready to get the interview under way. However, first she said, "Off the record, I read your book *Flyy Girl* when it first came out *years* ago, and now it just seems like your whole *Hollywood* mission is selling out all of the young sisters who related to what you went through growing up as a teenager in the 'hood. I mean, we all figured that you would get back with your first love and work it out on the black family side of things, and be more community related. You know what I'm saying? And I just wanted to say that to you for all of the sisters who really believed in your message. But now it seems like you're all out for the love of money."

I looked at Jabari, and he raised his brow at me as if to say, "Damn, she gave it to you!"

I was perfectly calm about it. I asked her, "How old are you?"

"Twenty-four," she snapped at me.

"And how old were you when you first read my book?"

"Seventeen."

"Did you go to college?"

"Yes I did."

I nodded and said, "Good. And did you learn anything from my book?"

"I learned plenty."

"Good. So, now that you've read and liked my book, you think that you can control my life now? Is that it?"

She backed down and responded, "I didn't say that."

"Well, what *are* you saying?"

"I'm saying that *you led* a lot of people *a-stray.*"

She was clever. I smiled at her. I said, "First of all, Victor married another woman, and I had to grow up from that. Second of all, no one can succeed with all that I've done up to this point because of money. Third of all, you need to read my *next* book, because you only know *half* of my story. Okay? You don't know how hard I had to work to get here, *nor* do you know where I'm going. I turned *down* money to get to where I am today! And I'll tell you another thing, while we're talking about the so-called *love* of money. Nobody flew in to interview me when I was a damn schoolteacher in Philadelphia!"

I couldn't help myself. The fire just rushed out of me and started growing:

"So, if you want to represent for the young sisters so much, then why don't you go back to the 'hood and interview the brothers and sisters who are still there in Philadelphia, or Washington, D. C., and Baltimore, and New York, and Chicago. Why don't you go and interview the *broke,* grassroots people in Atlanta, Dallas, Detroit, and in South Central Los Angeles?

"Better yet, why don't you call your editors up and tell them that you'd rather do a story on a community activist instead of the *sellout* Hollywood sister, and see what they tell you?" I asked her. "But *please* don't hold your breath, because you'll *die* before they get back to you, since we're talking about *the love of money!* You're out here to interview me because I *have* money! So don't get it twisted, sister. You know *damn well* how it works! If it don't make money, it won't make the press!"

I was *incensed.* The young sister had really pressed my damn button. She had *no idea* how much I had been through!

When she opened her mouth again, she nodded to me and showed me my respect. She said, "Well, you're right, but that doesn't mean that you can't look out for the community in the films that you *do* decide on."

"Films like what? *The Queen of Harlem,* so my *own* people, who *asked* for it, can *ignore it* when it comes out. How many people went to see Oprah Winfrey's *Beloved? I* supported the movie."

She said, "Well, nobody *asked* to see that movie. Oprah Winfrey doesn't ask us what *we* want. She does her *own* thing."

"Well, what do you want, sister?" I asked her. "Let *me* know."

"How about making *Flyy Girl* into a movie?"

I asked, "And how many theaters do you expect me to be able to get?"

"Does it matter?"

"Yes it does matter. Because if we don't get enough theaters to show it in, we'll have more of the shooting and fighting and all of that other nonsense."

"How do you know that? You don't have faith in us to go to the movies like we have any sense?" she asked me.

"The people who own the theaters don't, and that's all that counts."

"Well, why don't you make it into an HBO special."

I shook my head and smiled. The young sister just didn't get it. I said, "George Lucas gets the *world* with *Star Wars,* and I get a goddamned bubble-gum machine with HBO, right? Is that how it works? You'd rather have *anything* than the *right* thing? That's why we can't ever *get* the right thing; we're always settling for less."

She finally folded her cards and said, "Okay, well, let's just do this interview then."

"Good," I told her.

She said, "Well, how did Terry McMillan get *two* of her books made into movies?"

"Is this a part of the interview?" I asked.

She smiled at me and said, "No."

I answered, "Because Terry McMillan sold millions of copies of her books, that's why? For the love of money is how *Hollywood* works. So if you want to see *Flyy Girl,* the movie, then you buy a million copies of the book first."

The young sister laughed and shook her head. I know it sounded capitalistic of me to say something like that, but it was the truth. If Hollywood could not see an automatic return on their investment, then they were not trying to make it, not even HBO.

We finally got into the Q & A interview with her first question.

Q: "Is Hollywood the vehicle for strong black films to be made?"

A: "No, but independents will never get the job done for the mass community."

Q: "What about Spike Lee's movies?"

A: "What Spike Lee movie was ever filmed in Hollywood?"

Q: "I guess you're right. His movies have mainly been in New York. Do you ever think that Hollywood will change, and black cinema will begin to address more of the normal people of Black America?"

A: "No. Nothing will change in Hollywood until Black America can own a thousand of their own movie theaters nationwide. So if you want something to change in Hollywood with black cinema, then more black businessmen have to follow Magic Johnson's lead and own their own theaters."

**$  $  $**

I called my parents that night, just trying to stay in touch like I had promised. It must have been after three in the morning in Philadelphia, but my father said that it didn't matter when I called, so . . .

"Do you know what time of night it is over here, Tracy?" my mother whined when she answered the phone.

I said, "I couldn't sleep, and Dad said that I could call anytime."

"Well, you talk to *him* then," she joked, wearily.

I said, "I'm serious, Mom, I just needed to talk."

"And you had to wait until *this* late at night to call?"

"We're shooting a movie over here. I had to prepare for my scenes tomorrow."

She took a breath and asked, "Okay, what's on your mind?"

I said, "How do you really feel about my acting career, Mom?"

"I'm proud of you."

"What about the sex scenes and stuff?"

She responded, "How you think you got here? America can be so damn *childish* about sex sometimes."

I laughed. I didn't expect my mother to be so crystal clear on that. I guess she said it because she was sleep talking or something, and the truth had slipped out.

"How would you feel about me making a *Flyy Girl* movie?" I asked her.

She chuckled and said, "Who would play me?"

"I don't know. Lynn Whitfield or somebody."

"That's a good choice. I like her. Who would play your father?"

I laughed and said, "You're really getting into this."

"You *asked* me about it."

I said, "Well, what do you think about a sequel to *Flyy Girl*? I've been trying to get a new book deal signed for *months* now."

My mother responded, "Tracy, why are you asking me this? You're gonna do what you want to do anyway."

"I just wanted to get your opinion on it."

"Well, why would you *want* to do it? That's what you have to ask yourself. Why?"

*Good question,* I thought. "I guess to see how people would respond to it, you know. I never expected *Flyy Girl* to be as big as it has the potential to be," I answered. "It's almost like a cult following going on, and I really want to see what the numbers would be like if we went all the way with it. I'm just *mad* curious, like they would say in New York."

"And that's why you want to do this, just because you're curious?"

"I mean, why not? God said, 'Let there be light,' right? And Confucius said, 'If you build it, the people will come.'"

My mother chuckled and said, "Tracy, you don't have to philosophize. If you want to do it, then go ahead and do it. You're gonna do it anyway. If you wasn't, you wouldn't have called up so late to talk about it."

I said, "Well, I'm sorry, go ahead and go back to sleep now."

"Sure, after you ruined my *good* dream."

"What were you dreaming about?"

She paused. "That I was nineteen again."

"Get out of here," I told her, smiling.

"Same to you," she said. "You'll be having those same dreams soon yourself."

When I hung up with my mother, I felt a poem in me. I wrote it down immediately and called it "Genesis." I decided that when I had a chance the next day, I was going to call up Susan at home and ask her about the progress on the book deal.

**$ $ $**

Seven o'clock in the morning, before we began to shoot, I was on the phone with Susan.

"What's the progress on the sequel book deal?" I asked her.

"Oh, Tracy," she whined. "I'll call you back later on from the office."

"Well, just tell me right quick. I don't want to have to think about your phone call while I'm acting. I have a lot to shoot today," I told her.

She said, "Nothing has happened yet. I still say we pass it on to Eric Jerome Dickey. I could have it over to him by tomorrow."

I decided to stick to my guns. "No, we have to wait first. Maybe Omar is right between projects."

"Okay," Susan breathed. I heard movement in the background that didn't sound like her own. Usually Susan was willing to talk to me no matter what.

I smiled and said, "Tell Michael I said hi."

She chuckled and gave herself away. "I'll call you on the book deal as soon as I can."

I said, "Oh, and I came up with a title for the sequel too."

"Okay, let's hear it."

*"For the Love of Money,"* I told her.

She paused. "Why would you want to call it that?" she asked me. "That's like the total *opposite* of what you're all about."

"Exactly. It's an irony," I told her. "I mean, I haven't been busting my ass for *free,* but if you don't *make* any money, then nobody cares."

Susan paused again. She said, "I see. That sort of makes sense, like an ironic poem."

"Now you're thinking," I responded. "Get those morning cobwebs out of your ears, girl. Or that *wet* tongue," I joked.

Susan laughed and said, "I'll call you later on, Tracy."

When we hung up, I thought about my idea for a title again. *For the Love of Money* was *perfect;* the perfect irony.

# Direction Is:

*Lights!*
*Camera!*
*Action!*

*Or, in other words:*

*Ideas!*
*Focus!*
*Execution!*

*Think about it,*
*and make a feature film*
*of your OWN life.*

# Led Astray, The Movie, 1999

$ $
$

I had never been in a theatrical play before in my life, let alone a feature film. I didn't really know what to expect while on the set, but I was prepared to handle anything that they threw at me. First, they gave me the title of associate producer, because I had done so much to push the film forward. They made me *earn* that title too. Since I had written the script and would be on the set full-time in the lead role, nearly every actor asked me about making changes to their lines and delivery, while explaining this and that. On some of their changes, I agreed with it, but on other changes I had to tell them no and explain why. It was still my vision, and I had to make sure that things never got out of hand. However, the four main "Players" did get to choose their character names, making them feel closer to their roles.

As a director, Poncho Morales was a good choice. He worked with me closely on everything, where he could have been a typical *director* and taken over. He brought along plenty of people who he had already worked with while directing music videos, and they had a chemistry that was poetry in motion. We had a lot of hardworking people on the set who were all looking for a big break in their professional careers. I had to give credit to Jonathan Abner as the producer and Janet Krantz as the casting director for doing a hell of a job in their choices. And then the magic began, taking the script to the screen.

On day one, the cinematographer told me not to act so much. He said, "We have you in focus, and we need you to be more natural with your movement. There are many things that we'll do to imply seduction. We'll shoot your lips, your leg, your neck, a piece of your shoulder. So don't worry so much about performing for us. We know that you want the audience to get into Cynthia as a character, and it's *our* job to make sure that comes across on the big screen. So just be natural for us."

It made perfect sense to me. I nodded my head and said, "Thanks. So I can conserve some of my energy then?"

"Yeah, but don't conserve *too* much energy. We don't want you to come off as dull."

I smiled and responded, "Oh, I'm *never* dull. Trust me." However, by that time, I didn't know if it was *me* talking or Cynthia, because I was fully committed to my character.

Poncho worked more on the feel, the pacing, and the overall look of the film. He and the production designer came up with an ingenious idea to execute drastic environment changes as Cynthia climbed the Hollywood ladder of power. In her own apartment at the beginning of the story, there is no glitz or glamour at all, but at each level, the scenery brightens and looks more Hollywood. With that in mind, the costume and makeup people had to develop stages of Cynthia's appearance from the alleyway to the ballroom, so to speak, where she looks more attractive and lively at each new level, until she looks *fabulous* at the end. They got all of that through reading and breaking down my screenplay, where *I* hadn't even thought about it. Moviemaking was truly an art, and there was no way in the world that one person alone could make a good film. *Everything* had to work perfectly, from the script, to the actors, and to the sound.

Speaking of the sound for the film, in a word, it was *great!* We had a sound editor named Billy Jole, who wanted to hear *everything*. We had microphones placed near everything that moved, and then he added *extra* sound which would all raise the human sensory level when watching the film. However, Billy made sure that our voices would always stand out by recording our lines alone in silence *first*, and then adding everything else later. The soundtrack followed suit with Poncho's lead of directing the story from dark blue moods to bright yellow radiance. We even got a closing song (called "Led Astray" of course) from super sister Queen Latifah, and Poncho shot the music video with her.

In the process of getting everything done, I had two major issues to handle; one, there was a catch on the use of my name when going through the Screen Actors Guild; and two, how would I deal with the sex scenes in the film, knowing that I was nervous about performing them, whether it was just camera work or not?

I had to be signed into the SAG because *Led Astray* was a union film, and I was not a unionized actor. That's when I found out that my name fit too snugly between a Tracy *Ellis* and a Tracy *Ells*. I just could not get that thought out of my mind. I wanted a separation from those other two actresses. I guess it was my ego talking, but I wanted to stand out, so I asked Janet, the casting director, to write me in the Actors Guild as Tracy Ellison *Grant*.

She smiled and said, "I like that. It has a ring to it. Is Grant a family name?"

I smiled back at her. "No. It just popped into my head, and I liked the way it fits."

"Well, you know that people will think that you're married with that."

I nodded. "Yeah, I thought about that, but let them assume what they want, and when they ask me about it I'll tell them."

I called my parents about the name addition at home, and it was no big deal to them.

My mother said, "Well, if you had gotten married your name would have changed anyway. But what happens now when you *do* get married? You'll drop *both* names?"

I smiled. Marriage wasn't even a questions of *if* with my mother, it was *when*.

I answered, "I'll decide on that *when* or *if* it happens."

All of my friends liked the name, they just felt that it would create confusion down the road for me. So Tracy Ellison *Grant* it was, as of April 1999.

However, shooting the sex scenes for *Led Astray* was a whole different monster for me.

I knew that those sex scenes would cause a stir, but when I wrote them in the script I had no idea that I would be playing the part. I had done enough sleeping around when I was younger, and playing that back out on camera just didn't settle too well in my stomach. Nevertheless, I had to figure out a way to deal with it and make it happen because I had the lead role.

I had written in two hot sex scenes, one with the screenwriter character, David Bassenger, to let him know how serious Cynthia was about him writing the screenplay to her story, and the other with Player #2, so that she could get more inside information on Player #3.

To execute my plan, I thought about Theresa Randle in the movie *Girl 6* again, with her many delusions. I had to delude myself in order to perform *my* role, and I couldn't count strictly on my acting. I had to go deeper than that. I had to relate the sex to real feelings and emotions of being used and using others, like I had learned in acting class. I had done some using in my youth myself, but the difference was that I *liked* the guys who I used (as crazy as it sounds), where on the set of *Led Astray*, it was only acting. Not that the white actors were bad looking, because they were not, I just had a problem being able to jump right in and make the hot sex scenes happen with them.

In thinking about it, I finally came up with my *own* ingenious idea, or ingenious *delusion*. I thought about the day I caught Mercedes in a crack house, where she had been performing tricks for drugs, and I tried to imagine how she could do that to herself. I tried to imagine being high and fiending for cocaine, while using my body to get it. At the same time, I imagined Victor watching me, and wanting to be with me again. I rehearsed those feelings to myself until I could feel it and get it right.

When we shot the first sex scene at Cynthia's apartment, my delusions worked like a charm. I just did it! I took my clothes off in front of all of the lights and cameras and production people (including Jonathan Abner), and just imagined myself wanting the high and willing to fuck anyone to get it. Once we began the choreographed sex scene, I imagined that everyone watching me was Victor, and that they all wanted to get in on it. Needless to say, it worked, and the scene was dynamite? I left the production team all in awe of me, or in *lust* of me.

"Splendid job, Tracy," Jonathan told me with his mouth open.

I said, "I know," and turned to Poncho. "Let's set up the other sex scene and get it over with." We were not ready with the setup for the scene with Player #2 yet, but I wanted to get it done before my delusion wore off. I just wanted to have it over with and out of the way so I could concentrate on the rest of the script without having to worry about the sex any longer.

Poncho just stared at me. I guess he was still in shock. "It may take a few hours before we're ready," he answered.

I shook my head, wearing a robe with only my underwear on. "I don't have a few hours. If we can't set up the scene at *his* place immediately, then we do a rewrite where he comes over to Cynthia's. And in a way it makes sense. She's sucking them *both* into *her* plot, and playing things out on *her* terms."

"But then he would know exactly where she lived," Jonathan commented.

I said, "It doesn't matter. Her diary has already been sent home to her mother in Detroit. He can't touch her regardless. And if he *really* wanted to find out where she lived, that would be easy to do. It wasn't as if she was *hiding* from anyone, they just didn't have any reason to stay in contact with her."

Poncho nodded and looked at Jonathan.

Jonathan nodded back to him and said, "It sounds like a plan to me. And it saves us more time."

Poncho said, "Okay. LET'S GET READY FOR THE SECOND SEX SCENE! THERE'S BEEN A CHANGE OF PLANS! WE'RE SHOOTING IT AT CYNTHIA'S PLACE NOW!" he informed everyone.

The production assistants flew into action.

"AND GET HER SOME NEW SHEETS!" I added. "BLACK SATIN!" I looked at Jonathan and Poncho and smiled. "We can even shoot a scene where she's ironing the wrinkles out of the sheets and throwing the plastic wrappings and price tags away. After all, William Hicks"—the chosen name for Player #2—"is worth much more money than David Bassenger. She has to respect him that way. So let's jazz up her apartment a little bit. She's gaining more confidence in her plot now."

They both smiled and agreed with me again.

"Are you *sure* this is your *first* feature film?" Poncho joked with me. "You seem like a veteran actor to me."

Jonathan said, "She wants *my* job, that's what she wants."

I shook my head and grinned. "I just like things getting done, and I'm not the type to sit around and complain without coming up with any solutions."

"You got that right," Poncho said.

"Tell me about it," Jonathan added. I could just imagine both of them wondering which one of them would get to sleep with me before the shooting of the film was all over. Jonathan made his move first, while we began to set up for the second sex scene.

"When will we get to go out for that lunch date?" He was smiling when he asked me, as if it were all fun and games, but I knew that he was serious. White guys didn't fuck around with the head games. They came straight at you. Or maybe it was just the Hollywood types, because I didn't really know too many white guys. Philadelphia, Pennsylvania, was not exactly a cross-racial town. We usually stayed with our own tribes in Philly. So blame it on my inner-city culture for having such a hard time with crossing over.

I grinned at Jonathan and told him, "We have a movie to make, sweetheart. Don't get it twisted."

"Well, don't call me sweetheart then," he joked back. I could tell that he was getting irritated with me. Poor Jonathan. He just didn't know who the hell he was dealing with. He had no idea how many guys I had turned down in the past fifteen years of my sex life. I could have fucked every man involved with the production of my movie, whether they were happily married or not. That was the pure power of the booty, in particular, *my* booty. However, I wasn't that kind of a sex fiend anymore, and even in my youth, I was very selective about *who* I chose to sleep with. *Always!*

We shot the second sex scene in less than a couple of hours, and moved right along ahead of schedule, mainly because of the well-prepared execution on Poncho's part as the director. He was proving that he was worth every bit of his five hundred thousand, *and* then some. I was quite sure that he would get his next big deal too, and so would I.

When we prepared the dailies for the sex scenes, I couldn't watch them. That was some *other* woman up on the screen, not me. Everyone else couldn't take their eyes away from it. That's when I knew that I would have hell to pay when *Led Astray* hit the theaters. However, just like with my book, *Flyy Girl,* I would have to live with it. I even wrote a short poem about it called "Human Hypocrisy": How can I write / what I write / how I write it / and then do / what I do / how I do it?

We all do things that are contradictory to what we think, write, or say in some form or another. That's just a part of living life as imperfect humans.

## $ $ $

We wrapped the shooting of *Led Astray* in five weeks, before the six weeks that we had planned, and we were well within our eight-million-dollar budget before the editing process began. It was easy to edit Poncho's work because he shot everything in long natural scenes. It was like fading out a song that had a long fade versus one with a short fade. Longer fades gave you much more material to work with.

For our opening credit scene, we came up with several glamour shots of Hollywood star nights, with fancy outfits, limousines, and photos flashing everywhere, to give the dizzying illusion that sucks us *all* into moviemaking in the first place; this is where the stars are made. It reminded me of my poems "Led Astray" and "Recognition."

When we had our wrap party, executive producer Danny Greene showed up with his wife. She could tell that everyone had the hots for me, and they were mostly white men. My *few* friends from Black Hollywood showed up to lend their support as well. After all, I was still black. Poncho invited some of his Latin friends to the mix, so it turned out to be a pretty colorful and cultural crowd there, all dressed to impress.

Richard Mack showed up with his girlfriend, Kendra was there with her man Louis, Yolanda came by herself (working the crowds as usual), and Tim Waterman showed up with a tall blonde and began to tell everyone how he had given me my start as a writer three years ago. However, my girl Susan shocked me by showing up with a confident, good-looking, dark-haired man on *her* arm. He was perfect for her, standing around five foot nine, right below me and my two-inch heels.

"Tracy, this is Michael; and, Michael, this is my good friend, and one of the most talented new stars in Hollywood, Tracy Ellison Grant."

I smiled and shook his hand.

He said, "I heard a lot about you."

"Good things?"

Susan playfully nudged him in the ribs. "Why of course," he answered. I grinned and let them fade into the crowd to mingle. I figured I'd pull Susan's strings about it later.

I was spinning like a ballerina for the majority of the night, talking to everyone who wanted to have words with me concerning the film. It was pretty obvious where the marketing emphasis would be. Tracy Ellison Grant: a new star is born!

After a while, Rich finally got a minute alone with me. He asked, "So, how does it feel? I can't believe that you actually pulled this off. It seems like yesterday when we had that first date."

I smiled and answered, "To tell you the truth, you know that saying, 'It's lonely at the top'?"

He nodded.

"Well, I seem to be the only one in the crowd with no date tonight." Even Jonathan Abner showed up with a tall blonde. When they say blondes have more fun, they were not *playing,* or at least not in Hollywood.

Rich looked at me and said, "This whole damn audience is your date. You're the star of the show. Are you kidding me?"

He didn't understand what I meant because he had a girlfriend. I was alone in a crowd, and I couldn't help but think about being with someone special to share the moment with.

At the end of the night, I ended up right back with my girls, Kendra and Susan and their dates.

"Well, what do you want to do now? You all want to go out for a late bite to eat?" I asked them. "We can do Kate Mantilini's."

"Sure," they told me. The night was still pretty young

and it was a nice Saturday evening. Before we all left, I noticed Poncho on a pay phone without his entourage of Latin friends, and I got curious.

"Hold on a minute," I told my friends as I approached Poncho at the phone booth. When he hung up I asked him, "Hey, super director, what are you doing for the rest of the evening?"

He looked at me and read me fast, with his sexy, macho self.

He tossed his hands up and said, "I'm game. Let's go." I smiled, feeling slightly embarrassed by it.

"Aren't you going to at least say bye to your friends?" He looked in their direction and immediately shook his head. "They know their way back to my place."

"What about your limo driver?"

He said, "I'll tell him to show my friends all a good time while we jump in *your* limo." Wide Vision Films had given us the full star treatment for the night.

I nodded to Poncho and said, "All right," before taking him over to introduce to Kendra and her date, because Susan already knew him. She had agreed to take him on full time as a client. I felt leery about inviting him along with us, but so what? I wasn't going to be the only one without a date, whether I was doing the star-fucking-the-director thing or not. Poncho and I hadn't gone there anyway.

I must admit, however, that as soon as the evening got under way at West Hollywood's Kate Mantilini's for a bite to eat and drinks, I couldn't take my mind off of getting naked with Eduardo "Poncho" Morales. He was talking everyone up about Puerto Rican culture and growing up in Spanish Harlem, and I was impressed with his easygoing personality. Some directors had reputations of being uptight. Nevertheless, I think that the drinks had gotten to Poncho a little bit too, especially when he started bragging about the legend of Latin sexuality. I couldn't take it anymore. I wanted to try him out, but I had no way of leaving with him smoothly.

Susan finally looked at her watch at close to one in the morning and said, "Well, it's getting late, you guys."

Kendra responded, "Yes, it is."

I thought, *Hallelujah! I need my damn privacy anyway!*

We all said our good-byes and went our separate ways, and Poncho's ass fell asleep in the limo on the way back to my townhouse. It was just my luck to have to carry his ass out of the car and into the house, but the limo driver did it for me.

He laid Poncho out on my sofa, and I went to get my macho man some orange juice with plenty of ice in it before I showed the limo driver out. I gave him an extra fifty dollars for his help. I had money to throw away by then, but that didn't mean that I would. Fifty dollars was enough.

I sat Poncho up and got him to sip the orange juice. I guess he had more drinks that night than I had noticed.

He finally came around and looked at me. He said, "Tracy, you are beautiful, my sister. *Muy bonita!*"

I just broke out laughing. I said, "Poncho, and *you're* drunk."

He didn't laugh at all. He said, "That doesn't affect my good vision." He shook his head and smiled. "When you shot those sex scenes, man, I had to go back to my place and jerk off."

I couldn't even look at him it was so embarrassing. It made me horny too, and Poncho was not going anywhere.

I asked him, "Would you like to kiss me?"

He chuckled. "Does a man have any balls?"

I laughed again. I had no idea Poncho could be so much fun. I was so concerned with doing the film that I hadn't paid much attention to anything else.

I took a sip of the orange juice myself and wet Poncho's lips with mine before his tongue found its way into my mouth. Puerto Ricans were not white, you know, and I was definitely going to fuck Poncho. He was my lucky pick, and he made it worth my while when he slipped down on me right there on my sofa and opened me up.

Poncho had me grabbing at the air and pulling at my own hair.

"Wait a minute, wait a minute," I told him, feeling myself rising too early to where I *definitely* wanted to go. Poncho wouldn't stop. He was a man possessed by his tongue, and then the walls came down, and fresh tears rolled freely from my eyes.

*DAMN!* I thought to myself. *Can he top that?* He did. *We* did, all night long, and in the morning time, I thought of another poem, "Puerto Rican Freakin'," and laughed.

Poncho asked me, "What's so funny?"

I answered, "You don't even wanna know," and I kept it to myself.

A few days after that, Kendra called me up and told me that she and her man Louis were engaged to be married on Saturday, December 18, 1999, a week before Christmas, back home in Maryland.

I hung up with her and said, "Damn! I hope she doesn't ask me to be *her* maid of honor at the wedding too, because I'm gonna have to turn her behind down. I can't take *two* of 'em." Nevertheless, I was happy for her, just like she was happy for me. I just wish that I had a man to get married to.

# $ $ $

When we began to travel during the summer and fall of '99, and enter into the different film festivals with *Led Astray,* we didn't win any awards, but everyone sure learned *my* name. The strikes against us were many. We were apparently up against too many independent, raw-energy films that made our natural shooting seem too smoothly done. With no guns, killings, blood, extra plot twists, drama, or other major stars in the film, I was the only thing that the judges, journalists, and viewers bothered to focus on. So naturally, despite not being able to score with me, Jonathan Abner decided to have Wide Vision market the entire film as Tracy Ellison Grant's breakout vehicle.

I was pretty tight with Poncho up until then, and his possessive ways made it much easier for me to be able to turn down so many advances. However, when he seemed to be out-directed by the same camera tricks that I didn't necessarily care for, and with everyone paying so much attention to me, it was more than Poncho could take. We didn't have any painful breakup, it was more of a mutual business and artistic thing. He figured that he would have to move on and try something new, and I agreed with him. That was simply Hollywood for you; everyone had to be concerned about their own career or be drowned out in the waves.

The next thing that happened was the interviews that poured my way. Plenty of them!

"Your rise to Hollywood stardom has been rocket-ship fast. How does it all feel?"

I smiled and answered, "I'm not a star yet. We don't

even release the film to the public until February of next year. And hopefully then, my rise to stardom will really happen."

However, the hype machine had already started. I was being interviewed by magazines that I had never heard of before, and they all took on a certain "spin," as they call it in the journalism field. I was the young 'hood sister that had caught Hollywood off guard with her street sass and sexiness. That was my story. *Period!* Few of the articles brought up my master's degree in English, or my three years as a scriptwriter for cable and network television. They had what they wanted to run with, and they all ran with it. I wasn't media savvy at the time to *spin* things back to what *I* wanted to say about myself, as opposed to what *they* wanted to write about me. I was simply answering questions as I was asked, but I caught on fast enough. Even my parents called me up to complain about it.

"How come all of these stories only talk about how sexy and street-smart you are?" my mother asked me. "What did you do in this film?" She hadn't seen it yet. "They don't know that you went to college and got a master's degree? What the hell is going on? Did you ask them to write this way about you?"

I answered, "Of course I didn't, Mom. They write whatever they *want* to write evidently."

I called up Susan and said, "You know what? I have an idea. I don't particularly like these interviews I'm getting, so I think I need to write a sequel to my book to let everyone know how I *made* it out here, because these interviews are getting ridiculous, and the movie hasn't even come out yet.

"What are they gonna write about when it *does* come out?" I asked rhetorically. "I don't want to become another black version of Madonna. We have enough of that shit going on with these young rap sisters.

"And by the way," I added, "the *original* Madonna *was* black." I was slipping into a fight-the-power mood, and the black magazines *loved* to report from that spin: The Hollywood sister tells of dirty laundry; either that or, The Hollywood sister counts her riches.

Susan said, "I agree with you, and I feel partially responsible for some of that, because I was the one who sent Jonathan a copy of *Flyy Girl*. I guess they all went overboard with that. But they *do* have the rest of your résumé. They know what you're capable of. They act as if your screenplay was pure luck, and as if you can't really write."

She said, "I don't like the spin on these interviews either, and I think that a follow-up book idea would be good to set the record straight. The media has a penchant for sensationalizing the women of Hollywood, black, white, or whatever; you're either the sex symbol or the bimbo that they want you to be, or no one wants to know you."

She added, "I warned you of that when we first began to shop the script."

I said, "Yeah, but I didn't know that I would be starring in it at the time," which was hypocritical of me because I was admitting that I was fully willing to allow another woman use *her* body in the role. I was having to swallow my own medicine.

"Would you like me to make contacts to ask about the sequel book idea?" Susan asked.

I said, "I was thinking about writing this one myself."

Susan paused. "Do you have the time to write it? This is a lot more time-consuming than writing poetry."

I said, "Not really, but I'll *find* time."

"I don't really know about that idea," Susan responded. "I mean, it would be great to write it yourself, but even better to get a follow-up book with Omar Tyree, since he wrote the first one. That's who people are connecting your story to as a writer. I mean, you would almost have to reintroduce yourself to the literary world, and many stars have not done too well in the book business. Everyone just assumes that Hollywood stardom will push you straight through the bookstores, but it doesn't always work that way.

"However, if you had another *combined* effort introducing the new Tracy Ellison *Grant,* as told by Omar Tyree, I think it would sell a lot stronger in the literary market," she told me. "After all, he *has* built up an audience now, mainly off of *your* story, and I wouldn't want to count that connection out."

That conversation took place in late November 1999. I nodded, while thinking everything over. I didn't want to say that I couldn't write a book myself, but Susan had a point. Bookstores were different from movie theaters and vice versa.

I finally conceded to it and said, "Okay. Let's make that deal then," only to have many of Susan's phone calls concerning my sequel fall on deaf ears.

In the meantime, Susan and I had found a steal of a three-bedroom house up on the hills of Marina Del Rey, next to Culver City. Some down-on-his-luck producer was vacating the house, dirt cheap, to pay off outstanding credit bills. I was able to take the place off of his hands for well below what it was worth. Talk about being in the right place at the right time with the right money, I must have landed on the other side of the rainbow. This house was the *shit,* with a hell of a hillside view! I was screaming about it for *days!* The neighbors were probably ready to call the cops on me already.

As far as my Toyota was concerned? I drove that thing back home to Philadelphia to attend my brother's graduation ceremony in June, and I handed the keys over to him as a graduation present. I replaced the Toyota when I arrived back out in California with a black, 1999 convertible Mercedes, loaded and with a car phone. So, outside of the media's spin job on my imagery, in late 1999, I had few things to complain about. I guess my girl Raheema was right: I was *born* to be a star!

# Give the People
# What They Want!

Sounds simple
enough of a quest
until you find that
some want more
and others want less.
So you settle in the middle;
in the middle of nowhere
with nothing of value,
while beautiful,
thousand-year-old candles
are snuffed out
inside of small, barren closets,
replaced by electricity;
electricity to appease the masses,
who learn to take the flick
of a switch, or the press
on a button for granted,
with no more strikes
of the match, or rubs
of the firewood.


And then, when the power goes
on that electricity,
so simplistically gained,
we ALL end up in darkness,
searching,

*searching,*
*for those candles*
*that the PEOPLE*
*ignored.*

# For the Love of Money, The Sequel, 2000 $ $

$

## $

*oad Kill* was a much different movie from the independent feel of *Led Astray. RK* had blockbuster potential if we could market it right and get a good deal of buzz going. The main obstacle was for us to get two thousand theaters or more to premiere the film the following summer.

By mid June, we were shooting scenes back out in California. I had a bunch of scrapes and bruises from doing a lot of my own stunts, but I wanted to step it up and earn my keep toward making the movie a success. I had even turned Pauly into a fan. He kept asking me, "Are you *sure* you want to do this scene? You really don't have to."

As long as the stunt couldn't kill me, and I was still making two million dollars *before* the film ever released to the theaters, I said, "Let's do it," and kept going. I had stopped taking interviews for the time being, because all they were doing was throwing off my concentration. I needed to focus more on Alexis and not Tracy. So when Susan visited me unexpectedly on the set, she ended up having to wait several hours before I had a break to sit down and talk to her.

I stepped inside of my trailer with her. I said, "Well, this *must* be important, because you're still smiling even though you just wasted four hours of your day by *not* calling me first."

Susan said, "It doesn't matter. I took the whole day off just to give you the good news in person."

"What good news?" I had nothing on my mind but *Road Kill.*

Susan smiled and pulled out a faxed document with Omar Tyree's signature on it. "He finally agreed to the deal, just as we wanted it," she told me. "I told him when you would be finished shooting, and he said he would fly out to California right after you wrap up. He said he'd spend a full week with you to get the sequel all on tape recordings, and then transcribe it to text."

I grinned. It was finally going to happen, a sequel to *Flyy Girl.*

"And what did he say about the poetry?" I asked.

Susan hesitated. "Well, he called me back personally, and we actually talked about it for a while. And he made it perfectly clear that *without* the poetry he wouldn't have been interested in doing the book."

"Why not?" I asked her out of curiosity.

Susan was still being choosy with her words.

I said, "Come on, girl, you didn't come out here to waste my time. You always give it to me straight, that's why I like you. So let me have it."

Susan clasped her hands together and said, "Okay, Tracy. Well, *I* never even asked you what happened with your relationship with Victor Hinson, because I just figured that *you* were in college and *he* was in jail, and to be honest with you, I just didn't see much of a future there. However, *Omar* seems to think that the young fans of your book *obviously* hoped for that, and he said that unless your sequel would reconnect you with Victor in some way, a lot of the *Flyy Girl* fans that you've amassed wouldn't want to hear about your rise in Hollywood."

I did my usual thing and remained calm in the beginning. I said, "In other words, unless I get my man back, they don't give a fuck about *what* I'm doing? That doesn't make any sense," I snapped.

"I'm just telling you what he said," my girl responded. "That's why we were on the phone for a while. I didn't particularly agree with that."

I sat there and thought about it in silence for a minute. I said, "I had an interview out in Nevada where this young sister from *The Black American* ranted that she thought I was selling out by coming to Hollywood and not picking the right movie vehicles to star in. She also talked about this Victor situation. Then she asked me to produce *Flyy Girl* the movie.

"But if what *you're* telling me is the case, from Omar's standpoint, since I'm not getting back with Victor, then my fans wouldn't be interested in *Flyy Girl* the movie either, because they would know that it wouldn't end happily ever after," I added.

Susan smiled. "You wouldn't have to put that in the movie, you just end it exactly the way that the book ended."

"By leaving them hanging?" I responded. "But if they read this sequel, then they'll *know* what happens with Victor, and that would spoil the movie idea."

Susan broke out laughing. The whole situation sounded like some kind of a jigsaw puzzle.

I shook my head, feeling a headache coming on. I said, "See, *this* is why I need to concentrate on finishing this movie, because this shit is pissing me off. Mary J. Blige said that we have to wake up from the dream and move on, and they *still* buy her music."

Susan said, "Yeah, but from what *I've* been able to hear, it seems like every one of her songs is about losing another man." We broke out laughing again, but the shit wasn't funny.

Just to be clear on things, I said, "So, Omar is saying that even *young* sisters are more concerned about their man than they are about their own futures? I thought that was Terry McMillan's crowd, all strung out over some man. I didn't know that the *young* sisters were strung out too. Damn!"

Susan smiled real calmly and responded, "*You* were."

I took a deep breath and thought about it. I said, "So *I* can't grow up, and that means that *they* can't grow up." I was really hurt by that. I shook my head and added, "That's a damn shame." I felt like crying for the young sisters all around the country who couldn't see past their confused passion for a man and get on with their own lives. Not that *I* still didn't want a man myself, but I was only twenty-eight years old, and still good-looking. I had time. I still didn't have any kids or anything.

I decided to tell Susan the painful truth about myself and Victor.

I said, "Susan, I wanted Victor so badly that I went back home for my girlfriend's wedding and tried to sleep with the man, even though I had just met his wife and two sons that same afternoon in their family-owned health food store. And he played me like an absolute *fool,* just to show me how *sick* I was.

"And oh, *he's* doing *great!*" I told her. "He's into real estate and entrepreneurship; the real grassroots work in the community. Victor has *never* been a dumb man, he's just not mine anymore," I said. I began to tear up again. "But he never was, to tell you the truth. You read the book, Susan. I was just his young girl. But I'm not that young girl any-more, and he had to embarrass me that night to make me finally realize that. I had to grow up and face reality."

I really didn't need that shit on my damn mind at the time. I stopped my tears from falling by holding my palms up to my eyes.

Susan moved to comfort me but I shook it off. "No, I don't need that shit. I'm trying to shoot a movie here. I'm supposed to be a tough bitch, remember. Alexis, from Chicago. But it hurts. Lost love is *always* painful. But how long are you gonna allow that pain and that damn dream to control your life, when there's so many other things that we need to be doing for ourselves?

"We gotta let these niggas *go* when they want to *go*! We can't hold on to the *bullshit* anymore!" I yelled. I looked Susan in her face and said, "I'm not even supposed to be saying this to you. This is *insider* information."

Susan stood up and asked, "Would you like me to leave?"

"No," I told her. "We're both human, and we're both women. And if you can't feel my pain, then yeah, leave. But if you *can* feel it, then sit down and listen to me."

Susan sat back down with tears in her own eyes, proba-bly because she had never seen me vulnerable before, and it was scary for her. I was the tough, super black girl from the streets of Philly who wasn't *supposed* to cry, which was all bullshit!

I said, "Susan, we're gonna put this sequel book out anyway. And then I'm going to take all of this money that I make over the next three years, and produce *Flyy Girl* the movie, because we *still* haven't had any sister stories to set us straight. And we *need* one. So if Tom Cruise can get twenty million dollars to make *Mission Impossible,* then

I'll just have to get twenty million dollars to make *Flyy Girl*."

"I'm well behind you on that," my girl told me. "But what are you going to do about the sex scenes in that?" she asked me with a smile.

I smiled back at her. "We need to grow up from that too. My mother told me that sex was how I got here. Did *you* get here some other kind of way?"

Susan said, "I don't think so."

"Well, we have to deal with it then. In the meantime, I'm really interested in how well this sequel will do *without* Victor as my man. And I'm not doing this for the money; I don't need it. I'm doing it for the art, and for inspiration to all of the sisters out there who need to learn how to move on."

Susan smiled and said, "You *go* girl!"

I looked at her and said, "Susan, if Martin Lawrence could collect just *five* dollars every time someone used that line, he'd be a *billionaire*. Then we could just go and ask *him* for the money."

When Susan left me and I had another moment alone, I came up with my opening and closing poem for the sequel, "Happily Ever After" and "Prophecy."

## $ $ $

"Tracy, your mother phoned the office trailer with a message for you to please call home, ASAP," one of the production assistants told me when my next break was on.

I took a deep breath and said, "Now what?"

I called my mother from the trailer and asked her what was so urgent.

"Your cousin Vanessa," she told me.

I stopped breathing. "What happened to her?" I was thinking any- and everything, a car accident, a drive-by shooting, pregnancy (God forbid), you name it!

My mother answered, "She got kicked the hell out the house."

I exhaled. I could deal with that one. I even chuckled at it. My mother had threatened to kick *me* out when *I* was Vanessa's age. It was just a "girls will be girls" kind of thing, and you get over it.

"Well, what did she do?" Vanessa was a Goody Two-shoes compared to me.

"I'll let you talk to her about that. And I don't think the shit is funny," Mom snapped at me. "So when can you fly her out to LA?"

I stopped smiling and said, "What? Mom I can't—"

"Tracy, you gon' *have* to, because *this* ain't *my* problem," she responded, cutting me off. "I told you about instigating shit, but you wanted to be the big, bad boss lady because you're all *grown up now* and making Hollywood money. Well, now you're gonna have to deal with it."

"Mom, you can't call up Trish and work it all out?" I couldn't fly Vanessa out to LA! I was in the middle of shooting my damn movie!

"What do you think I've been trying to do, Tracy? Vanessa has been here for *three days* already, and Patricia is acting a damn *fool!* So you're just gonna have to deal with your little cousin."

I took another deep breath. *I can't believe this!* I thought to myself. *What am I gonna do now? I can't baby-sit no teenager.*

"Let me talk to her," I finally asked my mother.

She went and put Vanessa on the phone.

"What happened?" I asked her.

"My mom is just tripping, that's all."

"How so?"

"Ever since that night you talked about me going out to LA, she just kept bothering me about *little* stuff. And then I was reading this magazine, and she just snatches it out of my hand, talking about, 'You don't need to be reading this' and threw my brand-new magazine in the trash. So I went to get it out, and we got in an argument about it.

"A *magazine!*" Vanessa told me. "Now you tell me that's not *tripping.*"

"Was it a Hollywood magazine?" I asked her. I could just imagine where my little cousin's head was.

Vanessa paused. "It was *Entertainment Weekly.*"

I nodded my head. Her mother had lost it, and it was *all* because of my meddling. However, I still couldn't imagine Trish kicking her daughter out because of *that.*

I asked, "So, is that it? You got into an argument over a magazine, and she kicked you out *for that?*" It just sounded too unbelievable. I was doing *far* more than *arguing,* and my mother let *me* stay.

Vanessa said, "Well, when we started arguing and stuff . . . she hit me, and, you know . . . I hit her back."

*Oh my God!* I thought to myself. I never even *thought* about hitting *my mom* back when she whipped my ass up against the refrigerator in *my* teen years. Vanessa had lost her damn mind!

I just shook my head. I didn't know what else to say. That introverted shit was crazy. I *knew* Vanessa had some craziness in her. The kind of girls who hit their mothers back are usually the ones who get sent the hell away to group homes and shit.

I asked, "So, what do you plan to do now?"

"I don't know. I was hoping you'd let me stay with you."

*SHIT!* I cursed myself. My mom had jinxed me again. I nodded my head and said, "I have to call you back. Okay? I have to figure this all out."

"Okay," Vanessa whimpered.

I immediately called my brother Jason at his apartment, praying to God that he would be in.

"Hello."

"Thank God," I told him. "Jason, this is Tracy. I need a *big* favor from you."

"What, you need another idea for your movie?"

I ignored him and said, "How do you get along with Vanessa?" I had no time to waste.

"Our *cousin* Vanessa?" he asked me to make sure.

"Yeah."

He said, "Oh, she's aw'ight. She's kind of quiet, but you know, she's cool. I guess."

*No she's not,* I thought.

"Well, how would you like to come out to LA with her? I'll get you that Lexus," I blurted out. I was desperate.

Jason laughed and said, "It sounds like you're trying to blackmail me."

"I am, I need you," I admitted to him. "I have a movie to make, and Vanessa got in trouble with her mom."

"What she do?" I guess he hadn't heard yet.

"I'll tell you about it later."

"Well, you got a *job* for me out there?"

"I can get one, for *both* of y'all."

Jason said, "Aw'ight, I'm down with it. You gon' get me the Lexus too?"

I had second thoughts already. "Well, we'll have to talk about that when you get here."

"Aw, here we go," he responded.

I had solved my problem for at least the summer, but what would I do after that?

I called Vanessa back at my mom's house and gave them the news. After that, it was Mom's turn to laugh.

"Well, you've made your new bed, *Boss Lady*," she joked. "And I'm just *scared of you*."

I hung up with her and shook my damn head again. "This is just fucking great!" I told myself out loud. "What the hell *else* can happen?"

I went ahead and called my answering machine at home in Marina Del Rey, expecting more bad news. First, I had nothing but the usual business and pleasure calls. Then the bad news came:

"Hey, Tracy, this is Mercedes, girl, back at home. I thought about writing you a letter about the house thing, but you know I ain't writin' no damn letters, girl, so I had to look up your phone number and call you.

"Well, I just wanted to tell you that I agree to it. You buy the house, and I'll just pay off the mortgage for it. So call me back and let's talk about it when you get a chance. All right?

"And thanks, girl. I love you too. And I mean that. Really.

". . . All right, well, bye. And make sure you call me back."

I hung up the phone and didn't know whether to laugh or cry. Mercedes actually agreed to my proposal. I had set myself up to have to deal with her once a damn month when mortgage time rolled around. I thought that maybe I should just buy her the entire house and have her out of my hair already.

"Shit, shit, SHIT!" I ranted to myself.

Another PA knocked on my trailer door. "Tracy, they're ready for you on the set."

I stood up, took one last deep breath, and stepped out of my trailer. I had to face the facts of the crazy shit that I had just got myself into.

I took it all in and nodded to myself. I said, "Well, here comes the Boss Lady, Mom," and I went right back to work.

# Recognition

I had a big date yesterday
with King Kong
on top of the World Trade Center.

Helicopters swung in,
news cameras taped it,
and reporters took notes with flashing light bulbs
all around me.

But my King Kong got pissed off, y'all,
with all of the noisy cock blockers.
So somebody shot him.

And he fell waaay
down.
BOOM!
Then I cried
while the whole world watched me
in silence.

But when I awoke,
I realized that my King Kong
was only a little brown Teddy Bear
that my momma gave me.

And nobody knew me.
Even worse,
nobody cared
to know.

*So I held that*
*little brown Teddy Bear*
*close to my heart*
*and squeezed it.*

*Because somebody did*
*recognize me.*
*And somebody cared.*

*And once I realized that,*
*I got my King Kong anyway,*
*and I was as happy as I could be.*

*Copyright © 1996, 2000 by Tracy Ellison Grant*

# The Premiere, February 2000

$$\$\$$$
$$\$$$

In December of nineteen ninety-nine, I did my girl Kendra's wedding in Baltimore, and in February of two thousand, after everyone had gotten past the hype of the Y2K bug, Kendra did my movie premiere back in West Hollywood for *Led Astray*, because the world could *not* shut down before my movie premiere. No way, no how!

I spent five thousand dollars to fly my family out for the big event, including Raheema and her family from New Jersey. I rented limos to transport all my entourage to and from the hotel. To where? Mann's Chinese Theater. I was lucky again. Lucky with hard work, that is, but I didn't want to arrive with my friends and family. It was my moment in the bright lights to shine alone. So I took a limo ride solo from my home in Marina Del Rey and arrived on Hollywood Boulevard at seven twenty-two, eight minutes before our seven-thirty start time.

I wanted to make *certain* that *no one* would miss my arrival that night. So I wore a red, beaded tank dress that shimmered in the light, with matching elbow-length gloves, all designed by Marvin Pratt. My hair was wrapped in a long bob, and dyed honey brown to the roots, to match my skin and eye color. I wore diamond-studded earrings, carried a small, beaded purse, and stood on high-heeled sandals that finished my knock-out ensemble.

I took a deep breath and prepared to step out of the limo with my purse in hand. "Well, here goes my dream," I told myself, as I climbed out with the help of my driver. However, I wasn't dreaming anymore. It was real, and people were waiting for me with their cameras. So I stood tall and proud and struck my pose as the cameras lit up and illuminated my dress and gloves. Tracy Ellison Grant, the black sister movie star from Philadelphia, Pennsylvania, had arrived. And I was as *flyyyy* as I *ever* was!

# Prophecy

*Assata*
*was revolutionary*
*for yesterday.*
*Camara*
*is revolutionary*
*for tomorrow.*
*But today*
*was wasted*
*again*
*on more parties*
*and bullshit.*

# About the Author

Omar Tyree is a *New York Times* bestselling author and winner of the 2001 NAACP Image Award for Outstanding Literary Work—Fiction. His books include *Boss Lady, Diary of a Groupie, Leslie, Just Say No!, For the Love of Money, Sweet St. Louis, Single Mom, A Do Right Man,* and *Flyy Girl.* He lives in Charlotte, North Carolina.

To learn more about Omar Tyree, view his Web site at www.omartyree.com.